Enthusiastic praise for

BARBARA DELINSKY

"One of today's quintessential authors of contemporary fiction...Ms. Delinsky is a joy to read. With the incisive skill of a surgeon and the delicate insight of true compassion, she deeply probes the quality and meaning of life....
Women's fiction at its very finest."
—*Romantic Times Magazine*

"The deserved popularity of Delinsky's novels resides in her ability to create appealing, believable characters who don't need to drop names and fashion labels to earn the reader's attention."
—*Publishers Weekly*

"When you care enough to read the very best, the name of Barbara Delinsky should come immediately to mind.... One of the few writers who still writes a great love story, Ms. Delinsky is truly an author for all seasons."
—*Rave Reviews*

Harlequin Romance®
Love stories that capture the essential dream of pure romance.

HARLEQUIN *Presents~*
Meet sophisticated men of the world and captivating women in glamorous, international settings. Seduction and passion guaranteed.

Vivid historical romances that capture the imagination with their richness, passion and adventure.
Harlequin® Historical

Sexy, fast-paced stories that reflect the attitudes, desires, lives and language of women today.
HARLEQUIN® *Temptation.*

HARLEQUIN *Superromance*
Longer romance novels featuring realistic, believable characters in a wide range of emotionally involving stories.

HARLEQUIN® AMERICAN *Romance*
Upbeat, lively romances about the pursuit of love in the backyards, big cities and wide-open spaces of America.

HARLEQUIN® *Duets~*
A fun, entertaining "lighter side of love" read that delivers romance with comedy.

HARLEQUIN® **INTRIGUE®**
Electrifying romance and heart-stopping suspense that make for an exhilarating read.

HARLEQUIN®
Makes any time special™

Visit us at www.eHarlequin.com   HINTSERIES2

BARBARA DELINSKY
Bronze Mystique

GAYLE WILSON
Secrets in Silence

 HARLEQUIN®

TORONTO • NEW YORK • LONDON
AMSTERDAM • PARIS • SYDNEY • HAMBURG
STOCKHOLM • ATHENS • TOKYO • MILAN • MADRID
PRAGUE • WARSAW • BUDAPEST • AUCKLAND

ISBN 0-373-83472-1

HARLEQUIN INTRIGUE 2-IN-1 COLLECTION

Copyright © 2001 by Harlequin Books S.A.

The publisher acknowledges the copyright holders of the individual works as follows:

BRONZE MYSTIQUE
Copyright © 1984 by Barbara Delinsky

SECRETS IN SILENCE
Copyright © 2001 by Mona Gay Thomas

This edition published by arrangement with Harlequin Books S.A.

® and TM are trademarks of the publisher. Trademarks indicated with ® are registered in the United States Patent and Trademark Office, the Canadian Trade Marks Office and in other countries.

Visit us at www.eHarlequin.com

Printed in U.S.A.

CONTENTS

BRONZE MYSTIQUE

Barbara Delinsky

CHAPTER ONE

IT WAS A CONSPIRACY of darkness. What with the gloom of the skies, the heaviness of the rain, the narrowness of the road and a preoccupation with his own somber thoughts, Doug Donohue never saw the motorcycle until it had rounded the curve and skidded sidelong into him. He swerved onto the muddy shoulder of the road and slammed on his brakes, but it was too late.

Within seconds he was out of the car and running back the several yards toward where the cyclist lay. "My God!" he exclaimed, then more softly under his breath, "Damn fool kid!" when he caught sight of the slender form beneath the bulk of the Suzuki. With strong hands he levered the heavy motorcycle up. "Are you all right?"

Setting the damaged vehicle aside, he knelt down just as the cyclist's head moved. "Wait!" he commanded. "Be careful! If it hurts, don't move!" A quick perusal of the prone figure showed neither sign of blood nor the grotesque posture that might suggest a bone break. When the head turned again and a shaky hand moved toward the helmet, he got there first, unhooking the strap, sliding the visor up, then pausing and quite helplessly catching his breath.

The face bared to his gaze had to be the most delicate

and feminine, not to mention the palest he'd ever seen. "My God!" he exclaimed again, though in a whisper this time. By sheer instinct he smoothed the thick fall of auburn bangs to the side, to expose gentle features to the rain's ministration. Heart pounding, he watched wide-set eyes flicker, then open.

It took Sasha Blake a minute to focus. Stunned, she blinked. The world was an amalgam of darks and lights, the shadows of trees and hedgerows, a nearby automobile, the contrasting glare of an overcast sky. She'd been riding home. Her front tire had hit something. She'd skidded, then slammed into a car. Now she was on her back on the road. Eyes widening, she turned her head toward the figure kneeling beside her. Then, brought to full sense by the steady patter of rain on her face, she struggled to sit up.

"Wait!" the dark figure by her side commanded, a firm hand at her shoulder restraining her. "Maybe you shouldn't—"

"I'm all right!" she moaned, ignoring small twinges of pain to shift cautiously in search of more serious damage. Her arms worked, as did her legs, though when she tried to curl them sideways to prop herself more steadily, she couldn't suppress a whimper.

"Something hurts?" the deep voice demanded instants before long fingers closed over the taut muscles of her thigh and probed carefully down the slim length of denim. Skipping to her other leg, they repeated the exploration.

"Everything hurts," she murmured, her breath coming faster as the enormity of what had happened hit her. She'd nearly been killed! Had she been inches farther to the left it would have been a head-on collision. Feeling suddenly hot and faint, she mustered as much strength as she possessed to shove the helmet from her head. The rain, her enemy earlier when it had come so suddenly and with such force that her ride home from North Tisbury had become an ordeal, was suddenly, almost patronizingly refreshing. She was only marginally aware of the arms that supported her when she swayed, of the broad chest against which her head was momentarily cradled. By the time she regained her equilibrium, the support was gone.

"It doesn't look like anything's broken," the voice came less gently. "And we'd be a damn sight drier in my car. Can you make it?"

Stunned or not, Sasha was hesitant. The sooner she could be on her way, the better. "No. I mean, yes! I can make it. But I'm fine." Experimentally she flexed the taut muscles of her neck by slowly swiveling her head. "If you could just help me get the Suzuki up—" she gasped as she put a hand down and tried to stand "—I'll be on my way."

It was the strong arm around her ribs that got her to her feet. "You can't get back on that damned cycle. I'm taking you to the hospital."

"No hospital!" she cried, imagining the spate of publicity such a visit would cause. In her three years on the Vineyard she'd successfully maintained a low profile. She wouldn't blow that now. "I don't need a hospital. I'm fine!"

"Fine?" was the harsh retort. "Then what's this?"

To Sasha's horror, her rescuer took her hand and turned it until she could see the raw heel covered with blood. Fighting a flash of dizziness, she struggled to keep her knees from buckling. Her voice was a distant, ragged protest.

"It's a scrape. It doesn't hurt. Really." Even as she whispered the last word she was being lowered out of the rain into the passenger's seat of a plush sports car. "But…my Suzuki…."

"I'll set it off to the side of the road," he growled. "It can be picked up later."

"I want it now! Really! I'm all right!"

Wondering at the stubbornness of the woman, Doug worked his way back through the rain to the disabled cycle. Pulling it erect, he wheeled it to the roadside.

"Wait!" she cried, stumbling after him. "Is it badly damaged?"

"I thought I put you in the car," he snapped, his glower made all the more forbidding by the rain dripping freely from his dark hair.

Sasha managed to tear her eyes from his ominous expression to peer at her motorcycle. "The worst is the front wheel, I guess," she said shakily, then grimaced. "But look at the rest. It's scratched up pretty badly."

"Humph." If she was well enough to worry about damages, he decided, he had a word to add on that score. "You wanna see scratches? Take a look at my car!"

Horrified, Sasha wheeled around. The sudden movement made her dizzy, and she stumbled as she went back to study the jagged tracks marring the Maserati's otherwise smooth flank. Shaking rain from her fingers, she traced the ugly grooves. "I'm sorry," she whispered, then looked up at the man who had come to join her. For the first time she was struck by his height, which was accentuated by the breadth of his shoulders as he loomed above her. His hair and face dripped, his leather bomber jacket was sodden, his hands were clenched on hips covered by denim nearly as drenched now as her own. Slightly intimidated, she took a breath. "I'll cover the cost."

Ignoring her offer, Doug shot an angry glance at the spilling clouds. "This is ridiculous!" he breathed. "Get in the car!" He grabbed her elbow to enforce his command, but she winced. With a soft muttered oath, he released her to place a more gentle guiding hand at her back.

Each step made Sasha more aware of the battering she'd taken as her cycle had skidded those few yards with her between it and the road. Her ankle ached as she walked, her hip and shoulder throbbed. When once again she found herself seated in the Maserati, she dropped her head back and closed her eyes. In delayed response to the shock of the accident, her limbs began to shake. Yet her mind was alert. No sooner had Doug climbed behind the wheel when she spoke.

"I will cover the expenses. I mean that."

"I've got insurance."

"But it was my fault. I was the one who barreled into you."

"Now that you mention it, why in the hell were you racing? In case you hadn't noticed, it's pouring out there."

Feeling her first flare of testiness, Sasha sat straighter. "I wasn't racing. And of course I knew it was pouring. I was *out* in the stuff, or hadn't you noticed!"

He cast a wry look at his saturated clothes. "Oh, I

noticed all right. I'd planned on staying dry.'' His gaze shifted, then narrowed. ''Damn. Look at that hand.'' Reaching across her to the glove compartment, he withdrew a small towel. ''Here. This is clean. Press it to your hand while I drive.'' With a grunt, he started the engine. ''Now where's the nearest hospital?''

After no more than a moment's pause, during which Sasha decided that his question made him an off-islander, she gestured stiffly with her head. ''It's back that way. You've got to return to Menemsha Cross Road, then cut over to South.''

Three deft moves reversed the car's direction. Within minutes Doug was headed back toward where he'd come from. Jaw clenched, he wondered how he'd managed to get himself into yet another sticky situation. Hadn't he left New York in search of peace? Wasn't Martha's Vineyard supposed to have that? It had been bad enough when the skies opened, he mused. Charming as they were, the narrow island roads were treacherous in a downpour, and he'd practically slowed to a crawl. Then, to have this woman plow her cycle into his car.... Peace? Hah!

''What were you doing out there anyway?'' he growled.

On the defensive, Sasha raised her chin. ''Visiting friends in North Tisbury.''

''And you don't have a car, or access to one?''

''It wasn't raining when I left this morning. For that matter, it wasn't even raining twenty minutes ago! It just...came.''

''So you decided to speed on home?''

''Look,'' she breathed unevenly, ''I've said that I'll

pay for whatever repairs are needed on your car. But please. No lectures. You can take my word for the fact that I didn't run into your car on purpose. You can also take my word for the fact that I'm a responsible person…and that I didn't want, didn't *need* this any more than you did!" The gingerly way she pushed a long strand of wet hair up into the catch at the top of her head illustrated her point. Her voice grew more weary. "Something happened. I don't know what it was. I must have hit a stone or something going around that curve…."

Her voice trailed off and she frowned, staring out the rain-smudged windshield. If only her imagination weren't as fertile. But then, her imagination was her stock and trade. Unfortunately, it did nothing but frighten her now. Of course she had hit a stone. Or a piece of glass. Or a nail. And if the incident was reminiscent of *Autumn Ambush?* Pure coincidence. A simple blowout, that was all it had been. "Make a left here," she murmured, forcing her thoughts along a saner route. Yet the fingers holding the towel to her palm were white knuckled and her expression was grim.

Doug drove in silence, the rhythmic slap of the windshield wipers echoing his vacillation between worry for, then annoyance at his tight-lipped passenger. Hesitant to take his eyes from the road, he saw her from the corner of his eye—her body drawn into itself, wayward strands of hair plastered to her neck, one hand clutched to the other, her eyes straight ahead. She was a soggy water rat; she was a lost and injured lamb. She was a hazard on the road; she was an innocent victim herself. However he viewed it, though, she was the last thing he'd

needed in kicking off his new life. He wanted nothing
more than to deposit her at the hospital emergency room
and be done with it. Actually, he amended, squinting
with impatience at the roadway ahead, he wanted nothing more than to *find* the hospital.

"Where is the damn place?" he mumbled half to himself, then cast an anxious eye at Sasha.

"Almost there," she returned. "Go left up ahead."

He slowed at the crossroad, turned left and acceler-
ated. Sasha winced at the slight jolt to her bruised body,
but caught herself in time to say, "There's a road coming up on your left." Her voice sounded weak and tired.
She felt cold and wet, and wanted only to submerge her
aching limbs in a hot bath and stay there forever.
"Here," she directed, pointing with her uninjured hand.
"Turn here and go straight for a bit. You'll be coming
to a fork in the road. Make a right at the fork and we're
all set."

Doug turned the small car onto a road even more narrow than the first. As the car jounced over several
bumps, he shot a glance at his passenger to assess her
condition. Her face remained pale, her jaw tight. "I
don't believe this!" he exploded anxiously. "What kind
of civilized place hides its hospital down long bumpy
roads?"

"You haven't been here long?" Sasha ventured, relieved as the route leveled and smoothed, and the physical punishment subsided.

"Not quite," was the terse response. Attention riveted
to the muzzied view beyond his windshield, he managed
to spot the fork and bear right onto a road that, though
narrow, was well kept. When soon after he found him-

self in the circle of a dead-end drive, he was forced to stop. "What the...this isn't a hospital!" He turned his eyes from the single-storied rambling farmhouse to see Sasha slip stiffly from the car.

"It's my house," she answered quietly. "Thanks for the ride. As soon as you get an estimate for the repairs to your car, drop me a note. The name's Sasha Blake." Before he could get in a word, she slammed the door and, head bowed against the rain, started at an uneven trot up the stone walk.

Doug was out of the car and halfway up the walk when the front door closed behind her. Stopping in his tracks, momentarily oblivious to the rain, he stared. She'd tricked him. In her own quiet, insistent way, she'd tricked him! Momentarily indignant, he wondered if he should go after her. Perhaps he should insist she have a hospital checkup. After all, if she'd broken a bone or done some kind of internal harm, she could sue him. That was all he'd need. New town. New home. New lawsuit.

Shaking his head in renewed admiration at how silently she'd bested him, he turned and headed back to his car. He doubted she was seriously hurt; he hadn't felt a thing out of place when he'd touched her. Nor did he truly fear she'd cause him trouble. To the contrary. She seemed more than eager to put the entire incident behind her. There was something quiet, something private, something somehow off limits about her.

Puzzled, he started the car, turned in a wide arc and headed back toward the main road. Sasha Blake. Sasha Blake. Her name had a pretty ring to it. It was pixieish, like her. Small and elusive. And wily. It had been a long time since a woman had sidestepped him as skillfully as she'd done. His lips curved at the corners in a subtle smile of appreciation. If Sasha Blake was an example of what he was to find on Martha's Vineyard, his man-in-control image was apt to be well tarnished before long. Strange, he observed, that that thought didn't bother him as once it might have done. Strange how he felt lighter. Strange how Sasha Blake, accident and all, had knocked those darker, more serious thoughts from his mind.

He did like the Vineyard, he mused as he hit South Road once more. Rain and all, it was what he wanted. Fresh air and space, freedom and privacy. New York had become claustrophobic. And tiring. And boring. He needed a change. Midlife crisis? Perhaps. Or perhaps he had simply begun to reassess his goals. Something was missing in New York, in his career, in his life. Before he could begin to identify it, he needed breathing room. Well, he sighed, casting a skeptical eye toward the skies, he had that. He had the house that he'd built overlooking the Sound; he had rocks and grass and acres of rolling hills. And…he had a side full of scratches just waiting to be itched. Or was it the other way around, a whole lot of itches waiting to be scratched. Sasha Blake was a woman. He'd handle her.

"AHHHH!" SASHA CRIED aloud when the leather boot finally relinquished its grip on her swollen ankle. Dropping it on top of its mate with a despairing look, she pushed herself to her feet, unsnapped her jeans and wrestled the soggy denim over her hips. Moaning again, she eased herself back onto the small bathroom bench, carefully worked the fabric down her legs, then tossed it aside and sagged back against the wall. It was from that position that she unbuttoned her blouse and pushed it unceremoniously to the floor.

Removing her inner polo shirt was something else. Sitting forward, she crossed her arms and drew the material up over her ribs, then off with a yelp of discomfort. Half wondering whether she'd cracked a rib, she gently poked around a bit. When she sat still she felt fine—well, not exactly fine. Her hand stung like hell, her side ached, her ankle throbbed. But there was nothing sharp, as in broken bones. For that she had to be grateful.

Slipping from her underwear as gingerly as possible, she hobbled to the bathtub, stepped into hot water laced with scented oil, carefully eased herself down, then sank back with a sigh of relief and let her body float.

It was tense. She was tense. The last thing she'd expected when she'd left the house to visit Janine and Paul had been an accident on the way home. In three years of driving the Suzuki around the island, she'd never had any trouble. She was a good driver. Cautious. Even today in the rain, she hadn't been going terribly fast. But the road had been slick and something had sent her into a skid.

With a slender hand, she reached up to adjust the barrette that held her hair atop her head. Wincing as her muscles rebelled against even that simple motion, she gritted her teeth and slowly returned to her original position.

Thank heavens she'd been wearing a helmet. Thank heavens the man in the Maserati had been there to give her a ride home. She laughed sardonically. Perhaps if he hadn't been there she wouldn't have needed a ride home.

Had there not been a car in her path she might have recovered from her skid. On the other hand, had there not been a car in her path she might have gone headlong into a tree by the roadside and been knocked unconscious or worse. Aches and pains were a small price to pay, she decided, in the face of that other possibility.

Absently dunking the washcloth she'd set out on the tip of the tub, she drew it up over her stomach and between her breasts. Who was he, the man in the Maserati? She'd never seen him before. Was he from Boston? New York? Phillie? He was city; she was sure of it. Wetness notwithstanding, his clothes had that look of designer casual. And his car, well, that was proof of the pudding.

Sighing deeply, she settled more comfortably in the tub and brought the hot cloth over one breast, then the other. Made slick by the oily water, the terry square slid with sensual ease. Eyes closed, she concentrated on her muscles, willing them to relax, letting the moist heat work its magic. Her hand was only scraped. Raw, but nothing worse. It would heal, as would her bruises, though by morning she'd surely have a slew of purple patches to show for her mishap.

Who was he? She didn't know his name, but his face had made an indelible impression on her. Ominous. Forbidding. Yet…gentle beneath his glower? She recalled the hand that had carefully probed her legs for breaks, the arm that had circled her ribs to help her stand. Letting the washcloth sink to the bottom of the tub, she slid her hand to her thigh, inched it back along toned muscle to her stomach.

He was strong, that much she knew. And aside from the occasional brash outburst, he had treated her with care. Care. Her lips thinned. Sam had known nothing about care. He had taken her when he'd wanted her, used her to satisfy his needs. If he was hungry, he'd expected her to cook. If he was tired, he'd expected her to run his bath, turn down his bed, spend the evening alone while his snoring echoed through the house. If he was in the mood for love, he'd expected her to turn on at will. No, Sam had known nothing about care. Did any man?

With a small snort of disgust, she turned to happier thoughts. Her outline was almost done. Tonight she'd put the finishing touches on it. Tomorrow morning she'd begin. She had six months, more than enough time to write this book at a leisurely pace. And actually the six-month deadline was her own. By contract, the book wasn't due on her editor's desk until well after that.

Number six. Would it be up to par? Having been writing steadily now for eight years, she well knew the feeling of insecurity that would hover about her for the next few weeks. Creating her characters. Getting to know them. It was challenging and exciting and infinitely rewarding, if frightening. But she had her setting and her plot outline down pat, and her characters had been brewing for days. It was time to start.

FIVE O'CLOCK the following morning found Sasha at work, the light of her study cutting a blazing swatch through the predawn darkness. She was sore all over and, as she'd expected, slightly discolored along the side that had borne the brunt of the road's hard fury. But her mind was primed and ready, and her fingers sped over the keyboard, registering line after line on the screen before her.

By nine, though, she was stiff and in need of a break. After another long hot bath she tried to dress, finally deciding that her silk robe was the only clothing her battered body would abide. It was soft and light, slitted at the sleeves and leg and belted ever so gently at the waist. Of a pale apricot hue, it brought out the auburn tint of the hair she'd characteristically parted in back and loosely caught up in matching clips at the crown of her head. Her bangs fell thick and low on her brow. With a dash of blusher to cheeks whose lingering pallor spoke of yesterday's trial, she headed for the kitchen and breakfast.

What to have. As she stood staring at the contents of one open cabinet, preoccupied with thoughts of what she'd written, of what she planned to write when she returned to her study, the doorbell rang. Puzzled, she looked up; she hadn't expected anyone. Her mind ran through the possibilities: her friends knew she was working, she hadn't ordered anything to be delivered, the mail never arrived until early afternoon. When the bell rang a second time, she turned, then flinched when her muscles rebelled. Walking stiffly, favoring her sore side, she headed for the front door by way of the living room. Opposite the window she came to a standstill, eyes glued to the dark green, sun-misted Maserati sitting calmly in her drive. Inexplicably, her heart began to thud.

It was the third ring that set her legs in motion again. She hesitated a final time before the door, her hand on its brass knob. Then, with a deep breath for encouragement, she opened it.

For a moment they simply stared at each other, Doug as stunned as she. He had seen her in the rain yesterday, dripping and pale. Now, though, her skin gleamed. She looked fresh out of the bath, her face warm, her hair damp with escaped tendrils curling ever so slightly. Nothing in his vivid imaginings had prepared him for the vision of gentle femininity before him.

As for Sasha, she'd been aware of ominous and forbidding, even of the softer streak that had broken through from time to time. Today, though, confronted with near-black hair that was well trimmed, newly washed and combed, a straight nose, fresh-shaven jaw and stunning gray eyes shaded by the thickest lashes, she was taken aback. If she hadn't been rendered speechless by the male intensity of those eyes, she might have been by the rich bronze sheen of his skin, warm and bold but infinitely touchable. Raw breathtaking virility was something for which she hadn't been prepared.

"Hi," he said at last, his voice faintly rough in a sensual kind of way.

An awkward smile toyed with her lips. "Hi."

"I thought I'd make sure the hospital treated you well."

Her smile relaxed, though her hand held the doorknob for dear life. "It did."

"You look…fine." The understatement of the year, he mused. It was all he could do to keep his eyes on her face. Her robe clung to slender curves he'd somehow missed yesterday. Pixieish, elusive, even delicately feminine he'd thought her then. Nothing had prepared him for downright sexy.

In an unconscious nervous gesture, she dabbed the tip of her tongue to the corners of her mouth. "I am."

"No...aftereffects of the accident?" he asked, daring a fast once-over by way of elaboration.

She followed his gaze, then, self-conscious, showed him her palm. "It's dried up. I'm sure it'll scab over in a day or two."

He nodded, sensing her awkwardness, feeling his own as acutely and being appalled by it. Where was Doug Donohue, the ladies' man? Where was the playboy of the northeastern world? He could take her hand in his, run his forefinger around her bruises, raise her fingers to his lips and suck each in turn as his eyes seduced hers. He could put her palm to his cheek and then kiss away her hurt. For that matter, he could forget the preliminaries and sweep her into his arms for the sole purpose of feeling her body against his.

He cleared his throat. "Well, I guess I'll be going. Just wanted to make sure you were okay." Pivoting on his heel, he took a step down to the walk, then stopped and half turned back to Sasha, his dark brows drawn together. "I stopped on the way to see your cycle but it was gone."

"I had it taken care of." A call to the gas station was all it took. Hank Rossi had been more than eager to jump to her aid. The only price, above and beyond the cost of repairs, would be the sidestepping of another pass, and she was becoming quite adept at that.

"I see," Doug answered, impressed by the independence of such a vulnerable-looking woman. He wondered if there was a man somewhere in the picture. She wore no ring; he'd made note of that yesterday. At least he'd been on top of *something*. Damn, but he was curious. "Well, see 'ya around."

Sasha gave a half smile and a nod, and watched him resume his walk to the car. Wearing stylish gray cotton slacks and a plaid open-necked shirt with a charcoal sweater thrown across his shoulders, he looked decidedly dashing. A man to admire. A man to avoid.

By some twist of fate, admiration won out. "Uh...!" she called, lifting a hand on impulse. When he turned, she blushed again, and let her hand drop. He stood straight, expectant. Startled herself that she had halted his exit, she wondered what she was doing. But there was precious little time to analyze her motives. "Your name," she improvised. "I—I didn't catch it."

"I didn't say it," he replied with a crooked smile. "But it's Doug."

"Doug." She said it once, then nodded again. As when first she'd opened the door, they stared silently at one another. There was an undercurrent of something Sasha couldn't begin to identify. She'd never felt as simultaneously drawn to and unsure with a man. She knew she should let him go, but she couldn't. She moistened her lips. "I was, uh—" she cocked her head toward the back of the house "—I was just taking a break for breakfast. Would you, would you like something? Coffee? Eggs? Juice?"

His smile spread. "I'd like that."

"Of...course, if you've got to be somewhere—"

"I don't."

She moved back then in silent invitation. Seconds later Doug stepped over her threshold, his tall form nothing less than imposing as it passed. Struck by a wave of trepidation, she hesitated, then half reluctantly closed the door.

"Nice place you've got," he said, taking in the open space of the hall and living room. The house was a Cape, as were so many on the island, actually a "half" Cape, with the door and the chimney to the right and two large front windows to the left. Numerous additions had been added at later points in its history, allowing for an oversized kitchen, extra bedrooms and a study, and lending a sprawling air to the house Sasha had fallen for on sight. "Like white, do you?"

She blushed again and followed his gaze. "You noticed." The walls were white; the furniture was white. The floors were brightly sanded oak. She'd added color in cushions, rag rugs and artwork, leaning toward the softest shades of beiges and pinks, giving the house the airy quality she'd sought.

"Hard to miss. But I like it." His gaze turned back to Sasha with a warmth that made her tingle. It also made her suddenly aware of her clothing, or lack of it. She shot a glance downward and raised her hand to her throat. Her robe was high necked, with a mandarin collar and small buttons. All in all, she was well covered, though the cover was all she wore.

"Um, maybe I'd better change," she stammered. "I wasn't expecting anyone." Head down, she made for the stairs, only to have her wrist caught.

"Don't."

She looked up quickly, stunned by Doug's quiet intensity. The sooty gray of his eyes was rich and positively riveting.

"You look fine," he went on softly, waiting to hear himself make a more suggestive quip, as was his normal style. Something about the cling of her robe being good for his appetite. Something about his liking his women soft and sleek. Even something as simple as that she looked sexy as hell.

Strangely, those words eluded him. Reluctantly, he released her hand. "I didn't mean to disrupt things. It's enough that I'm imposing on you for breakfast."

"You're not imposing," she said, pink-cheeked as she recalled her body's present aversion to anything that might bind it. Acceding to that fact, and that fact alone, she led the way back to the kitchen. "What'll it be?" she asked without turning as she opened the refrigerator door and made ceremony of peering inside.

"Coffee. Eggs. Juice," came the voice in passing as Doug walked through to the round kitchen table framed by a semicircle of windows. "Whatever you were planning to have. It'll be a treat for me, in any case."

At the lack of pretense in his tone, she looked up. "You don't usually eat breakfast?"

He snickered. "I'm not much of a cook." He'd never had to be. Over the years he'd had an abundance of cooks. All of his women had cooked. He'd left that chore to them. Since he'd been on the Vineyard, though, he'd been on his own and without. If Sasha Blake wanted to take up the slack, he mused—then caught himself. "But I could try to do something to help, if you're in the mood to instruct."

She smiled. "That's all right. I think I can manage. Why don't you sit down. You can talk to me while I work."

Rather than sitting, he circled the table to stand with his back to her at the window. Sasha studied him for a minute, noting the dignity of his stance, the sense of control exuded by his large frame. A controlling man—the last thing she wanted. For that matter, she didn't want a man, period. Then why, she asked herself, had she invited this one in for breakfast?

Clenching her fingers on the refrigerator door, she turned her attention to a carton of eggs, a tub of butter and a bottle of orange juice. After setting each on the counter in turn, she fished a package of breakfast sausages from the freezer. Perhaps she owed the man, after what she'd done to his car. At least she'd make it good. Then he'd be on his way and they'd be even.

"Your view is beautiful," Doug commented, his voice aimed toward her backyard. "Have you lived here long?"

"Three years."

"That's how long you've been on the Vineyard?"

"Uh-huh."

For as far as he could see there were open fields, broken only by clusters of low shrubs and trees, and crisscrossed at intervals by rambling stone walls. "These were all farmlands once, I'm told."

Pausing to guess at how many eggs to crack, she finally placed half a dozen in a large bowl. A blob of butter already sizzled in the skillet. "I guess so, though there aren't any sheep nowadays. It must have been pretty then."

"It's pretty now," came the voice suddenly headed her way. "I've got an ocean view. Yours represents a whole other aspect of the island."

An ocean view. Janine and Paul had an ocean view. It was that ocean view, wild and white capped, that she'd spent hours contemplating not long before her accident...or whatever. Stifling a shudder, she asked with studied nonchalance, "You live here then?"

"As of two weeks ago."

"Ah. A newcomer." Reaching for the sausages, she struggled to separate the frozen links, hampered by muscles that groaned with even the slightest exertion. Pulling a knife from the drawer, she tried to chop them apart. Her ribs protested.

"Of sorts. Here." He crossed the room. "Let me do that." Effortlessly he separated the links, pleased to see a weakness in the woman, though as yet unaware of its cause. Taking advantage of the excuse to come closer, he simply leaned back against the counter when his job was done. "Don't tell me you have something against newcomers, too?" he asked, arching a wry brow.

Sasha didn't have to glance up to sense his closeness. It was a warm fact not two feet from her, a line of heat that seemed to sizzle along her side. Frightened, she swallowed hard, then turned to set the table. It didn't occur to her that in denying her guest one source of satisfaction she was supplying another. For each time she moved—slow and easy in keeping with the demands of her bruises—the brush of her robe's silk added stroke upon stroke to a vivid picture of her body.

"You've met Old Willie," she observed dryly.

"Old Willie?"

"The big weathered guy at the Menemsha docks who—"

"Who hates the sight of anything from the mainland? I've met him. Charming fellow."

"Oh, he's not really all that bad. Just wary."

"Wary? I don't know. He came across pretty strong

when I was down there last week. Really lit into me about how things just aren't what they used to be.''

She grinned fondly. "Old Willie can do that, all right. He's an islander from birth. A fisherman. A tourist attraction in and of himself. I think he enjoys his soapbox almost as much as the sermons he delivers from it.''

Returning to the stove, she turned the sausages, then pulled the bowl of eggs a safe distance from Doug, cracked each egg in turn, and concentrated on beating them. True vigor was impossible; the best she could do, given her stiffness, was to put added wrist action into play. She prayed he wouldn't notice…and question and prod. She felt shaky enough as it was.

"He's got a point, when you come down to it," she resumed, half hoping to distract him with her chatter. "Things *aren't* what they used to be. Each summer is a little worse than the last. Suddenly the population is five times what it's been. There are lines at the markets and banks and post offices. The roads are more crowded, the beaches and restaurants filled. It's almost enough to send a person packing.''

"Almost…."

She grinned sheepishly. "But not quite." For a split second her hazel eyes met his. Then she looked away again.

"You didn't leave."

"This is my home," she stated with the force of simplicity. "I choose to live here. I can go to the market early, before the rush. Same thing with the bank or the post office. Summertime is crucial to the island's economy. For us year-rounders, it's simply a matter of accommodating ourselves to the population swell for the few months a year it exists. Besides—'' she set the eggs back ''—I kind of like the crowds. They're cheerful and carefree and colorful.'' Her eyes grew momentarily distant. ''A place like New York, well, that's different. Crowds there are somber and less personal. They're in a rush. And if you don't hold the pace, you stand to get trampled.''

''Tell me,'' Doug drawled, drawing Sasha's thoughts from herself.

''You're from New York,'' she stated.

''Not originally. But since my mail's been going there for the past twenty years, I guess you'd have to call me a New Yorker.''

Sasha found New Yorkers distinctly threatening. Tearing her eyes from Doug's she took a large bread knife from the drawer. Thus armed, she reached for the loaf of bread she'd bought fresh baked yesterday morning— *before* her fateful trip to Janine and Paul's—and began to slice it. ''Are you here to stay?''

''If things work out.''

''Things like…?''

''Courier service and long-distance calls. Hey, I hope you're not cutting all those slices for me. Two is my limit.''

To her dismay, she saw seven slices of bread on the cutting board. Suddenly the emotion that had inspired her spree was spent and she gave a self-conscious grin. ''Guess I got carried away.'' Was it New York? Or this stranger in her kitchen? Confused, she quickly knelt to ferret a second frying pan from a low cabinet. Her limbs screeched. She clenched her teeth. Rearranging the pots with far more noise than was necessary in hopes of buying herself some recovery time, she finally slid the pan she needed onto the counter, closed the cabinet and, fingers clutching the edge of the countertop, eased herself up.

"You look a little stiff."

"I'm okay."

"You were favoring that ankle when we walked in here."

"I'm okay!"

"You should really see your doctor—"

"Damn it, I'm fine!" Angry at him for pushing, angry at herself for being angry, angry at her body for having put her on the spot to begin with, she impulsively stretched toward a new package of coffee filters stowed on a high shelf. "Ahhhh...!" she moaned helplessly, then whispered, "Damn!" as she pulled her arm back and tried to catch her breath.

Doug was suspiciously quiet. She stood, head bowed, for a minute, then, unable to stand the suspense, glanced his way. His eyes were dark, his bronzed face grim as he focused on her arm. With a touch so light that it might have been imperceptible had she not been watching, he slowly parted the slit of her sleeve, gently eased the fabric up over the curve of her shoulder and stared. Sasha could do nothing but hold her breath, her eyes large, her heart pounding.

When at last he spoke, his voice was low and ominous. "This is quite a sight. I thought you said you were okay."

"I am," she mustered shakily, terrified by something beyond Doug's simple discovery. He was close. Too close. And his fingers on her bare skin.... "It's just ugly," she managed, confused and upset.

"And painful." He lifted his eyes to hers. "Why didn't you tell me?"

"It wasn't your business."

"But I asked. And I'm half responsible."

"You're not! It was my fault! *I* was the one who skidded into you! You were doing fine on your own side of the road. It was my fault! All mine!"

His fingers slid down her arm to her elbow, then inched back up ever so lightly. All the while his eyes held hers. "But I was willing to help."

"I didn't need your help."

His gaze dropped to her lips. "You have someone else to look after you?"

She pressed her lips together as though in an attempt to dislodge his gaze. Her mouth felt dry. Her voice was meek. "I look after myself. I don't need anyone's help."

"Ever?"

"Just about." She would have elaborated had it been appropriate. But she knew this man didn't want to hear about her agent or her carpenter or the bear of an islander she'd hired to plow snow on the rare occasions it fell. He wasn't thinking of that kind of help. And increasingly, as her blood seemed to heat, neither was she.

"You're that self-sufficient?" he asked, beginning a slow perusal of each of her features in turn.

"I try," she whispered and attempted to shrink from the tangibility of his gaze, but it was unrelenting.

His hand crept to her shoulder, then slid over silk to her neck. His fingers curled around its nape, his thumb caressed the gentle line of her jaw. "Any special reason?"

She felt as though she was stifling. Something was building inside. She burned. She throbbed. She'd never reacted to a man's touch this way before. And a stranger's...? "One." She managed to think and speak only with the greatest of effort. "I like self-sufficiency."

If her voice was breathy, his was hoarse. "But why?"

"Because."

His thumb traced her jaw, gliding back and forth as his eyes followed the gesture. "That's a lousy answer," he murmured. "You have to have reasons."

If she did they were her own, but she could barely think of them now. The feel of Doug's thumb on her chin, inching ever closer to her lips, mesmerized her, as did the power of his gaze scouting the terrain.

"Well?" he prodded in a very masculine whisper.

"I guess," she whispered back.

"Care to share them?"

"No."

"Too painful?"

Had Sasha been fully aware of the conversation, she would have been appalled by her transparency...or this stranger's uncanny insight. But she wasn't fully aware. Far from it. She was spellbound. Drugged. Unable to think beyond the fiery crinkles inside, beyond the dark head slowly lowering, beyond the thumb stroking her lips. She couldn't think, couldn't protest, could only wait, wait until, after what seemed an eternity suspended, his lips touched hers.

CHAPTER TWO

HAD SHE KNOWN this would be coming, Sasha would have been terrified. She didn't know this man, his character, his motives. Had she been able to think, she would have balked. But she hadn't known this would be coming, and she couldn't think. Doug had corralled her senses, heated them, primed them, then focused them on his lips.

Firm but gentle, almost hesitant, those lips touched hers. They were warm, tasting her lightly at first, barely sampling. His fingers slid forward on her neck, his thumb easily propping her chin, holding her face where he wanted it. She couldn't move, couldn't breathe, could only experience a new world of delightfully arousing sensations.

Her name was a breeze on his lips, soft against hers, sending gentle flutters to her chest. Eyes closed, she waited as he hovered, waited for something more than the sampling he'd given. For, quite without her knowing what was happening, her appetite was whetted.

When, with innocent allure, her lips parted, he captured them more surely, sipping thirstily, savoring her sweetness. Alive with a rioting awareness of pleasure points radiating outward from his touch, Sasha felt her lips respond, tentatively at first, then with growing conviction as even her slightest movement doubled the pleasure.

Moisture and warmth, with a lining of fire—she'd never known anything like it. She'd heard, she'd read, she'd written, but never known. Oblivious to all but the glory of the moment, she sought to sustain it, opening her mouth to Doug's gentle prodding, drinking in his breath, his heat, the exotically tempting scent of his skin.

"Sasha," he gasped as he drew back to relish her expression of need, as stunned by its innocence as he'd been by the newness of her kiss. He'd expected...he hadn't known what he'd expected. Certainly not the kind of unaffected, spontaneous, utterly guileless response he'd received. Sasha Blake was different. He felt different himself when he was with her. Not that he understood it; his caution and consideration were new to him. Perhaps there was something in the Vineyard air that made a person slow down, appreciate the finer things in life, strive to draw time to its limits and make the lovely things last. Yet the emotions he felt had come in a torrent. Slow? No way.

His hands trembled beneath her chin. His smoky gray eyes absorbed the soft pink of her cheeks, the moisture of her parted lips. A lovely thing—that she was. Lovely and warm and apparently alone.

Bereft without his kiss, Sasha struggled to open her eyes. Her lashes fluttered, then lifted. She saw Doug's face, inches above hers, his hair falling dashingly over his brow, his color heightened in male counterpoint to hers.

"Sasha..." he whispered, then, with a soft groan, slipped his arms around her and, for the first time, brought their bodies into full contact. It was the stunning evidence of his arousal that made its mark.

Surrender. Humiliation. Pain. A world of memories long suppressed surged to the fore in Sasha's mind. With a groan of her own, not soft as his had been but anguished, she stiffened.

"What—?"

"Let go," she gasped, levering her arms against his chest. "Let go!"

Stunned, Doug did just that. "I've hurt you," he said, his voice thick with self-accusation. "God, I'm sorry! I should have remembered how sore you are. I guess I got carried away."

Braced against the counter, her body trembling with something far removed from desire, Sasha lowered her head. Her breath came in large gulps. She pressed a shaky hand to her brow.

"I'm sorry," he repeated in alarm. "Is it very painful?"

Neither pausing to correct his misconception, nor lying, she nodded.

He swore softly. "Damn, I knew it." He thrust his fingers through his hair, which promptly fell forward again, then hooked his hands low on his hips. His dark brows knit in frustration. His tone held a tinge of reproof. "You really should see a doctor, you know. Something may be chipped or cracked."

"I'm all right," she whispered, slowly regaining control. "I just wasn't prepared...for...." She doubted she'd ever be prepared for what this stranger had so obviously had in mind. Ten years. It had been ten years since she'd felt the force of that particular male appendage against her thigh. Ten years, and yet the memories remained. She'd been seventeen when Sam had married her. Seventeen and utterly innocent. What he'd done to her over the course of two years had been dreadful. And yet…and yet…this man she didn't know had kissed her, and she'd enjoyed it. She'd been oblivious to everything for a few minutes there, and it had been more than she'd ever dreamed.

"Can I get you something?" came the worried voice close by her side. "Some aspirin or something? A heating pad? Maybe you ought to sit down. Or get into bed. Will that help?"

His concern touched her. Looking up, she forced a tremulous smile. "I'm okay. It was just a pang. It's better now."

Oblivious to the hidden meaning of her words, Doug looked doubtful. He was likewise unaware that it was precisely this doubt and its underlying concern that had helped ease Sasha's pain.

This wasn't Sam, she told herself firmly. It was a man named Doug Donohue, a stranger, a man to whom she owed nothing, a man to whom she was in no way bound. He held none of the power over her that Sam Webster had held by virtue of the document proclaiming her his wife. She was her own woman now. Doug Donohue couldn't force her to do anything. And somehow she sensed he wouldn't try, as the other had done with gusto so very many times.

"You're sure you're okay?" he prodded gently. He still felt she should have medical help, but he couldn't force her. She was an adult.

She nodded, feeling better by the minute. "I'm sure." To prove her point, she turned to confront the eggs.

"Hey, you don't have to do that—"

"I want to. I'm hungry."

"Listen, why don't you get dressed and we'll get something in town."

She shot him a pithy glance, then gave a strangled laugh. "Clothes don't seem to agree with me today." More awkwardly, she added a quick, "It'll be easier this way. Besides, everything's out and ready. The sausages are just about done."

"You must be some kind of masochist. To hell with the sausages!"

"You don't like sausages?"

"Of course I like sausages."

"And scrambled eggs? And toast?"

"Those, too. But I don't think I can bear to sit here watching you suffer to cook for me."

"I'm not in pain. Not anymore. I told you—it's better." It was the truth. Having thrust what had happened between them to the back of her mind, she was relieved of those other memories as well.

Doug reached out to take her shoulders, but let his arms fall away when she inched back a step. He hesitated for just a minute. "You strike a hard bargain, babe." He looked down at the bowl of eggs, back at Sasha, then down again. "Okay—" he rubbed his hands together "—you'll have to tell me what to do. I'm not very good at this. I can't guarantee anything."

"Oh, you don't have to—"

"Either you sit in that chair and direct me, or I'll

leave.'' He issued his ultimatum with quiet finality. ''That's the choice.''

Astonished, Sasha gazed up at the figure towering over her. A man had never cooked breakfast for her. Sam wouldn't have dreamed of it. She recalled a time she'd been sick with the flu. Nauseous and weak, she'd stood at the stove preparing the feast necessary to bolster his lordship for a day on the farm. It hadn't mattered that she'd had a raging fever, a throbbing headache, more aches than she'd known she had muscles. The only thing that had mattered had been Sam Webster and his empty pit of a stomach.

This man, on the other hand, was offering. He was different, so different it scared her. *Call his bluff,* one part of her cried. *Let him leave!* It would be safer, far more sensible. Bronze-skinned, golden-lipped Doug Donohue wasn't for her. No man was for her. She'd had one once and been ravaged. Now she had all the heroes she wanted, strong men, loving men, men who if they acted up were sentenced to life with a villainness, thrown into bankruptcy, exiled to a Siberia of sorts, or simply written out of her book. She had what she needed. And yet…and yet….

What demon possessed her she was never to know. With an expression of utter helplessness, she meekly took a seat, forearms braced on the table, oddly comfortable.

''That's better,'' Doug sighed. ''Now then.'' He faced the counter full of breakfast in the works. ''First things first. If the sausages are done, I guess the eggs go on.''

He was neither helpless nor dumb, Sasha mused as she watched him work. Granted, he was no expert. The eggs were dashed with brown from butter that had begun to burn, the toast bore uneven clusters of jam, the coffee was laced with its own grounds, ones that had missed the filter and gathered on the plastic holder to be washed down with hot water from above. There were dribbles of raw egg on the stove and crumbs galore on the counter. But the juice was poured perfectly. And grounds and brown stuff and blobs of jam notwithstanding, everything tasted wonderful.

"Not bad. Perhaps you've discovered a new talent," Sasha quipped between bites. She paused, then scrunched up her face. "What kind of work do you do, anyway?"

"I'm in clothing."

"You make it?"

"Um-hmm."

"Out of New York?"

"Yes."

She nodded.

"And you?" he asked, spearing a sausage. "What do you do out here all by yourself?"

"I write." She gave a shy smile. "One of the many here on the Vineyard."

"Writers?"

"Um-hmm."

"What kinds of things do you write?"

She wavered. "Oh, short stories, novels."

"Published?" he asked with the arch of a brow.

"Um-hmm."

"Have I ever read anything of yours?"

Her cheeks grew warm. "Oh, I doubt it." She wrinkled her nose and made light of her accomplishments. "Not unless you're into romance."

"No, I've never exactly been into that," he reflected, momentarily pensive. He'd always taken his women at face value, seeking nothing more than light conversation, home-cooked meals, sex. He'd never had cause to be romantic, if being romantic entailed truly sharing himself as a person. He was a selfish bastard. He was the first one to admit it. As a matter of fact, he mused, looking down at his eggs, this was a first. He'd never waited on a woman before.

"No matter," Sasha said to cover the awkwardness she felt. "Most men prefer to read adventures or nonfiction."

"Or thrillers. There's nothing like a book that drives you into a corner on a dark rainy night with the doors and windows locked and every light in the house burning."

"Ahhh, you're one of *those*."

"On occasion. But don't tell anyone I told you. It doesn't do much for the image of a strong, fearless man." He wasn't quite sure why he'd told *her*, but the damage was done.

She chuckled. "So why do you do it? Why do you read things that scare the wits out of you?" She was well familiar with the genre, though the intrigue she wrote into her own books was of a far less nerve-shattering form.

Doug shrugged and gave a decidedly sheepish smile. "I don't know. Maybe for kicks. Or excitement. Maybe to take an entirely different view of the world every so often."

She eyed him thoughtfully. "You're bored with your life?"

She'd hit on the truth. He felt instantly defensive. His gaze narrowed. "Are you love starved? Is that why you write romance?" As soon as the words were out he regretted them. Even more than the words themselves, his tone bothered him. Cynicism seemed totally out of place here in Sasha Blake's peaceful kitchen.

Peace was the last thing Sasha felt at that moment. He'd hit on the truth. She felt instantly defensive. But it wasn't in her nature to snap back as he'd done. Rather, she simply avoided the first of his questions. "I write romance because I enjoy it. It's fun. It's a challenge." She eyed him with quiet conviction. "And it pays the bills. It enables me to be totally independent."

"Totally? Or simply financially?"

She tipped up her chin. "Totally. As I said before, I'm a self-sufficient person. Believe it or not, I wouldn't have starved had you not made my breakfast."

He knew it to be fact, and it disturbed him. Men liked their women to be dependent. The weaker sex. "Humph," he scoffed, scowling toward the window. "The liberated woman."

"Yes, liberated!" she exclaimed, a sudden fire in her eyes. "And proud of it. I live as I do out of choice. And I've earned the right to it. No man can force me into something I don't want. I made that vow a long time ago. And," she added, her thoughts straying back in time, "if you think that making my breakfast entitles you to a round in my bed, you're mistaken!"

Doug stared at her tense features, then dropped his

gaze to her fists clenched on the table. "You've been hurt," he stated softly.

"You said that before."

"I'm not talking about the accident." And well she knew he wasn't. He looked her in the eye. "I'm talking about a man. You've been hurt. Badly."

For a minute she wasn't sure what to say. No way would she go into her past with this man who was little more than a stranger. Lowering her voice, her vehemence spent, she murmured, "Haven't we all?"

It was Doug this time who wasn't sure what to say. Had he hurt his share of women along the way? He supposed he had, though he'd never promised more than he'd delivered. But that was another life and one he'd wanted to escape. Perhaps simply because she was part of this newer life, Sasha Blake was one woman he wanted never to hurt.

"Look," he said, pushing his fork idly around his plate, "I'm sorry. This isn't exactly what I'd planned."

"What had you planned?" she challenged impulsively.

He raised his eyes. "To check up on you. To make sure you were okay. It's not every day that I'm in an accident with a motorcyclist. The least you could do is to give me credit for having a conscience." It was asking a lot, he realized. He wasn't sure he deserved it. His motivations for coming this morning were far more complex. He had been curious. He was still. About this woman. About her life. And now about the man who had hurt her once. He sensed, though, that his questions would have to wait. Very obviously, Sasha prized her privacy.

"I'm sorry, too," she murmured, eyes downcast. "And you're right. It was sweet of you to come by." She looked up. "Thank you."

Their eyes held for an instant, mirroring a strange kind of bond. It was Doug who finally broke the spell with a self-conscious laugh. "Well—" he jutted his chin toward his near-empty plate "—I got more than I bargained for. It was good." He stood. "But I'd better be running."

Sasha gave him no argument. It was for the best...even if he *had* left her with the dishes.

UNTITLED WORK NUMBER SIX progressed well that week. As her characters built slowly, Sasha grew fond of them. Her hero was tall and dark haired with sun-bronzed skin. Bold and compelling, he was a man who designed and built race-class sailboats and luxury yachts, a man who had started from scratch armed with equal parts engineering genius and daring, and had gone on to fashion a small empire. Her heroine was a far more private sort, an artist who lived in the small coastal town to which the hero had come for the summer to test out a revolutionary sailboat design. Their life-styles were different, yet from the first they were drawn to each other. True, a strong physical attraction arced between them. But there was something more—a sense of curiosity, of intrigue—that promised to bring them together again and again.

"DAN?"

"Yeah, Doug! Damn it, where have you been? I expected this call two hours ago!"

"I was out." Walking the beach again, thinking. But that was none of Dan Pfeiffer's affair, and Doug had no intention of explaining. "You've got the papers on your desk?"

"Right here."

"Okay. Start from the top. I'm listening." Swiveling his large desk chair around so that he wouldn't have to look at the unpacked cartons of books piled in random stacks around his den, he stared blindly at the ocean. Within minutes, his concentration sped southward, arriving in New York, homing in on the words of the proposed contract his executive vice president was reading.

"Whoa," he ordered after several quiet minutes. "Run that by me again." He paused and listened, then stiffened. "That wasn't what we agreed to."

"They're getting fussy."

"Have them change it."

"I don't know if they—"

"If they won't, drop the whole thing. When we worked this out last month, that clause was very clear. It's in all our foreign contracts. It'll be in this one."

"And if they—"

"Change it. As a matter of fact, take the wording from the Austrian contract."

"Doug, that's stiffer than—"

"I like it. If Perkins won't go for it, he's got a problem. There are other distributors in Sydney. Okay, read on."

Twice more Doug interrupted to have things changed. At the end he took a breath. "Send it to legal for a good going-over and then express it to me." He grinned.

"Maybe I can think of some other changes to rock the boat."

"The Aussies may tell you to take a flying leap."

"I'm not all that sure I'd mind it. We've had trouble with Perkins and his crew from the start. What do you think, Dan?"

"I think that they're the best ones to do the job for us. You know that. It's just unfortunate that Perkins is nearly as headstrong as you are. The two of you test each other."

"But doesn't he know I'll win?"

Dan Pfeiffer gave a wry chuckle. "He will soon. Listen, I'll get these up to you by the first of the week. Or do you want me to hold them here? If you're flying in—"

"Send them. I may not be in for another few weeks."

"You like it up there?"

"It's quiet. And restful." He sighed, his thoughts slowly returning to the Vineyard. "I like it."

"You're not bored?"

"Bored? With the piles of papers I get from you guys every day? Hell, the post office knows me. Good thing they're used to prima donnas pestering them about when things are going out. By the way, I sent a packet of preliminary sketches up to Prosser. Tell him to get to work on them."

"Sure. Anything else?"

"Not now. I'll call if there is. You do the same." Doug knew Dan would, though he also knew that his CEO was perfectly capable of handling things in New York. Well trained and insightful, what Dan Pfeiffer lacked in toughness he made up for in sheer business acumen. He'd been a perfect foil for Doug in New York; now he was a perfect right-hand man once removed.

Tipping his chair back, Doug grew pensive. Somewhere along the line he'd grown hard. Had it happened when he'd first started the business, when so many things had seemed to go wrong? Had it happened over the years as a kind of accompaniment to corporate success? Or did its roots go further back, back to a childhood of scrimping and scraping and forever being without?

The jangle of the telephone tore him from his thoughts.

"Donohue here," he barked quite by habit.

"Douglas?"

Recognition of the drawl at the other end of the line brought a twist of impatience to Doug's lips. "Lisa."

"How are you, Douglas?"

"Not bad."

"I've been waiting for you to call."

"I've been busy."

"Busy? Up there?"

"Busy. Up here."

"Work kind of busy? Or play kind of busy?"

"A little of each," he replied in truth, though large hunks of his time during the past three days had been occupied with thoughts of one Sasha Blake. They were serious thoughts, curious thoughts, far from work, yet not carefree enough to be play.

"You must miss the city."

"Not particularly. It was my decision to leave."

"But you'll be back. Janet said she expected you next week."

Janet Mason was Doug's personal secretary, Lisa's sister and the instrument of their introduction. "Janet had no right to say that. Anyway, she's wrong. There's no need for me to rush back."

"But I thought that was part of the deal, that you'd be commuting."

"It is an arrangement strictly contingent on the business, Lisa. You know that. When the business needs me, I fly down."

"I need you."

"I doubt that."

"But I do."

"I'm sorry."

"You're a bastard, Douglas Donohue. A cold-hearted bastard. Do you know that?"

"Yes, Lisa. I do. That's precisely why you need to find someone else, someone who really cares."

"But you could if you tried—"

"Lisa...." The warning in his tone hung in the air for long moments before Lisa finally swore and hung up.

He *was* a bastard, Doug mused, returning to the thoughts that his ex-lover's call had interrupted moments earlier. He was callous and arrogant; and proud of neither. As a matter of fact, he didn't particularly like himself. Which was one of the reasons he'd left New York. He needed a change, a break from the whirlwind of a life he'd led for twenty years. He needed inspiration.

Like...Sasha Blake. She brought out things in him he hadn't known existed. Patience. Concern. Self-restraint. Even now he could feel his muscles begin to relax. His face, hard and immovable when he'd talked with Lisa, softened at the thought of Sasha's name. His insides warmed. His anger thawed. She was the antithesis of the world he'd known. Bruises, fiery temper, independent spirit notwithstanding, she excited him. He was looking forward to seeing her at the Slater's tomorrow night.

KNOWING SHE'D BE THERE, Doug had an advantage on Sasha, who, having no word from him since their breakfast together, had spent the better part of the week when not lost in her work trying to convince herself that it would be for the best if this intruder simply vanished from her life. She wasn't terribly successful. She couldn't seem to forget the warmth of his expression or, to her chagrin, the heat of his kiss.

The call from Ginny Slater had come at a time when she very definitely needed distraction. Ginny and Rob were having the group over for a spontaneous, last-minute dinner party on Saturday night. Nothing formal. Strictly casual. No, she couldn't come early to help in the kitchen. Yes, she could bring a dessert, but only if she promised not to leave the instant it was served.

Ginny and Rob were two of the first people Sasha had met when she'd first come to the Vineyard. They'd been introduced by a mutual friend, Sasha's agent, Diane DeScenza. As the publisher of a nationally distributed monthly magazine, Robert commuted to New York as did so many other islanders. Ginny spent her time working at home translating manuscripts and research papers from English to German or Spanish, or back, at the whim of scholars at universities in Boston and New York.

The first few evenings Sasha had spent with the Slaters had been quiet ones, just the three of them. Though Sasha half suspected that Diane had warned the Slaters about what an introvert she was, she didn't mind, for those early times she spent with Ginny and Rob were warm, intimate ones, the perfect antidote for the chill she'd acquired while living in New York. Gradually other islanders were invited along, and when they took to Sasha as readily as she took to them, Sasha became one of the group. It was a small group, no more than eight or ten together at any given time, but its members were friendly, and all were drawn to the Vineyard for its peace, its protectiveness and its privacy.

It was therefore in anticipation of a pleasant evening with friends that Sasha bathed and lightly made herself up, gathered her hair softly atop her head, tugging tendrils to fall here and there, put on a silk blouse, wool gabardine slacks and stylish leather pumps, took a wool blazer against the October evening's chill and her chocolate rum cheesecake and drove to the Slaters.

Doug was the very first person she saw. Granted, he was taller than the others and, to Sasha's eye, the most attractive man there, but the fact of his presence had telegraphed itself to her central nervous system the instant she stepped inside the door. Stunned, she simply stood at the entranceway for a minute, knees locked, gaze frozen. She didn't notice the presence of her friends or the gentle hum of conversation. Only when her hostess approached did she manage to tear herself from the hold of the silver eyes across the room.

"Sasha, come on in and shut that door." Ginny hugged her, then set her back. "You look gorgeous, as usual. Here, let me have your masterpiece." Taking the large round plastic container in one hand, she ushered

Sasha toward Rob. "Sweetheart, why don't you get Sasha a drink to warm her up."

"How are you, Sasha?" Robert Slater asked with a smile. Taking Sasha's hands in his, he pressed a fatherly kiss to her cheek. "Hmm, you *are* cold." He squeezed her fingers, then put an arm around her shoulders and drew her toward the first cluster of people in the living room.

"Sasha! Good to see you!" This from Tim Carlin, a retired economics professor, whose wife, Susan, chimed quickly in.

"How have you been, Sasha?"

"Very well, thanks. And you two? Tell me about your trip. Was China an experience?" If she was babbling, she didn't care. Anything to be nonchalant, to try to forget the virile presence nearby.

"What'll it be, Sasha?" Rob murmured. "White wine?"

She smiled and nodded, watched her host walk toward the bar, then turned back to the Carlins.

"We were just telling Maggie about it," Tim said, tapping an older woman on the shoulder, drawing her attention back from the next group.

Margaret Powell was a sculptress who had lived and worked on the Vineyard for more than twenty years. At the age of sixty-eight, she was the matriarch of their group. Sasha had always been touched by the sensitivity of both her work and her person. In her own gentle way Maggie had come to be a sort of favorite aunt to Sasha. Their affection was mutual.

"Sasha," the older woman cooed, a smile lighting her

weathered face, "how wonderful to see you." She extended an arm and Sasha immediately met it with a hug.

Though touching and kissing was spontaneous with these people, Sasha had been skeptical until she'd realized it accompanied a genuinely fond attachment to one another. Feeling that fondness now, she grinned. "How are you, Maggie?"

"Not bad for an old lady. But you—" she poked a finger at Sasha's ribs "—you're doing beautifully. Was that *Midnight Rogue* I saw on the *Times*'s list? No, not *Midnight Rogue*. *Raven's Revenge*. Was that it?"

Sasha blushed. "That was it."

"And you're working on something new, I gather."

"Always," Sasha admitted with a dash of self-mockery. "But I want to hear about Tim and Susan's trip." Still holding Maggie's hand, she turned back to the other couple. "Come on. Tell."

Managing by some miracle to look enthralled, she barely heard a word they said. Her mind was at the far end of the living room, on the figure dressed in hunter-green and navy—slim-fitting slacks, turtleneck jersey, Shetland sweater—and the eyes that seemed to meet hers every time she dared glance his way.

When Rob returned to push a glass of chilled wine into her hand, she jumped, managing to recover only momentarily before her host had his arm around her waist again.

"Excuse us, folks," he said to the others. "Sasha hasn't met Doug. She'll catch you later."

Sasha had no choice but to acquiesce as gracefully as possible, a monumental challenge on legs that seemed strangely and suddenly uncoordinated. Doug was standing with Paul O'Hara, her good friend and fellow writer, and Jonathan Macoubrie, the rising young multimillionaire of the group. The two turned to her with smiles of welcome; Doug simply stared intently.

"Hey, Sasha," Jonathan drawled, slipping his arm around her waist for a momentary hug. "How's it going?"

"Okay," she said breathlessly, then offered a hand squeeze and a kiss to Paul. "Hi, Paul. I'm glad you two made it—hey, where is Janine, anyway?" Looking frantically for a diversion, she scanned the room.

"In the kitchen. She'll be right out."

"Maybe I could do something—" she began in Rob's direction, only to have her feeble attempt at escape nipped in the bud.

"Two in the kitchen's plenty. Besides, I want you to meet Doug. He's just moved here from New York. Douglas Donohue...Alexandra Blake."

For a split second, Sasha wondered whether to acknowledge that they'd met before. Douglas Donohue...his name, spoken in full for the first time, was as familiar as his face, and she suddenly wondered whether she should have recognized it from the start. Each member of this group was renowned in his or her way. Douglas Donohue...Douglas Donohue. Stifling tiny frissons of trepidation, she let Doug take the lead.

Without so much as the slightest pause, he extended his hand and enveloped hers in its warmth. "Alexandra." He nodded once. "It's my pleasure." Then, to her perverse satisfaction, he offered a legitimate frown. "Alexandra Blake. Why does that sound familiar?"

"No doubt you've seen Sasha's name in bookstores,

supermarkets, drug stores, etcetera," Rob put in proudly. "She's the queen of romantic intrigue. She's written five bestsellers, the most recent of which is on the *New York Times*'s list now."

"Five best-sellers," Doug repeated with quiet concentration. His eyes held Sasha's, his hand gripped hers all the more tightly. "I'm impressed. This is truly an honor, Alexandra."

"Sasha, please," she corrected, her voice weak in response to his imperceptibly sardonic note. Or was it his meaningfully firm clasp of her hand, or her own imagination? Was it simply her own guilt she felt? "Here on the Vineyard I'm Sasha Blake. I—I prefer it to the other."

"No need for excuses—or modesty, Sasha," Rob went on. "Doug, here, is renowned in his own right. I'm sure you've heard of his clothes. The Douglas Donohue label carries its share of clout in high-fashion circles."

It was Sasha's turn to be stunned. Douglas Donohue. Of course! Those gray eyes that sun-bronzed face, the near-black hair falling rakishly across his brow—Douglas Donohue! How could she have been so stupid! With great effort she tugged her gaze from his and let it fall to the small insignia on the breast of his sweater. Back-to-back D's. Freeing her hand from his, she raised it, lay a forefinger on the initials, then looked helplessly up again.

"I should have recognized the name instantly," she murmured dumbly. She might have, had he not made light of what he did. He was "in clothing," he'd said, and had admitted that he made it. But designing it was something else, and selling it in only the finest men's stores and boutiques in the country and abroad was another thing entirely. "This *is* a pleasure, Mr. Donohue," she said, less able to hide her sarcasm than he had been. Suddenly aware of a fire beneath her fingertips, she pulled her hand away and thrust it into the pocket of her slacks.

"Not that we're hung up on occupations, Doug," Paul felt called upon to explain. "It's more a matter of making the association, then forgetting it. We're pretty protective of one another here. We respect each other's need for privacy. Take Sasha, for example. If she wanted constant adulation, she'd have stayed in the city. The Vineyard is a place where she can come and go without people staring or treating her any differently.

As though to disprove his point, Geoffrey Briggs chose that moment to arrive, offering boisterous hellos to the others in the room but seeming to make a beeline to Sasha.

To her chagrin, though she hadn't expected much less, he came up behind her, slipped his arms around her waist and gave her a sound kiss on her cheek. "How's my favorite bestselling author? Mmm, you smell good."

"Geoffrey," Sasha pleaded, color rising from her neck. She tried to free herself with as much grace as possible, but succeeded only in endangering the wine in her glass. Not daring to look at Doug, she sent Paul a silent plea for help. Rob had disappeared in response to an urgent wave from his wife, and Sasha needed rescue.

"Geoff," Paul began, "why don't you let go of Sasha and say hello to Doug. Geoffrey Briggs...Douglas Donohue." Satisfied when Sasha was momentarily freed,

Paul turned to Doug. "Geoffrey is the island's resident photographer. When he's not on assignment, that is."

His composure fully intact, to Sasha's dismay, Doug shook the newcomer's hand. "Geoffrey Briggs. *LIFE? National Geographic?*"

"Right on, man," Geoffrey said, beaming. "I mean, it's not the kind of stuff you need for *your* ads, but it sells, if you know what I mean."

"I'll say it sells," Doug returned. "It's beautiful."

Geoffrey nodded his thanks, then turned his gaze back to Sasha, who stood quietly beside him, feeling awkward and unsure. "I've done models' portfolios in my time, but this little lady keeps refusing me."

"I'm not a model and I don't need any pictures," Sasha insisted self-consciously.

"Book jackets, publicity—you must need something."

"My publisher takes care of all that in New York. You know that, Geoff. We've been through it before."

"Yeah, yeah, but why won't you humor me and let me photograph that beautiful face of yours?"

Sasha sighed. "I guess I'm not the humoring kind. Sorry, friend."

Geoffrey shook his head and sent the other men a conspiratorial wink. "Shot down again. The woman's a witch. She's got me half in love with her and she won't even let me take her picture. No heart. No heart at all."

A welcome female voice came from behind just then. "Is this lecher after you again, Sasha? Here, guys, have an hors d'oeuvre."

"Janine," Geoffrey exclaimed, taking a toothpick-skewered something from the tray Janine held, "you look great! Hey, what is this?'' The last was said with a mouthful of food. ''It's great!'' Still juggling the item in his mouth to counter its oven-fresh heat, he reached for another.

''That was *rumaki*, these—'' she pointed ''—are mushrooms rolls, and these are miniature quiches.'' She extended the plate in one hand, a pile of cocktail napkins in the other. As the men helped themselves, she leaned over to kiss Sasha hello. ''How're ya doin', sweetie?''

Sasha raised her eyes skyward and took a big breath. Between Douglas Donohue and Geoffrey Briggs, she felt at that moment squished between a rock and a very hard place. ''I'm fine,'' she murmured, though she shook her head when Janine passed the plate her way. ''Did you make all these?''

''Ginny did. Looks like she's been on a cooking binge. I think this party was an afterthought, a necessity to dispose of all she's made. She's outdone herself this time.'' As the two women inched off by themselves, the men picked up conversation of their own. ''Are you okay?'' Janine whispered. ''You look a little peaked.''

''Peaked? Oh, no, I'm fine.'' Sasha smiled. ''Working on my book, though, I barely step foot outside. Jailhouse pallor, I think they call it.''

''How's it coming?''

''The book? Okay. The beginning's always tough. I can never tell whether it's really going to be any good.''

Janine drew Sasha farther from the men and leaned closer. ''Did you get a look at him?''

''At who?'' As if she didn't know.

''Doug Donohue. Gorgeous, isn't he?''

''Janine, you're a happily married woman!''

"And a good five or six years his senior, but that doesn't have to tarnish my eye. You're single. And just the right number of years his junior. *You* take a look. What do *you* think?"

Given good cause by her friend, Sasha cast a glance over her shoulder to find Doug's eye on her. She looked quickly back. "He's dangerous, that's what I think. Looks like the kind to love 'em and leave 'em." He was a slick New Yorker, wasn't he. And *Douglas Donohue* to boot!

"That's what they say."

"They do?" Sasha asked in unbidden dismay.

"Mmm," Janine replied. She looked down, popped a tiny quiche into her mouth, then deposited the plate into the hands of Tim Carlin. "Make yourself useful," she teased, her voice lowering again once he'd moved on. "The word is that he's a pretty hard guy. A tough businessman. An even tougher ladies' man. Strange." She seemed genuinely puzzled. "He doesn't look that bad from here."

Strange, he hadn't looked *that* bad on the two other occasions she'd seen him. "Maybe it's the Vineyard. It brings out the best in people. Maybe he's planning to turn over a new leaf."

"I hope so, for your sake. He hasn't taken his eyes off you."

Sasha scowled. "He must be taken with my work. Men like that assume that a woman who writes bestselling novels with sex in them have to be wildly erotic creatures themselves."

"And you're not a wildly erotic creature?"

"Hardly."

"I wonder...."

"Come on, Janine. You know me as well as anybody does."

"Which is only to say that, woman to woman, I find you a warm and caring person. What you'd be like with a man, if you ever gave yourself a chance, is something else. It's in there, Sasha. I've read your books. You wouldn't be able to write what you do without feeling something."

Sasha sighed. "Dreams, Janine. Not only mine, but those of millions of women. My heroes are ideal, imaginary. They are men who truly love, who care enough for their women to risk everything, to *be* there." Her expression saddened. "I'm not sure I've ever met a man like that...or that I ever will."

"You've never been in love."

"No. I suppose not."

"You never loved Sam?"

Sasha shook her head. "My marriage was more practical than anything else. Love was never an issue."

"But surely you're capable of love."

"Surely," she drawled facetiously. "That's what makes me a bestselling author of love stories."

"Hey, such a sober face," Paul O'Hara quipped, coming up behind his wife and slipping an arm about her waist. "Discussing your latest villain, Sasha?"

"Could be," Sasha mused moments before she felt the warm body behind her. Tensing imperceptibly, she tried to steel herself against its presence, but her pulse already raced, her nerve ends buzzed.

"The lady's dangerous, Doug," Paul joked. "Better

watch out for her. She's got any number of evil ways of disposing of unwanted men.''

''Oh?'' came the deep, faintly smug reply. Obviously, Doug Donohue wasn't frightened. ''I'll have to read her books then. Forewarned is forearmed.''

Sasha grimaced. ''While you boys are having fun at my expense, I think I'll see if Ginny needs a hand.'' It was the perfect excuse for the perfect escape, which would have been perfectly executed had it not been for the fact that, with a wink to Paul and Janine, Doug followed her.

CHAPTER THREE

THE KITCHEN was empty. Knees weakened by a world of conflicting emotions, Sasha leaned against the counter, facing the large window above the sink. She took a deep breath, then sucked it steady when she saw Doug's reflection join hers. She didn't turn, simply regarded him warily in the glass, taking comfort in the sense of distance though she knew it to be an illusion.

He took a bold stance, his hands flanking hers on the counter, his long arms imprisoning her. Though his body touched hers but lightly, it was enough to set her blood pounding through her veins.

"So you're *the* Douglas Donohue," she forced herself to say, unable to bear the silence, praying that the sound of her voice would hide the thunder of her pulse.

"And you're *the* Alexandra Blake," he retaliated softly.

"Why didn't you tell me?"

"Why didn't *you* tell me?"

"I had my reasons, and they were probably a lot more sound than yours."

"Try me."

"Privacy, for one thing. I like it. New York takes care of publicizing my books. I don't. For another thing," she raced on, gripping the counter, "I like to come and go without people staring...or leering."

"Why would they do that?"

"They stare if they are curious about a bestselling author. They leer if they are curious about a bestselling author of romance. Don't tell me you aren't curious." Her gaze narrowed with the cynicism of her tone. "Don't tell me those wheels haven't started going round and round in your head. Don't tell me you're not wondering just what's in my books and how juicy it gets. I've been doing this long enough to know your type. New York was full of them."

"So you came here."

"Yes."

"And you wish I'd leave you alone."

"Yes."

"Why, Sasha?" he asked, his voice disturbingly gentle as he talked to her reflection. "What are you afraid of?"

"I'm not afraid of anything," she lied, even then tormented by the manly scent of the body so close to hers. "I just don't *want* anything from you."

"Your mind says that. So why is it you're trembling?"

"I'm...upset."

"About me? About who I am?"

"Maybe. You could have told me, you know. Why didn't you?"

"For many of the reasons you didn't tell me about yourself. I had my motives for moving to the Vineyard."

"Why did you move here?"

"To get away. To break a pattern I didn't like. To try to think things out, to decide where I want to go in life."

"Humph. Sounds like you're already there."

"Are you?"

"Yes. I have what I want."

"A man?"

"I don't want a man."

"Is that why you write the stories you do?"

She swallowed hard, unable to take her eyes from their dual images in the glass. Her body, smaller, more slender, fit in front of his perfectly. The top of her head barely reached his chin. "So we're back to that?" she muttered weakly.

"It's a legitimate question." He paused then, lowering his head, closing his eyes to breathe in the lemon fragrance of her hair. "I'm attracted to you," he said thickly. "You know that."

She did. And she couldn't deny the warmth that surged through her at his touch.

Bowing his head until his mouth touched her cheek, he kissed her ever so gently. "Give us a chance, Sasha. That's all I ask."

Mesmerized by the sensual tableau before her, she couldn't move, much less breathe. It was as though after a buildup of hours—no, days—the air was suddenly charged with erotic sparks, a fantasy in the works. Without realizing what he was doing, she relaxed back against Doug, absorbing the strength of his body, giving in to the mindless demands of her own. The fact that she barely knew him was irrelevant at the moment. He seemed so gentle, so caring. And her body responded in ways that were new and infinitely exciting.

"I won't hurt you," he murmured, his breath a warm caress on her cheek. "Please believe that. It would only be good and filled with pleasure."

"But...." She couldn't remember what she wanted to say, for his hands left the countertop and slid up her hips to her waist. His thumbs inched higher, drawing exquisite circles on her silk-sheathed skin before touching the outer swells of her breasts. She sucked in a breath, but he was speaking again before she could protest.

"You're soft, so soft and delicate." His thumbs moved inward. She watched their progress, his bronzed skin so very masculine against the white silk of her blouse. She felt the betraying hardening of her breasts, and when her breath came faster, she bit her lip. This man was a stranger, an unknown to her, yet he courted her in ways that sent swirls of heat curling from her breasts to her toes. The effect of his touch fascinated her, as did the seeming naturalness of his hands as they came to curve beneath her breasts. By the time his thumbs found their mark, her nipples were already taut. He rubbed them and a burst of pleasure surged within her. Her eyelids slid shut, her head fell back to his shoulder. Fear was in another world, another time. What Doug was doing to her was warm and erotic and too good to be denied.

"So sweet," he rasped. "Oh, babe, it's happened so quickly, but if you only knew how much I want you...."

She did feel wanted and, for the first time in her life, very, very feminine. Her body craved something she'd only dreamed about and had a mind of its own as it leaned toward that dream.

A loud burst of laughter from the other room broke

the spell, bringing with it a harsh reminder of where she was and what she was doing. Stiffening, she brought her head forward, eyes wide open, and leaned against the counter once more.

Having heard the laughter too, and appalled that he'd so forgotten the time and place himself, Doug moved to the side, turned his back to the glass and took several great gulps of air. "Damn it, Sasha. I don't know what's gotten into me. I haven't been able to think of much else this week besides holding you again."

"You didn't call," she managed in a whisper, trying desperately to catch her breath.

He looked sideways at her. "I wasn't sure you wanted me to." When she didn't answer but continued to stare down at the sink, he went on. "You're feeling better?" She nodded. "Soreness gone?" She nodded again. "But you didn't drive that damned cycle here tonight, did you?"

"No. It's still in the shop."

"Good. I'll drive you home."

She looked up quickly. "No! I have a car."

"Then I'll follow you home. We have something to work out."

"No!" She shook her head, feeling soft wisps of hair against her cheek. As though he'd felt them too, Doug reached out and fingered one long silken strand. He was about to argue when the swinging door opened and Ginny bounded through.

"Hey, this is *my* kitchen," she exclaimed, smiling as she bustled toward the stove. "You're not supposed to be out here." Slipping her hand into an oversized oven mitt, she pointed toward the living room. "You're supposed to be out there, eating my hors d'oeuvres and mingling with my guests.'' She gestured with the mitt. ''Now, scoot!''

Doug had the grace to give a sheepish smile first to Ginny, then to Sasha. ''Yes, ma'am,'' he said to the former, with a low-murmured, ''Later,'' in Sasha's ear as she passed through the door a breath before him.

He might have yelled it, or plastered it in bright red paint on the wall, for try as she might to forget it, that one word reverberated through Sasha's being for the rest of the night. To her surprise, Doug left her pretty much on her own to talk with her friends. He kept his distance, fitting into the conversation easily but always in a different group. She half wondered if he didn't trust his control; each time she caught his eye it held the same promise he'd made at the door. *Later.* The word grew nearly tangible as the hours passed, and Sasha grew more and more afraid.

Douglas Donohue. *The* Douglas Donohue. From the fast lane, for sure, and certainly not for her. Yet she couldn't help but warm each time she thought of the way he'd leaned into her, the way he he'd kissed her neck, the way he'd held her breasts—so gently, almost worshipfully. Oh, yes, it was a purely physical thing, yet she felt cherished, and to her surprise, she liked the feeling. It was something new, albeit something that frightened her with its sudden force.

Doug, too, was in his way frightened. He'd never met a woman like Sasha Blake before. Amazed at her success, he wondered at her innocence. For that was what he'd felt in her responses, both to his kiss that first morning at her house and to his touch earlier this evening.

Innocence. Simplicity. But she was right; though he had no idea what went on in the bedrooms of her books, he was downright curious. Was the innocence all for show? Was she truly a woman of the world?

All week he'd harbored the image of her sitting alone in her house writing, eking out the scant living most authors did, praying that her latest masterpiece would sell. Hell, in advances alone she probably made a million. And here he'd spent hours thinking of the little luxuries with which he might dazzle her. Thinking of giving, a new experience for him. And to find that there was probably little she couldn't buy for herself—it was damned frustrating. As was, he mused, the quiver of arousal he felt each time he looked at her. Damned frustrating! The evening couldn't end fast enough.

Not so for Sasha. Had she not promised Ginny she'd stay, she would have run out the back door right after dessert. But she had promised. And as though suspecting her second thoughts, Ginny seemed to stick close by her elbow until, guest by guest, the gathering broke up. Having missed her chance for an early escape, Sasha waited, prolonging the inevitable. But if she'd hoped Doug would leave graciously with the others, she was mistaken. He, too, waited. The inevitable was, it seemed, indeed inevitable.

When it was only Sasha and Doug and Ginny and Rob lingering over refills of coffee in the Slaters' living room, Sasha finally stood.

"I guess I'd better be running," she said with a sigh of regret that held its share of resignation. "I'm planning to be up at five to work tomorrow."

"It's today," Ginny said, "and you can't do that. It's Sunday. You deserve a day of rest."

The other three had risen with Sasha, who tried to ignore the fact that Doug had taken a step closer. "Days of rest will have to wait until this manuscript is done. And since I've just started...." What was meant to be a subtle hint to Doug only succeeded in bringing Ginny and Rob down on her.

"You work too hard," Rob said with a frown. "The book will wait. You deserve a day off now and then."

"We were planning on taking the ferry to Falmouth and driving into Boston for the day," Ginny added. "Why don't you join us?"

"Oh, no, I couldn't—"

"Why not? It would be fun."

"Actually," Doug broke in, his voice a deep lure, his eyes echoing the sentiment, "I was hoping she'd show me around the island. Just a few hours. She can't refuse."

"Oh, Sasha—" Ginny grinned enthusiastically "—why don't you? Doug is new to the Vineyard, after all. And if you could get some work done in the morning—"

Sasha sent Doug a withering look and promptly ignored his offer. It was to Ginny and Rob collectively that she spoke, as polite a smile on her face as she could muster. "You're sweet to worry, but don't. I'll be fine. I do love what I'm doing, remember?"

Rob arched his brows, then headed for the closet and her blazer, which Doug took from him and put gently around her shoulders.

Sasha smiled at her host and hostess. "Thanks for a lovely evening. It was great seeing everyone."

"We should do it more often," Ginny said, then leaned forward and gave her a hug. Rob repeated the gesture and stood back, his arm curling comfortably about his wife's waist, emerging only briefly to shake Doug's hand.

"Thank you both," Doug added. "It's a lovely group of friends you've got."

Ginny grinned smugly. "You'll join us again soon, won't you?"

"My pleasure." With a final nod of goodbye, he put his hand on Sasha's back and escorted her out of the house. Only when the door had closed firmly behind them did he reach out to catch her hand in his. "Where're you going so fast?"

"My car."

"Shall I follow you?"

"No."

"I'd like to talk."

"It's late. Like I told Ginny and Rob, I've got to be—"

"What's another hour? Besides, you don't really want to send me home to that big empty house with cartons all over the place."

The darkness hid his expression. Unable to tell if he was mocking or serious, she sent him a quizzical look. "You mean you've been here a month and you haven't unpacked?"

"Not quite a month, and no. I'm not good at that type of thing."

"Don't you have a houseboy or a maid or something?" Surely *the* Douglas Donohue would have help.

"No," he answered curtly, reading her thoughts. "I left the servants back in New York. I would have thought you'd guessed that after my enthusiasm for breakfast the other morning."

"Poor Doug."

"Not really. It's nice to have breathing room for the first time in years." Quite a turnaround, but he meant it. Though he could remember the days when thoughts of having a maid were second only to those of eternal salvation, he did enjoy the freedom.

"You mean that, don't you?" They arrived at her car and she fished in her blazer pocket for the keys.

"Yes." He paused. "Is that yours?"

"Um-hmm."

He choked on a forced cough. "A step up from the Suzuki, I'd say."

The night hid her blush. "You can see why I like the Suzuki," she said in a tiny voice.

"Oh, I don't know. There are many people who'd kill for a little number like this." He whistled and stepped back to admire the car. "A Mercedes two-seater. Not bad."

"Mercedes, Maserati…not much difference," she murmured, opening the door, sliding quickly inside. But Doug wasn't so taken with the extent of her means that he'd let her escape him as easily. Before she could shut the door his hand was on it, holding it ajar.

"I'll follow you."

"Please. You don't have to. I'm sure we'll bump into

each other another time.'' Only after she'd said it did she wince. Doug mirrored the motion.

"Hell, I hope not! My car hasn't recovered yet. Neither have I, for that matter.''

"Look,'' Sasha began with a weary sigh, "this really won't work out. Please, I've got to run.''

Doug stared at her for a long moment, the moon just catching the silver of his gaze. Then, with a nod, he shut her door and stepped back. Needing no further encouragement, she started the car, turned around and headed down the long driveway toward the main road. No more than a minute passed before the Maserati's headlights glared at her in her rearview mirror.

Swearing softly to herself, she tightened her grip on the wheel. There was always the possibility that he was headed home. After all, this was the major road along the north shore of the island, and he'd said that he looked out on the ocean. Any one of the upcoming drives led to private homes with ocean views. Any one....

By the time she'd turned onto Menemsha Cross Road, though, she'd given up that hope. He was following her, just as he'd said he would. What was she going to do now? The last thing she needed was "to talk'' with a man who stirred such new and overwhelming sensations in her. True, she was curious, and excited even as she thought of it. But she'd been hurt so badly once, and in ways above and beyond the physical. She didn't need that kind of hurt. She didn't need Doug Donohue.

Unfortunately, she didn't have much choice in the matter. Doug kept her in sight, turning when she did first at South, then her private road, then the fork. She'd no sooner pulled into her garage when the Maserati drew to a halt outside her front door. Doug was waiting for her there.

Trying to make the best of an uncomfortable situation, she said nothing as she unlocked the door, stepped into the house and flipped on every light in sight. Only then did she turn, interlace her fingers, and eye him guardedly.

"You wanted to talk?"

"Yes."

"Well?"

He glanced toward the chair. "May I sit down?"

"Be my guest." She watched as his leggy frame settled itself comfortably, then, feeling more awkward than ever, she took refuge in a protective corner of the sofa. "Okay, what is so urgent that we have to talk tonight?"

"Your friends are nice, Sasha. I enjoyed them."

"*Urgent,* Doug. There's nothing urgent about my friends." She thought for a minute. "How did you come to be there, anyway?"

"Maggie and I have a mutual acquaintance in New York. He told her I was moving to the Vineyard. When Ginny invited her to the party, Maggie mentioned me. Naturally, consummate hostess that she is, Ginny called me."

"I see."

"It is an interesting group, each renowned in his way." He paused. "Has Geoffrey really tried to photograph you?"

"He's a pest."

"But a talented one, you have to admit."

"I'll grant him that."

"And he's good-looking."

"He's a kook."

"Because his hair passes his collar and his jeans are worn to threads?"

"Because his idea of photographing me is only the first step in a very deliberate seduction scenario. But come on, Doug. There's nothing urgent to discuss about Geoff. What's on your mind?"

Doug took a deep breath, then let it out. He'd hoped she'd relax, even offer him coffee, though he'd had more than enough to keep him up all night. But it wasn't the coffee that would keep him up all night, was it?

"Who was he, Sasha?"

She tensed. "Who?"

"The guy who hurt you."

Expelling a ragged breath, she shook her head and looked away. "You don't mince words, do you?"

"You wanted to know what I thought to be urgent? Well, I'm telling you. Something's happening between us and I think that whoever *he* is, he's standing in our way."

"Whatever gives you that idea?" she snapped defensively.

"You," he said more thoughtfully. "Your reaction to me. Your reaction to your reaction to me."

"This is getting complicated." Her attempt at humor fell flat. Doug wasn't to be deterred.

"It doesn't have to be. Just tell me who he is. Or was. Then I'll have an idea about what I'm up against."

"You're not up against anything…or anyone. I'm me. What I want is what *I* want."

"Look who's playing with words now, Sasha. We're

both fairly intelligent people. We know that what we are is a product of a whole series of life experiences.''

"Then tell me about yours, Doug," she burst out. "You're an enigma to me. I mean, here you are, a world-renowned fashion designer who's probably had the most glamorous women at his beck and call, and yet you're chasing me. Why? What attraction could I possibly have for you?"

He didn't blink. "You're here. And you're alone. And you seem unbelievably innocent and fresh."

"Innocent? Hah!"

"Who was he?" Doug growled this time, beginning to lose himself to his frustration.

At his tone, Sasha jumped up from the couch and crossed to the fireplace. Fingers gripping the marble mantel, she stared at the compact lineup of ancient mystery books, then raised a hand to one that had been removed from the lot and lay open. When had she taken it out? She couldn't recall. With an impatient scowl, she closed the book and returned it to its awaiting slot.

"Who was he?" Doug asked again, this time more gently and from directly behind her.

"My husband," she said, a note of contempt in her voice. "My husband!"

"When?"

She sighed, regaining control. "A long time ago."

"Couldn't be that long. You're not old enough to—"

She swiveled around to face him. "I was seventeen when we married. But you're right. I wasn't old enough to know better."

"That wasn't what I was going to say."

"It's okay. It's the truth."

"What happened?"

Wondering how she'd let Doug Donohue get further than most people had, she grew self-conscious. Unable to meet the intensity of his gaze, she lowered her head. "Oh, the usual. It was a bad match, that's all."

"So you've turned off to men as a group?"

"Men as a group can be vile. I thought it would be better in New York, but there was only one thing on *their* minds, too." She sent him a scathing glance. "Don't you all think of anything but sex?"

He arched a brow in humor, unable to help himself. "It can be pretty nice to think about."

"Pretty boring."

"Were you bored before?" All humor was gone. "Tell me, Sasha. I need to know. Did you feel anything for those men in New York?"

She dropped her gaze in soft admission. "No."

"Did you feel anything with me before?" When she didn't answer, he curled a finger beneath her chin and turned her face up. "Did you? Or was I imagining it because I wanted it so badly?"

At that moment his expression was one of a longing she'd never seen the likes of before. Something tugged at her, something far beyond the physical. "No," she murmured, unable to lie. "You didn't imagine it."

"Then you felt something?"

"Yes."

"And it frightens you?"

"Yes." Her voice caught on that single word and was further choked by the utter gratitude in his gaze.

"Oh, Sasha," he murmured, his voice velvet soft. "I

wouldn't ever hurt you. I've told you that. I think you're...precious.''

"A newborn kitten is precious," she whispered, wide-eyed.

"Not precious as in one of a kind."

She didn't know what to say. She'd had compliments before, but none offered in as heartrending a tone from a man whose expression was so utterly devoid of pretense. Her pulse skipped a beat, then raced on double-time.

"Doug—"

He put a long finger to her lips. "Shh. Don't say anything. Just kiss me. I've been wanting you to all night. I've been needing you to all night. Just kiss me. Once."

There was no way in the world she could deny him, not when he was so close, so warm, so lean and tall and every inch a man. Her lashes fluttered, then fell as his lips touched hers, and as had happened before, she felt herself melt.

His mouth was gentle at first, then opened more hungrily. And she met its demand, giving of herself freely, driven by the unsolved need that sprang from her depths and took control. His arms circled her back, her own crept to his shoulders, then coiled around his neck. He drew away, then returned, tempting her with the tip of his tongue until she welcomed it. She actually welcomed it. Far from her mind were memories of Sam, of men in New York who'd grabbed her and kissed her this way. Then she'd gagged. Now she could only revel in the feel and texture of Doug's tongue as it skimmed across her teeth then plunged deeper. Only when she gasped for air did he retreat, and only then to lift her and carry her to the sofa she'd bounded from in frustration moments before. When she tried to protest, he soothed her.

"Shh, babe. It's all right. I won't hurt you."

"But you...you said...once."

"It's still going on."

And it was. His lips returned to hers, tasting and consuming, exploring and conquering as rational thought became a thing of the past. High on its newness, wanting the delight of it all to continue as badly as he did, Sasha held him closer. Her fingers were in his hair, celebrating its thickness. His own were near her face, caressing whatever was missed by his lips, then moving lower to frame her neck and shape her shoulders. Everywhere he touched she bloomed, arching toward him, seeking an answer to the raging quest of newly awakening sensations.

When his hands moved inward to work at the top button of her blouse, she gave a faint moan, but her protest was lost in his mouth and the moistness of his tongue diverted her. When she felt the cool air on her chest, though, she mustered a frail resistance.

"No..." she whispered against his lips.

"Let me touch you. Oh, Sasha, it's so good."

"But I barely know you. You...barely know me...."

"Let me," he crooned, brushing aside her objections along with the silk of her blouse and deftly unhooking the catch of her bra. Then his hands were on her and she had no idea what she'd fought. "Oh, babe, so soft. Silk beneath silk."

And beneath that, fire. Her body flamed where he touched her, burning, needing. His hands spread over her ribs, her breasts, moving in large sweeps, tracing her fullness as though imprinting an image of her nakedness in his mind. She was devastated with desire. One moment he would caress her breasts, the next he would stroke her shoulders or her neck and her breasts would swell in frustration. And all the while he maintained the mind-drugging kiss that muffled her tiny whimpers of pleasure.

When at last he raised his head to look down at what he'd only felt she was too dazed by passion to demur. Her breasts were of exquisitely molded ivory crowned with firm auburn buds. Stunned by their beauty, Doug shook his head in astonishment.

"You're beautiful, Sasha. Very beautiful."

She bit her lip and felt positively helpless.

"You believe that, don't you?" he asked in a soft but husky voice.

"I never have," she managed somehow to whisper. "But you...you almost make me...believe...."

"Believe, babe. Believe every word." Still holding her gaze he slid his hands to her breasts, capturing them fully, caressing them, straightening his fingers until only his palms manipulated her nipples.

"Ahh!" she cried, stunned by the jolt of heat that shot from her breasts to her loins.

"Beautiful. Soft there. Hard here." His fingers closed in on those twin turgid buds, and unable to bear the sweet pain, she closed her eyes and pressed her face to the cushion. "No, no, Sasha, don't look away. Kiss me. And tell me what you feel."

She doubted she'd ever be able to speak again, but she needed his kiss desperately and met it with an ardor more eloquent than any words. Swept up in the force of his passion, she drifted higher and higher, sighing her delight at the continued play of his fingers, aching for the something more that her insides demanded.

"Is it good?" Doug whispered against her lips.

"Oh, yes," she answered in kind, eyes closed, arms wound tightly around his neck.

"Do you feel it here?" He rolled her nipples between his thumbs and forefingers in waves of gentle eroticism.

"Yes," she breathed.

"And here?" One hand pressed against her heart. It's thudding was a visual thing.

"Mmm."

"And here?" His hand fell to her trembling thigh, then slowly slid upward.

"Oh, yes…yes!" Her voice was little more than an airy rasp as his hand found her warmth and caressed her tauntingly. "Doug!" she exclaimed, her senses aflame.

When his mouth covered hers, he quickly released the button of her slacks, lowered the zipper and slid his hand along the warmth of her abdomen beneath the band of her panties. He found her unerringly, his touch a silken brand on her feminine heart.

"Doug…no!" she whimpered in a moment's fright. "Please, no!" She clamped her legs together, succeeding only in holding him closer. No man had ever touched her there since Sam, and he had pawed her and mauled her such that she'd been in pain. The pain she felt now was different, though. It was hotter, sweeter, more fluid and demanding.

Doug caressed her face with his free hand. "I need to, Sasha. I need to pleasure you. Please let me. Please."

Eyes still closed, she moaned softly, for already his

hand had begun to move in a slow, rhythmic lilt that calmed her, excited her, eradicated all thought of pain as though it had never been. Caressing her gently, his fingers stole deeper. Never in her life had she imagined the pleasure of such intimacy. She gasped, tried to hold back, then arched up against the rising of a deep, deep heat. It was all new. All new. She'd never felt....

His pleasure inexplicably interwoven with hers, Doug sensed her bewilderment as though it were his own. "It's all right," he murmured thickly. "Don't fight it. Let it come, babe. It's good." Brushing the weight of her bangs free of her brow, he moved up against her to kiss her forehead while his fingers brought her ever higher.

Reaching, reaching, she gave a breathless cry. "Doug!"

"Oh, yes," he crooned hoarsely. "That's it. That's it, Sasha."

"Oh—" She caught her breath and her body stiffened. Then, as she clung frantically to his shoulders, her being exploded into a myriad of sun-burst spasms that went endlessly and gloriously on and on.

It seemed forever before she could breathe again, and even then her lungs labored for what seemed an eternity of gasps and sighs. Only slowly, as the trembling of her limbs yielded to a kind of lethargy and the high haze of passion began to dissipate, did Sasha realize what had happened.

Stunned, she opened her eyes. Doug's were warm and waiting, but his face held a subtle tension. "Was it good?" he asked softly.

She stared, then covered her eyes with her hand and whispered, "My God!"

"Was it good?"

"Oh, yes!"

Within seconds he'd scooped her up and had sat on the sofa, hugging her to his side. "Then what's to be shy about?"

She buried her face in the wool of his sweater. "I've never...I've never...."

"Never climaxed like that?"

"Never...."

"Never climaxed *at all?*" It was his turn to be stunned, though in hindsight it explained the bewilderment he'd felt in her. She'd been married. She wrote stories of love and passion. Yet she'd never experienced this pleasure? Feeling strangely awed, he sucked in a ragged breath. "Ah, Sasha, what a gift that is."

"A gift?"

"To me. To know that I was the first to show you...and there's so much more. So much more. It's beautiful. Not painful or ugly or something to be ashamed of." He turned her face up with a gentle hand and was startled by her look of doubt. "You didn't know that, did you?" When she didn't answer, he swore softly. "You must have been married to a jackass!" He paused, frowning. "But what about other men, Sasha? Surely there were—"

"There weren't—"

"In New York?"

"No."

"My God," he breathed, "you're practically a virgin." When she tried to push herself away, he simply held her more tightly. "What is it, babe? What's the matter?"

Eyes downcast, she tugged at the edges of her blouse. "I feel foolish."

"But why?"

She thought for a minute, struggling to gather her wits as her pulse rate steadied. "Because you're practically a stranger and that was so...intimate. Because you're... very experienced. You knew what was happening to me before I did."

"Oh, you knew," he chided, his tone velvet and soothing. "And I'm no real stranger, not in my heart or yours. You let me pleasure you because it felt good and right. You were just frightened by its force. It's like that sometimes."

"For you?" she asked with an upward glance.

"Sometimes," he said, but he couldn't recall when he'd enjoyed it as much as he'd enjoyed pleasuring Sasha just now.

His eyes spoke to her, reaching out. It suddenly occurred to Sasha that while she was physically sated, Doug could not be. He'd been so good, so gentle, so generous. She'd been trained.... She was frightened, yet it seemed her role.... "Doug?" she began unsurely. "You haven't...I mean...." She shot a pointed glance downward by way of elaboration. "If you want..."

He was very quiet for a moment. "Why?"

She shrugged and told herself that he was right, that he wasn't really a stranger anymore. "It—it's only fair."

"You mean you'd make love to me just to even things up?" When she looked away in agony, he studied her sadly. Then, very slowly, he began to set her clothes to rights. "No way, Sasha Blake," he said softly. "When we make love—when we *really* make love—it's going to be because we're both positively burning with need.''

"But aren't you...." Again she faltered. This time, Doug stood and drew her up with him, then took her face in his hands.

"Believe it or not," he said, faintly incredulous himself, "my satisfaction came from yours."

"Then your need isn't...."

"It's there, all right. And I'll probably have all hell to pay for my nobility when I get home. But for now—" he lowered his voice "—it's enough for me to know that you've felt good."

Unbelievably touched, Sasha could think of nothing to say. There had to be something very special about a man who could defer his own gratification this way. While the heaven he'd taken her to had been one kind of awakening, this self-control was another. *The* Douglas Donohue—or *any* man, for that matter—putting her pleasure before his own? It had to be pure fiction....

The sound of a steady, distant ringing tore Doug's eyes from hers. "What's that? Not the telephone. An alarm?"

As puzzled as he, she made for the stairs, to return moments later with silence restored. "Strange, I must have flipped it on by mistake."

"It's nearly two in the morning. That's quite some mistake. I thought you said you got up at five."

"I do." She frowned a minute longer, then shrugged and forced a smile. "I must have been really out of it yesterday when the stupid thing went off. Lucky thing I wasn't sleeping just now."

"I'll say," Doug drawled, then threw his arm around

her shoulder and swung her toward the door. "How about if I pick you up, oh, say, twelve hours from now?"

"Pick me up?"

"You were going to show me the island."

"You've been here for days," she argued, feeling more than a little awkward. "Don't tell me you haven't already seen the island. It's not that big. Besides, I really do have work to do."

"Then do it in the morning."

"I'm not sure how early I can get up."

"I'll be here at two."

"Four."

"Two-thirty."

"Four."

"Two-forty-five."

"Four."

"Come on, Sasha! Give a little! Three o'clock is my last offer." He released her and opened the door. "Three o'clock. Take it or leave it."

As he turned to await her decision, Sasha felt the weight of it. After what she'd just experienced, she reeled in uncertainty. On the one hand, if she agreed to go out with Doug she was admitting to wanting to further the relationship. True, he'd opened her eyes in several respects tonight. But there was far more to a relationship than sex. And in spite of the delirium he'd produced in her, there were memories too harsh to ignore. Yet, if she did refuse his invitation, what was she to do about the strange and unbidden curiosity she felt?

Take it. Leave it. Take it. Leave it.

"Well?" he asked softly, all banter forgotten.

"Three o'clock," she murmured softly. "See you then."

The purr of the Maserati had long since faded when she double-checked her doors and put out the lights. Starting up the stairs, she paused, then looked back at the sofa. What had happened there still stunned her. And frightened her. And made her blush. What was the hold Doug had over her? What was it that made her quiver when he came near, that made her melt in his arms and come alive, that made her accept an invitation to drive around the island when she knew her time was better spent at work?

She shook her head. It was a mystery—a mystery, involving this dark-haired, bronze-skinned man of the silver eyes and the golden touch. Just last week her life had seemed well-ordered and relatively complete. Suddenly things had changed. Doug Donohue challenged her; he fascinated her. And her own curiosity after all she'd been through and had sworn to avoid—therein lay the mystique.

Loath to agonize, she sighed and climbed the stairs, entered her room, idly stepped from her pumps and reached to remove her earrings. Suddenly she stopped arms midair, and stared at the bed. Her hairbrush lay there. But she'd left it in the bathroom, hadn't she? Puzzled, she skimmed the room, only to have her eye catch on the dresser and her favorite perfume, it's glass stopper lying uselessly by the side of the bottle. How could she have been so careless?

Crossing the room in annoyance, she replaced the stopper, turned and, frowning, leaned back against the dresser. Within seconds her gaze was on the small alarm clock that had gone off earlier. The alarm, the hairbrush, the bottle of perfume—had she been that distracted lately? She recalled the book downstairs on the mantel, the book she could have sworn she hadn't touched in months. A shiver coursed through her. Her eye crept slowly around the room as though in search of a presence lying in wait.

Then she straightened and took a deep breath. Coincidence. That was all. There was nothing to fear. She'd been careless and forgetful, but then, who could blame her, with a new book in the works and a man the likes of Doug Donohue toying with her peace of mind? It'd be perfectly understandable for her to displace a book or a brush or accidentally twirl the alarm setting of her clock to an ungodly hour. If it was *Autumn Ambush* again, that too was chance. Life didn't mirror fiction; it was the other way around. Wasn't it?

CHAPTER FOUR

The Sunday Times lay forgotten on the kitchen table, the instant coffee remained dry powder in his cup. After no more than three hours' sleep, Doug spent the morning walking the beach.

Reliving the party and the hours immediately after, he felt stunned. Sasha Blake had to be the most intriguing woman he'd ever known, and he realized it not for the first time. Rather than being satisfied as, one after another, the pieces of the puzzle fell into place, he was more curious than ever…about himself as much as her.

Self-control. He'd never, never experienced the likes of it before. To have held her, kissed her and brought her to the heights of passion and then held back…it was mind-boggling. She'd even offered to complete the act, and he'd refused! But he'd been honest with what he'd told her, though even now it confounded him. He *had* found satisfaction in hers, more so than he'd ever imagined possible. Was he going soft in his old age? Oh no, not soft, he mused, shifting his hands in the pockets of his jeans to alleviate a pressure that had even now begun to build. Not soft, but gentle? And considerate? Or was it simply his ego that screamed against having a woman offer her body out of duty?

He wondered what her husband had done to her.

Beaten her? Taken her with brute force? Indeed, when she'd offered herself to him in the wee morning hours there had been a look of resignation in her eyes. The whore selling herself for the money she needed? No, the wife accepting her dismal fate in life.

Swearing softly to himself, he kicked at the sand with his booted foot and walked on. Her body was beautiful. He couldn't imagine any man wanting to hurt that. And her passion was something to behold. But that was new, perhaps well hidden even to herself over the years. She'd been startled by the pleasure she'd felt, the pleasure he'd given her. And yes, his own pleasure had been nearly as great as if he'd taken her fully. Nearly...but not quite.

He wanted to make love to her. But how, and when? She was frightened. He couldn't do anything to add to that fear. From what she'd told him, it had probably been close to ten years since a man had touched her as he had earlier. And things were happening so quickly now....

He'd have to take it slow, another first for him. But he'd meant what he'd said. When they made love, he wanted her to burn for it as he did, to ache so badly that the past was nothing.

It could be very easy. He already knew that he could produce near mindlessness in her by his kiss alone. But that was *too* easy, and he resisted its lure. Perhaps it was a sense of total conquest that he needed. Or perhaps, just perhaps, he wanted more from her than sex. Perhaps.

As he took refuge atop a cluster of rocks and stared out at the sea, he wondered what she was thinking just then.

HER WORK FORGOTTEN along with the Sunday paper and

the super breakfast she'd promised herself, Sasha paced
the floor. She didn't understand what had gotten into her
that she'd allowed Doug Donohue, a man she'd known
less than a week, the freedom she had. It could only lead
to pain of one kind or another. Hadn't she had her fill
of that years ago?

After he'd left, sleep had been slow in coming and
even then, brief and filled with troubled dreams. Now,
tired and unbelievably keyed up, she had to face an afternoon with Doug. How could she? She felt confused
and frightened and not at all comforted by the memory
of what she'd let him do. It had felt good. Oh, yes. And
though she fought it, she couldn't deny the speck of
eagerness she felt at simply seeing him again. He was a
man, through and through. But would he turn on her
when passion seized him? A relationship with him might
prove a magnificent illusion around his leanly muscled
frame, his dark face and hair, his warmth and his gentleness. An illusion built...only to be crushed? She
wasn't sure if she could bear it.

The clock ticked irreverently on, minutes into hours
as she wandered, distracted, from one room to another
of her house. She couldn't work. She couldn't read. The
only thing she seemed capable of doing was taking one
outfit after another from her closet, studying it critically,
then discarding it as all wrong. By two-thirty she could
delay no longer. Finally choosing a faded pair of jeans
and a comfortable sweatshirt in hopes of blending name-
lessly with the islanders, she dressed, piled her hair on
top of her head, applied a trace of mascara and blusher,
and went downstairs to wait.

She prayed he'd be late, but he wasn't. On the stroke

of three her doorbell rang. She pressed her dry lips together and rubbed her clammy palms against her jeans, then answered the door.

His jeans were as faded as hers, his shirt a dashing plaid wide open at his neck. He wore the same leather bomber jacket she'd first seen him in, and boots as weathered as her own, he looked gorgeous.

"All set?" he asked eagerly. She gave a jerky nod as his gaze skimmed over her. "Will you be warm enough? There's a breeze off the ocean. Maybe you should bring a windbreaker or something."

She cast a glance at the swaying grasses on the moor, so much more serene than she felt at that moment. "I guess so," she murmured, bypassing more chic jackets to ferret from her hall closet a simple corduroy one that Doug promptly threw over his elbow. They walked to the car in silence.

"So where should we start?" he asked. "You're the guide."

She sent him a look of skepticism before refocusing on the scenery. "South Road is fine. It's a pretty route into Edgartown." She was safer in a crowd, she reasoned, and even this late in the season there were bound to be day-trippers galore.

Sensing her awkwardness, he didn't speak until they hit the main road. "How do you know the Slaters?" he began, trying a less personal approach in hopes of settling her.

"My agent knew them. She introduced us when I first moved here."

"Your agent has a place here?"

She shook her head. "In New York. She knows Rob

professionally. She's submitted things to him from several of her other clients from time to time.''

"Have you been with her from the start?''

"Diane sold my first book, but only after I'd written several smaller things and sold them on my own.'' She gave a shy laugh. "I wasn't sure I'd sell *anything* way back then. It was a shot in the dark. I wouldn't have had the presumption go get an agent at that point.''

"How did you finally get her?''

"A mutual friend.'' For the first time she smiled. "Seems to be the way things work.''

"This friend was a writer too?''

"Uh-huh. He'd had a mystery published and was forever working on his second.'' Her eyes took on a look of fond remembrance. "Simon was a character. I think his efforts were misplaced. He should have been in the theater. The man had a way with makeup and disguises, not to mention accents and physical deformities he could put on at will. There were any number of times he put on a show to cheer me up.''

"You needed cheering up?''

Awkward again, she looked down at her hands. "When I first moved to the coast, I was kind of down.''

"The coast?''

"Maine. It was soon after…soon after my marriage broke up. I was very alone and pretty unsure of myself.''

"He filled a void?''

She glanced up quickly. "Oh, not in that sense. He was a friend. That's all. And I needed one badly.''

"You don't have family?''

"I have family.'' Her gaze returned to the passing landscape.

Doug waited, then dared prod. "You don't sound thrilled."

"They're the ones who aren't thrilled. I was a disappointment to them. I was supposed to marry and raise a family and be a good, loyal, obedient wife." Her bitterness was ill-hidden.

"But you didn't."

"No. I wanted something more."

"Like...?"

"Like—" Like love. And romance. And trust and caring and loyalty. "Ach, it's not important."

Doug knew it was. He also knew, though, that he could only dig so deep at one time. She was talking. She was opening. It would come, all that deeper stuff, in time.

"Your family must be proud of you now."

"Not particularly. They're potato farmers. Not," she hastened to add, darting a glance his way, "that there's anything wrong with that." She took a breath. "Sam is a potato farmer too. They all work hard. But they're not terribly sympathetic toward a dreamer."

Doug took his eyes from the road for a minute to study her grim expression. "Is that how you see yourself? A dreamer?"

"That's how *they* see me. Head in the clouds. Eye on the stars. Me? I suppose I am a dreamer of sorts. Even more so an idealist. What I write expounds on an ideal." She sighed, her voice tainted with defeat. "They can't understand that."

"Do you ever see them?"

"No. They live in Aroostook County. Inland Maine. I haven't been back since I left."

"Not even since you've become famous?"

"I'm not famous, at least not in my mind. I'm a writer who has been very, very lucky. I feel good about myself, self-confident at last. To go back there and have to deal with *their* image of success, well, I don't think I could stand it."

"Do you...miss them?"

She looked at him and let out a short laugh, then pressed her fist to her mouth and stared out the side window. There was something comforting about the windswept moors, the ripening of wild apples, the brilliant color of the huckleberry thickets.

"I suppose I do," she admitted softly. "There are some good memories, memories of when I was a child, memories of my mother holding me after I'd had a nightmare or my father carting me around on his shoulders." The warmth of her tone faded. "But times changed. Money grew tighter. The weather didn't cooperate. And the expectations of a child were very different from those of an adult."

As they approached Edgartown, Doug slowed the car to accommodate the growing traffic. Brought back to the present, Sasha felt suddenly self-conscious. She brushed a strand of hair from her cheek and frowned.

"What is it?" he asked softly.

"I shouldn't have gone on and on like that. It's all really irrelevant." And startling given the fact that the story she'd held in for years was now spilling itself for this compelling newcomer.

"Not at all," the compelling newcomer replied with sincerity. "I think it's fascinating." It was, though he'd never been particularly interested in a woman's history before. Now he couldn't seem to hear enough. "Did you always want to write?"

"Me?" She coughed. "You're talking to the woman who practically flunked English in high school."

"Those teachers must be dying now."

"I hope so. They gave me lousy grades on one paper after the next because my ideas were impractical, so they said."

"Ah. Potato country school."

"You bet."

"So when did you start? Writing, that is."

For some reason, astounding given the fact that she'd never revealed as much about herself to a living soul in years, the words flowed. "Actually it was Simon who got me going. I was working as a waitress at one of those little lobster places on the coast. I was reading everything I could get my hands on. He suggested I take a course at the state university."

"So you did?"

She nodded. "English literature. Then creative writing."

"Did your teachers think your work...impractical?"

She chuckled embarrassed. "No. They liked it."

"And encouraged you to submit for publication?"

"No. Simon did that. At first I thought he was crazy. Then I realized that I had nothing to lose. I did love to write. And if a few rejection slips were the price of satisfying my curiosity...well, it seemed a small price to pay."

He brought the car to a halt in a parking space near the center of town and turned to face her. "And you sold instantly."

"Not quite. There were rejections at first."

"Were you devastated?"

"Not really. After all, it was only a short story, and I hadn't expected anything."

"Then…"

"Then that first acceptance came, and…"

"And the rest is history."

She blushed and averted her gaze from the silver eyes that so bound her. "Pretty much." She sat silently for a minute. It was Doug's gentle voice that finally made her look up.

"Thank you."

"For what?"

"For telling me all this. You don't tell many people, do you?"

"No."

"Then I feel honored." When she blushed again, he squeezed her hand. "Come on. Let's take a walk."

The streets of Edgartown were as delightful as ever, small shops and eating places intermixed with large houses of the Georgian and Federal styles set flush to the street in the old-English fashion. People browsed idly along, islanders and off-islanders alike with their jeans and sweaters, shoulder bags and sneakers. Occasionally they passed a more colorful character, a young woman in trendy peasant garb, an old-timer decked out in wing tips and bow tie, a bearded, slightly surly looking cad who stared at Sasha until she was pulled by Doug into the nearest bookshop. There Doug proceeded, to her mortification, to buy a copy of her latest book.

"Doug!" she protested, turning beet red and tucking her chin to her chest.

"What's wrong?" he asked with an innocent grin.

"You don't want to buy that," she chided in a hushed whisper.

"But I do. I want to see what juicy things you've put in it. See, you've piqued my imagination."

Her high color persisted. "You won't like it."

"Of course I will. You'll autograph it for me, won't you?"

"I'll write something lewd," she scoffed.

He lowered his voice, the eager wolf. "All the better to get me going on a cold and lonely night, my dear."

Sensing he'd best her in any further repartee, she simply stood by the door examining the magazines, pretending not to know him while he paid for his choice. Then, with the book tucked safely in the back pocket of his jeans, they started out again.

It was a glorious day for a walk. The sun was warm to counter the breeze that gave the air a fresh salt tang. Wisps of Sasha's hair fell to wave down her neck; Doug's hair was likewise windblown and infinitely attractive. As they wandered through the town, he threw his arm around her shoulders. She couldn't protest. The fit was ideal.

They passed the courthouse and the town hall, then strolled farther, past the newspaper office, then a museum. "Hey, there's the library," Doug teased. "Shall we go in and see if they've got a copy of your book on their shelves?"

"It's closed. And they don't."

"You've checked?"

"In Chilmark. I go there to do research. Let me tell you, that librarian would just as soon I move back to

New York. She made it very clear that she doesn't particularly care for my brand of literature.''

"Snobbery? On the Vineyard?''

"A little.'' She smiled, amazed at how relaxed she felt. "But not often. Besides, it's all a matter of taste.''

Doug squeezed her shoulder and they ambled on. Their hips knocked together, then meshed again and their easy strides were well mated. Sasha found herself wondering whether Doug often walked down streets with his arm around a woman, found herself wondering about the kind of woman who had last come under his spell. For she was, without a doubt, under his spell. All her forewarnings were for naught when he was as amiable, as innocently companionable beside her.

Retracing their steps, they found themselves headed for the waterfront, where they stopped to quietly watch occasional fishing boats return from an abbreviated Sunday outing.

"Hungry?'' he asked her. The sun had lowered dramatically on the horizon.

"Um-hmm. All this walking and neither breakfast nor lunch must do it.''

He smiled, a broad, endearing, man-of-the-world smile that tickled her all over. "Let's get something to eat. Okay?''

"Okay,'' she said, returning his smile with a warmth that made Doug wonder whether he'd simply missed the boat all these years. Perhaps the way to a woman's heart was through her stomach.

Hand in hand they turned and began to walk. Lost in a world of momentary pleasure, Sasha barely heard the slow roll of a dull thunder. Doug heard though, looked up and tensed, then with lightning speed crushed her close and dragged her back several paces. He was just in time. A contingent of large barrels fell from a roof to the pavement, pounding the very spot where they would have been standing at just that moment had his reflex not been as fast.

Both round-eyed, they stared in horror as the barrels rolled to a halt. Sure concussion, if not skull fracture or worse—they'd missed it by seconds.

"Holy Moses!" Doug exclaimed, holding Sasha tightly against his own trembling body. In anger he looked toward the roof. "Where in the hell did those come from? My God, you could have been killed!"

"Your head is harder than mine?" she teased shakily. Had she been alone she might have panicked. But Doug had saved her from both harm and panic. Burying her face against his shirt, she soaked up his strength.

For a minute they simply stood clutching each other as the impact of what might have been hit them. "That was close," he breathed at last, then growled, "Damn it, how could something like that happen?"

"Very simply," she stated. "Those are empty oil barrels, the kind the old whalers used to use. They've probably been piled up there for years, slipping slowly. Maybe a gust of wind did the trick, maybe a gull."

Doug looked down at her. "How do you know so much?"

She grinned, liking the fact that he hadn't seen fit to let her go just yet. "I used it once in a book. *Midnight Rogue.* It can be real spooky, especially if the heroine suspects that someone is out to get her." In *Midnight Rogue* it had been a jealous stepbrother who had given the barrels that final push. But that had been fiction, and a very convenient ploy. Things like that didn't happen in real life.

"Did the heroine survive?"

"Oh, yes."

He arched a brow. "How?"

"Her true love was there to pull her out of the way in the nick of time," she responded smartly, then swallowed hard when she realized what she'd said. "It's all make-believe," she added quickly. "It's what romantic intrigue is all about."

Her belated attempt at rationalization fell flat. Doug's gray eyes held hers with uncompromising heat as the words echoed in his mind. *Her true love.* He wondered if he could ever be that to Sasha, wondered if that was what he wanted. He'd never been in love before. Was there an explanation for the protectiveness he felt, for his sudden willingness for self-sacrifice? When he'd hauled them from the path of the barrels, he'd thought only of her. Was it love? Or simple chivalry?

"Doug?" she whispered, unable to stand the tension a moment longer.

The sound of her voice, the look of fear in her eyes drew him from his trance. He raised his eyes to passersby who bystepped the barrels and cast curious glances toward the roof. He followed their gaze. The roof was empty, marked only by the darkened shingles where, as Sasha had suggested, for years the barrels must have lain.

Stifling an eery feeling at the pit of his stomach, he muttered a sober, "Let's get out of here," and fixing an arm firmly around her shoulder, led her around the barrels and away.

He walked briskly, staring straight ahead. Sensing his need to work off the fright they'd had, Sasha pushed herself to keep up. They were nearly back to where he had parked the car when he finally relaxed and recalled their original intent.

"I'm sorry, babe," he said, looking down at her in surprise. "I forgot. You're hungry—"

"I'm okay," she was quick to assert, but Doug quelled her protest by ushering her across the street toward a small restaurant.

"Well, *I'm* hungry," he informed her, the corner of his mouth twitching in mockery. "Heroic acts take their toll, you know. I'll have to keep my strength up if I'm to rescue you from future calamity." True love or not, he recognized his need to do that. It was a very pleasing thought.

To Sasha as well. "My knight in shining armor?"

He opened the door to the restaurant and let her pass through. "Maybe a little rusty around the edges," he mused only half in jest, "but nothing that a little oil won't cure. Look, there's a table just waiting for us. Come on." Taking her hand, he led her there, then leaned down as he seated her to whisper in her ear, "They've got terrific fish chowder here. And fresh zucchini bread."

"Hey, I thought you were the newcomer to the island," she protested in fun and was rewarded by an appealingly crooked smile.

"But a noncook. A man has to survive," he drawled, and for a minute, with his bronzed skin, his windblown hair, his shirt open to reveal dark tufts of very masculine chest hair, he was pure rogue.

When push came to shove, she'd known all along that Doug hadn't sought a sightseeing guide when he'd asked her out for the afternoon. He'd wanted her company. And, in truth, she'd wanted his. The dinner they proceeded to share convinced her that, whatever the consequences, she'd been right in yielding to that whim. Their conversation was light and relaxing, focusing mostly on the Vineyard and each of their experiences living here.

It was only later, long after Doug had dropped her at her house with a gentle kiss to her cheek and a promise to call during the week, that Sasha realized she'd done most of the talking. Yes, she'd been a guide of sorts, but a guide to her background, her occupation, her everyday life as an islander. Other than his attentiveness, his wit and the occasional hint of a passion held strictly in check, he offered nothing of himself, of who he was, where he'd come from, where he was going. Not that she'd asked. It stunned her to realize that she'd been so blinded by his engaging presence that she'd simply followed his lead, and he'd led right back to her time and again.

Alone in her bedroom that night, propped against the pillows on the bed with a red pencil in her hand and the latest printout from her word processor in her lap, she realized how little she knew. Here at home once more, though, she wondered if it was for the best. True, she'd enjoyed her time with Doug today; demanding nothing but her company, he'd managed to put her fully at ease, a remarkable feat given the awkwardness she'd felt when he'd first picked her up. He'd made no mention of the little episode on the sofa. Perhaps he'd sensed she'd be having trouble coming to terms with it herself. Which she was. Even now the thought of it brought a faint flush to her cheeks.

But she couldn't dwell on it. She wouldn't dwell on it. Doug hadn't seemed to, nor had he thought less of her for it. It had happened, and she had enjoyed it far too much for self-castigation. She was also too realistic to deny the fact that, while their outing today had been an outwardly innocent one, the biological attraction between them was as strong as ever. She'd been vitally aware of him from the start, aware of the strength of his arm about her shoulders and the muscled cord of his thigh as it bumped hers. She'd been fascinated by the way he arched that dark brow of his, by the compact movement of his lips when he talked. His hands, his hands had tormented her—sun-toasted skin, the faintest sprinkling of soft dark hair, long strong fingers manipulating his fork when he ate. And the memory of what those fingers had done to bring her such intimately exquisite joy…she sucked in her breath and shook her head, but there was no way she could deny what she'd felt. She was a woman, convinced of it for the very first time in her life.

And Doug was a man. He'd want to make love to her. He'd promised as much even as he'd rejected her immediate offer of satisfaction. What had he said—that they'd make love, *really* make love—only when they were both burning with need? One week before she would never have imagined a day such as that ever coming. She'd never burned for a man in her life, yet now, after such brief exposure to Doug Donohue, she felt an insidious ribbon of smoke curling its way through her system. A smoldering? The first step toward that "burning" Doug had predicted? Or an invitation to disaster?

Bewildered, she picked up pencil and paper. How much safer writing romance was than living it, she mused, her brow furrowing in frustration. Regardless of what happened, she was always in full control. If her hero did something she didn't like, she simply took her red pencil and crossed it all out. If her heroine took a wrong turn and found herself in an untenable situation, there was similar recourse. And there was always a happy ending, a guarantee that the trials and tribulation in a particular plot would be to good avail.

Yes, writing was safer, safer yet nowhere near as titillating as what she'd felt in Doug's arms last night....

DOUG DIDN'T CALL on Monday. Immersed in her work, Sasha told herself that she didn't mind a bit. When the phone rang on Tuesday morning, though, she jumped a mile. She counted to ten as the second ring came and faded, reached for the receiver, drew back, then finally answered it in a voice schooled to calmness.

"Hello?"

"Sasha? It's Diane."

Her disappointment was curbed by the pleasure of hearing from her agent. In the three years Sasha had spent in New York, Diane DeScenza had come to be like family. It had been Diane herself who, having seen Sasha's unhappiness in the city, had suggested she think of moving out.

"How are you, Diane? Gee, it's good to hear from you."

"I'm fine. Wondering how you are. Everything all right?"

"Great. The writing's going well. No name yet for this thing, but then it never does come until later in the book."

"Are you pleased with the characters? They sounded really good in the proposal."

"I'm pleased with them, now that I'm finally getting into them. The hero is very special, I think."

A spirited chuckle came from the other end of the line. "So are all your heroes, if your sales figures are anything to go by. You've heard about *Raven's Revenge* making the list, haven't you?"

"Uh-huh. That'll please M.P.I." Madison Publishing had handled all of her books.

"To say the least. In fact, that's why I'm calling. They're going back to press with re-releases of *Devil Dreams* and *Autumn Ambush.*"

"No kidding? That's great!"

"Um-hmm. But they want another tour."

Sasha's face fell. "Oh, Diane. You know how I hate those things. Twenty cities in as many days, with every hair in place and a smile plastered on my face. I end up with bleary eyes, sore feet and writer's cramp. By the time I'm done, I need a month to recuperate, and then when am I going to write?"

"Calm down, Sasha," Diane said gently. "It wouldn't be that bad this time. They're talking about ten days. That's all. Major cities. Television spots, media interviews, a few signings."

"But I've just started a book!"

"And you've got a whole load of time to finish it. Besides, the tour wouldn't be for another three or four months. By then you'll be needing a break, if you haven't already finished the thing," she cajoled.

"I never need a break in the middle of a book," Sasha declared perversely. "It ruins my concentration." Strange how her concentration had been broken repeatedly in the past week, and still she'd managed. Doug Donohue was a stimulant...in many ways.

"Well," Diane said with a sigh, "I'll try to hold them off. Or at least keep it to a minimum. Maybe we can limit it to a week. Does that sound fair?"

"Fair?" Sasha echoed in resignation. "I guess so. After all, I should be grateful that they're doing what they are. New covers?"

"Yup." Diane lowered her voice to simulate bold typeface. "By the author of the bestselling *Midnight Rogue* and *Raven's Revenge*."

"Poor *Demon Woods*," Sasha teased, thinking of the one of her children that hadn't been mentioned. "It's being left out."

"Maybe not. They're...oh, I shouldn't tell you...."

"Diane...." When a silence persisted on the other end, Sasha raised her voice. "Diane, tell me!"

Her agent hesitated for just a moment more. "They're talking of trying to sell *Demon Woods* for a TV movie."

"You're kidding! When did this come up? You've never breathed a word!"

"I've never *known* a word until this morning. And it's purely in the talk stage, which is why I probably shouldn't have opened my mouth at all. You'll have your hopes up, and then nothing may come of it.''

"I know," Sasha breathed in awe. "But still. Just to be considered!''

Diane laughed then, a warm, affectionate laugh. "That's what's so wonderful about you, love. You're as innocent and enthusiastic today as you were the day I sold your first book. Fame hasn't gone to your head, that's for sure! And it's a relief. You should see some of my other clients. Speak of un-bear-a-ble…!''

Mention of her other clients touched a gentle cord in Sasha, whose mind homed in on that one in particular of whom she had coincidentally spoken to Doug two days before. "Have you heard from Simon, Diane? I feel really badly. I haven't spoken with him in months.''

"As a matter of fact, I got a call from him a few weeks ago. He was his old beguiling self, regaling me with stories of his latest adventure. He's diving for deep-sea treasure. Did you know that?''

"I didn't. Is he really doing that?''

"Ach, who knows. With Simon, spinning the tale is half the fun.''

"Has he written anything lately?''

"Not that *I've* seen. He talks about it…but no cigar. He asked about you. Wanted to know all about your latest book.''

"Raven's Revenge?"

"No. This new one you've started. I told him about the proposal. He was excited.'' She paused, momentarily unsure. "You don't mind my telling him, do you?''

"Of course not. He was right with me on those first few books, reading my proposals, discussing them with me. I feel guilty losing touch with him like this. With you as a go-between, it's not so bad.''

"Why don't you give him a call? He'd love to hear from you.''

For the first time Sasha grew hesitant. "Oh, I don't know. I feel awkward.''

"Because of your success? Sasha, you shouldn't. Simon of all people is pleased for you.''

"But he tried so hard there for a while, writing and writing, selling nothing.''

"Maybe he only had one book in him. That's true of many writers. He may have realized it, if he's into diving for sunken treasure.''

"Sunken treasure." Sasha chuckled. "That does sound like Simon. I miss him. I really do.''

"Then call him. Just to say hello. Uh-oh. There's my other line blinking. Gotta run. Listen, I'll talk with you some time next week. Okay?''

"Sure. Take care, Diane.''

"You too, love.''

Sasha hung up the phone feeling infinitely grateful to have a friend like Diane. From the first, when Simon had introduced them, Diane had taken her under her wing. When, with two bestsellers under Sasha's belt, it had seemed the thing for her to move to New York, Diane had been the one to help her find an apartment, to show her around, to introduce her to people. That Sasha had hated New York was no fault of Diane's. Despite lavish dreams of dash and glamor, Sasha was a small-town girl at heart.

Emboldened by Diane's urging, Sasha flipped through her Rolodex, picked up the phone and dialed Simon's number. When there was no answer after eight rings, she hung up, vowing to try again another time.

Returning to work, she put in another two good hours, then paused for a light lunch before attacking her keyboard again. It was late afternoon when the phone rang this time. She looked up sharply. Her heart skipped a beat. Pressing her hands to her thighs, she took a long steadying breath, then lifted the receiver.

"Hello?"

A faint but telling static forewarned her that again the call was a long-distance one. Not Doug, Sasha realized, but her disappointment took a back seat to uncertainty at the sound of her sister's voice. "Sasha? It—it's Vicky."

It had been several months since Sasha had spoken to any member of her family, and then too it had been to Vicky, her senior by three years and the only one of her four siblings who'd been even marginally tolerant of the path she'd chosen.

"Hi, Vicky." Sasha's voice was tinged with wariness. Over the years she'd been hurt once too often by her family's lack of understanding and interest, which was why she rarely called home. "How are you?" she asked, her thoughts skipping ahead to the reason for Vicky's call. It was Tuesday, not yet five o'clock. The telephone rates would be at their prime. Sasha experienced a ripple of apprehension.

"I'm okay," her sister answered, but there was obviously something on her mind.

"Is John well? And the kids?" Vicky had a hard-working husband and four growing children. Her parents were pleased.

"They're fine. But," she took a breath for courage and raced on, "it's Mom."

Sasha felt a silent pang. "What is?" she asked quietly.

"She's sick."

"Sick...how?"

As though still debating making this call and then suddenly realizing that it was too late to turn back, Vicky sighed. "She's in the hospital." When Sasha remained silent, she elaborated. "She went to the doctor for a regular checkup and he took her in to do more tests. She's got a tumor. They're going to do a hysterectomy." She paused and lowered her voice to an apologetic murmur. "I—I just thought you should know."

Sasha stared at the floor in anguish. The silence was deafening, yet she didn't know what to say. Finally she cleared her throat. "When? When are they doing it?"

"First thing next week. They want her to get some rest before that. You know how hard she works."

"I know," Sasha said with a glimmer of anger, but it was an anger directed as much at her father, who'd allowed a woman to bear such a tremendous physical burden, as at her mother for having borne it as her lot in life. As Sasha thought back on it, her mother had always been tired. That fatigue had taken the form of impatience with others in general, and in particular with one not quite as prone toward martyrdom, in a word, Sasha herself. "Is she very uncomfortable?"

"No. But she's worried about not being home. She feels guilty. And I'm sure that behind that stony facade of hers, she's probably scared to death."

Sasha was as stunned by her sister's tone as by her

words. It was the first time, the very first time, she'd
ever heard criticism on Vicky's part of her mother's sto-
icism. True, as a child Vicky had complained with the
rest about the endless string of chores their mother
seemed always to have up her sleeve, but Vicky had
been a true Blake, marrying young, working beside her
husband, bearing and raising the children just as her
mother had before her. Sasha had always wondered just
how like her mother Vicky was. Vicky's criticism was
a sign of hope.

"What do the doctors say, Vicky? Are they hopeful
that...that the surgery will take care of it?"

"They don't know. They won't know until afterward.
They're talking of the possibility of some follow-up
treatment, but it's all so undefined right now."

"I see."

"Well, uh, I just thought you ought to know. I didn't
want you to be upset later." She began to stammer,
"You know, with whatever, with whatever happens."

"Sure, Vicky." Sasha paused. "Does Mom know
you've called me?"

"No. I didn't want to upset her anymore than was—
Oh, God. That came out wrong. I mean she's been upset
and trying not to show it and I didn't want her to get
her hopes up or think I had called you because she's
dying."

"Is she?" Sasha heard herself ask in a small unsure
voice. The hand she raised to her forehead trembled. "Is
she dying, Vicky? Tell me the truth."

"I don't know," was the quiet reply. "We'll know
more next week. But listen, there's no need for you to

run up here. I mean, she's all right for now. The surgery itself is no more dangerous than any surgery.''

Sasha bowed her head, eyes closed for a minute, then looked up. Her voice was as gentle as could be in announcing her decision, though she took no pride in it. She was a coward. Despite what Vicky had said about the lack of immediacy of the situation, Sasha knew she should get on the first plane and fly up to Maine. She knew it, yet she couldn't go. She just couldn't.

"Can I call you…after the surgery?" she asked at last, then waited cautiously for Vicky's reaction.

"Sure, Sasha." There was a touch of resignation…and relief. Vicky had done what she'd felt she had to do in alerting her sister to the situation. Anything beyond that was up to her.

"Well, then, I guess I'll talk with you next week," Sasha began. She half wished Vicky would fight her, would tell her in no uncertain terms to come home. In the absence of such direction, though, she could only make a graceful exit. "What hospital is Mom at?" When Vicky named the one, Sasha nodded. "Do they need any help? I mean with money? I'd be glad—"

"It's okay, Sasha. Insurance will cover it."

And Jerome and Natalie Blake wouldn't want to touch her ill-earned money anyway, Sasha realized bitterly. "Well," she said with a sigh, "if there's anything I can do—"

"I'll let you know. Bye-bye, Sasha."

Sasha stared at the phone for an age before she pushed herself from her desk to wander aimlessly around the room. Hands thrust in the back pockets of her jeans, she stopped before the window and looked out. The surgery wasn't really risky. Vicky had said so herself. And after that, well, her mother was a woman of iron. She'd make it. There was nothing to worry about.

Returning to her desk, Sasha reread the last paragraph she'd written. But her mind wandered and she had to read it a second time. Finally she typed one sentence, then another. She read them over, deleted the first, substituted something she liked even less, deleted it as well. She returned to read the page from the top, added a new sentence in place of the one erased, stared at it and shook her head. It was wrong. All wrong. With a soft oath, she stabbed at the button to save what she'd written, waited until the machine had finished its work, then turned it off and stood up.

It was unfair, damn it, she reasoned unreasonably. Things had been going along so well. She'd come to terms with the estrangement from her family long ago. Between her work, her new life and friends such as Diane and the Vineyard contingent, she had everything she wanted. Now her mother's illness stirred up a host of unwanted feelings, not the least of which was guilt, and second to that regret. But why should she run back to Maine? Had her mother stood beside her when she'd needed her? Had she been there with sympathy and understanding? No! She'd been no more supportive than Sasha's father or her brothers or sisters or her oaf of an ex-husband, Sam Webster!

Angry and hurt, Sasha stormed from her room. In the kitchen she filled the kettle, set it down hard on the stove and turned on the gas. Crossing her arms over her chest, she leaned back against the counter to scowl at the crisp white ceramic tile underfoot.

The tea did little to settle her. She tried to push thoughts of Vicky's call from her mind, to concentrate instead on her storyline, or Diane's earlier call, or even the prospect of hearing from Doug, but it was useless.

Doug. Hah! And what could *he* give her? He'd string her along, toy with her, imply a kind of security that in the end he'd rob her of without a second thought at all. Wasn't that the way it worked?

Plunking her half-empty cup of tea into the sink, she headed for the front door. Her hand was on the knob when the phone rang. Stalking back into the kitchen, confused and annoyed, she snatched up the receiver.

CHAPTER FIVE

IT WAS A startlingly impatient "Hello!" that Doug Donohue heard.

"Sasha?" he asked cautiously. "It's Doug."

As if she didn't know. She'd recognize that voice anywhere. Its deep vibrancy was firmly etched on her brain. Had he called an hour earlier, she might have been pleased. But he hadn't called an hour earlier, damn him. He'd let her down. Now he'd have to endure her sour mood.

"Hello, Doug," she stated coolly.

There was a brief silence on the other end of the line, then a controlled query. "Is everything all right?"

"Of course. What could be wrong?"

"You sound angry."

"Me? Angry? I don't get angry," she snapped. "I'm just a sweet writer sitting here in all her innocuous glory. Nothing fazes me."

"What happened?" There was no hesitancy in his voice this time. Doug had never heard her sound this way and he was genuinely worried.

"Nothing at all."

"Sasha..." he warned.

Feeling shaky all over, she took a deep breath. "Look, Doug. Maybe I should speak with you another time. I'm going out.'' Without giving him a chance to respond, she hung up the phone and made good the escape she'd begun moments before. She needed fresh air. A brisk walk would be just the thing to work off some of the tension she felt.

All but running from the house, she headed for the moor. The distant burr of the telephone was quickly swallowed up by the whistle of wind through the grass. It was nearly dusk, that gray, eerie time that came earlier and earlier as fall progressed. And it was cold. Protected by nothing but the jeans and sneakers, turtleneck jersey and wool sweater she'd worn in the house all day, she welcomed the chill. Anything to take her mind from that other...

Maintaining a steady pace, she half walked, half ran up a hill, then down the other side. When she was out of breath, she stopped for a minute, tossed her head back and breathed in the sharp night air, then resumed her step more sanely.

Darkness fell quickly. By the time she had turned and headed back in the direction of her house, the moor was enveloped in a murky shroud. Passing close by a clump of pines, she nearly stumbled over an exposed root. Swearing softly, she shoved her hands into the pockets of her jeans and steered toward more open spaces.

In the distance the light from her study blazed into the night. With a sigh of defeat she propped her hip against a rambling stone wall and turned her back on the warmth. She wasn't ready to go in yet. There was still an anguished tugging in the vicinity of her heart that had been only marginally eased by her walk.

Lowering her head, she closed her eyes and put her

hand to her brow. The tightness in her throat was something else. She hadn't cried in months and months, certainly not about things that were over and done. Swallowing convulsively, she gulped the cold air, but it didn't dislodge the images that flitted through her brain. Her mother, her father, Sam, Doug—one face was as painful a vision as the next. If only she could blot them out.

As though in answer to her silent plea, the sound of footsteps broke through her brooding. The crisp grass crunched rhythmically. The occasional fallen leaf, dried and waiting for the wind to carry it to a more sheltered spot, crackled as the footsteps neared.

Sasha stiffened. She raised her head, too frightened to turn, a rabbit sensing imminent danger and counting on sheer immobility for its salvation. For a split second her imagination ran away with itself and she wondered whether *he'd* come to get her. In place of those other images that had haunted her moments before came ones of a motorcycle sabotaged, of barrels pushed from a roof, of the gardener's shed whose door had stuck, of personal belongings picked up and rearranged. Someone seemed to be after her. But why?

Heart pounding loudly, sure to give her away, she huddled into herself. The footsteps neared, then came to a halt. The darkness—was it friend of foe? Would it hide her from her pursuer?

"Sasha?"

The sound of Doug's voice, unsure and concerned, sent shafts of self-disgust through her. She'd done it again, imagination and all, the creative urge gone awry. She was a fool!

Several more steps sounded on the crisp grass. He stopped. "Sasha? What are you doing?"

She shook her head and tucked her chin to her chest. With the dispelling of her wildest fears, those other sorrowful thoughts returned. She squeezed her eyes shut against the moisture that gathered.

"Sasha?" His voice was softer, closer. Several more footsteps and he was within arm's reach. "What's wrong?"

Had he been angry or impatient, as he had a right to be given her curtness and the fact that she'd hung up on him, she might have been able to muster some sort of defense. Instead, she merely tucked her chin tighter and wrapped her arms about her middle. One by one, slow tears worked their way down her cheeks.

"Oh, Sasha," came the heartfelt sound behind her. With a single step, Doug absorbed the distance between them and threw his leg over the low wall to straddle the stone. Then, with one hard thigh against her backside and the other bracing her leg, he put his arms around her and tried to draw her close. When she resisted, recoiling into a self-contained knot, he grew adamant.

"Damn it, you're freezing." Unbuttoning the front of his dark pea jacket, he forced her body against the warmth of his, wrapping her in his arms and holding her tight. "Where's your common sense? You'll catch pneumonia!"

"I won't," she murmured, though the sudden warmth was as welcome as anything she'd ever known. "I can take...care of myself."

"Could've fooled me," he scolded with all the sympathy of a dictator betrayed. "You get yourself into a stew about something and don't even have the guts to talk about it, then you storm out into the night hell-bent on self-destruction! What's the matter with you, Sasha? Don't you know who your friends are?''

''Don't yell at me,'' she rasped against the seeping warmth of his sweater.

''Then don't do anything to give me reason!'' he growled. When he shook his head, his chin rubbed against her hair. ''Damn it, that was quite a welcome! Here I'd had to spend two days in New York—much against my plans *and* will—and all the while the only thing keeping me marginally civil is the thought of seeing you when I get back, and what happens? You hang up on me! Then pull this crazy stunt! I searched every inch of that damned house for you before I headed out here!''

''Don't yell,'' she whimpered, touched by an emotion she couldn't explain. And the tears came then, faster and stronger, accompanied by the softest, most heart-wrenching sobs Doug had ever heard.

Burying his face in her hair, he pulled her closer. His arms circled her back and held her to him with a fierce possessiveness, offering her a warmth and protection she simply didn't have the strength to refuse.

''It's all right, babe,'' he crooned throatily. ''It's all right. Let it out. It's good for you.''

What was good for her was the sure comfort of his embrace. Slipping her arms around his lean waist, she clung to him as though he were the only stable thing in her existence. He wasn't, she knew, but she went along with the illusion nonetheless. It had been so long, so long since she'd truly leaned on another human being.

With his words of reassurance and the sturdiness of his body supporting her when she felt so weak, she was helpless to resist.

Very slowly her tears ebbed. Eyes closed, cheek flush against the commanding beat of his heart, she took long drags of his clean male scent. Gradually her strength returned. It was only with reluctance that she finally pulled her head back and withdrew her hands to blot from her cheeks the faint wetness his sweater had missed.

With the same reluctance she'd felt he released her, but only to take her face in his large hands and turn it upward. "Better?" he asked, very gently kissing away the last of her tears.

She smiled, suddenly embarrassed. "Yes," she whispered and lowered her eyes. "I'm sorry."

"For what? For being human?"

"Crying is a wasted emotion."

"Not if there's no other way to express what you feel. And you obviously weren't about to talk. You must have been holding that in for a good long time. Hmm?"

"Actually, no," she murmured. "Just for an hour or so."

"Like fun," he scoffed, but with an exquisite gentleness. "Something must have happened to trigger it, but it's deep down inside you simmering for far longer... Want to talk?"

She raised her head and took a last hiccuping breath. "I don't know."

"Well, while you're deciding, what say we head for the house. They didn't tell me about this November chill when I agreed to come live here.'' He feigned a shiver. ''It's cold.''

At the moment Sasha felt strangely warm, oddly content, as though in the protective cushion of Doug's arms she might forget the ills of the world. But it was dangerous, very dangerous to grow dependent on this type of support. She should know.

Doug drew her up, helped her over the low stone wall and tucked her inside his jacket again. As they walked to the house in silence, she savored those last moments of warmth. Once inside, he released her, tossed his jacket on a chair and looked toward the fireplace.

''Mind if I light it?''

''Be my guest.'' Sinking into the nearest chair, she watched as he lay first kindling, then logs on the grate. When he looked wordlessly around, she bounded up and headed to the kitchen for a match. Within minutes a warm fire had taken hold.

''There.'' Standing, he rubbed his hands together, ''Now, where's the brandy.''

''Brandy?''

''To take off the chill.'' He scanned the room for sign of a bar. ''And if you don't need it, I do.''

She tossed her chin toward the alcove she called her dining room. It was simple but elegant, a white table, four chairs upholstered in pink and ecru, and behind them a long buffet. ''In the cabinet on the right. Way back.''

He had no trouble finding the spot, hunkering down to remove a bottle and two snifters. Sasha made no move to help, finding that she enjoyed watching the movement of his body. He wore jeans, a rust-colored sweater and a shirt whose rust-and-gray plaid coordinated both the sweater and his eyes. There was a fluidity to his walk, a natural grace. That the narrowness of his hips made his shoulders look all the more brawny was simply frosting on the cake.

"Here," he said softly, handing her a half-filled snifter. "Drink."

"I'm really okay."

Before she knew what he was up to, he'd taken one of her hands in his. "Your fingers are like ice. Now, drink."

As a form of diversion from the unguarded sensuality of his touch, if nothing else, she raised the snifter to her lips and let the amber liquid warm its way down her throat. She kept her eyes downcast as Doug settled onto the sofa, his long legs stretched before him, crossed at booted ankles. He took a healthy dose of his own drink, frowned at the swirling amber stuff, then looked up.

"I'm really sorry I couldn't call sooner. There was something urgent in New York that I didn't find out about until early Monday morning. I just about had enough time to pack my things and catch a plane and, well..." He'd thought of calling so many times while he'd been in the city. But then he hadn't known what he'd say. Miss you. Wish you were here. When I get back we'll do naughty things together. One was worse than the next. Besides, he hadn't been ready to confess his fascination with this auburn-haired waif with the deep hazel eyes. Not yet. Things had happened so fast. But soon. It was bubbling inside, near to overflowing. If only he knew she was ready. Even now, though, there was a wariness in her. He could see it in the way she sat, in the way she avoided his gaze. She regretted having leaned on him before. She wanted so badly to be self-sufficient....

"Is it—did you work everything out?" she murmured, taking another sip of brandy.

"Oh, yeah. It's all set. They're just having a little trouble getting used to my being away." In another man there might have been arrogance. In Doug there was none. Feeling a shaft of admiration, Sasha looked away.

"You're very successful," she stated.

"I wasn't always."

He had her interest. She met his gaze. "You mean, when you first started the business?"

"That...and before." When she frowned, he explained. "I came from nothing. My parents were dirt poor. My father was a laborer in a textile mill. I worked there after school as soon as I was old enough. When I began to balk and talk of something better, he was furious. We didn't see eye to eye there for a while."

"He didn't want you moving up?" She couldn't understand that, any more than to this day she could understand her own parents' resistance to her success.

"Oh, yes. He wanted better for his son than he'd had. But I was talking on a grander scheme than anything he'd ever envisioned. He was frightened. Frightened that I'd dream, then fail and end up right back there at the mill."

As Doug described it, it made such sense. She had to hear more. "What happened? How did you break out?"

"I was lucky. I won an art scholarship. Without it, college would have been the first of those dreams to fall."

"Did you go right into designing when you graduated?"

"Slowly. I free-lanced while I got a graduate degree in business. Then I took out every possible loan I could get and opened shop." He offered a grimace of a smile as he remembered those earliest days on his own. "It was tough. The rents in New York were staggering and anything I earned by way of profit was poured back into repaying those loans plus interest. Several times I came close to folding."

"What kept you afloat?"

He looked at her hard. "Pride. And sheer grit. I was determined to make it, if for no other reason than to show my father he'd been wrong."

"You did."

Doug's eyes softened and he looked down sadly. "Yeah. Too late. He died just when things were beginning to look up. My mother lasted a little longer, but I was never able to do the things for her that I might have been able to do today." He didn't want to go into the frustration he'd felt at being robbed of giving to those he'd loved. Perhaps it had been that anger that had made him so hard. He'd never know.

"I'm sorry," Sasha said softly. She was struck by the depth of feeling the man had, a depth etched now over each of his rugged features. "You must have been... disappointed."

He nodded, leaving it at that. "Anyway," he resumed with a sigh, "things went well, and here I am. Oh, there were setbacks here and there, but for every step backward there have been two forward. I can't complain."

Nodding, she studied the brightly blazing fire. "It

sounds as though you've got a very satisfactory life.'' For the first time since he'd found her outside, she recalled her own frustration. In that instant she felt an irrational twinge of jealousy spiked with the self-pity she'd bordered on earlier.

Had he been truly caught up in his tale, Doug might have missed the shadow of bitterness Sasha was unable to hide. But he was looking at her, studying her delicate features, attuned to the moment when her jaw hardened so slightly, when her lips grew faintly tight. He hadn't been truly caught up in his tale because there had been a purpose in the telling. He'd wanted her to know about him, though he'd been miserly with every such bit of information in the past. He wanted her to hear him, to trust him, to open to him.

"Professionally I'm satisfied," he offered invitingly.

Sasha bit. She'd been curious since the day she'd met him. If he was talking about himself, there was far more she wanted to know. "And personally?"

He shrugged. "Personally…leaves something to be desired."

What had Janine said, that he had the reputation for being a tough ladies' man? "Come on, Doug," she chided. "Don't tell me you haven't had your share of fun."

"Fun is one thing, but even then there are different kinds of fun. There's the fun you have when you're eighteen and experimenting, the fun you have when you're twenty-eight and rather high on your own success. By the time you reach thirty-eight," where he was, "fun is a little more elusive." This wasn't quite the direction he'd anticipated the conversation to take, but he was helpless to stop the flow of his words. Suddenly he wanted Sasha to know where he stood, what he needed, what he wanted. Suddenly *he* wanted to know.

Sasha eyed him doubtfully. "The women are still there."

"Oh, yes," he admitted grimly. "Eager and empty."

"Empty? I can't believe that."

"For me, at any rate." His silver gaze caught hers on a thread of intensity. "Which was one of the reasons I left New York. I've just about had it with making small talk, with abiding by jokes that aren't funny, with being bored. And with being judged, above all, a 'good catch.'" His snarling of the words waxed eloquent on his legitimate disdain. "I even had a paternity suit slapped on me last year." At her look of surprise he went on, though his gaze grew distant, his voice hard. "Oh, I wasn't the father, as the courts easily decided. But the ugliness of it all churns my stomach to this day. To use a poor child..." He made an angry gesture with his hand. "It left me with a pretty lousy taste in my mouth."

Pausing for a breath, he refocused on Sasha. "I want something more. Something deeper and longer lasting." His voice lowered with menacing calm. "I want a future with a woman who's as intriguing as she is adoring. I want someone who will be impeccably loyal and infinitely understanding. I want a home. And I want kids." He made a disparaging sound and shifted the force of his gaze to the window and the bleak darkness beyond. "My...friend in New York just got herself in trouble, then tried to capitalize on her mistake. Most women today, though, are either more concerned with their careers

or their waistlines to figure children into the bargain.''
He looked back at Sasha, his message clear. "But I was
an only child and I want kids. Three, maybe four or
five." He took a breath then, egged on by the look of
astonishment on her face. His voice gentled and he bid
his muscles relax. "Didn't you ever want kids?"

It took Sasha a minute to register his question, so
swept up had she been in the force of his declaration.
This wasn't the man she'd expected to find in *the* Douglas Donohue. Was he putting her on? Could he be, given
the undercurrent of vulnerability she sensed in his every
word?

"Hmm?"

"Children. Have you ever wanted them?"

Had she ever wanted them? Her breath caught in her
throat and she swallowed the knot that had formed there.
Pushing herself from her chair, she crossed to stand before the fire, then knelt, seeking its heat to combat the
sudden chill that stormed her insides.

"I wanted them," she said in a very small voice, her
thoughts drifting back to those days so long ago. "I almost had one, too."

The fire chose that moment to spark, its loud crackle
covering Doug's approaching footsteps. When he squat-
ted by her side, she was startled. "What happened?"

She stared at his face, all bronzed and intent with the
firelight playing over its manly terrain. Sam had been
handsome in his way, though there hadn't been a touch
of softness in him. As though being soft was to be un-
manly. Yet Doug was as manly as ever, even more so,
with that glimmer of concern flaring from within.

Her lips were dry and she moistened them with her

tongue, then looked down at the fire and let herself recall. "I lost it," she stated baldly. "Or rather, it died at
birth. I was seven months pregnant." Her voice softened
with remembered yearning, and she tipped her head and
turned pleading eyes to Doug. "I wanted that baby. Oh,
how I wanted a baby to love. It was a boy. A little boy."
She gasped for air. "When you have a miscarriage early
on, you never know. But I knew. It was a boy. A beautifully formed boy—" her brows met and she struggled,
as she had so many times in those days, to understand
the justice of it all "—who was strangled by the umbil-
ical cord when his mother didn't know what to do."

Doug raised a hand to lightly touch the hollow of her
cheek. Though the fire burned hot before her, the chill
within her seemed to have taken possession. "My God,
Sasha. You can't actually blame yourself. Surely the
doctors—"

Pulling from his grasp, she stared blankly at the
flames. "There weren't any doctors. It all happened so
quickly. The baby wasn't due for ten weeks. He was so
tiny and weak and I was nineteen and scared and at
home all alone."

"Your husband—"

"Was out celebrating with his buddies. The harvest
had been good that year." She snorted. "Fat lot of good
it did me. Pregnant and all, I'd beat my tail helping him,
then he wasn't there to help me. He wasn't there when
I'd needed him. He was *never* there when I needed
him."

"But your parents—"

"It was too late," she said stonily. "By the time I
could get to a phone, it was too late." Her voice sank

to a whisper. "I couldn't help him. God, I tried, but I didn't know what to do."

Before she could resist, Doug shifted until he was behind her on the stone before the fire, his thighs on either side of hers, his arms drawing her back against his solid frame. Her limbs were stiff and unyielding, but he persisted, fitting himself to her taut form, wrapping his arms around her middle as though to protect the child she'd lost so long ago.

"It wasn't your fault, Sasha. Things like that happen."

Her hair slid against his sweater as she shook her head. "Not where I came from, they didn't. Births weren't complicated. You had your baby and, bam, went back to work. I was a grand disappointment to them even in that."

"Then that was *their* problem," he said, feeling anger that anyone should be so unfeeling, particularly toward Sasha, who deserved so much more. "And you're just as well without them."

She sucked in a breath and tried to control herself, but her emotions were strung tight, too tight, and snapped. "But now she's sick, and I don't know what to do!" Her wail was an anguished one and her eyes flooded anew.

They'd come full circle. Doug realized that in her own way and time, and, he was sure, quite without intending it, Sasha had answered the question he'd first asked when he'd found her outside in the cold. "What happened, Sasha?" he asked gently. "What happened today?"

Taking a staggered breath, Sasha spilled her heart out

of sheer necessity. "My sister called to tell me that my mother's sick. She's got a tumor. They're operating on Monday."

"Do you want to go to her?"

"Yes. No! I can't!"

"Why not?" he asked in that same gentle tone.

"I just can't!" Unconsciously she clutched Doug's hands as they crossed her stomach. "There's so much anger and hurt and I haven't been there in so long, and the last thing I want to do is to see her lying all pale and weak in some hospital bed."

"You do love her."

"She's my mother!" Her voice broke into a pitiful moan. "And it hurts...."

"I know, babe," he crooned, rocking her gently, wishing only to relieve her of some of the pain. "And it'll be all right."

"But how? If she dies..."

"What did your sister say? Is it as serious as that?"

Sasha sniffled and blotted her cheek with the back of her hand. "No. Not yet. Maybe not at all."

"So there. Then it's not that bad."

"But the issue's still there. And if it's not today or tomorrow that I have to face it, it'll be next week or next month or next year or the year after that." Running short of breath, she gasped, then quieted, sagging back against him in despair. "Don't you see? I've avoided the whole thing for years. I want to go on avoiding it. But can I? If it's not my mother, it'll be my father. I don't know...I don't know if I have the strength to face them."

"You, Sasha, have the strength. I do believe you've got the strength to do anything you want. Hell, look what you've done—starting from scratch, all alone, building a career and a home. If that's not strength, I don't know what is. There must be millions of women out there who stand in awe of you.''

She snorted. "The grass is always greener..."

"Life is never perfect," he argued softly. His breath warmed her temple, stirring her bangs ever so slightly. "It's a question of finding the best compromise."

"I don't want to compromise!" she cried bluntly. "I want it all. I want peace and happiness, love and success and respect."

"Perhaps that's fiction though. An ideal. It may be fine to write about, but—hey, wait a minute!" Sasha had wrenched herself from his hold and was on her feet, fleeing to the other room. "Sasha!" He took off after her, nearly running head-on into the swinging door to the kitchen as it closed in her wake. Pushing it angrily, he forged ahead. "Listen, Sasha, I wasn't criticizing." She sat huddled in a chair by the window, her defeated form a wrenching sight. Crossing the room, he knelt by her side. "I can understand those ideals. Don't you think I haven't wrestled with them myself? And I'm not saying that I've given up. Hell, I want all those things, too. Wasn't I the one who presented some pretty firm demands just a few minutes ago? It's just that, well, to be miserable because one or another of them elude us..." His voice trailed off as he gazed into her face. Her cheeks were moist, her eyes downcast. "I read your book," he coaxed softly.

For a minute he feared she'd say something smart and bound up and away from him again. But she sat very still. Then her eyes flickered, not quite meeting his but signifying that she'd heard.

"You did?" she asked timidly.

"Cover to cover. It was wonderful."

She scowled and darted him a brief, skeptical glance. "You're just saying that."

"Would I do something like that?" He frowned in puzzlement, then thought aloud. "Actually, I might have...before. If it suited my purposes, I'd have been patronizing as hell." But he raised his eyes to hers with a candor she couldn't doubt. "I'm not being patronizing now. I could very easily have said something bland about understanding why women like your books. But I said it was wonderful, and I meant it. Not only was it well written, but the characters were real and thought-fully drawn, and the intrigue was a very potent thread. But the emotions, those were the key. And as for the idealism of love, well, to tell you the truth, I was envious as hell of your hero. To have found a woman like that, a woman who trusted him with her life, who adored him, who believed that her future would be nothing without him..."

Very slowly, the warmth that had eluded Sasha began to seep into her being. The need in Doug's eyes was a tangible thing, reaching out, aching. Patronization? Not possible. Could it be he truly understood?

Deeply touched and unable to express it in words, she reached out to brush his cheek. It was warm and glow-ing, its beard-shadowed roughness a heady contrast to the softness of her hand. In that instant she felt closer to him than she had to anyone in her life. Her eyes must have mirrored the feeling, for he smiled then, an endearingly vulnerable smile. When his long fingers closed around the back of her neck and he drew her head forward, she didn't resist.

He kissed her gently, expressing the overwhelming reaction she inspired in him. His lips sucked hers and his tongue filled her mouth, all with that same exquisite care, that same tenderness that had been so lacking in her life until now. For the first time she responded in kind, offering her moist warmth by way of a thank-you for his understanding. To her astonishment, the pleasure she felt in the giving returned the thank-you tenfold. And stirred a desire that shocked her. She suddenly wanted to run her fingers through his hair, to explore the strength of his shoulders, to feel the warmth of his flesh beneath his sweater, beneath his shirt.

When he drew back, she was disappointed, but the huskiness of his voice suggested that she hadn't been the only one stirred. "I think maybe," he cleared his throat, "that we ought to get something to eat." He slapped her leg in a gesture of nonchalance that didn't quite go over. "Come on. Let's go out."

"Oh, Doug," she whispered, reeling still from the power of his kiss. Then she brought her hands to her tear-ravaged face. "I don't know. I'd be a sight to take into a public place. I look awful!"

"You look beautiful," he said, and meant every word. She looked soft and vulnerable and very much in need of him. He liked that.

"Why don't I just make something here? I've got some steaks in the freezer. And some potatoes and salad makings."

"But that's a lot of work."

"I don't mind." The thought of cooking for him somehow appealed to her.

He reflected on her evident enthusiasm, then cast her a sheepish glance. "A home-cooked meal. Pretty tempting."

"And I'd do it all," she coaxed, recalling the morning he'd waited on her. It was her turn. And she was eager.

"You would?" he asked with a little boy smile. "I could just sit back with my legs up and watch?"

She met his smile with a soft one of her own. "If you wanted."

He stood quickly. "You're on, woman." Then he stretched lazily, looking all the more massive and appealing. "I could stand a little pampering. This living alone bit is harder than I imagined."

Feeling strangely in her element and suddenly more sure of herself, Sasha stood and bodily ushered Doug back to the living room. "Sit," she commanded, then relented momentarily. "Would you, uh, would you like some music or the newspaper or something?"

"Music would be fine. Something quiet and appropriate for daydreaming in front of the fire."

In light of their talk of ideals, he could have said nothing to make Sasha more comfortable. With a lighthearted smile on her face, she flipped on the radio to her favorite FM station—always quiet and appropriate—and returned to the kitchen to make dinner. As the microwave defrosted the steaks, she made salad, then exchanged the steaks for potatoes and grilled the steaks on the Jenn-Air. As she set the dining-room table, with an occasional glance at a closed-eyed, thoroughly relaxed Doug, she marveled at how successfully he'd rescued her from the grip of so many troubling thoughts. Somehow they seemed more in perspective now. At 'least she was determined not to brood on them, not tonight, when she had more pleasant things to keep her busy.

Dinner was a resounding success, eaten in island elegance with two tapering candles and the bottle of wine she'd prevailed upon Doug to open. Stomachs replete, they sat before the fire finishing the wine, talking softly and of nothing at all in an utterly comforting way. Sasha felt more relaxed than she'd remembered feeling in far too long, and she didn't delude herself into thinking it was the full stomach or the wine or the music. It was Doug, sitting beside her in such undemanding, companionable fashion.

When, thanks to the early hours she'd risen to write and the tension that had taken its toll later in the day, her eyes grew heavy and her head nodded, she very happily curled against his shoulder and fell asleep. He woke her gently several hours later.

"Sasha?" he whispered, brushing a feather kiss to her cheek. "Babe, it's time to go up." Lingering in a half sleep, she cuddled closer.

"What time is it?" she murmured groggily.

"It's nearly one. I fell asleep myself, but if I don't get you to bed and get home, I'm not sure I'll ever make it." Slipping his arms beneath her, he lifted her carefully.

"The fire, Doug," she murmured, struggling to think straight. "Is it out?"

"Cold." He took the steps two at a time.

"And the…lights in my study? I think they're…still on."

"I'll check them before I leave." Only one door was open, very obviously her bedroom. He turned in to it, not bothering to flip on the light, guided by the slice of illumination from the hall to her bed. Freeing one arm, he flipped back the covers and laid her down on the sheets. Knowing he should simply kiss her good-night and leave her, but utterly incapable of such sanity, he began to undress her. He drew her sweater up over her head, then her turtleneck. The sight of her full breasts sheathed in delicate wisps of silk and lace made his hands tremble. But he steadfastly attacked the snap of her jeans, then the zipper, and turned to remove her sneakers, then tug the denim from her legs.

When he turned back, his eyes were drawn to hers, which were suddenly wide open and very much alert. She said nothing, simply stared at him, her gaze questioning his in the shadowed room. His heart hammered. He told himself to leave while he could, but her pale, slender length was too much of a lure.

Her name was a trembling hosanna on his lips, and somehow his hands found their way to her legs and slid up their smoothness, over her hips to her waist. Then, bracing himself on arms less than steady, he leaned toward her lips and worshiped them with small, pleading kisses until her mouth opened in helpless invitation.

He took all she offered, but ever gently, exploring her lips and their soft insides, tracing the even line of her teeth, sampling the deeper, darker warmth. He kept his ardor leashed, though the strain was huge. He simply couldn't get enough of her. He wanted to strip the wisps of silk from her body and feel naked flesh against him. He wanted to throw off his own clothes and bury himself in her. He wanted her body, her soul, her everything, but his greed frightened him as much as, instinctively, he knew it would frighten her. Things had happened so fast...so fast. But as he'd told her before, it was a matter of compromise. For now he would only kiss her and hope that the fire he kindled would bring her to him in time.

Sasha felt his lips on hers, so warm and sensuous, and her lashes fluttered down as she yielded to the sensation. There was a dreamlike quality to his lovemaking that made her weak and pliant in such a feminine sort of way that thought of anything real or practical had no hope for existence. She liked the gentle coaxing of his mouth, the tempting moisture of his tongue, so different, so tender, so new. A hunger grew within her and she opened to him happily. If this was what caring was about, she knew what she'd been missing.

Almost hesitant, as though fearful the dream would be shattered, she raised her arms to his shoulders, letting them rest on the sinewed swells. Then slowly, curiously she began to knead. When he deepened the kiss, she was with him, reveling in the way he filled her mouth with his breath, his tongue, his moistly erotic essence.

Her hands crept to his neck and wove through the thickness of his hair to hold him closer. She felt the tremor that passed through him and marveled that she might stir him so strongly. But it was only fair, she reasoned dizzily. Her own body felt suddenly alive and strong and needing something from his as it had never needed anything before.

And she wanted to touch. Bidden by a strength of their own, her hands fell to his waist and worked their way beneath his sweater, pushing it up, flattening over his shirt in frustration.

"Take off your sweater, Doug. I need...I need to touch you." Was that really her own voice, a whisper, true, but making demands nonetheless? Did she have the right to be forward? Sam would have punished her all the more for it, not that she'd ever ached to touch him as she did Doug. For a minute she wavered, fearing what Doug would do. When he leaned back and whisked the sweater over his head, she sat up and watched him tremulously.

Then he was back before her, his silver eyes glittering. "I need that too," he rasped, his tone and his gaze quelling her fear, the promise of his broad chest replacing fear with desire. Thinking only of satisfying the urge to touch him, she reached for the button of his shirt and, fingers stumbling but intent, she released it, then another and another.

For the first time his bare chest was before her. Even the dim light couldn't hide its utter perfection. Firm muscle corded his shoulders, then swelled even more before tapering to the leanness of his middle. His skin was firm, its dark pelt of hair an irresistible lure. She touched him and felt the echo of the shock that sizzled through him. He was warm beneath her fingertips, then strong as she opened her palms and began to move them up his vibrant torso with innocent expertise.

Doug moved closer, spreading his thighs to bring her kneeling form against him. He whispered her name, burying his lips in her hair, and his hands floated over her flesh as though he, too, were afraid she'd simply disappear in a cruel cloud of smoke.

"Sasha, Sasha," he murmured, eyes closed, body afire. When her hands brushed his nipples, a shaft of sweet pain shot to his loins. His own hands slid down her silken skin to the small of her back, and he arched his hips and pressed her closer.

Sasha couldn't believe the tension she felt. Where she'd thought to find satisfaction in finally touching his skin, the hunger only grew, feeding upon itself. For a fleeting instant she wondered if she was truly sex starved. But no, there had been men who'd made passes over the years and she'd felt neither curiosity nor desire. Geoff Briggs had fairly broadcast his eagerness, yet…nothing. Only Doug stirred her. Only Doug.

Driven by womanly instinct, she lowered her lips to his shoulder and tasted him, her tongue lapping gently, then sensuously. He was clean and fresh smelling with a tang of salt from the sheen of perspiration that had crept to his skin. It was an aphrodisiac to her untutored senses, sending her into a mind whirl of ecstasy from which only his shaky fingers on the thin straps of her bra brought relief.

She sat back then and met his gaze, aware of the race of her pulse, of the rapid rise and fall of her breasts. Speaking his need through his simmering gaze, he haltingly eased the straps from her shoulders. He had no way of knowing that his near-timidity inflamed her all the more. Her memories were of roughness. This tenderness was something new and wondrous.

The straps rasped softly against her arms in their downward glide. With their descent, the cups of her bra slowly lowered, baring her by inches to his lambent gaze. When the bra was at her waist, he lifted her arms free of the straps, then held her hands to the side as, swallowing hard, he stared at her. It wasn't the first time he'd seen her, though well it might have been for the raw electricity that charged his senses. Her breasts were full and aroused, their peaks taut and eager. The chill of the air was nothing compared to the heat engorging her.

Bolstering himself higher on his knees, Doug slipped his hands down her bare back and brought her forward until the fullness he'd feasted on was pressed to his chest. A low moan of elemental pleasure escaped his throat, and he closed his eyes to savor the sensation to the fullest. Had he never taken the time to enjoy a woman this way? Had he always been too greedy, too anxious to satisfy his own primal urge? But it was beautiful, this slow torment. And it was Sasha, Sasha who began to move against him, Sasha who held the key to this exquisite heaven.

When she raised her arms and coiled them tightly around his neck, he thrilled to the rise of her breasts against his chest. With his hands at her back, he gently shifted her body in a rhythmic way that rubbed her against him with excruciating sureness. He moaned again and murmured her name, then slowly eased her back to the sheets. Hands free, he placed them on the silky skin of her thighs, spreading them apart and lowering himself against her. Then, taking her hands in his and anchoring them by her shoulders, he took the taut nub of her nipple into his mouth and sucked hungrily. When she strained upward and moaned her delight, he began to move against her, slowly but inexorably telling what he needed, what he wanted.

Though brought from her haze by the blatancy of his

thrusts, Sasha wasn't frightened. Rather, this time his tumescence aroused her all the more as it temporarily eased the ache she felt inside. His shirttails flared to the side as he adored her body. The heavy fabric of his jeans was abrasive against her in a most erotic way. She dug her fingers into his shoulders and arched, that he might have more of her.

And suddenly she wanted everything. If there would be pain, she wanted pain. If there would be fury, she wanted fury. She wanted Doug. She needed Doug. And she wanted to know, or she was sure she'd positively die with this agonizing need unsalved.

"Make love to me, Doug," she whispered roughly, rolling her head from side to side in torment. "Please, make love to me. I need you. I need to know. I need to forget. To forget everything." Her short bursts of speech were punctuated by a tortured moan when he went suddenly very still. The tension in his limbs was of a different sort now and it terrified her. Catching a ragged breath, she waited, half expecting him to erupt and take her with the callous force she'd known from Sam. He was a man, wasn't he? Could she have been so stupid as to expect anything else?

But he didn't erupt. He simply held himself still, then sagged to the side, his face on her stomach. She looked down, only vaguely registering her own knee bent near his outflung arm. He took several long staggering breaths before finally meeting her gaze.

Sasha was stunned. Never before had she seen such raw pain on a person's face. What had she done? God, *what had she done?*

"I didn't mean this to happen, Sasha," he began, his

voice hoarse, his dark hair falling damply over his brow. "I swear to God, I didn't. I wanted to give you time. Time to get used to me, to get to know me. Things have happened so fast, maybe too fast. I wanted you to need me."

"But I do!" she cried, her throat tight.

"I want you to need *me*," he said more forcefully, then lowered his voice to a sorrowful murmur. "Not as an escape, Sasha. Not to wipe out whatever horrid memories you may have of the past. But *me*. I want you to want me, and me alone. That's what I meant by a burning, babe." Very slowly he pulled himself up and began to button his shirt while she watched, dumbstruck and incredulous. When he scooped his sweater from where it lay on the floor, he turned to her one last time. "I won't sell myself—or you—short, Sasha, or we've lost it all." Shoulders burdened by the weight of his ideal, he left Sasha in darkness to ponder what he'd said.

CHAPTER SIX

SASHA THOUGHT long and hard, frightened to believe, terrified not to. What kind of a man would leave her high and dry this way? A cad? A playboy? Or a man who cared, very deeply, that there should be something very special to their joining?

She'd been wild with passion, begging him on. Yet she knew neither embarrassment nor regret. For Doug had been fully aroused and in dire need himself, and had it not been for the depth of a certain ideal, he'd most certainly have taken her there and then.

But he'd wanted more than a simple roll in the hay. He wanted her to want him. Him, and only him. Did she? Oh, no, it wasn't a question of her wanting other men. But did she want him as an antidote to the venom lingering from Sam, or did she want him solely for the unique sustenance that was Doug, and Doug alone?

As her frustration wore off she thought back upon the evening. It had been unbelievably lovely, despite its inauspicious start. She'd enjoyed making dinner for Doug. When was the last time she'd cooked for a man? Strange, after Sam's unrelenting demands she'd sworn off her role as chief cook and bottle washer. But she'd enjoyed it with Doug, *for* Doug. And the quiet compan-

ionship they'd shared before the fire had been the nicest
dessert possible.

When sleep finally came that night, it was deep and
relaxing. She awoke in the morning filled with a strange
sense of hope, and sat down to write with an abundance
of words at her fingertips. If she was aware that the hero
she'd created smacked strongly of one Doug Donohue,
she ignored it. If she realized that she was imbuing her
character with the most idealized form of the qualities
she'd glimpsed in Doug, she chose to call it coincidence,
or habit. Quite quickly she was falling in love with her
hero, as was her heroine, and if things were moving far
faster than normal, she simply called it poetic license.

DOUG, ON THE OTHER HAND, couldn't work. He couldn't
read. He couldn't sketch. He could do nothing but think
of Sasha and how wonderful he felt by her side. When
he was with her, he liked himself. Once before he'd
thought it, and he'd more or less chalked it up to chance.
Continually now, though, he was pleased, pleased with
his patience and consideration, pleased with the kind of
decent and devoted guy he was in her presence.

And he was pleased with her response. From the
woman he'd first met who'd seemed wary of his slightest
move, she was more confident, more comfortable. And
passionate. He still couldn't believe how she'd writhed
beneath him. He still couldn't believe how he'd stopped
in the nick of time! He'd been prudent, if cruel, given
the states of both their arousals. Hell, if a woman had
dared do that to him he'd most probably have taken her
by force. But Sasha wasn't him. In physical strength
alone she'd have failed without his cooperation. He re-

called her slenderness and experienced a surge of protectiveness. She was so small, so vulnerable. Had he gone ahead and made love to her, without doubt she'd have had regrets the morning after. He didn't want that. Thank heavens he'd pulled back. Twice, now. Incredible!

Also incredible, to himself as well as perhaps to her, was what he'd told her with such vehemence. But it was true. He wanted a home. He wanted kids. And he wanted a woman, to have and to hold. He wanted Sasha. It was as simple as that.

Now all he had to do was to convince her that she wanted him as much. Not only in bed, but forever. All he had to do was to work through that final barrier. True, the bricks were crumbling one by one as her story came out. He knew that neither her family nor her husband had understood her, that she'd felt unwanted and unloved. He knew that she'd lost a baby she'd desperately wanted in part because her husband hadn't been there, because no one had been there to help her. She'd been all alone. Perhaps, used to being alone now, she was frightened to commit herself to another person. Perhaps she feared that she'd be hurt again.

In a million years he could never hurt her. Had she been his wife expecting his child, he doubted he'd have left her alone at all. Hell, though she wasn't his wife and certainly wasn't pregnant with his child, he still had trouble leaving her! With a snort of amusement, he glanced at the papers on his desk awaiting his attention. How to concentrate? How to earn a living with a woman such as Sasha Blake monopolizing his mind? Perhaps the years he'd spent in total devotion to the corporation had been well spent after all. The company was a strong, going concern, with a staff carefully chosen and perfectly capable. They could do with only his halfhearted attention for a bit. What the hell—they wouldn't have any choice!

And his time? It would be spent dreaming dreams of Sasha, planning the hours they'd spend together, plotting the best way to reach her. He had his direction for the first time in months. With the vision of a future without her strangely bleak, he had nothing to lose.

Thus determined, the first thing he did was to go into town, ball out the librarian for not carrying Sasha's books, then march to the nearest bookstore and buy a copy of each of those that were in stock. He wanted to know everything about her, and her books spoke volumes. Having already read *Raven's Revenge,* he managed to pick up *Midnight Rogue* and *Demon Woods,* then had special orders placed for *Autumn Ambush* and *Devil Dreams.* Returning to his house, he sat down with *Demon Woods,* from which he stirred only to call Sasha at midafternoon.

"Hi, babe," he said in soft response to her voice. "How's it going?"

"Not bad," she acknowledged with enthusiasm. "I've written fifteen pages already."

"Is that good?"

"You bet. Some days it's a struggle to eke out four or five. Fifteen, just rolling off my fingertips...." She gave a self-satisfied grin. "It's good."

"I'm glad. Wanna take a break?"

Did she ever! And with Doug? But...maybe she shouldn't. Temptation was a potentially dangerous thing.

"I'd love to, Doug. But I don't know. The juices are flowing. Maybe I shouldn't trust fate and run out just yet. They may be all dried up by the time I get back."

There were creative juices and there were creative juices. The type she had in mind at that moment had little do do with writing and everything to do with Doug. The vivid memory of what she'd felt in his arms was slightly overwhelming in the light of day. She needed a little time to adjust.

"But you'll have to stop some time," he reasoned.

"I will."

"When?"

"It's...hard to tell." She looked from her computer screen to the clock, which read nearly three-thirty, then back to her screen, as though to convince herself that her hesitancy was indeed work induced.

"By dinnertime?"

"Probably."

"Want to go into town for something light? Really fast. Just an hour or so. Then you can get back to work."

If there had been sign of his resenting her work, Sasha would have heard it. She was looking. Oh, she was looking. Over the years, as her career had taken hold, she had wondered how any man might want to share his wife with a career such as hers. Not that she'd ever consider remarrying, for she truly hadn't. But in theory she wondered. Her work took such time and energy. A man would surely never stand for that.

Doug, however, seemed to be standing for it. She was amazed. "You—you really wouldn't mind something quick like that?"

"Well," he drawled, "I'd prefer more time, but if it's an hour or nothing, I'll take what I can get."

She hesitated only a minute longer before smiling. "You're on."

"About six-thirty?"

"Fine. See you then."

She hung up the phone still wearing a smile, feeling lighthearted and warm all over. She cast a glance at her computer screen, grinned smugly, then saved what she'd written and turned the machine off. In the kitchen she made a fresh cup of tea, sat with her legs up on a chair and sipped it slowly, thoughtfully.

She wanted a bath, but first there was something she had to do. Returning to her study, she extracted a piece of her personal stationery and began to write. The pen moved slowly. She wondered if she'd simply gotten so used to the word processor that her thoughts didn't come as well this way, then she caught herself and put the blame where it belonged. She just wasn't sure what to say. Sorry to hear you're ill? Get better soon? An apple a day…?

She spent a good long time at the task, writing and crossing out, then finally copying the finished product over from scratch. But in the end she was pleased…well, relatively so. Addressing the envelope, she put a stamp on it and set it by her purse, to be dropped in the mail while she was in town.

She took a bath then, long and hot and relaxing, and finally dressed in a pair of clean jeans, a bulky turtleneck sweater and boots, and hoped that she'd look as though she'd just come from work. Her cheeks were flushed. The ends of her hair were damp from the steam. She used no more than a touch of makeup around her eyes. With a final look in the mirror, she headed downstairs and edited what she'd written that day until Doug arrived.

They ate in Oak Bluffs at a small fish place overlooking the harbor. The food, though fresh and good, was incidental to the company. At Sasha's urging, Doug talked about his work, about plans for upcoming shows, about expansion into foreign countries. At Doug's urging, Sasha talked about her work, about her characters, about the friends she'd made in the field, even about the exciting news Diane had given her the day before.

"A TV movie? Sasha, that's great!" The genuine nature of his enthusiasm was a relief to Sasha, who had half feared he might resent her success. Many another man would, she knew, and she had memories to prove it. More than once in New York she'd been the subject of snide remarks, and though she hadn't cared a whit about the men making them, she'd been stung.

"It's really nothing," she said quickly, looking down to find her hand in Doug's, which echoed the warmth of his tone. "I mean, it may not amount to anything."

"But to be considered...!"

She laughed shyly. "That's what I told Diane. I was pretty excited myself."

"I should think so!" As a new thought struck, his expression sobered some. "If it does go through, will you have to supervise things? To leave here?"

"Not if I can help it," she vowed. "I may write the books, but I don't know the first thing about script writing. I'd leave that to the experts, though I guess I would have some say in the final product. But that can all be done by mail. I won't go on location. As it is, Diane says that M.P.I. wants me to tour when they re-release *Devil Dreams* and *Autumn Ambush*." She scowled. "I hate those things."

"They're not that bad," Doug chided gently.

"You can have them." Even as she said the words, she realized that he did. "Don't you do a certain amount of traveling, celebrity status and all?" He was the handsome fashion designer. Though she wasn't a television watcher herself, she was sure he'd gone the talk-show route.

"I've done it."

"And liked it?" If she was subconsciously looking for a source of incompatibility between them, it was to be soundly dismissed by his reply.

"No. I've never liked them. But—" his fingers began a slow caress of hers "—if I had someone with me, someone special, the whole thing could take on a different light. Like a second honeymoon, or a third or fourth." His eyes glittered, their silvery beams ricocheting into Sasha. "You have to admit that for people like you and me who had none of the advantages growing up, traveling has its excitement."

She grew thoughtful, lulled by the gentle stroking of his thumb against hers. "I thought it would. And I suppose it did at first. Then it…it lost its glamour."

"But *with* someone…?"

For a split second, her eyes held captive by the smoldering in his, she let herself imagine what it would be like to tour the country, even travel abroad, with Doug by her side. A second honeymoon, a third or fourth? It sounded…nice. Without realizing what she was doing,

she moved her fingers to hold his tighter. They were firm
and strong and warm, just right to give her a boost when
she was tired or lonely. Quite helplessly, a tiny smile
emerged to match the softness of her voice. "Yes. That
would be different."

Without releasing her gaze, Doug brought her hand to
his mouth and whispered a soft kiss against her knuckles.
"I think we could both survive it," he murmured
thickly. "Late-night dinners, breakfast in bed." Uncurl-
ing her fingers he sucked on her pinky and was rewarded
by the burst of flame in her gaze.

Sasha held her breath. Breakfast in bed…breakfast in
bed after a night of… She wanted it, she didn't, though
her senses flared wildly even at the simple gesture he
made next. It was highly erotic, the movement of his
cat's tongue up and down her pinky. She felt drawn in,
ready to drown and quite happily so, but…

"Please, don't," she whispered, unable to fathom the
power of what she felt.

Sensing her sudden bewilderment, Doug removed her
finger from his mouth and enclosed her hand in the cocoon of his fists. "Why not?" he murmured a trifle
tautly.

"It's…it's too much."

"Too fast?"

She nodded.

His hands tightened around hers and, eyes closed, he
bowed his head against them. He stayed that way for
several minutes during which Sasha agonized at her response. She wanted to please him, more than she'd ever
thought to please a man. She wanted to give to him, and
she'd tried. But he'd turned her down, and he'd been

right. Given what he'd told her, Doug deserved to have only the best. And the fullest. Yet at moments like this, in a place that could not help but remind her of what she'd made of herself and how far she'd come, she was still…frightened. Too much, too fast.

Eyes pleading for his understanding, she waited for him to look up. He didn't at first, simply spoke with his eyes shut, his brow creased as though he was in pain. "I know, I know," he muttered, trying to convince himself as he spoke. "It's scary, after all these years, to find someone…and feel so much…so fast." Then he opened his eyes with a look of dire determination and spoke through gritted teeth. "But it's right, Sasha. I know it is. We'll be good together in every way. One day you'll see that yourself. I'm not giving up. I can wait."

Stunned by his vehemence, Sasha needed a moment to recover. He was talking about a future together. A *real* future together, not simply some whimsical imagining. But she'd signed on once before for a future with a man, and it had been a disaster.

"Good together?" she echoed shakily. "You look like you want to throttle me."

Her accusation brought a slow relaxation to his features. He lowered her hand to the table, though he didn't release it, and the far corner of his lip quirked. "Throttle you for sitting there turning me on, throttle me for being so susceptible and disgustingly noble—how could I choose?" His voice became a sensual drawl and he leaned intimately forward. "Throttle you? Oh, no, my lady. What I'd *like* to do is—"

"Doug!" she pleaded, fully serious.

So was he. In point of fact he was tired of being noble.

He wanted to spend the night with Sasha, to make love to her until she nearly died of the pleasure and then named him her bona fide savior. And that day would come. He'd make it come, by hook or by crook. "What I'd *like* to do," he resumed, but forced a more casual smile, "is to be like Sean."

"Sean?"

"You know. Sean—in *Demon Woods?*"

She went beet red. Of course she knew Sean. She'd created him. Yet he'd been the last man on her mind at the moment. "How did you know about Sean?" she asked guardedly.

"I'm more than halfway through the book."

"Do-ug," she drew his name to two syllables in protest, "wasn't one enough?"

"You're embarrassed. Why, Sasha?"

"Because…I don't know, because…"

"Because there's so much of you in those books? But I know that, babe. I discovered that early on in *Raven's Revenge. Demon Woods* is very different in its way, but the same depth of feeling is there. Sean is a saint. And it seems he's well on his way to satisfying Nicole's needs."

"You've read the love scenes," Sasha intoned sternly. "Douglas Donohue, don't tell me you're one of those who skims around looking for sex?"

He beamed. "Skims around looking for sex? Hardly the phrase I'd have used, and not at all appropriate when you consider my recent self-restraint—"

"In *books*," she scolded. "In *books*."

He took pity on her discomfort. "No, I don't skim the pages for hot spots, but I have reached that first big love scene in *Demon Woods*. It's quite something. Strong. Highly passionate. But tender. And very emotional...."

Sasha shot him a challenging stare, only to find the most gentle expression on his face. In that instant she believed him; he did envy Sean. And he obviously wanted Sasha to be his Nicole.

Suddenly they were back where they'd been moments before, eyes locked, air sizzling. Sasha felt Doug's pull far beyond the physical. The need in his eyes spoke of an even deeper commitment, one she was no more ready for than the other. But she'd barely opened her mouth to protest when Doug gave a sigh of resignation and spoke.

"Anyway, I think the book is every bit as powerful as *Raven's Revenge*. When Nicole found that snake draped around the hanger in her closet...." He gave Sasha a pointed stare and asked, "Where *do* you get your ideas?"

She smiled and shrugged. "Sometimes from the newspapers. They often report weird things like that. Sometimes from other books or television. Mostly, I guess, from imagination." She cleared her throat. "Mine is fertile."

"Why the grimace? You've certainly managed to channel it along very productive lines."

"I suppose," she began thoughtfully. "Unfortunately I sometimes get carried away with it. I begin to imagine things like that really happening."

"Really happening to *you?*" His brow furrowed. "What do you mean?"

When Sasha realized what she was about to say, it occurred to her to quickly laugh and pass it all off. Doug was apt to think her positively paranoid. On the other hand, she half wanted to air her fear, to share it, to be told how foolish it was.

"I mean," she spoke hesitantly, keeping her voice low, looking up to make sure the waitress wasn't around, "that there are times when little things happen to me and I begin to imagine that it's not all by chance." She blushed. "It's really awful." She crinkled her nose. "And silly. I guess I'm so used to writing scary things into my books that I grow suspicious of very innocent occurrences."

"Things like what?" Doug asked quietly.

Sasha looked down at her plate and pushed crumbs around with her fork. "Like things out of place in my house. Like barrels rolling from a rooftop. Like the accident with my Suzuki." She forced a chuckle and sheepishly met Doug's gaze. "I even got stuck in the gardener's shed a month or so back. The door hinge jammed. For a minute I couldn't get out."

"What happened?" Doug asked, eyes wide.

"I panicked and hit the door with what had to have been either superhuman strength or sheer luck. It opened."

He let out a breath. "But you wondered, in that minute, whether someone was trying to trap you?"

She nodded and laughed. "Silly, isn't it? That's what I mean by a fertile imagination. It can work for me…or agin' me."

Doug didn't laugh. "Yeah, and when it's agin' you, you're probably miserable. I hope you're not worried now."

"Right now? Of course not. I'm with you." What had

emerged on impulse made a very special statement. Doug acknowledged it with a warm smile.

"Maybe you're getting there after all," he mused softly, then tossed his head in the direction of the door. "Come on. Let's get out of here." He left money enough for their food and a tip on the table, then ushered Sasha to the door, throwing his arm around her shoulders when the dark of night enveloped them. "I hope you know that if you're ever frightened you're to call."

"It's only my imagination. Vivid and bothersome."

"But still. Call. Do you hear me, Alexandra Blake?"

She returned a mocking, "I hear you, Douglas Donohue."

He reached into the inner pocket of his jacket and took out Sasha's letter. "Now, let's walk over to the post office to mail this, then I'll get you home. Okay?"

"Okay." Though Sasha was sure he'd have to have seen its address, Doug had been tactful enough not to ask questions about the letter she'd written to her mother. And she was grateful. She was still in a turmoil on that particular issue. Though she felt better for having written it, the letter had been little more than a stopgap measure. For the moment, though, she was simply unable to do more.

Presumably as a consequence of their discussion of vivid imaginings, Doug brought Sasha into the house, turned on the lights and saw that everything was well before he turned to leave. Sasha found comfort in his consideration.

"I'm fine," she laughed after he'd asked a third time. "And as soon as you leave I'll double-latch the door. Have I warped your imagination too?"

"Oh, yes," he drawled, reaching out to take her into his arms. "My imagination has worked overtime since the day you ran into me in the rain." He frowned and studied each of her features as though trying to understand it himself. "Hard to believe it was less than two weeks ago. I feel as though I've known you far longer."

So did she. His long lean body had a familiar feel now. But, she chided silently, that was beside the point. "You're stealing the lines from my books, Doug Donohue!"

"Am I? Naw, I've never read that one in yours."

She thought for a moment, cocking her head to the side. "Come to think of it, you're right. That line was from *Devil Dreams*. Humph! Maybe you're just catching it from me."

"Catching what?"

"Romanticitis," she announced with a sly half grin. Doug's arms were coiled around her waist. Her hands settled easily over his shoulders. She felt comfortable and secure with his compelling presence towering above her, with his bronzed skin aglow and his silver eyes brilliant.

"Is it serious?" he asked, suppressing a grin.

"Sometimes."

"Painful?"

"On occasion."

"Terminal?"

"Only once in a great while, as in Romeo and Juliet."

"I see," he said with an exaggerated nod. "Then there is hope?"

All pretense gone, she returned his soulful gaze. All along she'd known they were talking about themselves and the ailment that had seized them by storm, rather than some fictitious illness. Doug's final question brought it all home.

"I think so," she whispered.

"I know so," he said moments before he kissed her. What started as a gentle brushing of lips, though, quickly evolved into something far more heated. Doug hadn't intended it, any more than had Sasha, but the need had been building all through dinner and could be denied no longer. Their kiss was thorough and soul shaking, leaving them both breathless when Doug finally disengaged his lips.

He moaned thickly and his long limbs quivered. "Oh, God, I'd better leave or I won't be responsible for my actions. Call you tomorrow?"

Unable to speak, she nodded, watched him walk to his car, then put a hand to her lips as though to preserve the heat of him. But when the Maserati disappeared from view, she felt chilled. Closing the door, she double-latched it as promised, then returned to her study to finish editing what she'd written that day.

She was good for all of ten minutes. Suddenly she wanted simply to be in bed, buried beneath her heavy down quilt, dreaming. It had been a long day in so many respects. She was exhausted. And the sooner tomorrow came...

Sasha was still thinking of Doug when she awoke at five the next morning. She brushed her teeth and threw cool water on her face, then made a fresh pot of coffee and nestled in her study to work. The love scene she proceeded to write was as steamy as any she'd ever composed. She half expected to shock her computer, but it took it quite gamefully, with nary a curl of smoke. She, on the other hand, was trembling from head to foot when she sat back to reread what she'd written.

Her hero and heroine, boat designer and artist respectively, were very definitely in love. It had happened so quickly as to stun them both, and Sasha, too, for that matter. Usually she spent far longer building her love story, weaving the web of love and intrigue slowly and carefully around her characters, establishing side characters and subplots. This book was different, more simple in some respects, but unbelievably intense. She had a hero and heroine who had been attracted to one another from the start. Their relationship, growing from acquaintance to friend to lover stage, had dominated these first eighty pages, leaving neither room nor energy for awareness of other people, other happenings. Theirs was a pervasive, all-encompassing attraction that had grown and grown until its only proper outlet was in lovemaking.

Sitting back in her easy chair in the corner to the left of her desk, Sasha reflected on the cataclysmic scene she'd written. From page one it had been inevitable. The hero and heroine had been fascinated with each other, intrigued, aroused. Neither of them had ever experienced such instant and overwhelming attraction before, and it had been only the force of it all that had, ironically, held them off so long. But it had to be. The craving of their bodies went hand in hand with a mental craving that cried out for fulfillment—a oneness that, when it came, was devastatingly joyous and incredibly electrifying. It was a true merging of bodies and souls, a mind-altering experience, taking man and woman and producing far more than simply the sum of their parts. It was, quite breathlessly, magnificent.

Sasha closed her eyes and took a long breath. Her body tingled. It was Doug's face she saw. Her hero? She wondered. If only she could be a fly upon the wall of the heavens, looking down at the plot outline of her life as she looked down now at the outline of her book. What was in store for Doug and her? Would they be going through a trial by fire, as her hero and heroine would be soon?

For not everything was rosy in her book. While her hero and heroine had been totally engrossed in each other, a sinister force, unbeknown to them, had arrived on the scene. The archrival of the hero, his one-time mentor, a man now half-demented by dreams unfulfilled, was in residence, convinced in his warped mind that the hero's latest design was a copy of one of his own, stolen quite unconscionably years before, only now put into construction and tested. How to get back at the hero for stealing one's true love? It seemed obvious. Tit for tat.

Sasha shivered as she pictured the villain. He was a large burly man with a full beard, one eye that tended to wander, and a perpetual scowl. He reminded Sasha of the man who'd glowered at her when she'd been with Doug in Edgartown the past Sunday. Perhaps she'd even modeled him after that one. He'd seemed angry, his beard unable to hide the rigid line of his jaw, his eyes hard, his chin set in a pose of uncompromising resentment—the perfect villain, the man with the long-standing grudge, the embodiment of dementia.

Another shiver brought Sasha from her seat to stand before the window and open the shutters. She'd been working, totally absorbed, for nearly four hours. It was almost nine-thirty. Looking out on the day for the first time, she saw that it was raining, dark and gray. How lovely—and meaningful—that she'd produced such a beautifully strong love scene wrapped in her own private world on such a potentially gloomy day. Now that the day was exposed, though, she couldn't escape it…or, strangely, escape the more somber trail her thoughts had taken moments before.

Before the next chapter ended, the heroine would be earmarked as the villain's prey. Oh, there would be nothing sudden, no instantly terrifying event. That would be too fast for the villain, who, mindful of the years he'd felt slighted, then betrayed, wished to build the torment slowly and prolong it for both hero and heroine.

Sasha tugged her shawl more snugly around her shoulders. Could it really happen? Could a person set out to slowly and steadily terrify another? *Could,* of course. But *would?* What kind of perverted mind would want to hurt Sasha. And *why? Had she ever hurt someone that badly? Who?*

For all her skill, she couldn't begin to imagine who might be after her. Certainly no one related to Doug. Weird things had started happening to her well before she'd met him. Coincidence? So she'd tried to convince herself. But it was getting tougher and tougher with each little occurrence, because there was a pattern. Whoever was after her had read her books. Either that, or she was a seer herself.

On that very interesting possibility she stepped away from the window and padded to her desk. If it was true that what she wrote could come true, would it also hold that if she wrote what she wanted the future to hold, it would? So much of what she felt for Doug was embodied in her heroine's heart. Doug Donohue, in even the short time she'd known him, had aroused thoughts and cravings she'd honestly given up on in real life. At this moment she realized that she desperately wanted Doug to be her hero, to be there for her always. But the question remained as to whether he would be. Fiction or reality—was she asking too much?

The lights flickered. She looked up and froze. In *Devil Dreams* the phone lines had been cut, the electricity had mysteriously gone off. She held her breath. But after that momentary wavering, the lights were steady. Just the wind or the rain whipping at exposed wires? Very possibly. Then again...

Shaking her head, she left her study, showered and dressed, then made herself some breakfast. Wandering through to the living room, she stared out the front window at the drive. It was empty, its gravel glistening beneath a steady patter of rain. It was a gloomy day, indeed. She wrapped her arms about her middle, then shot a glance behind her. The fire. She'd work in front of the fire for a while. That would warm her up.

After setting kindling atop the cold ashes on the grate, she reached for several logs, only to realize that her supply in the copper basket was low. She stood and crossed to the cellar door, flipped on the light and started down. She'd barely put her weight on the third step when the plank gave way. Had she not been holding the open rail, she would have fallen. As it was, she stumbled and twisted around, held from a fall by the reflexive grip of her fingers on the steadying wood.

It took her a minute to recover. Heart pounding, fingers relaxing their grip on the rail only when she was sure her seating was firm, she pressed her hands to her knees and took a long ragged breath. From where she sat more than halfway down the steps, she stared back up at the plank that had yielded. It lay innocently if lopsidedly atop the stair frame, very obviously relieved of the nails that should have held it in place. With a shaky hand she touched the wood, raised the plank, tipped it up. Then she dropped it as though burned and stood quickly.

This was no accident. Someone had been in her house. But when? Her nervous eye skimmed the dank cellar, but nothing else seemed out of place. There were storage cartons piled as always in one corner, the furnace and hot-water heater in another, the washer and dryer side by side against the concrete wall. Atop the latter lay the white cloth that Doug had pressed to her hand that day in the rain. She'd washed it; it was clean. Scrambling from the stairs, she grabbed it, then retraced her steps, cautiously lest there be another plank out of place, stepping gingerly over the one designed to trip her.

She had to get out of the house. No longer could she simply imagine that someone was after her. And there was no doubt in her mind as to where she wanted to go. A quick call to Maggie gave her the information she needed. Within minutes she was in her car, speeding over the rain-slick roads en route to Doug's.

Someone had been in her house. More than once? But she worked at home. She was there for most of her waking hours. Lately though, there had been times out with Doug. She recalled the book on the mantel that had been taken from its place, the alarm clock reset, the brush misplaced, the perfume stopper set aside—now her cellar stairs sabotaged. Tallying the signs, she realized that she had indeed been out of the house for a span of several hours before each of these small incidents. Someone was watching her, aware of her comings and goings. It was a terrifying thought and one from which she was still trembling when, as per Maggie's instructions, she turned off North Road, found the private driveway marked by a bright red mailbox, and approached Doug's house.

Only her periphery vision absorbed the ultramodern structure with its pervasive glass and its commanding ocean view. She just wanted to see Doug. Then she'd relax.

He was on his phone in the den, carrying on a heated discussion with his West Coast distributor, when the doorbell rang. His first impulse was to ignore it. The mailman would leave whatever he had at the door. When he realized that most probably his signature would be required for at least one of those pieces of mail, though, he relented.

"Damn it, Frazier, hold on. That's my doorbell." Frustration bade him slam the receiver onto the desk, irritation marked his step as he made for the door. His face was a mask of aggravation when he hauled it open, then his pulse careened when he found a startled Sasha Blake before him.

"Sasha!" She looked much as she had when he'd first seen her, when she and her motorcycle had run into him in the rain. Though only spattered with drops this time from her dash from the car, the same damp tendrils stuck to her cheeks, the same pallor dominated her skin, the same look of fright filled her eyes. "My God, Sasha, come on in." He reached for her and tugged her out of the rain, shut the door behind her, then stood for a moment staring at her, unable to believe she was here on his doorstep. Without thought, he brushed the wisps of hair from her cheeks and ran his fingers around the back of her neck while his gaze devoured her features one by one. Then, as he hadn't done that first day in the rain, he lowered his head and kissed her. He couldn't help but feel the tremor of her lips or the way she seemed suddenly to cling to him. When he raised his head once more, she sagged against him and breathed a great sigh of relief.

"Thank heavens you're home," she murmured against his shirt, taking courage from the solidness of his arms around her back. "I was so worried you'd be out and I needed to see you." Her voice sounded as weak as she felt. Doug set her back.

"What's wrong?"

"Oh, Doug…" Meeting his gaze, she let her voice trail off. He'd think her crazy. Absolutely crazy. But… he hadn't that other time. He'd been concerned. Even now she could see that same worry in his eyes.

"What is it?" he whispered hoarsely.

"I'm—I'm—" She lowered her gaze and, in a moment's cowardice, reached into her pocket and drew out the white cloth. "I wanted to return this," she murmured, unable to look up.

Doug stared at the cloth. "You're not trembling over a stupid cloth, babe. What's wrong?"

She looked at him then, her eyes filled with trepidation. But she needed his comfort too much to hold back. "I'm—I'm scared, Doug."

"About what?"

"Something happened this morning. And I'm probably imagining it all, but I'm scared." The words came in a rush as her limbs began to shake. Doug took her into his arms and held her tightly for a minute. Then, an arm firmly about her shoulder, he held her beside him and began to walk.

"Come on." Returning to the den, he grabbed the phone with his free hand. "Frazier? I'll have to get back to you. There's an emergency here. You'll be in later? Fine." Without another word he hung up the phone.

"Oh, I'm sorry, Doug. I didn't mean to interrupt. This is really foolish of me—"

One long finger stilled her babble, touching her lips, sealing further apology within. "Nothing is foolish where you're concerned, Sasha. Didn't I tell you to call?"

"Didn't quite expect me at your door, though, did you?" His presence had taken the initial edge off her fear, allowing self-consciousness to peek through.

"How did you find me?"

"Maggie."

He nodded, then leaned back against the desk, brought her between his legs and hooked his hands at the small of her back. "Now, will you tell me what's wrong? Another...accident?"

She swallowed hard and nodded once. "Almost. I was going down to the cellar to get more logs for the fire and I nearly fell. One of the wooden treads had been unnailed. If I hadn't been holding on to the railing..."

Her voice faded, replaced by the image of her toppling the length of the hard wooden steps.

Doug swore softly and hugged her to him. He pressed his cheek to her hair and drew reassuring circles on her back with his hands. "It's okay," he murmured, "you're safe here. It's okay." Perversely her body shook uncontrollably for several minutes, during many of which he repeated his whispers of comfort. It was only when Sasha began to relax that she noticed the corresponding tension in Doug. At that moment he set her back and looked at her hard.

"The cellar stairs? As in *Raven's Revenge?*"

She shrugged, momentarily embarrassed. "It's a common enough occurrence—"

"But one too many. Now, I want you to tell me everything that's happened. Everything. Do you hear me, Sasha?"

CHAPTER SEVEN

THERE WAS TO BE no compromising. Doug's stern expression stated as much. Not that Sasha wished it, for she desperately needed to air the extent of her fears. When she'd first broached them the night before at dinner, she'd simply tossed them out as examples of her overactive imagination. Now, though, they seemed totally legitimate.

"I'm not sure where to begin," she murmured.

Doug coaxed her softly, patiently. "How about the beginning. Tell me the very first thing that happened, and when."

She frowned, trying to think back. It was hard, since at the time she hadn't thought much of it. "I guess about five or six weeks ago. That was when I thought I was stuck in the gardener's shed. I mean, I got myself out quick enough, and it was a perfectly understandable thing. The shed is nearly as old as the house and not as well kept. Wood swells. Hinges rust."

"What next?"

"My lights have gone out once or twice." She tried to rationalize that too. "It happens a lot on the Vineyard. The wind blows, lines get tangled, conformers shake."

"Did anyone else lose their electricity at the time?"

"I'm not really sure. I didn't check. The lights came back on after five minutes or so."

"Was this during the day?"

She shook her head and shuddered. "At night. Always at night."

"Leaving you in the dark and afraid."

"I'm not that bad," she drawled. "I've got plenty of candles and flashlights. And, like I said, it didn't last long."

"You never called the light company?"

"No. Had the darkness persisted, I would have, I suppose. Once the lights came back on, though, it seemed unnecessary. I assumed they'd had plenty of calls and wouldn't need another one."

Doug sent her a punishing glare. "You may have been too thoughtful for your own good." He sighed. "Okay. What next?"

"I suppose the bike accident was next."

"But it was rainy. You skidded," he argued, playing the devil's advocate.

"That's what I told myself. And I'll never really know for sure."

"The bike's repaired, I take it." She nodded. "Did the repairman have anything to say?"

"I didn't ask. I may have simply skidded, for all I know. Then again it may have been—"

"—a tiny bullet piercing the tire."

Sasha looked at him in alarm. "I guess I *did* do something to your imagination."

"No," he stated baldly. "I'm just anticipating what I might read in one of your other books." When she continued to stare at him, he elaborated. "I've already finished *Raven's Revenge* and *Demon Woods,* and I'm three-quarters of the way through *Midnight Rogue.*''

"You are?"

"Uh-huh." For the first time since she'd arrived, he cracked the semblance of a smile. "Couldn't seem to concentrate on much else after you left last night. Couldn't seem to sleep, either. I read for most the night." The smile, what there had been of it, faded. "*Raven's Revenge* takes care of the cellar stairs, *Midnight Rogue* the barrels toppling off that roof in Edgartown and, if we exchange wine cellar for gardener's shed, the incident there. Nothing from *Demon Woods* yet, though."

"I hope not! That's the slimy one, with snakes and muddy pits and wild wolves!" Her expression was one of revulsion. She was trembling again.

When he smiled this time, it was with affection. "How did you ever write that one if you have such an aversion to creepy, crawly things?" He ran his fingers up and down her spine, though if he was trying to scare her, he hadn't a chance in the world. His touch never failed to affect her, but not in creepy, crawly ways.

She wriggled in response and mustered a half grin. "I had plenty of nightmares through that one. I think it was my own terror that made the book."

"I doubt that," he growled, just imagining the wealth of love held in that book too. Pushing himself from the desk, he led her to a chair and sat her down, then pulled a matching one closer and sank into it, leaning forward, his hands clasped between his outspread thighs. "There's a definite pattern here. Anything else? What about things in your house being misplaced. You mentioned that last night.''

Sasha sat stiffly. "Do you remember that alarm clock that rang at two in the morning? I may have misset it by accident, then again I may not have. The same night there was a book lying open on the mantel, but I don't remember taking it out. After you left, I went upstairs and found my hairbrush in the middle of the bed and my perfume bottle left uncapped.'' She sighed and shrugged. "In all fairness, I may have just been careless. But I'm not usually.''

"Which book?" he asked pointedly.

"Autumn Ambush."

"And the motorcycle?"

She averted her gaze. "The same.''

For a long time Doug said nothing. When he finally broke the silence, it was in a voice taut and controlled. "Have you called the police?"

Sasha's eyes shot to his face. "No!"

"Why not?"

"Because this is absurd!"

"Is that why you came to me—because it's absurd?"

"I needed reassurance.''

"Because *you* believe it all."

"I'm beginning to," she said meekly.

"Then why not the police? Surely if someone's on your trail—"

"The police are apt to think I'm daft! Either that, or they'll think it's a publicity stunt I've dreamed up!"

His silver gaze held hers steadily. "But you've told me. And I don't think you're daft. Nor do I think you'd do anything for publicity, least of all this.''

"That's because you know me."

"Thank you," he said a trifle stiffly, then reached for her hand and took it in his to counterbalance his tone with the warmth of his touch. "But I do think we should call the police."

"No," she declared firmly.

Not quite giving up, Doug took a different tack. "Okay, then, who could it be? Who could possibly be out to hurt you?"

"That's the bizarre thing!" she cried. "I don't have the slightest idea! I mean, I'm not a cruel person. I haven't exactly raced through life leaving a trail of injured parties in my wake."

"People can be sick sometimes."

"Tell me," she quipped rigidly. "My present villain is a jealous maniac hell-bent on revenge for something he imagined happening."

Doug scowled. "Your present villain?"

"In the book I'm writing." She waved aside the divergence. "But I don't have any enemies. And I can't imagine who could possibly hate me that much."

"Think."

She did, studying her hand wrapped in his larger, stronger one, trying to concentrate on whom she might have clashed with on the Vineyard. Finally she sighed in bewilderment. "I suppose there are those people who may be annoyed with me."

"Such as?"

"Ruth Burke, the librarian who thinks I write trash, Hank Rossi, the auto mechanic I turn down every time he asks me out, Joseph Marovich, the postal clerk I pester—I mean the list can go on and on. There's old Willie

Dunton who hates everyone. But this is ridiculous. I've never really argued with any of these people. And I've never been rude—''

"I know, babe. I know," he said kindly, squeezing her hand reassuringly. "But if we're dealing with a sick mind, you never know. Who else?"

"I suppose you'd have to add Geoff Briggs to the list. You heard *his* complaint."

"Yeah. I heard."

"But I can't go to the police, Doug. These are all decent people, despite what insignificant differences I may have with them."

Releasing her hand, Doug sat back thoughtfully and pressed his fist to his chin. "What about your ex-husband?"

"Sam? Oh, no! Sam would never do something like this!"

"You are divorced. That has to leave some kind of hard feeling. Maybe the guy's jealous of your success."

"Sam jealous? Hah! He's too wrapped up in his spuds to even notice," she sneered. "Besides, he would never take the time away from his work to come down here to haunt me. And whoever is doing this has to be nearby. The incidents are spread out pretty far time-wise."

"But getting closer," Doug suggested. "Most of those things have happened during the past ten days."

It would have been a sobering thought had not Sasha already been stone-sober. "I know," she whispered frantically. "I know."

"Then the police it'll have to be."

"No!" she exclaimed once again, then lowered her voice to a pleading murmur. "At least, not yet."

"You've got a better suggestion?"

If only she had. She shook her head in misery. Then she sprang from her chair and whirled in the direction of the door. "I shouldn't have come. I'm sorry."

Doug was behind her in an instant, grabbing her, drawing her back against him. He wrapped his arms around her and bent his head until his lips grazed her cheek. "Never say that again to me, Sasha. You did the right thing. I want you here." Very slowly, he turned her in his arms until she was facing him. "This is where you belong. With me. Don't you realize that yet?"

Suddenly the air changed and all thought of danger receded. In its place was the spark that had been there from the first. It was both sexual and emotional, binding them irrevocably closer. Looking up into Doug's eyes, Sasha knew then.

"I guess I'm beginning to," she whispered, timidly lifting her arms to his shoulders. "There had to be some reason why the only place I thought to run to was here."

"Then you admit that the cloth was a ploy?" he asked, his firm male lips curving crookedly.

She studied them and moved a finger to trace their strong lines. It felt right. Everything felt right just then—his hard, lean body against hers, the whipcord strength of his thighs, his enveloping arms. She felt safe and secure and warm and excited. She felt that strange knot of desire forming beyond the pit of her stomach. Oh, yes, everything felt right.

Standing on tiptoe, she replaced her fingers with her lips, tentatively at first, then, feeling Doug's welcome, with greater conviction. His arms tightened around her back, practically lifting her off her feet, and she knew she'd come home. This was what she wanted, this sense of needing and being needed, of cherishing and being cherished, for that was what came through his kiss. She was a woman, needing this man and only this man to make her life complete.

At his probing, her lips opened fully, but the hunger was mutual, a sparring for depth and possession. She trembled for more, arching her back, thrusting her fingers into his hair to hold him closer. She'd never imagined such wanting, such aching to be part of another person. And it was Doug who inspired it, only Doug.

The hands that had been holding her lowered her gently, then slid around her waist and rose to her breasts. She moaned into his mouth and felt herself swell, loving the moment he found her hard nipples through the layers of clothing, wanting more, always more.

Suddenly a thought intruded on her heaven, though, and with a strength born of pride she pushed herself back. "Oh, no, Doug Donohue!" she cried, staring at his stunned expression. "If you think you're going to do this to me again, you're the crazy one! Twice now you've taken me to near-forgetfulness and then left me unfulfilled." Her breasts rose and fell sharply with the raggedness of her breathing. "But I won't have it this time! Do you hear? I don't know what's happened to my life in the last two weeks, but you've turned it topsy-turvy! I thought I was satisfied! Hah! I didn't know the meaning of the word!" Her voice lowered to a beseechful tone. "But, God, I want you! You, damn it, *you!* And if you're leading me down some primrose path only to abandon me at the last, you can forget it!" Her hand shook as she raised it to her mouth and whimpered, "I don't think I can take it, Doug. I don't."

For what seemed an eternity Doug simply stood where he was more than an arm's length away, staring at her. Then, as she watched warily, his stunned expression took flame. His eyes glowed, their lambent gleam spreading to the bronze of his skin. Neither saying a word nor releasing her gaze, he kicked off his deck shoes. Tugging his shirt from his pants, he ignored buttons to whip the soft fabric over his head. Hooking his fingers beneath the elastic band of his trendy cotton sweats, he pushed them and his shorts over his hips and stepped out of them in one fluid move.

Still trembling from her heated monologue, it was Sasha's turn to be stunned. Doug stood before her naked, as gloriously masculine as she'd imagined, as strong and lean and proud. Her eyes dropped from his face to his corded shoulders and then to his chest, covered with its dark brush of hair that was as broad at the top as were his shoulders before tapering to a thinner line below. His waist was slim, almost indistinguishable from the virile narrowness of his hips. His thighs and calves were carved of sinewy twists, his feet well formed and planted firmly in the thick brown carpet.

He was a bronze god, his skin a teak treasure broken only by a paler swath across his loins. It was to this paler swath that Sasha's gaze was drawn, to the essence of Doug's masculinity, long and strong and quite helplessly responding to her visual caress.

He made no attempt to hide from her, but stood his ground with the realization that for Sasha this was something new, this slow admiration of a man's bare body.

He saw her pleasure in the flush of color on her cheeks, saw her arousal in the flash of hazel in her eyes, saw her need in the rapidity of her breathing, the clenching of her fists, the tautness of her stance.

And he felt utterly exposed. For aware as he was of his own body and of the fact that Sasha admired it, he was abundantly aware of the broader implication of what was happening. In offering himself so blatantly he was asking a corresponding commitment of Sasha. She may have been the one to stand back and dare him to deny her this time, but with these slow moments' perusal of what he offered, she was being offered a chance to refuse him. It was her turn. Standing before him neither held in his arms nor drugged by his kiss, she was being given a choice. Awaiting her decision was perhaps the hardest thing he'd ever done in his life.

By the time Sasha's gaze returned to his eyes, he wore a look of infinite vulnerability. In view of the beauty of his body, she marveled at his lack of arrogance, his lack of pretense. It was as though the tables had been turned, as though it was he who now feared she'd leave him. He had no way of knowing that it was precisely this fear, this vulnerability that bound her to him as nothing else might have.

Feeling suddenly shy, she spoke in an unsure whisper. "I don't know what to do, Doug. I mean, I've never had a choice before."

For a split second his expression hardened. "You want to leave."

"No!"

"What do you want?" he asked cautiously.

She bit her lip and allowed her gaze to fall once more

along the manly contours of his body. "I want...to touch you," she whispered.

He spoke one word, no louder than hers and held out his arms in invitation. "Well?" But he didn't move. She was the one who would have to take those last few steps.

In that instant Sasha knew how truly different Doug was from what she'd known in the past. He saw her as a woman with a free, if heavy, choice to make. He'd meant what he'd said before, that he wanted her to want him and only him. And she realized that he was purposely forcing her to move that last distance simply because he had to know.

With one step the distance was halved, with another it was obliterated. Only when she reached up and put her hands on his chest did he touch her, and even then it was with the lightest grasp of her shoulders. She was to lead the way, to do what she wanted, to show him what she needed most.

Swallowing once, Sasha fought a rising fever. She wove her fingers through his hair, finding his chest beneath to be strong and warm. She lowered her hands and traced his hips, trailing her fingers up his thighs to his groin, settling her palm against the rock hardness of his indrawn stomach, moving it slowly down.

She'd never touched a man this way before. Intermingled with awe was a tiny surge of power, dizzying yet self-perpetuating. Her fingers drifted lower, tangling in a more coarse thatch of dark hair, feeling beneath it a softness, a hardness, a throbbing.

Doug was the one who trembled now. It was all he could do not to thrust against her, and the force of his restraint coiled his muscles all the more. But he waited, his breath laboring as her fingers crept lower, finally touching him timidly, experimentally, measuring his length in airy strokes of silk, at last circling his thickness and holding him as he needed to be held.

A deep animal sound escaped his throat and she released him in alarm. But he grabbed her hand and returned it to him, his own fingers holding hers firm.

"Oh, no, babe," he rasped. "Don't let go. I've waited so long. Don't let go."

His urgency was all the encouragement she needed. Bowing her head to his chest, she closed her eyes and pressed her lips to his warm blanket of hair as she stroked him steadily. Her hand fed on his turgescence, delighting in its strength. Her thumb found the silk of its tip and marveled at its butter smoothness. Was this the instrument she'd once thought to be a tool of pain and degradation? It seemed impossible, for there was nothing but beauty in the full rise of Doug's manhood.

As though sensing her astonishment, Doug called her name. His voice seemed to come from a distance at first, from the far reaches of arousal. On second calling, it was stronger.

"Sasha?"

She looked up, her eyes dazed in admiration. "Yes?"

He took her hand from him then and held it against her other on his chest where she could feel the drum of his heart. His voice was thick. "I need to know, Sasha. I need to know what he did."

"He?" she asked blankly. At that moment there was only one "he" in her world and it was Doug.

Pleased, Doug offered a gentle smile and brought her hands to his lips for a kiss before returning them and holding them tightly to his chest. "Sam. I need to know what he did so that I can make it really good for you. I'm frightened, babe. So afraid of hurting you. Of doing something that may remind you—"

"Shhh," she whispered, loving the feel of his hard length pressed intimately to her body. "I'm not thinking of him, Doug. Only you."

"But tell me Sasha. I need to know."

For an instant she resented the intrusion. Sam was of another world, an alien being to this new heaven. But she saw that same look of urgency, of vulnerability in Doug's face and could deny him nothing, least of all this glimpse of her past. He cared. And if his knowing everything would set his mind at ease, she cared in turn.

Letting her head fall forward until it was cradled atop their entwined hands, she gently kissed his fingers, then took a deep breath. "He was rough. That's all."

"He beat you?"

"No. He just took me without care or consideration." Momentarily reliving the humiliation, she couldn't look up. Her words spilled forth with a will of their own. "He was little more than a rutting animal. When he felt the urge, I was his receptacle. I was a virgin when we married. My wedding night was a nightmare. Over and over again. Oblivious to my pain, my bleeding."

Doug freed his hands to hold her in his full embrace. "It didn't get better after that?"

"It might have had he ever tried to arouse me. But he didn't. My pleasure wasn't part of his definition of the act. He was only concerned with relieving himself." She looked up then. "It sounds dirty, doesn't it?" When Doug nodded she went on, holding his gaze unwaveringly. "Well, it felt it too. When I was embarrassed or humiliated he only pounded all the harder. When I was dry—which I always was—he seemed to take pleasure in my cries. It was his way of exerting his authority over me, I suppose. I half wish he *had* hit me. If I'd been unconscious I wouldn't have had to feel what he did to me. Not once was I proud to be a woman. Not once."

Running out of breath, she fell silent and awaited Doug's response. That he was appalled was obvious. But there was something else in his expression that snagged her pulse. "Oh, God," she cried softly and covered her face with her hands. "I *feel* dirty! And I've turned you off!"

"You could never turn me off!" Doug declared, taking her face between his hands and gently forcing it back up to his. "Never, Sasha! It's just that...just that I feel...guilty."

"Guilty? You?"

"Yes, me." He sighed and sent a pleading look over her head. When he returned his gaze to hers it was with humility. "I've taken women that way. Too many times. And I'm ashamed of it! You know, before I met you I didn't like myself very much. I've used people, men in business, women in bed. Since I've met you, I feel different. With you I'm different. I think that for the first time in my life I truly respect myself as a man." A fine tremor shimmered through his limbs. "Maybe...maybe that's what love's all about."

Sasha's breath was caught in her throat. "Love?" she warbled.

"Yes, love." Suddenly it was in his eyes, in the fingers that stroked her finely sculpted features with wonder. "I love you. Is that so hard to believe?"

"No one's ever said that to me before," she whispered.

"And I've never said it to anyone before, so it's a first for us both."

Sasha's heart swelled until she felt it would burst. "And you mean it?"

He gave a crooked smile. "Would I be standing here naked as the day I was born, exposed and unprotected, and lie?" The smile waned, yielding to a more sober set of his mouth. "I need you, Sasha, in ways I've never needed another human being. Oh, I've taken in the past, taken what I've wanted and then turned my back without regret. But I've never needed to give this way, to make things good for a woman, to make her life happy. And I want to do that for you, Sasha. More than you can imagine, I want that. But I need your help. And I need *your* giving. The whole thing isn't one-sided anymore. That was why I had to know that you only wanted *me*. Because I only want you, babe. No one or nothing else."

"Oh, Doug," Sasha murmured, her eyes awash with tears. "You make me feel so...special."

"You are! Dear God, you are!" Wrapping her in arms made of steel, he hugged her then. She half feared her ribs would crack, but she welcomed the pressure and returned it through arms coiled tightly around his neck. She held and held, and he did too. For the moment kisses were secondary—but only for the moment.

Tipping his head back, Doug smiled down at her, eyes shining, dazzling her with their brilliance. Then his mouth was on hers with the same hunger as earlier, yet with an openness that was loving and needing and aching combined. It seemed to go on forever, a dialogue of lips and tongues and teeth. Only reluctantly did they separate, and then to set about soothing the ache.

"Aren't you warm?" Doug asked, kissing tiny dots of perspiration from her nose. When she nodded, he reached to the hem of her sweater and gently eased it over her head. Without pause he went to work on the buttons of her blouse, tossing the unwanted covering to the floor before releasing the catch of her bra. He bent his head then and found haven in the damp valley between her breasts, breathing in the sweet scent of her skin while she buried her face in his hair.

His lips were everywhere, on her throat, her ribs, the soft undersides of her breasts, then their crests. Sasha cried her delight when he opened his mouth on her nipple and drew it in, dabbling with the wet point of his tongue, then sucking so strongly that a shaft of raw heat sizzled to her loins. Eyes closed, holding his head tightly, she moaned and he released her, but only to slip to his knees and trail kisses to the hollow beneath her ribs while his fingers attacked the zipper of her jeans.

Then he was slow, tantalizingly slow, and she fought the urge to push him away and strip as quickly as he had. His hands inched the denim lower, taking her panties with them. His mouth worshiped each bit of flesh as it was revealed to his exultant gaze. His tongue found her navel and plunged. His lips dealt more gently with the soft ivory flesh of her belly. The fabric receded farther and in a burst of desire he peeled it to her thighs. Hands cupping the warm roundness of her bottom, he kissed the dark triangle of hair that protected her inner-most secrets.

Sasha arched her back and whimpered, still clutching his head, fearing that her legs would give way. Her body quivered wildly, every muscle, every bone, every nerve end aflame. She felt more alive than she ever had, more needed, more cherished, and she wondered how she'd ever managed to put such feelings in words...and knew she hadn't. If her writing held emotion, it was the emotion born of dreams. This, though, was real, and that much more rapturous. Though she may have come close in her imaginings, she'd never truly known or expressed this exquisite emotional joy of being with a man she loved. And she did love him. As her clothes left her body, so all pretense left with it. There was no room for prevarication, no time for playing with words. To say that Doug was unique, that he was warm and caring and intelligent and charming and companionable, was only to say that she loved him.

"Oh, Doug," she breathed on a note of ecstasy, aware that her jeans had been tossed aside only when the man beneath her slowly stood. "Doug," she whispered, look-ing into his eyes then, needing to be as open as he. "I love you."

Had he been waiting for the words? Somehow she believed that even without them he'd have adored her without reservation, but the joy she saw in his eyes made the adoration that much more breathtaking.

His face said it all—the light in his eyes, the flush on his cheeks, the smile of awe on his lips. No words were needed. Nor were they offered. Lowering his head, he kissed her tenderly, then again, hunger momentarily taking second place to sheer devotion. He opened his eyes and lifted his head, and his gaze went to her hair.

"I've never seen it down," he said in a rasping murmur. "Do you know that? I've never seen it down."

Sasha watched in wonder as he reached for first one clasp then the other, tossed them aside, threaded his fingers through the thickness of her auburn tresses and very gently combed them down to her shoulders.

"Beautiful," he whispered, unable to take his eyes from the vibrant tangles. "Beautiful and wild and sexy. Do you know that?" His gaze returned to hers for a moment, then fell to her full breasts, her flat belly and finally that harbor he'd kissed so eloquently moments before. "You're beautiful, Sasha. Beautiful and warm and wonderful. And I think that if I don't make love to you now I'm going to die."

"Don't do that," she whispered back, a smile on her face. "If you die, I'll never know, will I?"

"Never know what?" he asked, wrapping his arms about the small of her back and drawing her intimately closer.

Her own arms settled around his lips, her hands pressing against the leanness of his buttocks. She didn't falter. "Never know what it's like to be made real love to," she breathed, entranced. "Never know what it's like to give you pleasure. Never know what it's like to feel you deep, deep inside me."

Doug sucked in a sudden breath. His body jerked, inflamed by her words. "Oh, God, I want you," he gasped, sweeping her into his arms and setting off in what direction Sasha neither knew nor cared as long as his strong arms were cradling her, holding her close.

Suddenly, almost comically, his tone changed. "Hell, the bed's not made. I never made the bed." His frustrated apology was offered on the threshold of his room.

Sasha grinned, finding his dismay all the more endearing. "We don't need it made."

"But I want you on clean sheets. Satin sheets. The finest."

"It's you I want. Not satin sheets." Her back came down on cool cotton, perhaps rumpled, but of a manly checked design. "And it's your bed I want to be in," she whispered, looking up at the face so close to hers, "not some sterile peacock showcase."

Doug chuckled and kissed her hard, lowering himself to her side while his hands began to reacquaint themselves with the body they'd never forget. He touched her everywhere, then followed with his mouth, licking her flesh, kissing it, nibbling here and there until she began to writhe with the desire he unleashed.

Breathing as hard as she, he finally raised himself to lie by her side, and turned her to face him. "Touch me again, babe. Please."

His pleading sent the flame higher and she yielded instantly, adoring his flesh as he had hers, feeling her own body weep in response. At last, her face a mere breath from his, her eyes riveted to the silver ones she so worshiped, she caressed him as intimately as she had before. She felt his fullness and his hardness, sensed him swell all the more in her grasp. Then she felt something else, a hand sizzling down her belly, finding her, opening her, stroking her with such gentle fire that she thought she'd drown in flame. She'd written steamy before, but nothing could compare with the imminent conflagration that threatened. Moaning softly, she arched onto his fingers, then the fingers were gone and she was on her back. Doug on his knees, spreading her thighs, giving thanks to the light of day that illuminated the portal of her sex.

Unashamed, she lay still, though the roughness of her breathing and the faint tremor of her limbs bespoke of the need he'd created, the need he'd have to fill. He came forward then, one hand lingering to feather stroke her a final time before joining its mate as a brace by her shoulders.

"You're ready for me," he whispered. "All wet and warm. You're not afraid, are you?"

She nodded. "I'm afraid you'll keep me waiting longer." It was her turn to beg, but it was new and wondrous. "Please, Doug. I need you."

"And I love you," he said, holding her gaze as he slowly undulated his hips, moved closer, touched, gently entered, then penetrated completely. She held her breath, aware of a gliding, a slow filling, then the most heartrending sense of possession she'd ever dreamed. Who was the possessor? Who the possessed? One was the other, each was both. Their sighs of satisfaction were in perfect harmony.

"Oh, Doug," she whispered, wrapping her legs around his hips, her arms around his back, arching up from the bed to receive his kiss. He didn't move as he kissed her but used his tongue provocatively, inspiring her to do the same, while they both savored the sense of satisfaction down lower where their bodies were joined.

Then, slowly, he began to move, and what happened

was pure fantasy to Sasha. With each thrust she rose hotter, higher. With each hungry twist she burned. She wanted to die and be reborn as part of this man, to have all of him, to devour him as she was being devoured by his magnificence. If this was what being loved and in love was about, she was more than willing to toss self-sufficiency to the winds. One couldn't be self-sufficient and have all this, this mind-boggling joining of minds and hearts and bodies that built a tension that coiled and knotted and was relieved by her writhing only to renew itself and soar onward.

"I love you, Sasha! I love you!" Doug cried, his face a mask of sweet pain that she saw for only a moment before, eyes shut tight against the unbearable agony of reaching, her body exploded into multitudinous fragments of flame. Seconds later Doug cried out again, this time from his own powerful climax, his body irrupting to quench her flame, succeeding in making it all the more grand as he collapsed atop her and held her close until the last of his shattering spasms subsided.

It was only later, long moments later, that either of them moved, and then it was Doug to roll to her side and Sasha to curl snugly against the damp warmth of his body. The air was rent with panting, then sighs. The sweet smell of their lovemaking lingered as a heady aura about them.

"Never before," Doug rasped. "I never knew…"

With a catlike grin of satisfaction, Sasha teased, "That should have been my line."

"Is it?"

"Yes."

Heads sharing a pillow, they looked into one another's eyes. "How do you feel?"

Her grin persisted. She couldn't have stifled it if she'd tried, which she wasn't about to. "Free. And warm. And tired. And happy."

"I'm glad," he crooned, smiling back.

"How do *you* feel?"

"Free. And warm. And tired. And happy."

"Free? I thought I was the one released from her fears."

"Oh, no. I had fears, too." He gently stroked the tangled mess of her hair. "I wondered if I could satisfy you. If I could give you what you deserved."

"You sure did, bub."

"I'm not kidding, Sasha." He was stone-sober. "I had no idea there were so many insecurities where the heart's concerned."

"You've a heart condition?" she asked, feeling far too giddy to think of being serious.

"You bet I do. And it's only partly relieved."

"Only partly?"

"Marry me, Sasha. Be my wife. Promise to spend the rest of your life with me."

His words took Sasha by storm. Wide-eyed, she stared at him, all giddiness suddenly gone. "Oh, Doug," she murmured sadly.

"What's 'Oh, Doug'? You said you love me."

"I do."

"Then marry me."

There they were again, those two gut-wrenching words. She took a sharp breath, her eyes pleading for something she couldn't quite fathom. "I—I don't know. It's so sudden."

He was up on an elbow then, single-minded and intense. "No more sudden than our falling in love. You've accepted that, haven't you?"

"Yes."

"Then why not marriage?"

Her face twisted painfully and she looked away. "Because I've been through it once before."

"With a jackass."

"Perhaps, but a jackass who took license to control from a bunch of meaningless marriage vows."

"Ours wouldn't be meaningless. We love each other. Did you ever love Sam?"

She rolled onto her back and stared at the ceiling. "No."

"You see? That'd be the difference."

It certainly was a difference. He had a point. But the fact remained that the thought of marriage unsettled her. Irrational? Perhaps. But until she worked it out...

Turning her head on the pillow, she faced Doug once more. "I need time," she pleaded. "Everything's happened so fast. Can't you give me time?"

"And do what in the meanwhile? See each other every once in a while? Date? Catch sex on the run?" He grunted in frustration, shot a glance at the window, then looked back. "Don't you see? I want you with me all the time. I want to spend every day with you and every night, all night."

"Can't we do that sometimes?"

"Oh, sure. And in the in-between times I'll sit here stewing, fearing that I may lose you. That's my insecurity, Sasha. And what about this crazy who's after you? What about him? How can I protect you if you're not mine to protect?''

She offered a faint gesture of dismissal. ''Oh, it may be nothing. Really.''

''Come on, Sasha,'' he growled. ''Face facts.''

''I am, and I know that I need more time!''

Doug stared at her, his eyes hard as stone. Then, before she could reach out, he rolled from the bed to his feet and headed for the door.

''Doug…?''

He didn't stop, and when her cry was swallowed in silence, she didn't follow him. This was a new side of Doug, a darker side, and she wasn't quite sure how to handle it.

CHAPTER EIGHT

SASHA TUGGED at the sheet to cover herself and lay quietly listening to the thunderous beating of her heart. She couldn't hear Doug, but then, did she really expect him to stomp around the living room in a temper?

Very slowly her eyes wandered and she took in her surroundings for the first time. Doug's bedroom was huge, made even more so by high vaulted ceilings painted a fresh beige as were the walls, and a multitude of windows. The carpeting was brown, as it had been in the other room, the furnishings slate gray and strictly contemporary, with a simplicity of line that broadcast masculine elegance. It was a fitting room for Doug, she decided, knowing that he'd have decorated it himself and admiring his skill.

Cocking her ear, she listened again. There was nothing but silence. Rolling to her side, she gathered the sheet to her breasts and recalled the wonder of what had happened earlier. Breathing deeply, she caught Doug's unique scent and felt the echo of a tremor deep within her. She loved him. And she loved what he'd done to her. But she was right, she knew, in demanding more time. Even now she felt slightly breathless at the thought of the turn her life had taken in barely ten days. Too fast. She felt caught up in a whirlwind of emotion. Yet

there was so much more to the man that she still didn't
know. And if she was to marry, to marry again, she had
to know exactly what she was getting into. No longer
was she a seventeen-year-old innocent. At the age of
twenty-nine her eyes were open wide. And she had to
look, to know, to be sure.

Until now, Doug had been the near-saint he'd thought
Sean to be. But he was human. His stalking from the
bedroom moments before was testimony to that fact. Human. Man. He'd been magnificent even as he'd strode
away, tall, athletic of build, compelling and quite nude.
Again she felt a quickening inside, and she shifted on
the bed in a vain attempt to quell it.

He was hurt and frustrated. In a bad mood? Most
probably. But, she mused, perhaps he had a right to be.
Wouldn't she have been the slightest bit disappointed if
he'd accepted her demand without a fight? If he cared
for her as much as he claimed he did, he'd most naturally
be upset. And she could accept that. She wasn't so
starry-eyed as to believe that even two people deeply in
love didn't have differences on occasion.

Hugging the pillow his head had shared with hers, she
rolled to her other side and stared at the window. It was
still raining out, drops creating a slow-changing pattern
on the glass. Bad moods, petty differences notwithstanding, would he be there for her? This was the crux of her
worry, the bottom line to her demand for time. Before
she agreed to marry Doug she had to be certain she
wouldn't be let down. She'd been so hurt once before,
and then there had not even been a pretense of love in
the relationship. But marriage, however farcical it might
be, implied that kind of commitment. And loving Doug

as she did, she couldn't bear the thought of coming to count on him, then losing.

He'd come through today. A slow, feline smile worked its way through her sober expression. He certainly had come through. He'd been home when she'd needed him, offering comfort and security. And when other needs had taken hold, he'd been there for her. He'd even put off his own work—that phone call her arrival had interrupted—to be with her.

Quite coincidentally at that moment the phone rang again. Out of habit she raised her head and speared a glance at the instrument beside the bed. This ringing was more distant, though. A business line in the den? The sound came again and was picked up midring. Smiling with the knowledge that he hadn't gone far, Sasha sat up. Then, strengthened by the love she felt and half-curious to see the rest of the house, she slipped from the bed.

A robe of thick chocolate-colored terry cloth hung inside the bathroom door. Reaching for it, she put it on. It fell to her knees; she imagined the midthigh point it would reach on Doug's hair-spattered legs. Feeling simultaneously lost in the volumes of fabric and deliciously cushioned, she loosely knotted the tie and rolled the sleeves. A quick glance in the mirror told her that her hair was unsalvageable. A double take told her that it was strangely sexy. Or was it the robe? Or the way she felt in the robe? Or the fact that the last body it had covered would have had to have been Doug's?

For a lingering minute she stared at herself, mildly stunned by what she saw. Her cheeks had a natural pink flush. Her hazel eyes seemed more green than usual. Her lips were moist and faintly puffed from erstwhile kisses. She looked very feminine. She *felt* very feminine. More than that. Enveloped so richly in Doug's thick robe, she seemed small, fragile, vulnerable. Strangely, though she thought she'd sworn off fragility and vulnerability years ago, she didn't mind.

Leaving the mirror, the bathroom, the bedroom behind, she silently made her way down the long hall she hadn't seen before to the living room she hadn't seen before. The lush brown carpet appeared to run through the entire house, as did beige walls and a thoroughly modern decor. The large living room, though, was furnished and accented in hunter green, rather than the gray of the bedroom, and while it looked every bit as masculine it seemed more...social. She smiled at the observation, thinking how irrelevant it was as she admired the sectional sofa, the glass-and-marble tables, the freestanding shelves that bore nothing at all, the unopened cartons at their foot.

Unopened cartons. So he really hadn't unpacked yet! Odd that a man in such a beautiful house would have put off such a chore. Odd. On second thought, not so. Typical. She smiled, and felt not disdain but fondness. For a man like Doug, so willing to give of himself, she would gladly do the unpacking, make the bed, do the laundry. In Sam's house it had been just another drudging task to perform. In Doug's it would be a privilege.

At the sound of a rising voice, she continued through the living room and entered a shorter hall from which branched the den. Pausing at its open door, she peered inside. Doug was at his desk, dressed now, though his shirt hung open. He looked quickly up when she appeared and she saw an instant's flicker of unsureness in his gaze. When he looked down again and continued talking, his voice was quieter.

Aware that he might want privacy, Sasha turned to leave, only to be waved back in by his sweeping gesture. Warmed, she slowly entered the room and looked around. Doug continued his conversation.

"What's wrong with Hasselfromm?...I know he's got other assignments, but he's the one I want.... Damn it, we've paid him enough in the past to expect some kind of preference. Offer him more. Give him some stock. He's the only model for this campaign. I want him."

Sasha let the discussion flow around her as she studied the den. So very like the rest of the house it was, yet different. This was the working room. Doug's large lacquered desk sat on one side, a drawing board on another. The easy chairs on which they'd sat earlier stood in the middle, their deep leather sheen almost identical to the carpet's hue. A long low table stood nearby, its top cluttered with open magazines and papers. One wall, that behind the desk, was sheer windows, another backed a long credenza atop which several smartly framed ad blowups were propped. The remaining walls, allowing for the door and a closet, held floor-to-ceiling shelving units of various depths and sizes, very obviously custommade and as obviously bare but for an occasional book or sculpture. More conspicuously sat the cartons nearby, piled as high as three, even four in a bunch.

Curious, Sasha wandered to a stack of two, the topmost of which reached her waist and stood with its flaps open. Inside were books on fashion design and marketing. As well there should be, she mused, lifting first one out, then another, piling them in her arms and nonchalantly finding the shelf she thought to be most appropriate, setting them carefully upright. She returned to the carton, extracted several more volumes, flipped through one on the history of design, then placed them on the shelf with the others. She paused momentarily to arrange them by height before returning for another batch.

"Okay, Dan. See what he says to that. But I want him, remember that.... Fistran's lined up for the shoot, isn't he?... Good. Hey, what about that silk fabric? Did it come in?... Hell, what's it taking, a slow boat?... I know, but it should have been in two weeks ago."

Having filled one shelf, Sasha stood back to admire it, then shot a glance at Doug. His eyes were on the papers before him, brows drawn low with his frown, one hand fisted, the other rubbing the back of his neck. The casual muss of his hair did little to ease the air of tension surrounding him.

On silent cat's feet she walked around the desk, pushed his hand away and began to gently knead the taut muscles at his nape. Questioningly, he half turned, only to be urged forward again by knowing hands that then resumed their work.

Sasha took delight in her ministrations. Though his hair was thick and full it was well-shaped and trimmed. Her fingers brushed against the soft stubble at his nape and would have returned for a second velvety feel had not Doug's voice wavered sharply. She hadn't wanted to distract him, only make him more comfortable. Stoically keeping her attention on his muscles, she was rewarded when she felt them begin to relax.

Then the doorbell rang. Doug sent a sharp glance toward the hall, but it was Sasha who squeezed his shoulder and headed for the door. Only when she remembered what she was wearing did she come to a dead halt and slither an awkward grin toward Doug.

Covering the receiver, he murmured with a smile, "It's okay. Probably the mailman. Look outside. Anyone you don't recognize, give a yell."

Reassured first and foremost by his smile, she answered the door. It was indeed the mailman, mercifully one she'd never seen. She signed for two of the bundles, took the rest in her arms, backed the door shut and returned to dump the load on Doug's desk.

"Yeah, Dan, that's okay.... Well, let me know what he says. I'll call him myself if need be and twist his arm." He grinned at something his CEO said. "Only a figure of speech, Daniel. Only a figure of speech.... Sure. Talk with you later." He hung the phone up soundly, but rather than reaching for one of the packages that had arrived, he half rose from his chair to catch Sasha's hand and draw her around the desk again. Swiveling sideways, he imprisoned her between his thighs.

"It's nice to have you here," he said softly, his hands propped loosely on her hips.

"It's nice to be here," she answered, her wrists dangling over his shoulders.

He cast a glance at the shelf she'd filled. "You didn't have to do that."

"It's about time someone did. I think you need a caretaker, Douglas Donohue."

"I think so, too," he said, so humbly that she knew his mood was eased.

She hesitated for only an instant. "You're not mad at me?"

He knew she wasn't talking about the books. A look of gentle resignation gave his features a softer slant. "Of course I'm not mad. I can't have my way all the time, can I?" He arched a brow. "Not that I wouldn't like to force you to the altar, mind you. But that wouldn't be good for either of us. You need to be sure that marriage is what you want. I need to be sure that you're sure." One corner of his lips quirked upward. "In the meantime, you look sexy as hell." Drawing her closer, he pulled loose the tie and spread the robe to the side, then buried his face between her breasts. "Ahhhh—" he gave a muffled moan "—if a volcano erupted right now I could very happily stay this way for eternity."

Sasha laughed against his hair. "What a morbid thinker you are."

"Not morbid. Imaginative." He lifted his face and Sasha met his gaze, stroking the hair at the back of his head, as proud of her near-nakedness as she'd ever been. "I love you, Sasha. Do you love me?"

"I've said as much."

"Well, say it again."

"I love you, Doug."

"Mmmm." Spearing his hands inside the robe to her back, he crushed her to him and hugged her. "I can wait," he murmured gruffly. "If I'm a bear every once in a while and tear out of the room, you'll just have to understand. But I can wait. I can wait."

The phone couldn't. It jangled a second, a third time before either Doug or Sasha noticed. At the fourth ring, Sasha spoke. "Doug? Aren't you going to answer it?"

"No," he murmured. "They'll call back."

"But it may be important."

"Nothing's so important as to take precedence over this."

"I didn't come here to disturb your work."

"Like hell you didn't," he teased against her stomach. "You came for a good lay, and you know it."

"Douglas!" Not sure whether to laugh or scold but definitely needing a show of dignity, she reached for the phone herself. "Good morning. Douglas Donohue Enterprises, Martha's Vineyard Headquarters. May I help you?" Her sing-song professionalism brought Doug's head slowly up. He was in the process of eyeing her askance when she covered the mouthpiece and whispered, "It's Sergio Martin?" She added a mouthed, "Sounds weird," before presenting the receiver to Doug.

He returned a mouthed, "He is," before donning his most commanding smile. "Sergio, my friend! Good to hear from you!"

Rolling her eyes skyward, Sasha squirmed from his grip, retied the robe, and returned to the cartons. By the time she'd completely emptied the first, what with skimming tables of contents here and there, she'd had a crash course on the history of clothing and clothiers. By that time she was also aware of Doug's returning tension. His grimace gave him away, where his voice had not.

"You're sure it has to be tomorrow?...I know, and I appreciate that. But I wasn't planning to be back in the city for another week or two.... I understand.... No, no. It can be arranged." His lips thinned and he scowled at the phone, though his voice retained its cordial ring. "Fine. See you then."

This time when he hung up, Sasha stayed in front of the desk. "What's wrong?" she asked softly.

"Damn!" Doug sat far back in his chair and swiveled to the side in disgust. "Just what I didn't want to have to do."

"Go back to New York?"

He shot her a fast glance. "Mmm."

"Who's Sergio Martin?"

"My Italian coordinator. He was supposed to be in the city for the month. I was going to meet with him later. But he's got a family problem and has to cut his trip short. Damn! But I didn't want him coming *here*."

Sensing an apology in the offing, Sasha felt all the more sympathetic. "If it can't be helped, it can't. When will you go?" The thought of his leaving the Vineyard was a disturbing one.

"Tomorrow morning," he mumbled. With his elbows braced on the arms of the chair, fists pressed to his mouth, head bent, he was obviously thinking. Slowly he raised his head and swiveled back to face her, a look of cautious hope on his face. "Come with me, Sasha. We can fly down tomorrow. I'll have my meeting. Then we can spend tomorrow night and the weekend together. I promise to get you back here by Sunday night. That way you can be around on Monday...."

Monday. She tensed, remembering things she'd tried so to push from her mind. She looked down and fumbled with the cord of the robe.

"It'd be good for you, Sasha," he went on, leaning

forward in urgency. "Sitting here you'll only spend the time worrying."

"I was hoping to work," she said in a small voice. "That usually keeps my mind occupied."

"But I don't want you to work. I want you to be with me. Even if I weren't going to New York, I'd want you to stay here. I'm not sure how safe your place is."

Another dilemma, also far from solved. Sasha helplessly met his gaze. "I can't go into hiding. I mean, if someone's after me, he can find me wherever I go. Those barrels are a point in fact. I wasn't even at home then."

"But I was there. And if you come to New York with me, I'll be there. When we get back, you can stay here with me."

"I have to work. I can't work here."

"Why not?"

"I'd—I'd be distracted."

"Not if I'm working," he reasoned. "Try again."

"My computer."

"I'll bring it over."

"But my house! I love my house!"

"Don't you like mine?"

"Of course I like yours," she wailed, casting a sweeping glance around the room. "It's light and beautiful and—"

"Large enough for both of us. There's even a den you can have all to yourself. I mean, what the hell, Sasha. When we're married—"

"Doug!" she whispered, shaking her head in confusion. "I haven't said I'll marry you."

"But you will. In time." His smugness faded when

he sensed imminent rebellion. "And you've got that, Sasha. I can wait. I told you that before. I can wait."

Knowing now how her clothes felt swirling round and round in the washer, Sasha sighed, blew her bangs from her brow and turned, sinking into one of the nearby easy chairs. Doug's voice came quietly from his desk.

"Will you come, babe? Tomorrow. To New York. With me." When she remained silent, staring at her hands, he sugared the deal. "I promise I won't mention marriage again. Not until you bring it up. And when we come back we'll reach some kind of amicable agreement on living conditions. Does that sound fair?"

It did. Oh, it did. For as much as she loved her house, she loved Doug more. The thought of spending time with him was infinitely pleasing…and perhaps just what she'd need if she ever hoped to find the answer she sought to that one lingering question.

"Sasha?"

As she'd been thinking, he'd come from the desk to squat by her side. She lifted her gaze to encounter the raw need, the vulnerability that could sway her each and every time.

"I'll come," she agreed softly, then manufactured a scowl. "But if my career's shot to hell because I'm so distracted that I can't get back into my book, it'll be your fault." As she spoke, she poked a finger against his chest. He deftly captured it and brought her hand to his lips, then called her bluff in a muffled tone.

"I could get your machine now and let you get to work."

"No!"

"Why not? I've got all this mail to go through and

there's probably a tape from my secretary to listen to and then a score of letters to dictate and send back.''

"I'm not in the mood," she said crossly. "And besides, if I'm going to spend any time *here* I want those cartons unpacked."

"Aw, Sasha, they'll wait. Unpacking is a drag."

"You work. I'll unpack."

"I can't let you do that."

Her tone softened. "But I want to. It's fun learning about all your little treasures. You do want me to get to know you, don't you?"

"Of course, but—"

"Then it's settled," she declared, bounding up before an openmouthed Doug and heading toward another carton. No more than halfway there, though, she stopped in her tracks and began to look around, puzzled.

"What's wrong?"

"My clothes. They were—" she pointed to the spot on the floor where she thought they'd landed once upon a time "—there."

Doug stood, drawing himself to his full height. "Now they're there." He pointed to a small shelf behind the desk upon which her clothes were neatly folded. "I may hate unpacking and be lazy about making my bed, but when it comes to clothes, I have the utmost respect."

"Figures," she said, but she couldn't be angry. "Does that mean I won't find piles of laundry waiting in another room?"

He went beet red and grimaced. "Well, I don't know…there may, uh, be some things on top of the washer…."

"Um-hmm."

"But you don't have to do them," he was quick to advise.

She sent him a feminine smile and turned to retrieve her clothes. "Of course not," she murmured as she set off quite happily for the bedroom.

BY MIDAFTERNOON she'd changed the sheets and made the bed, done two full loads of laundry, made lunch for them both and put a stew on to cook for dinner. She'd unpacked four cartons in the den and three more in the living room, admiring each and every item along the way, and she'd watched Doug work with pride she couldn't fathom.

For the most part she simply eavesdropped as he talked on the phone or spoke into his tiny tape recorder. She couldn't help but straighten and look his way, though, when he played the tape his secretary had sent. It was primarily a rundown on calls that had come in, on correspondence he didn't have to bother to read, on appointments set for his future trips to New York. At its end was something else.

"Oh, and Doug," the pleasant voice added, "Lisa thinks you're a bum. I'm afraid she's taking your exit pretty hard. Maybe you could put in a gentle word while you're here? Ta-ta." The recorder clicked off with a deafening thud.

"What was *that?*" Sasha asked, more bemused than threatened.

Doug had the good grace to look uncomfortable. "That was my smart ass of a secretary putting in her two bits about my private life."

"Who's Lisa?"

"Her sister. We dated for a while."

Sasha gave an exaggerated nod. "Ah. I see. So...will you?"

"Will I what?"

"Put in a gentle word while you're there?"

"To Lisa? I've already put in as many gentle words as I can." He shook his head. "The woman won't let a dead dog lie."

Crossing her arms over her breasts, Sasha leaned against the arm of a chair. "What's she like?"

Doug stretched back in his chair, folded his hands across his stomach and sighed. "She's very pretty. And very nice. But not terribly bright. And she's a clinger."

"You don't like that? Some men would."

"I suppose I did at one point. In the big ego days." He widened his eyes for emphasis as he drawled the words in self-mockery. "But those days are gone. The woman I want now can stand on her own two feet. She's got a successful career and prides herself on being self-sufficient. She's independent, sometimes too much so. But I love her, faults and all."

Silently bidden by his gaze, Sasha came to stand before him, her hands on his shoulders, her knees braced against his. "I'm not sure whether to be flattered or offended."

"The first," he declared, then mistook her deep, happy sigh for one of fatigue. "You must be beat. You've worked hard today."

"I've had fun. You know, it's strange," she began softly, raising her eyes to the window beyond which the ocean thrashed in the rain. "I used to resent doing things for Sam. I mean, I had to do everything around the house, and then some. I felt like a slave. But today was different. Maybe it's the fact that I have a career of my own. Self-respect. I had none then.'' She returned her gaze to his face, her eyes glowing with feeling. ''Maybe it's the fact that I love you. Doing for you is…nice. Then again,'' she cautioned, lest his head grow too big, ''maybe it's that I have a choice. That makes all the difference in the world.'' She reached out on impulse and brushed the hair from his brow. It was an exquisitely gentle gesture, touching Doug at his core.

''You'll always have the choice here, Sasha. Even if I'm not good at doing things, I'll try.'' He'd already showed her that the morning he'd fixed breakfast in her kitchen. ''And when you're busy with your writing, we could hire someone to help. I want things to be as easy, as enjoyable, as rewarding for you as possible.''

Sasha beamed. ''You're a sweet man, Doug Donohue.''

''Humph. I do believe you're the first person to describe me in quite that way. I'm not sure whether to be flattered or offended.''

''The first,'' she said, echoing his own words with a grin. At the pressure of his fingers on her back, she leaned forward to receive his kiss. It was filled with love and sincerity, and was very sweet indeed.

And it was only the beginning. After a delightfully intimate dinner at his house, they returned to hers, where she packed a bag and closed things up while Doug saw to renailing the stair that had been tampered with. Back at his house, atop his clean checkered sheets, they made love again, slowly, gloriously. With his greatest urgency released that morning, Doug was more tender than ever, the epitome of selflessness even at the height of his passion, worshiping Sasha's body in ways she'd once have thought sinful but discovered to be profoundly erotic. It was all in the approach, in the state of mind that in turn primed the body. Where love was involved there were no bounds, she decided quite joyously before falling into a deep, deep sleep in Doug's strong arms.

NEW YORK WAS startlingly wonderful given the fact that in the years she'd lived there Sasha had developed a strong aversion to frantic crowds, looming skyscrapers and taxis. With Doug by her side, all was different. She was oblivious to the crowds, uncowed by the skyscrapers, and aware of taxis only as places to steal a kiss on the sly.

Though the nip in the air signaled winter's approach, they spent hours walking the avenues arm in arm, stopping now and again to window-shop, doing touristy things neither would have dreamed of doing before. They soared to the top of the World Trade Center, took a hansom ride in the park, paid their respects to the Statue of Liberty. If Doug was wowed by the sight of Sasha in a dress, she was no less impressed by him in a suit. They ate well, slept well and made love particularly well.

There was only one snag to the weekend and that was the fact that when it ended Sasha would have to face two issues she desperately wished to avoid. The first was the matter of her mother, whose surgery was to take place on Monday morning. The second was the matter of the deranged faceless someone who was systematically plotting her harm.

Doug faced both of these, plus another. He had no idea how to get Sasha to finally say yes. In the time they spent together his love for her grew to frightening proportions, such that the thought of ever losing her sent him into a cold sweat. At every opportunity he did what he could to prove his love, no effort at all since the feeling was every bit there. But what it would take to secure that final agreement on her part—that was where he was stymied. He'd promised her time, and he'd give her that. But, Lord, he was impatient.

They were a straight-faced duo returning to Martha's Vineyard on Sunday evening. Mindful that Sasha would want to be near the phone on Monday, they spent the night at her house after thoroughly searching it to make sure all was in place. Sasha found it a novelty having Doug there, watching him shave before her mirror, do sit-ups on her rug, virilely stretch his bronzed body on her large white bed. He distracted her from more somber thoughts with the sheer force of his presence, the fiery dominance of his lovemaking. But Monday morning came, as Sasha knew it would, and she was tense.

While Doug read the paper, then pretended to doze, Sasha made ceremony of writing. The phone rang twice, one call from Maggie who, after trying her all weekend, had been worried, the second from the office-supply store to tell her that the computer paper she'd ordered was in. Both times she jumped a mile. Both times Doug was alert and as tense as she.

By the time noon arrived she'd produced nothing worth saving. Turning the machine off with a muffled oath, she went to Doug, took the newspaper from his knees and slipped down onto his lap, then slid her arms around his waist and rested her head on his chest.

"Oh, Doug," she murmured wearily. "I feel so helpless."

Rising quickly from his half nap, he traced her spine, then caressed her back with his palms. "It's only natural."

"Maybe I should have flown up there."

"Would you have felt any less helpless then?"

She sighed. "No, I suppose not."

"Then there's nothing to do but wait." He pressed a warm kiss to her bangs, then, bending his head farther, the bridge of her nose. She sighed again and yielded to his comfort, only to push herself to her feet after several moments and head for the phone.

"I'm trying Vicky."

"She may not be home yet."

"Then I'll call the hospital."

"I doubt they'll give you the information you want."

"I've got to do something!" she cried, lifting the receiver and punching out Vicky's number.

Doug was right. Vicky wasn't home. And a call to the hospital merely said that Natalie Blake was in the recovery room.

"At least she made it through surgery," Sasha breathed shakily.

"You never doubted that. Come here, babe." Docilely she returned to Doug's outstretched arms. "Ya' know," he suggested softly, "I do think you ought to consider going back for a visit." When she opened her mouth to protest, he sped on. "Not necessarily right away, assuming your mother's all right. But in time. I mean, look at you, babe. You're a nervous wreck worrying about your mother's condition and you haven't even seen the woman in years. You care.''

"Of course I care," Sasha responded thoughtfully. "And it's because I care that it's so hard for me to go back. I hurt when I think of them. I want their acceptance and respect, not another rejection."

"Who says they'll reject you now?"

"I say. You don't know them, Doug. They're dogmatic as the day is long. They're not going to change. Not at this late date. If they'd wanted to patch things up over the years, they could have."

"Perhaps they're afraid."

"Afraid? Of *me?*" She gave a dry laugh. "They were never afraid to tell me what they thought of me then."

"That was then. This is now. And you happen to be an internationally known writer who is sophisticated in what may be a threatening way to them. Perhaps they feel that *they're* the ones who won't fit in."

"Humph. I doubt that. They go through life with blinders on. I doubt they know what they've missed."

"Sasha," Doug chided softly, "where's your generosity?"

She raised her head to look at him, then bowed it, ashamed. "I don't know, Doug. I just don't know. It's become such an emotional issue with me. Strange, I never really dwelt on it before. Maybe that's why it's boiling over now."

"Maybe. But I'm glad it is. You've got to settle it, babe. After all, you said it yourself. The issue is there. It's not going away. At some point or another, something's got to give."

Tipping her head back in the crook of his shoulder, she slanted him a curious stare. "Have you always had these analytic tendencies?" she asked softly.

He shook his head with a smile. "Only since I've met you, and it's because I care that I want things settled. More than anything in the world I want you to be happy. I don't want any shadows hanging over us when we're—" He caught himself just in time. "Sorry about that," he murmured, though he really wasn't. He meant what he'd said and he knew she'd heard the word he hadn't. "What if I went up there with you?"

Sasha chuckled lightly. "That would be great. Mom and Dad, I'd like you to meet my lover, Doug Donohue. They'd die. I mean, they'd really die."

"You could always tell them we were engaged," he dared, quite expecting Sasha to come down on top of him. Instead, she gave him a high laugh.

"Then they'd *know* I was beyond hope. No offense intended," she added as a pert aside, "but you're from that sinful world, too. A designer of men's haut couture?" The accent she drawled into the words through pursed lips would have been funny had it not been blatant evidence of her highly emotional state. "They'd assume you were gay," she announced baldly, then broke into wild laughter. "They sh-should only know how wr-wrong they'd be!" she gasped. "They should only know what we've done in bed! H-how good you are!" Suddenly her laughter dissolved into tears and Doug held her very tightly.

"Don't go hysterical on me, babe," he growled. "Everything's going to be all right."

"Oh, Doug," she said, sniffling against his sweater,

"if only I didn't feel s-so guilty about it. I mean, life has been good to me these past f-few years. And you're right. I should be more generous. I should feel sorry for them. But instead I'm angry. Why?"

"Because they're your parents. Because despite everything you love them. Because you're hurt and frustrated and confused."

"So what do I do?"

"You calm down and try Vicky again. It's the waiting that's always the worst. Once we know what's what, we can think about what you ought to do."

"What's what" was very good news indeed. After trying Vicky a second time, then finally reaching her on a third, Sasha learned not only that her mother had come through the surgery well, but that an open exploration had revealed no spreading of the disease. Mild radiation treatment was being considered as a precaution, but the prognosis was excellent for Natalie Blake's full recovery.

Reassured of her mother's well-being and feeling slightly ashamed of her own emotional display, Sasha gave Doug no argument when he insisted she pack up her computer and more clothes and stay at his house for a while. She left his number with Vicky in case of emergency, with no explanation other than a general if-you-phone-me-and-there's-no-answer-try-this kind of thing, locked up the house and returned with Doug to his ocean-front retreat.

THE NEXT FEW WEEKS were strangely peaceful and very happy ones for Sasha. She and Doug were constantly together, if not in the same room of his house then within easy calling distance. To Sasha's amazement, both her computer and her concentration survived transplantation. Comfortably set up in Doug's spare den, she found plenty to write, and though she'd begun to have her doubts about ever submitting this particular manuscript for publication, the story sped along.

"Tell me about it," Doug said one night as they lay naked together in his bed. "I mean, you've been typing away there for days and all I get to see is the flash of a skimpy synopsis you wrote months ago."

Sasha snuggled closer to the body that was now like her second skin. She rubbed her cheek against the warm hair on his chest, slid her arm over his ribs to rest on one leanly masculine hip, tucked her leg down between his, sealing her lower self in intimate collusion with his thigh.

"It's a lovely story," she began lazily, gazing up past his strong chin and nose to his eyes. "My hero and heroine meet quite by accident, fall in love and live happily ever after."

Doug gave her a squeeze. "Even the synopsis said more than that. Come on. Give."

"Naw. Romance always suffers in the retelling. You'll just have to read it some day."

"Have you decided on a name?"

She hadn't, until that moment. Craning her neck, she placed a soft kiss on his cheek. "I think I'll call it *Bronze Mystique*."

"*Bronze Mystique?*"

"Mmmm. *Bronze* for the very masculine color of the hero's skin—" she brushed her nose against Doug's "—and *Mystique* for the heroine's unbelievable fascination with him." Her gaze slid up to lock with the intent silver one above her. "She's never known a man like him before, and there are times when she can't begin to fathom the extent of her feelings for him."

"She loves him, though."

"Of course. Wildly and to distraction."

"Will she marry him?"

Sasha took a breath. "In time, I think. But first she's got to work out one or two last things for herself."

"What if he gets tired waiting?"

"He won't."

"Why not?"

"Because he's as fascinated with her as she is with him. And besides, there's got to be a happy ending. Isn't that the way it works?"

"I hope so," Doug murmured, then kissed her tenderly.

Whoever the villain was in Sasha's life, he was making himself scarce. She couldn't quite understand it, other than to assume that his original plans had been thwarted by Doug's continual presence. As the days passed, she began to wonder if he'd simply given up. Yet she couldn't help but think of him from time to time. And she couldn't help but imagine what would happen if he was simply lying low and revising his plot.

More and more, she found herself thinking of marriage. Living with Doug on a day-to-day basis proved to be almost idyllic. True, there were times when he was tense, when his mood was lighter or darker. But he was ever attuned to her, and she could find little to fault with his love.

Often while she worked he did the same in his den.

On more than one occasion he sat quietly in hers, a pad of paper on his lap, a pencil in his hand, looking at her, turning his attention to the paper, looking up again. When on one such occasion her curiosity was piqued, she slapped a finger to the save button and whirled around in her seat.

"What *are* you doing, Douglas?" she demanded, materializing at his shoulder before he could hide the sketch he'd been making.

"Aw, nothing really. Just doodling."

She reached down and stole the pad from him. "You've been so busy. Let me see. Hey…" She studied the top sketch, then flipped the pad back to find a dozen different drawings. "But these are women's clothes."

"Do you like them?"

"They're gorgeous," and they were. Casual clothes, slacks, sweaters, blouses with a sporty kind of femininity about them, smart business ensembles, formal wear that was soft and chic. "I love them! But…you only do men's things."

He cocked his head with modest smugness. "That doesn't mean I can't try something new."

Her eyes widened. "Are you going to? I mean, are you thinking of starting a line for women?"

"I wasn't…until I started sitting here looking at you." He smirked. "God only knows I've undressed you enough. I think I'd like a chance to switch it around." Squeezing over to make room, he pulled her down onto the chair beside him. "What do you think? Wouldn't you like to have a D D on your breast?" He raised a finger to the spot where an insignia might be and traced a tiny circle there.

"I've already *got* a D D on my breast," Sasha whispered naughtily. She caught his finger to stop its sweet torment and brought it to her lips. "But I'd love to wear your clothes! A new line...that's exciting!"

They spent the rest of the afternoon talking about it, until the excitement and the nearness made talk irrelevant. They made love there on the chair in her den, then showered together and took a ride into town for a quick dinner, stopping only for a quart of Sasha's favorite homemade ice-cream—a heavenly butter crunch—on the way home. Then they settled in for a quiet evening listening to music in the living room. They talked softly from time to time, the atmosphere one of peace and contentment. When Doug received a late call from a friend, Sasha stole to the kitchen for a spoonful of ice cream. She returned with one for Doug; when he shook his head, she licked the spoon clean, dropped it back in the kitchen, then retired to the bedroom to wait for him.

He wasn't long, but she found herself feeling strangely hollow. When he finally joined her, stripping and taking her into his arms, she breathed a sigh of relief. When the hollow remained, she simply pushed it from mind, immersing herself in Doug's lovemaking until they'd both reached dizzying heights and fallen slowly back to earth.

Strangely, her dizziness remained, yet she dozed. When Doug woke her less than half an hour later, her body was covered with sweat.

"Are you all right, babe?" he asked, concern written over his features. "You feel hot."

It took her a minute to focus. "I don't know," she murmured. "I feel weird."

"Weird like how?"

"Like dizzy. And...crampy."

"You had your period last week."

"I know, but..." She tried to sit up and her stomach churned. "Oh, God," she moaned, then bolted from bed and made it to the bathroom in time to be violently sick.

Doug was right beside her, holding her head, bracing her quivering limbs, propping her on the commode when she'd finished and bathing her with a cool cloth.

"Any better?" he asked at last. She looked deathly pale despite her body's heat.

"I think so. Must be a bug."

He carried her back to bed and let it go at that, but he was awake long after she'd fallen asleep, watching her, relieved when her forehead cooled and her breathing deepened. Only then did he get up, throw on his robe and head for the kitchen.

CHAPTER NINE

HE WAS WIDE AWAKE, propped upright in bed, when Sasha opened her eyes the next morning. "How do you feel?" he asked cautiously.

"Fine." Something about him brought her quickly awake. "*You* look awful. Didn't you sleep? You're not coming down with whatever it was I had, are you?"

"I doubt it," he declared with such conviction that she gave him a closer look.

"What do you mean?" she murmured timidly. Studying his taut expression, she had the fleeting impression that the past few weeks had been the calm before the storm. "What's wrong, Doug?"

The muscle of his jaw worked once. "That ice cream you ate last night? I do believe it was poisoned."

"Poisoned? You've got to be kidding!"

"I'm not." His eyes were the texture of slate. "I took a good look at it last night after you fell asleep."

"I saw it, too. It looked fine!"

"Did you happen to catch the tiny pinhole on the side of the carton just below the rim of the lid?"

She blanched. "Oh, my God!"

"Someone injected something into that tub."

She shook her head in stunned denial. "No...oh, no...."

"Come on, babe. Look at the facts. You were fine before that. Your health is excellent. You have one spoonful, two spoonfuls of that stuff, then you're sick."

"Oh, Doug," she whispered, her eyes filling with tears.

"It can't be anything else, Sasha. The only thing I can't figure out is where he got the idea. I've read every one of your books. There's nothing about ice-cream poisoning in any of them."

She bit her lip and sat up, clutching her stomach, rocking back and forth. One by one tears trickled down her cheeks.

"It hurts again?" Doug asked, leaning forward to give her support.

She shook her head. "Not here," she whimpered, pointing to her stomach. Then she pointed to her head. "Here. Oh, God! Oh, my God!"

His arms went around her, trembling but holding her steady. "What is it?"

"Oh, Doug. I *did* write that."

"But where? I haven't—"

"In this book. This new one. I mean, I haven't actually written the scene, but it was in the synopsis. Oh, my God!"

Doug looked away, his eyes darting from side to side. "The synopsis. I didn't think." Then he looked back at Sasha. "Who's seen it?"

"Diane. Diane...and my editor. Maybe some others at M.P.I."

"Anyone else?"

"Oh, God," she cried, burying her face in her hands.

"Who, Sasha? It's important!"

The eyes she raised were wet, frightened and held an agony beyond belief. "Simon," she breathed. "Diane told Simon about it! But—" her expression turned pleading "—it couldn't be! It just couldn't be! We were so close there for a while! He was like a big brother. I still think of him as my mentor." Her mind wandered for an instant to the plot of *Bronze Mystique*. The villain there had been the hero's mentor, a man made vengeful by jealousy and suspicion. She slowly shook her head. "He's not the suspicious type. He's cocksure of himself and adventurous and unconventional. And I've never taken an idea from him. I'm sure of it!"

"But he hasn't sold anything lately."

"No. Just his first."

"So you've soundly eclipsed him."

"But he's doing other things. Diane said so."

"That does mean he can't be jealous." Another thought came. "You said he had a flair for the dramatic. And that he used to disguise himself and play different roles. Is it possible, just possible, that you may have seen him around the island and not recognized him?"

"Oh, Doug, anything's possible! But he wouldn't! Simon loved me in his way. I'm sure of it."

"Maybe his way was different from the way you think," Doug suggested quietly.

Sasha was instantly wary. "What do you mean?"

"Maybe he loved you. Really loved you, while you thought of him as a brother and mentor. Maybe he wanted more. Did you ever get that feeling?"

"Of course. But he knew what I'd been through and that I wasn't looking for that type of involvement. He fully accepted it."

"Which doesn't mean that, as the years passed, he didn't think of it again. If his career had gone sour while yours soared, and he saw you getting involved with me—"

"But all this started *before* I met you."

"True," Doug admitted. He was pensive for a moment. "But suppose, just suppose, that his mind was warped enough to bring him down here with mischief in mind. Those early things were more frightening than harmful. On second thought," he added with a grimace, "you could have been killed on that cycle." He took a breath. "But suppose he only intended to scare you, to play a sick game. Then he saw us together and got really angry. Hell, Sasha, poison is something else! Lucky you only had a little of the stuff!"

"Lucky you didn't have any!"

"Damn it, I don't care about *me*. You were the one who was sick! But come to think of it, if the ice cream *was* poisoned, he had us both in mind, which makes it my affair as well. And *I* say we call the police!"

"Oh, Doug, I don't know. If it *was* Simon—and I still can't accept that it was—he needs psychiatric help, not criminal detention."

"That's fine for you to say now, babe, but what if you'd eaten a whole dish of that stuff. What if you'd been *really* sick. What if you'd died? I agree that he needs psychiatric help, but first we've got to find him."

"If it is him." She frowned, trying to clear her head. "I keep trying to think back to the ice-cream parlor. There were only a handful of people in there. And two guys behind the counter."

"How was it going to work in *Bronze Mystique?*"

"The villain was going to be one of those behind the counter." She caught her breath. "In disguise."

Doug nodded, his point well made. "One of those fellows was young, the other more middle-aged. How old is Simon?"

"In his early forties, I guess. But that man was sandy haired. And Simon is dark."

"But adept at disguise. How about the height and the build."

"About…right, I guess," she admitted miserably. "But Simon wouldn't! I know he wouldn't!"

Feeling that she'd had enough for the moment, Doug hugged her. "Okay, Sasha. Just relax. I want you to have a nice long bath while I make a few calls and find out how we go about having that ice-cream carton analyzed. Maybe it was just a bug. There's always that chance."

Much as she wanted to believe it, Doug had planted too many ideas in her mind. And the coincidence with her plot was far too startling to ignore. Obeying him without further fuss, she relaxed as long as she could in his large sunken tub before climbing out and toweling herself dry. She'd barely wrapped the towel about her when Doug joined her in the warm, steamy room.

"Well?" she asked timidly.

He took her by the shoulders and looked her gently in the eye. "The police will take a look at it."

"The police? You didn't, Doug!"

"I had to, babe. For your sake…and mine. If anything happens to you…" He shuddered and pulled her into his embrace. "I can't bear the thought."

"You didn't…you didn't tell them…"

"No. I didn't mention Simon's name. I simply said

you'd been violently ill and that I wanted the ice cream checked. They'll stop by for it in a little while. I think the hospital has a lab they can use.''

Sasha sagged against him with a sigh. It was done. Perhaps, despite her protests, she felt a little relieved. After all, if the ice cream was found to be untainted, the police would fade out as quickly as they'd been brought in. If not... She winced. Maybe Doug was right. Simon—or whoever—had to be found. She was no longer the only one endangered. And if anything happened to *Doug*—she couldn't bear the thought!

Within an hour two officers were at Doug's door to pick up the container of ice cream. Sasha stayed in the background, curled in a chair, while Doug talked with them. When he returned, he swooped down and took her hand.

''Come on. Put on a skirt. We're going to Boston.''

''Boston? At a time like this?''

''What better time could there be?'' he asked, a gleam in his eye. ''The police are at work and there's nothing we can do until we hear from them. Don't tell me you'd be able to concentrate on work today.''

''I suppose not.''

''It's settled then. Let's go.'' He had her clasped to his side and on her way to the bedroom before she could think of further excuse. ''Something warm and pretty. We'll have a day on the town.''

To her astonishment they did just that. To her astonishment she had fun. Doug kept her busy walking through the Marketplace, asking her opinion on pieces of art in various galleries, charming her with witty observations, regaling her with humorous anecdotes of one experience or another he'd had in his life. He was prone to self-mockery in a way she found endearing, but the modest pride he took in his accomplishments was unmistakable and contagious.

By the time they returned to the Vineyard it was late afternoon and a light blanket of clouds billowed through the skies. It was warm, surprisingly so for early December, a rare gift. "How about a quick trip to the cliffs?" he asked, tucking her back into the car they'd left at the airport.

"Now?"

"Why not?" He glanced at the skies. "It's been a nice day. The rain will hold off for a little while longer. Besides," he added more softly, "I don't think I'm ready to go back to the house yet. Let's prolong the fun…just a little?"

How could she deny him, when she felt the same. "Okay," she said with a smile.

Unfortunately the weather didn't cooperate. By the time they arrived at the Gay Head cliffs a light sprinkle misted the windshield. But Doug was determined.

"Wait here," he ordered, taking his keys and opening the trunk of the car. He extracted a large piece of what appeared to be canvas and, when unfolded, proved to be an oversized poncho.

"Designer, no less," Sasha quipped as he pulled it over his head and opened her door. "That'll keep you dry, but what about me?" All he had to do was to extend one arm and produce a rakish grin and she understood. "This is absurd, Doug," she said, but she scampered under the poncho nonetheless and managed, with his help, to squeeze her head through the same opening as his. "A two-headed monster." She sent a glance around. "Let's hope no one's watching."

"No one's watching. Look." They both did. "The place is deserted. No one else is crazy enough to be outside in the rain on a balmy December day."

"Sounds romantic," she drawled, feeling light-headed as sin. Doug's wandering hands did nothing to quell her mood.

"Most definitely," he replied in a deep husky tone that promised more to come. For the moment, though, he drew his arm back to her shoulder and glued her to his side.

The cliffs, as always, were breathtaking in their multicolored cloak of salmon and mocha and white. Doug held her carefully while they made their way through the damp grass above, down onto the clay itself, then farther, weaving along jagged outcrops and into valleys.

"This isn't swell with high heels on," Sasha observed as she tottered and clung more tightly to his waist.

"Yeah, but without them your head wouldn't clear the neckline of this thing. And anyway, if you fall, it's against me. Not so bad, hmm?"

"Not bad at all," she mused happily. The rain brought a fine sheen to their faces and hair, but otherwise they were warm and quite protected beneath the poncho.

Guiding her around one jagged crevice and down into another, he found just the right spot. It was a cozy nook, receding slightly into the cliff, just big enough to hold them both and offer a spectacular view of the sea. Nestling in as far as he could, Doug eased them down.

"There. Comfortable?"

She tipped up her head and kissed his jaw. "Mmm."

"Look." His eyes led the way. "It's beautiful, isn't it?"

"Yes. But I'm glad I'm up here. Those whitecaps look cold."

He tightened his arms around her and for long moments they simply sat as one, admiring nature's gentle fury. When his hand found its way to her breast, she took a deep breath and sighed. "Oh, Doug. This has been a lovely day. I'm not quite sure how you did it, but you did it."

"I'm glad, babe," he crooned, then bent his head and took her lips in a kiss that was warm and wet and as furiously gentle as the sea. His tongue traced the even line of her teeth, then plunged farther in search of her essence. Meanwhile his fingers did highly erotic things to her nipple, which thrust forward through a layer of cashmere in response.

He could arouse her. Always. Whether simply by standing straight and tall in an art gallery, brushing his thigh against hers beneath cover of a tablecloth in a restaurant, rubbing his thumb to her palm in the middle of a cobblestoned street. Now, in the middle of God's country, her breath came faster and she twisted to put her arms around his neck. Deftly he shifted her until she was on his lap facing him, her knees straddling his thighs. When he put both hands on her bottom and crushed her closer, she moaned.

"Doug, this is indecent!" she whispered hoarsely, but her legs clung.

"No one can see." He grinned, returning both hands to her breasts, squeezing them, taunting them, brushing his fingers against their crests until the fire beneath her was unmistakable. His eyes glowed into hers. "I love the feel of your body. So warm and firm and aroused all the time." Slipping his hands beneath the hem of her sweater, he pushed the fabric high on her chest. Then his fingers slid under the lace of her bra, tormenting her until she strained upward. Only then did he release the catch, freeing her hot breasts to spill into his palms.

"You shouldn't," she whispered against his lips.

"But it feels good, doesn't it," he whispered back, kissing her again in declaration of his growing hunger. She could feel that hunger, both in herself and in him. Retaliating against his intimate tugging of her nipples, she snaked her hand between their bodies and touched him, stroked him, felt him grow until the fine wool fabric of his slacks was sorely tested.

"Oh, yes," she breathed, against his mouth, "it feels good. I want—" The words were sealed into her mouth when he kissed her more forcefully, and though his hands left her breasts, the position they took up at her hips and the movement they directed did nothing to ease the physical longing. "We've got to stop, Doug," she whispered roughly. Her body was aflame with need of his, a flame that seemed to have grown hotter day by day. If either of them had thought their recent freedom to love would have taken the edge off their hunger, they were mistaken. Perhaps it was the late night's misadventure, perhaps this day of public restraint, but whatever, their desire at the moment was beyond bounds.

"Let's go home," she whispered even as she arched her hips and sought his hardness.

"Oh, no," he rasped, shoving her skirt to her waist. "Doug!"

"Shhhh. Easy does it." He slid a finger into the inner leg of her panties and found her unerringly. She cried out, then held her breath, only the occasional animal murmur coming from her throat. Arms around his neck once again, she raised herself slightly to give him room.

"Oh, please, no. Let's go home. I need you, Doug. Not your finger. *You!*"

"You'll have me," he stated, his voice hoarse and uneven as he began to wriggle beneath her.

"What're you doing?" she cried dazedly.

"Trying," he grunted once, then again, "to get these damned pants down."

She looked at him round-eyed and whispered a conspiratorial, "Here?"

His expression held the same urgency she felt in his body, in her own. "Yes, here," he gritted, rolling his hips from side to side as he worked his open pants to his thighs.

"Doug, we can't!" she croaked, but already his fingers pulled at the waistband of her panties, and elbows braced on his shoulders, she helped him. She had only time to free one leg from the silk when he brought her back down. Slowly, surely, he entered her, filling her as fully as she'd ever been filled before.

"I'll never get enough of you," he gritted, his hands at her hips, lifting her, lowering her, letting her feel his throbbing as he felt her sheathing. "I love you, babe. God, I love you!"

Their lips met then, tongues stroking in mime of that lower motion. And Sasha knew that just as each time they made love it was better and better, the physical was only half of it. The other half was the sheer joy they found in one another, which seemed so perfect it frightened her. But she loved him more than life itself. And the passion she showed him said as much.

In tandem, as the waves below thrashed against the rock, they reached a shuddering climax. Then they clung to each other as the waves subsided, and whispered soft words of love and praise. How long they sat there in their hidden nook, locked together in the most intimate of embraces beneath the sheltering cover of the poncho, they didn't know. Time had no meaning. Nor did place. It was only an increase in the rain that finally bid them repair their clothing and begin the trip back to the house.

IT WAS INDEED POISON. The lab technician had given it a fancy name, one the police repeated but which was foreign to Sasha. But then, that wasn't surprising. She hadn't mentioned specifics in her proposal.

At the prodding of the police and Doug's gentle insistence, Sasha related the sequence of events that led her to believe mischief was in the works on the island. With reluctance she told what she could about Simon, though her descriptions were heavily interspersed with denial.

"It couldn't be him," she repeated time and again, while Doug tried to reassure her that nothing would be done unless there was sufficient evidence to warrant it. When she stated that Simon was probably at home in Maine, the police suggested she try to call him. Again reluctantly, she did so. When no one answered the phone, she tried to rationalize. "He's into different things all the time. The latest was deep-sea diving. He's probably somewhere down in the Caribbean," she offered prayerfully.

"Could be," one of the officers said, but he made copious notes nonetheless.

At Doug's urging, the police agreed to keep their investigation as quiet as possible. Their approach, they claimed, would be simply to look for strange faces on the island. Their first stop would undoubtedly be the ice-cream store.

Left alone with Doug at last, Sasha reeled uncertainly. To have slid from such heights of passion on the cliffs to the doldrums the instant they'd returned, finding the police at their doorstep, was unsettling. Even more so was the waiting that commenced.

Both Sasha and Doug were tense. Though life went on, outwardly normal and blatantly uneventful for the next few days, they were cautious, watchful. Sasha called her sister several times, satisfied when told that her mother was recovering nicely, then was going home. She sent another note, this one addressed to the farm and more chatty than the other had been. Agreeing with Doug that at some point she'd have to visit, she paved the way with small talk about her house on the island and about her work.

Her work was another matter. Sasha wrote nearly every day, but *Bronze Mystique* was proving to be more a diary than a work of fiction. When her heroine brooded on her love for her hero, it was Sasha's feelings about Doug that lit the screen. When her heroine contemplated the future, it was Sasha's feelings about marrying Doug that achieved outlet. When, in those darker moments, her heroine wrestled with thoughts of the mysterious being who stalked her, it was Sasha's fears that were aired. Anticipation of the climactic scene in the book was what made Sasha particularly uneasy. The heroine, as per Sasha's proposal, was to be kidnapped and buried alive in a coffin-sized box with nothing but an air pipe to keep her alive. It would be a terrifying experience from which, of course, the hero would rescue her. Of course. And there would, indeed, be a happy ending. It was at this point that Sasha began to pray.

The balmy weather continued. Sasha and Doug took long walks on the beach, holding hands, silently contemplating the tide, waiting, waiting for the villain's next move. As mindful as her of the ending of *Bronze Mystique*, Doug was reluctant to let Sasha out of his sight for more than a few minutes at a stretch, and then only when necessity demanded it.

The police had dutifully interrogated the young man who'd been working at the ice-cream shop, only to learn that he was an off-islander working part-time who had thought nothing about an older man with an air of authority popping in to help. The young man had simply assumed him to be the owner's partner. But the older one had come and gone quickly, leaving no concrete clue to his identity. And he'd never shown up again.

Slowly the agony of waiting began to take its toll. Furious at feeling so helpless, Doug grew testy. He wanted to steal Sasha back to New York or to some other hideaway where he might keep her safe. But as the police had pointed out, that might either prolong the inevitable or, worse, land the couple in an even more vulnerable situation than their present one. At least the population of the Vineyard was small and somewhat watchable. Unfortunately there were no less than a dozen eccentrics, recent *and* not-so-recent arrivals on the island, who might be their man.

It was late on a Thursday afternoon when Doug stalked into Sasha's den and eyed her idle form. "Come on, babe. Let's go into town. We need a change of scenery and the refrigerator's getting bare."

"You go," she mumbled without turning, as tightly strung as he.

"Not without you. I'm not leaving you here."

"Oh, please, Doug," she blurted out. "I'm not a child who needs constant baby-sitting." She propped her chin on her fist and stared at the blank screen before her. "Nothing's going to happen. I'll be all right."

He came forward in two angry strides. "You're coming with me."

"I'm not."

"Sasha..." he warned quietly.

She turned to throw him a livid glare. "Damn it, you can't order me around! I'm tired of being guarded! I feel as though I'm under house arrest! Well, you know what? I hope the guy *does* attack! I can't take this much longer!"

Doug's eyes narrowed. "My company's that much of a punishment?"

"That's not it, and you know it! But I see no reason why we can't be apart for all of an hour!" Her eyes flashed. "I'm not going into town. Period."

Hating herself for her tone, feeling ungrateful and unloving and angry and frustrated, she gritted her teeth and turned back to her screen.

A day before, a week before, Doug might have been

understanding. But his anger and frustration matched hers and he was in no mood to be solicitous.

"Fine. You stay here. I'll see you later."

Without further word, he stormed from the room and the house, leaving rubber on the drive as he spun the Maserati around and off. Only then did Sasha bury her face in her hands and wonder how she could have been so cruel to the man she loved, to the man who was going through so much because of her. And *it was her fault.* Someone was after *her*—and after Doug whose sole crime was loving her. It wasn't fair, damn it! It wasn't fair!

Surging from her seat in irritation, she grabbed her coat and headed for the beach. She needed a change of scenery too, and though a ride into town with Doug would have been nice, had she not been so ill-tempered as to refuse him, the beach would be some solace. It had to be. When Doug returned, she owed him an apology.

It had been a sunny day, but already the skies were beginning to darken with scattered clouds and the setting sun. The days were so short at this time of year, she mused. Life was so short. So why was she putting Doug off when, in her heart, she knew she wanted to marry him? What was she waiting for? Some sort of divine intervention? Some mystical revelation of the future?

No one knew what the future held, least of all her and Doug. Were there ever guarantees? Doug had done everything in his power to convince her of his love. Could she continue to punish him for something Sam Webster had done over ten years ago? Could she continue to punish herself?

The tide was low. Walking slowly, head down, she

made her way far out across the damp sand, her sneakers leaving the ghost of a trail along intricately patterned ridges, between scattered clusters of seaweed. By the water's edge, she stopped to study the lapping foam, then the far horizon. There was something lulling about the constancy of the surf, lulling as Doug's arms, as his gentle voice, as his love. When she'd heard the Maserati roar off, she'd felt alone as she hadn't felt in weeks. Was this what life without Doug would be like, this gnawing emptiness? He'd given so much of himself. Wasn't it time she reciprocated? Wasn't it time she decided to take that chance on the future? Didn't she owe it to Doug? Didn't she owe it to *herself*?

After agonizing for weeks, the decision was simply made. Feeling suddenly lighthearted, Sasha turned to retrace her steps. The air had chilled noticeably since she'd been out. Her skin prickled.

She'd taken no more than two steps when she swayed. Dizzy, she shook her head and tried to walk on, but her legs felt strangely stiff and uncooperative. Lighthearted…light-headed? Too many emotions, she thought. Too much cold. It was, after all, December, and getting darker, darker….

Senselessness came fast and she crumpled onto the wet sand. Only then did the distant figure on the cliff lower his gun, take a long swig from his pocket flask and retreat.

A CIRCUITOUS DRIVE around the island had done little to curb Doug's anger. When he'd finally headed into town, he'd been hell-bent on satisfaction. The Maserati screeched to a halt in front of the police station and he was out in a minute, storming into the building. By a coincidence not surprising giving the limited size of the Vineyard's department, the officer on duty was one of the two who had dealt with the poisoned ice cream. Doug had been prepared to spill his guts regardless of whom he found there.

"All right, officer," he gritted, planting his elbows firmly on the high desk. "I think we've pussyfooted around enough. You've got that woman and me out there like sitting ducks and it's about time we do something."

The policeman raised his eyes from the form on which he'd been idly drawing. Though life on the Vineyard was usually quiet, particularly in this off-season, he'd had years enough of dealing with temperamental residents to be perfectly calm before Doug.

"Just what do you propose we do, Mr. Donovan?"

"Donohue. It's Donohue. And I propose we—you—start bringing people in and questioning them."

"Bringing *who* in?"

"Suspects! You said there were a number of people new to the island!"

The officer laughed. "Great. I should alienate citizens who've come here for peace and quiet? How would *you* have taken that sort of thing, Mr. Donohue?"

"*I* didn't come here with the express purpose of terrorizing an innocent woman!"

"No, and neither did any of the others, to our knowledge."

Doug's eyes hardened all the more. "Are you suggesting that we imagined that ice-cream incident?"

"Of course not. We've got the lab report on it. It was poison, all right. But we can't just go out and corral a

bunch of law-abiding people without any evidence pointing to one or the other. All we can do is to keep our
eyes open. We're doing that.''

Doug's gaze dropped to the officer's doodles and he
uttered a tight-lipped, ''Yeah. So I see.''

''Look. Someone has to be here. We can't leave the
office unattended. But there are other guys on the streets.
Take my word for it. You're not being forgotten.''

''But how long must we wait?'' Doug growled. ''I
mean, we're going crazy. *You* were the one who told us
to hang around here. But nothing's happening.'' He
slapped his hand on the desk and looked away. ''This is
ridiculous!''

''If nothing's happening, good. Maybe your fellow's
begun to realize that he won't get away with whatever
he's trying to do. Maybe he's left.''

''Who's left?'' Doug asked pointedly. ''Any of those
eccentrics you mentioned?''

The policeman took a deep breath. ''I can't tell you
that, Mr. Donohue. We have no way of monitoring every
coming and going. People arrive on the ferry for the day,
they leave. There are flights in and out. For every private
boat that docks, another shoves off. All I can say is that
we're trying to keep on top of anything strange. If this
person is as demented as you believe, he's bound to tip
his hand somewhere along the line.''

What had started as an excuse in patient indulgence
on the officer's part had become a staring contest between him and Doug. Neither was backing down.

''Sure,'' Doug seethed. ''But what if it's too late?''

''We're doing everything we can.''

Doug took a breath, ready to further lambaste his opponent, then he realized the futility of it all. With a look that promised harm if any was done to Sasha, he whirled on his heel and left. Hands on his hips, he stood beside the Maserati breathing hard in the cool night air for several minutes before slamming into the car and starting off.

The grocery store benefited from his frustration, since he threw one item after the next into his cart with hardly an awareness of what he bought. Three bundles sat beside him in the seat when he realized that he was still in no mood to return to Sasha. She needed his support, not his misdirected anger. Swerving onto the main street of town, he drove a block, then pulled the car sharply over and parked it. A bench stood nearby. He stalked toward it and sat, hands jammed in his pockets, legs sprawled carelessly before him.

It was dark. Cars moved slowly along the streets, echoing the leisurely pace of the pedestrians who passed. The tempo there was slow. Why then was he in such a turmoil?

Answers came to him in rapid succession. Love. He was a novice at it and it had thrown him for a loop. Sasha. He wanted her so badly that he didn't know what to do. Simon Tripoli, damn him. Making their existence miserable, complicating things. Who in the hell did he think he was to be able to control their lives this way?

Inhaling deeply, Doug let his head fall back, then he brought it forward with a remorseful sigh. It was his own frustration, and he'd taken it out on Sasha as though it had all been *her* fault. He'd stormed from the house as if she'd personally rejected him.

Now he had to look at things from her side. She'd

given so much, she truly had. She'd admitted her love, she'd asked for time, she'd even so much as hinted that she would marry him one day. Could he fault her that she was cautious? Could he fault her that she was as tense as he with the knowledge that that maniac was on her trail? Oh, she hadn't yet fully agreed that it might be Simon, but Doug knew that much of her agonizing related to that distinct probability.

And he'd left her alone. He'd left her alone to stew…just when she needed him the most!

Deeply engrossed in his guilt, he bounded from the bench and ran smack into a man who'd approached. "Whoa," the man said. "Where're ya goin' so fast?"

The smell of whiskey was as telling as the slow slur of his words. A drunkard, Doug mused. Just his luck.

"Excuse me," he gritted quietly, intending to sidestep the man. "The bench is all yours."

But when he would have continued toward his car, the man's sheer bulk restrained him. Though comparable to himself in height, Doug saw at a glance that it was multiple layers of jerseys, shirts and a loud plaid wool jacket that gave the deception of bulk in the drunkard, rather than muscle itself.

"All 'lone? Wha' fun'd thad be? Come sit wi' me a bit. We'll talk."

"I'm sorry. I've got to run," Doug said, making another attempt at escape, only to be snagged by one steely arm.

"'S too late," the man mumbled, and something about him drew Doug's closer scrutiny. Dark haired, with the thick stubble of a beard on his jaw, he could easily pass as a vagrant. Yet his clothes weren't quite worn enough or dirty enough. And the flask he raised to his lips was a far cry from the brown-bagged bottle a vagrant would carry.

"What?" Doug asked tightly, his every sense suddenly razor sharp.

The man seemed to be focusing on a distant dot in the dark. "'S too late. Ya can't have her."

"What?"

"If I can't have her, you can't." He took another drink. Something caught Doug's eye. On impulse, he grabbed the flask from the man's unsuspecting hands and turned it toward the dim light of a nearby streetlamp. A second after he'd absorbed the initials on the side of the flask he threw the metal to the pavement.

"Wha—?" The drunkard hadn't finished his first word before Doug seized him by the collar and threw him down against the bench with a rigid knee pressed to his stomach.

"Where is she, you creep?"

"Ya can't have her."

Doug shook him. "Where is she? What've you done to her?" His heart pounded in terror, but his body was coiled, a tool of potential murder.

"I wanted 'er...I wanted 'er an' she left...an' she's gotten so high and mighty thad she ne'r called...." From a wail to a growl, he widened his red-rimmed eyes on Doug. "Well, you can't have 'er! She's gone! I took care a' that. You won't have 'er!"

"Where is she, you bastard!" Doug roared, shaking Simon again and again out of sheer helplessness. One part of him told him to try to find Sasha; the other knew it might be futile without this man's help.

"Gone," the other gulped, seeming to collapse spinelessly.

"Tell me! Tell me, or so help me I'll personally see that you spend every last day of your life in prison. I don't give a damn if you're sick or not. You'll rot in hell if you don't tell me what you've done!"

A new voice joined the fray and hands hauled Doug from the sprawled form beneath him. "Hey! What's going on here?"

Doug fought with all his strength to get back to the man who held the only answer he wanted. "That bastard's done something to my girl," he gritted, struggling to free himself from the restraining arms.

"Donohue?" the policeman asked. "That you?"

Panting furiously, Doug looked back. "Yeah. It's me. And that's Simon Tripoli, the man you should have found days ago! He's done something to Sasha and he won't tell me what."

Sensing the urgency of the situation, the officer abruptly released Doug's arms and leaned over Simon. "Okay, bud. You're in trouble enough. Things would go better for you if you gave us some hints. Where is she?"

Simon shrugged and rolled his head, then craned his neck and looked for his flask. "She's nice an' peaceful. Ri' near home. Where's my whiskey?"

"Damn your whiskey!" Doug hollered and would have lunged again had not the policeman set a preventative hand flat on his chest.

"Come on, Tripoli. Where is she?" Doug retrieved the flask and held it just out of his reach.

"She's on the beach."

"What beach?" Doug growled.

"Yours."

"What did you do to her?" he demanded, waving the flask before the other man's nose.

"Nothin' much."

The policeman took over, placing a threatening knee at Simon's groin and beginning to apply a slow, slow pressure. "What? Exactly."

Simon made a face of annoyance. "A dart. Tranquilizer. The tide's comin' in." He grunted when the officer leaned forward, but the eyes that went to Doug's were defiant and without fear. "You can't have 'er, Donohue! You can't have 'er!"

Doug didn't stay long enough to hear the continuing tirade. Ramming the flask toward the bench, he turned and bolted for his car, driving like a man demented which he was in a way. If anything happened to Sasha... if anything happened...

When the windshield blurred, he swore and batted on the wipers, only to realize that it was his own eyes that were filled with tears. Sniffling, he mopped his face with the back of his hand and drove on, willing himself to be cool, willing the road to shorten, willing the tide to stay out, willing Sasha to wake up before it was too late.

Hands in a death grip on the wheel, he drove like a maniac, caring little if a police escort joined the race. But the only other cars on the road passed in a whir on the opposite side, or slammed on their brakes to yield to the whizzing Maserati.

The beach. He had to get to the beach. He had to get to Sasha. Damn, where was the moon when he needed it? Would he be able to find her? If he did, he'd take her on any terms he could. Marriage? To hell with it! If he could simply be *with* her....

Taking the turn onto his private road at a madman's pace, he jounced over ruts he'd never seen before. At his house he slammed on the brakes and burst from the car, leaving the door wide open.

At a full run, a nervous sweat pouring from his skin, he raced down the embankment, over ragged cliffs, ever downward. He tripped once and slid several yards, then pulled himself up and tore on. His eyes were trained on the beach, his pulse pounding as thunderously as the tide.

When he reached the level sand he stopped, gasping, squinting frantically toward the water for a form, any form. He paced to the left and the right as he searched.

"Where are you?" he gritted. "Where are you? Damn it, Sasha, where are you?" Then he raised his voice in a mournful wail. "Sasha! Saaaashaaa!" He ran forward into the surf, heedless of the frigid water that soaked his sneakers and jeans. "Saaaashaaa!"

CHAPTER TEN

SASHA CAME TO SLOWLY, feeling cold and numb and disoriented. She was sprawled on the wet sand, her cheek to the coarse grains. One hand lay across a strand of seaweed, the other was pinned beneath her. It was the foot that lay in the rising water, though, that jarred her to awareness.

Pushing herself up, she pressed a hand to her head and looked around in confusion. There was water...everywhere, save the small sandbar on which she'd apparently fallen. But...what had happened? She recalled having started back toward shore, feeling dizzy, falling...

Looking frantically about the ink-black sea, she gasped. Then she hugged her knees to her chest and tried to still her thudding heart. Where was shore? She was sure she faced it, but everything was so dark, so forbidding, so threatening.

Gradually understanding dawned and she realized that while she'd been unconscious the tide had come in. How long had it been? She didn't have a watch, though she doubted she'd have been able to read one anyway. It was dark, so dark. She could barely make out the vague outline of the cliffs, much less the house. And it was cold. All balminess had gone with the light of day. She was chilled to the bone.

She'd have to swim. That was all there was to it. With a great effort she pushed herself to her feet, only to find she was dizzy and frighteningly weak. Numb and oddly divorced from the rest of her body, her legs wobbled. She glanced in bewilderment at the encircling waves, then the shore. She had no choice. Even as she stood, her small hill of sand seemed to shrink. The water couldn't be that deep, she reasoned in a desperate attempt to encourage herself. She'd been unaware of any major slopes in the sand when she'd wandered earlier. But then, her mind had been on Doug. As it was, she couldn't believe she'd come out so far!

She took a step, swayed and crumbled to her knees, only to have her jeans become soaked within minutes. Of course. *This was what he'd planned.* If her legs wouldn't work and her head spun each time she tried to move, how could she possibly swim to shore? If she stayed there she would die of exposure or fright, unless of course she simply passed out and drowned the easy way.

But she wouldn't. She had to get in…there was something she had to say to Doug…there was too much to live for!

Swallowing a growing wave of panic, she struggled to her feet again. Her teeth chattered; her fingers were wet and frigid. She took one tentative step, then another. When the waves saturated her sneakers, she was momentarily paralyzed. But she tugged her coat around her and took another step. Head ablaze with an icy inferno of lights, she tottered; then, even as her mind screamed in protest, she sank helplessly into the waves. Too frightened to cry, she was shaken by dry sobs of terror. Doug! She had to get to Doug! She had to see Doug!

On hands and knees she crept forward, but each inch brought the water higher on her body and her clothing began to weigh her down. Doug. Doug. Where was he? *Help me, Doug! Please help me!* Rocking back and forth on her knees, she prayed softly. Then, above the ocean's din, she heard a voice in answer.

"Saaashaaa!"

It was distant. Imagination? Hallucination?

"Saaashaaa!"

She puckered up her face and screamed with all her might. "Doug!" She screamed a second time, drawing from hidden reserves, not caring if she was left with nothing. "Douuuuugggg!"

At the sound of her voice, Doug's heart nearly exploded. His eyes riveted in the direction from which she'd yelled and even as he began to run down the beach he was kicking off his shoes, dropping his jacket, scrambling out of his jeans. When he hit the water he wore nothing but his shirt and briefs, yet his blood was pounding too fast to allow for the cold.

"Sasha! Yell again! I can't see you!"

Frightened and weak, she cried his name again, but her voice seemed to drown in the waves the instant she opened her mouth. Again and again she tried, shaking uncontrollably, though mindful of nothing but that Doug had come. She'd needed him and he'd come. She knew that if she passed out and died in that instant it would be with the conviction that he'd loved her that much.

The thought gave her strength. "Doug!" she

screamed, head up though she was doubled over holding herself. "I'm here! Here, Doug!"

At last he saw her, farther east then he'd expected, a faint shadow on a frighteningly small piece of sand. Running through the shallow waves, he dived forward and swam, arms and legs miraculously endowed with the superhuman strength needed to counter the onrush of the waves.

Though Doug was the one making the exertion, it was Sasha who gasped for air. It was so cold and he was swimming against the tide. If anything happened to him...

"Oh, Doug," she cried softly. "Come on, Doug. Come on."

He stroked steadily, shortening the distance between them until the water grew shallow again and he was able to stumble to his feet and run the last few yards. Then he was on Sasha's tiny island, taking her into his arms, crushing her to his wet frame.

"Thank God," he murmured brokenly, his face buried in her hair. "Thank God you're all right."

Sasha clung to him as to life itself. "I was so frightened.... I c-couldn't stand...and it's s-so dark...."

"It's all right, babe. I'm here. I'll take you back with me now." Mindful of what lay ahead and of the continued urgency of the situation, he set her back on her haunches and quickly began to unbutton her coat. "This will be more heavy than warm." He tore the jacket off and let it fall, then reached for her feet and discarded her sodden sneakers. The wool sweater went too, along with the jeans. "Hold your breath and try to relax, babe. Let me do the work. It'll be cold."

She nodded, but she was already so cold that the temperature of the water held little impact on her. Doug carried her until the waves reached his ribs, then he plunged them both in and, one arm around her waist, stroked steadily toward shore. Arms looped around his neck, Sasha could feel the extent of his exertion, but he forced himself on, bringing them closer, closer to the beach. When he could more easily wade again, he scooped her up in his arms and began to run through the surf, at last reaching the beach, stopping only to get his bearings before heading straight for the house.

Sasha was never to know whether she'd passed out again or simply been so numbed by the cold that her senses went on hold. The next thing she knew, though, she was in Doug's house, in his tiled shower, being held upright by his strong arms while the warmest, most deliciously welcome water hit her skin.

Above her, Doug's face was a mask of worry. Throwing her arms around his neck, she burrowed into his neck and hung on until the lump in her throat allowed for speech. "I love you so much, Doug," she murmured through her tears. "I love you." She clutched him harder and was rewarded by a corresponding tightening of his arms about her back. "Don't ever leave me again. Please don't leave me."

"Shhhhh," he soothed, threading unsteady fingers through her hair, brushing it back from her face and kissing her forehead. "It's all right. I'm not going anywhere." Slipping his thigh between hers to brace her against the shower wall, he gently stripped off her blouse, her bra, then her panties and socks. Removing his own, he took her back in his arms, hugged her, rocked her beneath the regenerative spray. "Shhhh," he crooned again, as much for her benefit as for his own as slow tears trickled one by one down his cheeks.

Sasha cried freely, whispering his name between sobs. With her thawing came the full awareness of what had happened, and she was overwhelmed by the force of divergent emotions. By the time she began to calm, a thick steam filled the stall. Turning the water off, Doug reached for a towel, wrapped it warmly around Sasha, took one for himself, then led her into the bedroom where his heavy quilt awaited.

"Warm enough, babe?" he asked, softly, his face inches from hers, torso flush with hers, arms and legs intertwined with hers. He tucked the quilt more tightly around them.

She smiled and sighed a breathy, "Yes," then sent him a look of remembered terror. "I was so scared and confused," she whispered, round-eyed. "I kept trying to stand but my legs wouldn't hold me. I was dizzy and cold. If you hadn't come—"

Doug's warm finger sealed the words at her lips. "I did come. That's the important thing."

She breathed a ragged acknowledgment and simply held him for a minute, reassured by his strength and the warmth of his long lean body. Then she forced herself to speak. There was so much to be said. "Doug?"

"What, babe?"

"I...I guess it had to have been Simon." When Doug simply stared at her, she went on. "I know I resisted the idea for a long time, and I suppose if I'd been more open to it I might have been able to help locate him. But I'm sure it was him. The MO is too distinct."

"MO? What do you mean?"

"The technique. Simon used it in his book, that first one, the only one that sold. He waited until I was as far out as I could get, then hit me with a tranquilizer dart." She paused, bit her lip. "I know he's out there somewhere. Maybe in the light of day if we got the police and went looking...?"

"No need," Doug said softly. "They've got him."

Her breath caught in her throat. "What do you mean? If they've got him, then who did this tonight?"

"Simon did...before he came into town and got drunk."

"Got drunk? You saw him?"

Doug nodded, his nose rubbing against hers. Now that it was over and Sasha was safe, he felt no anger, but rather a strange pity for Simon. "He's a sick man, Sasha, and what he tried to do to you, to us, was wrong. But he's suffering. After he shot that dart at you, he tried to bury it all in a bottle. When that didn't quite work, he actually stopped me and told me about it."

"He *what?*"

With an indulgent smile, Doug backtracked a bit. "After I left the house, I stormed around the island for a while, went to the police station and gave the officer on duty a piece of my mind, blitzed my way through the market, then found a bench in town and sat down to gather my wits. I had finally reached a grand conclusion and had got up to come home to you when he approached. He obviously knew who I was. When he started to talk, I realized he knew something about you. Then I saw the flask he was drinking from—with the initials S.T. on the front. That was when I got a little, uh, rough.''

"What did you do?" Sasha asked, alarmed.

"Not much. Oh, I threatened, but the police came around and hauled me off before I could do any damage. Between the good officer and myself, though, we managed to get the information we wanted. That was when I came after you."

Sasha closed her eyes and moaned softly. "And the police took Simon?"

"Yes. They'll keep him in custody." When she winced, he stroked her arm. "They have to, babe. Don't you see? He needs help. Tomorrow morning he'll most likely be sent to a hospital for evaluation. But he can't be let out on the streets. Not after what he's done."

"But *why*, Doug?" she cried, eyes awash with tears. "Why did he *do* all these things?"

"For many of the reasons we suspected. Jealousy— of you and your career, of me and our love. His belief that you'd abandoned him. There are probably a whole slew of other things totally unrelated to you that brought him to this state. The important thing is that he get the help he needs."

Tears spilled down her cheeks. "Oh, Doug, I'm sorry. It's partly my fault. I should have kept in touch with him."

"Don't blame yourself, babe. That was only a small part of the problem. The fact is that you surpassed him both personally and professionally. It's possible he couldn't take the turnaround."

"Well, then," she said, sniffling. "I'm sorry for being so stubborn about him. And I'm sorry for what I said to you before, Doug. I was cranky and upset. I shouldn't have—''

"I'm the one who should apologize, Sasha. I was imperious and insensitive. I was upset, too, but you didn't deserve that—''

This time it was her finger that stoppered the words at his lips. "I love you, Doug. I should have understood, rather than send you off and then run out of the house like an idiot.''

His gaze narrowed. "Why did you do that? You have to admit that it was a pretty stupid thing to do given the fact that a madman was on the loose. What were you doing on the beach?''

"Same thing you were doing driving around the island. Calming down. Thinking. Putting things into perspective. I had finally reached a momentous decision and was starting back here to wait for you when Simon's dart knocked me out.'' Her voice softened to a sweet whisper. "I owe you my life, Doug Donohue. Do you know that?''

"You don't owe me anything,'' he said with a sudden gruffness. "If I hadn't arrived, you'd have swam to shore yourself. You're a pretty self-sufficient lady, Sasha.''

"Not that self-sufficient,'' she argued gently. "My knees wouldn't work and I was dizzy. I could never have made it to shore myself. And anyway,'' she mused more soberly, "self-sufficiency has taken on a different light since I've met you.''

"Oh?'' he asked cautiously.

"Yes.'' Her fingers found their favorite niche against his spine at the small of his back. "It's lost some of its glow. I used to think that it was the most important thing in my life. Not that I'm denying its importance now. But...there are other things that matter more.''

"Like?"

Facing his beloved bronze visage, she didn't hesitate. "Like my love for you, my need for you. The joy I get doing for you, sharing with you." She glanced down for an instant. "And the future."

"What about the future?"

"Is—is that proposal still open?" She heard herself say the words, then held her breath while Doug stared at her. When his lips thinned, her heart constricted.

"You mean to say that you'd marry me because I saved your life? You'd marry me out of gratitude—stemming from another man's connivances?" He set several inches between them. "No way, Sasha. I don't want marriage on grounds like those. In a way that was what I'd decided on the bench in town just before I bumped into your friend." His eyes darkened to a gleaming charcoal gray. "I love you. I want to spend the rest of my life with you." His voice gentled. "But I'll take you on your terms, regardless of what they are. If you don't want marriage, so be it. Because if you're not happy, I'm not happy. It's as simple as that."

As quickly as those cold fingers had closed around her heart, they warmed and began a heady massage. Sasha smiled slowly. "But I'd made a decision, too, remember? *Before* Simon's dart hit. I'd decided that you were everything I'd always wanted in a man, a lover, a husband, and that I was hurting both of us by letting my experience with Sam hold me back." Her voice, too, gentled, and she followed her fingers as they wove through the rich vibrancy of his hair. "I love you so much that I sometimes think I'm just wishing it to be so. I've lived so long on wishes, I guess. It's hard to believe this one's come true."

"It has, babe. Believe me. It has."

"Then you'll marry me?"

His eyes danced. "If that's what makes you happy."

"But what makes *you* happy?"

"Your marrying me. Will you?"

"Yes. Oh, yes."

"No more doubts?"

She shook her head. Though tears glistened in her eyes, a brilliant smile lit her face. "I love you," she whispered.

"I love you," he echoed through a tremulous smile, then cautioned her more playfully, "But this isn't a happy ending, ya' know."

"I know." She glowed. "It's a happy beginning. Right?"

"Smart lady," he said, and turned the first page.

SEVERAL DAYS LATER, before a local justice of the peace, Sasha and Doug were married. It was a brief ceremony made beautiful by its very simplicity. With neither family nor friends present, it was a statement of the very private nature of their relationship. They married for neither money nor business nor family convenience nor tradition, but rather because they loved each other. Very simply. They loved each other.

A week later, Sasha brought Doug to Maine to meet her parents, who, though very definitely of Grant Wood's "American Gothic" school, had as definitely

begun to mellow. Not that there were open arms and
tears and smiles of excitement all around, but then Sasha
hadn't expected that. Rather, as an initial wariness gradually eased, the visit became a pleasant one. There was
talk of Natalie's improving health, of the farm, of
Doug's work and of Sasha's—the last with a quiet if
cautious respect on the part of the elder Blakes. It was
a beginning. Sasha couldn't ask for more. Besides, she
was intrigued by her mother, who, under the guise of
following doctor's orders, let her father putter around
fixing lunch. There was something about that ghost of a
smile on Natalie Blake's face that held hope.

Simon Tripoli was indicted on multiple counts of attempted murder. Though Sasha might have herself chosen to drop the charges, the matter had been taken out
of her hands with the involvement of the police. Thanks
largely to the lawyer Doug brought in from New York,
the defendant was found not guilty by reason of insanity
and was placed in a private hospital for the care he so
badly needed.

Donohue for Women took off like a house afire, from
drawing board to sewing room to runway to boutique.
More willingly than he ever had, Doug promoted the line
nationwide, each new city an adventure with Sasha by
his side. At Sasha's request, M.P.I. coordinated her publicity tours to coincide with Doug's, a practice so satisfactory to author and publisher alike that when her sixth
and most critically acclaimed novel, *Scheherezade Sunday,* made its debut it received the finest send-off ever.

Bronze Mystique never made it to press. On the day
of their wedding, Sasha gave it to Doug, who promptly
had it bound in leather and set it on the nightstand by

their bed to be read only on special occasions when they were alone, together and naked. It became quickly dog-eared, for he found himself rereading various portions on the sly from time to time, just as she did. It was a diary, a treatise on trust and understanding and patience, as well as on jealousy and suspicion and fear. It was a story of the heart's victory. And it held the promise of love for a world of tomorrows.

SECRETS IN SILENCE

Gayle Wilson

For the faculty, staff, students and alumni
of The Altamont School,
a model for excellence in education

PROLOGUE

SHE ALMOST MISSED IT. Her eyes had begun to burn, her vision blurring with exhaustion. Her fingers had already found the edge of the photograph, ready to assign it to the stack of those she had examined, when something caught her eye. Something seemed slightly out of place. Something…

Her gaze never leaving the photograph, she reached out, groping on her desk for the magnifying glass. She held it above the image, leaning over for a closer look. As she did, her hair fell forward. Impatiently, using the spread fingers of her left hand, she combed through it, lifting it out of her eyes as she focused the glass over the section that had attracted her attention.

She held it there, transfixed, until her hand began to tremble. She laid the magnifier down carefully, afraid she might drop it. Her pulse thundered in her ears, beating loudly enough that everything else faded away. Everything except the photograph and the small, curving red line that disappeared under the fall of blond hair.

She lifted her head, closing her eyes and massaging them with the tips of her fingers. This was too important to be mistaken about. She had to be absolutely certain that what she was seeing was truly what she had been looking for all these months. As she did, she realized with a jolt of nausea how close a thing this had been. If she hadn't stretched her budget to hire the researcher who had sent her the material lying before her, she would never have seen it.

She took a breath, concentrating on slowing her heart rate and steadying her hands. She was almost afraid to look at the photograph again in case she had been wrong, but of course, there was only one way to be sure.

She removed her fingers and slowly opened her eyes. They fell again to the picture in front of her. The round eye of the magnifying glass was resting on the exact spot she had studied before. Exactly over the curving stem of a small red rose a murderer had drawn on the nape of his victim's neck almost ten years ago.

She took another breath, fighting a surge of elation this time. *The beginning of the end,* she thought. No matter the outcome of the quest she had begun more than eight months ago, at least one of the questions that had haunted her life had now been answered.

Even in the midst of this victory, she realized there was no one she could share it with. No one who would feel this same sharp rush of vindication. They were all gone. All the people to whom this might once have made a difference.

She was the only one left. *The only survivor.* It was up to her to speak for all of them.

Her eyes fell again to the photograph. Another child. Another little girl, her hair so blond it was almost white.

Her fingers turned the pages, going back to the front of the file to find the name. The letters were bold, printed with a thick black marker, and they were very clear.

Katherine Delacroix.

Katherine. She had had a name. And she had had a life. Until he had taken it from her. Taken everything.

She opened the folder again, looking carefully at each of the photographs it contained. And this time, she really saw them. She saw the child they portrayed. At least what he had left of her. The broken, empty shell of another child he had destroyed.

Her eyes filled with tears. They were unexpected, because she never cried. She couldn't remember the last time she had been moved to tears. Or to an emotion strong enough to evoke them.

Katherine. And Mary.

For you, she promised them, her lips moving silently as in prayer. And the image in the photograph before her blurred again. *For you. And for all of us.*

CHAPTER ONE

HEAT WAVE. Callie Evers had heard the words all her life, of course. She wasn't sure she had ever really understood their significance until now. Until here.

When she had driven her car into Point Hope late this afternoon, heat had roiled upward from sun-stoked sidewalks and lain heavily beneath the branches of moss-draped oaks. Humidity thickened the air, so that drawing breath became a conscious act, and moisture gathered in body creases, dampening clothing and occasionally breaking free to slide slowly downward.

Just as the bead of sweat rolling between her breasts was now. Ensconced in a cushioned wicker chair on the back porch of the bed-and-breakfast where she had rented a room, however, she was decidedly cooler now than when she had first arrived.

The reality of the house where she was staying was a little less picturesque than the photographs on the Chamber of Commerce Web site, but it was near enough to the center of town for her purposes. And the screened-in porch did, as promised, overlook the tranquil waters of Mobile Bay.

Startled at the sudden bang of the screen door amid all this peacefulness, Callie looked up to find her hostess coming toward her across the porch. The old woman was juggling two glasses of iced tea and a couple of white linen napkins in her palsied hands.

Callie smiled her thanks, reaching up to take one of the glasses, its sides slick with condensation, before the contents ended up in her lap. She laid the napkin she was handed across her knees. Her hostess wrapped the other around the bottom of her own glass as she sank into the cushions of another chair.

"Land sakes," Phoebe Robinson said, "this late in the day, and it's *still* hot."

She lifted the tea to her lips, her hand trembling slightly. She took a long, greedy draught, ice tinkling in the near darkness of the screened-in porch. Then she pressed the glass against her cheek before she turned to smile at her guest.

"I expect you aren't used to this kind of heat. Or are you? I'm never too sure about my geography. Too many years since I was in school, I guess. Is Charlotte near the water?"

"No," Callie said, considering the panorama before her.

The dark bay had become a mirror of the twilight sky, the dying sun's crimsoned golds and yellows spread across it as if someone had spilled paint over the surface of the water. The eastern shore was famous for its sunsets, and this one lived up to the advance billing.

It was already night, however, under the trees that lined the shore, their black branches eerily silhouetted against the spectacle. And for the first time since she'd arrived in Point Hope, it seemed possible that something as brutal as Katherine Delacroix's murder might really have happened here.

"I expect it'll take you a few days to get acclimated," Phoebe said. "Give yourself plenty of time, dear. It's the humidity and not the heat that takes the toll, you know."

Callie lifted her own glass, using it to hide the smile provoked by that oft-repeated Southernism. The coolness of the sweetened tea was welcome against her tongue. She resisted the urge to mimic her hostess and press the glass against her face, allowing her eyes to focus again on the water instead.

The light was fading, and the colors that had dazzled only seconds before were disappearing from the darkening surface. There were already a few stars visible, and soon it would be impossible to determine where sky ended and the bay began.

In the stillness, she could hear the rhythmic lap of the water. The comforting sound would make sleep easier tonight, despite her excitement. When she had made the decision to come here, she had felt as if she were at the culmination of a long journey rather than at the beginning of one. Now that she had arrived, however, her anticipation had begun to grow.

"Vacation?"

Lost in the relaxing, shore-lapped quietness and her own thoughts, she had almost forgotten her hostess. And the question seemed an intrusion. "I beg your pardon?"

"I asked if you're here on vacation?" Phoebe repeated. "We don't get many visitors this time of year. Fall's really the time for Point Hope. Fall's glorious," Phoebe said, the sound of the ice in her glass again whispering between them.

"Not a vacation, I'm afraid." Callie hesitated, but it would have to be said. "I'm here to work on a book."

"You're a writer? Anybody I've heard of?" Phoebe asked.

"Probably not," Callie admitted, amused by the bluntness.

Phoebe wouldn't be familiar with her name. Not unless by some strange accident she had stumbled across the small weekly for which Callie wrote her column. Or unless she subscribed to one of the regional magazines to which Callie sold the local color pieces that kept her solvent.

"Is it a romance?" Phoebe asked hopefully. "Sally Tibbs at the library always saves the new ones for me. They do make me miss Hobart, though. And him dead more than twenty years."

Phoebe's laugh was surprisingly deep, considering her bird-like frame. Callie turned toward the sound, intending to share in the laughter with her own answering smile. Night had descended so rapidly with the setting of the sun that she could no longer see the old woman's features, only the movement of a pale arm lifting the glass of iced tea.

Maybe it was that companionable darkness. Or the interest she had heard in Phoebe's voice. Or maybe it was simply that she had to start somewhere, and so she said, "Actually, I'm writing a book about Katherine Delacroix's murder."

The words lay between them for several long heartbeats before Phoebe's voice, flattened, no longer filled with any hint of friendliness, came out of the darkness.

"Kay-Kay? You're here about Kay-Kay?"

"Did you know her, Mrs. Robinson?"

"Everybody knows everybody in Point Hope," the old woman said scornfully, as if that were something Callie should have realized. "I taught Kay-Kay in Sunday school. First Baptist Church. She was there that very Sunday. The one before…"

The words trailed, but Callie knew those that would have completed the thought. *The Sunday before someone murdered her.* The Sunday before someone took the life of a little girl who would never feel the humidity of a summer night gather between her breasts. Who would never read a novel. Who would never make love to a man.

"Would you tell me about her?" Callie asked. Despite her resolve, emotion had gathered in her throat, making her voice husky. And it seemed a long time before Phoebe answered.

"We don't like to talk about Kay-Kay. Or about the murder. There was enough talk when it happened to last us a lifetime."

"I know it's painful for those of you who knew her, but… She was one of you. Somebody who—"

The wicker chair creaked as the old lady stood, the abruptness of her movement cutting off Callie's argument.

"We don't like to talk about it," Phoebe said again.

"Believe me, I understand," Callie assured her. "But a little girl died. And people have a right to know why."

"A right to know *who*," Phoebe said, the words an accusation. "That's all you're interested in. You and everybody else are only interested in the who."

"Of course," Callie said. *Of course* that's what people

were interested in. The identity of Katherine Delacroix's murderer was what they had been interested in for over ten years.

It was a question that had never been answered. Not fully enough to lead to an indictment, much less a conviction. And it looked now as if it never would be, not unless someone outside this small, elite Southern conclave took a hand.

"Tom Delacroix's dead. Best to let it alone," Phoebe said.

"Do *you* think he did it?"

"It doesn't matter what I think. It doesn't matter what anyone *thinks*," Phoebe said. Her voice rose sharply on the last.

"It matters if he didn't," Callie reminded her. Because if Delacroix *hadn't* killed his daughter, if he hadn't been the one who had strangled that little girl—

"Ben Stanton," the old woman said.

Her voice came from across the width of the porch, and Callie realized only then that Phoebe had already moved to the door that led into the house. She was standing beside it, an indistinct, almost ghostly shape in the darkness.

"Ben Stanton?" Callie questioned, although it was a name she was familiar with. Anyone with even a modicum of knowledge about the Delacroix case knew Stanton.

"If anybody knows…" The old woman's voice stopped, and Callie waited through the silence. "He knows *everything*," Phoebe said finally. "You talk to Ben Stanton if you want to know what all they found that day. Talk to Ben to get the straight of it."

Callie opened her mouth to ask for an introduction to the man who had been at the center of the decade-old investigation. The bang of the screen door put an end to that intent.

She could ask in the morning, she comforted herself. That would give Phoebe time to become accustomed to the idea that she was here about the Delacroix murder. And to the idea that no matter what the people of Point Hope

GAYLE WILSON 269

wanted, the outside world wasn't ready to forget the little
girl who had died that night.

A quiet, hot August night, which, from everything she
had read, would have been very much like this one. Callie
turned her eyes again to the water that stretched in front of
her.

Ask Ben Stanton, Phoebe had advised. And after all, that
was exactly what she had come all this way to do.

"GOING OUT, DEAR?"

As soon as Callie stepped off the last carpeted tread of
the staircase and onto the polished hardwood of the front
hall, Phoebe's voice floated out from the front parlor. Smiling at her hostess's timing, Callie walked over to its double
doorway.

Phoebe and three other people were seated at a card table
that had been set up in the center of the room. The drapes
had been pulled across the windows to keep out heat generated by the morning sun, making the room unnaturally
dim. It took a moment for Callie's eyes to adjust, and when
they had, she realized the people at the table were Phoebe's
contemporaries. And all of them were looking at her rather
than at their cards.

"Come on in, dear, and let me introduce you," Phoebe
urged.

Apparently the unease her hostess had felt over Callie's
project had dissipated during the days she had lived in this
house. Or perhaps Phoebe's innate good manners prevented
her from treating a guest with anything other than that
much-touted Southern hospitality. Obediently, Callie
stepped out of the doorway and into the dimness of the
room, smiling at the others gathered around the table.

The old woman seated opposite her hostess shared
Phoebe's magnolia-petal complexion. Unlike Phoebe's, her
hair had not been allowed to silver. It was almost henna,
with one streak of white sweeping back from her forehead.
Her drooping earlobes sported multicarat diamonds, and the
long, patrician fingers of her hands, as pale as her face,

were covered with rings. Green eyes studied Callie from behind bottle-thick glasses.

"Virginia Wilton," Phoebe said, gesturing toward her partner with the hand that didn't hold her cards.

"Tommy Burge," she continued, indicating the small, thin man to her right. Burge was in shirtsleeves as a concession to the heat, his seersucker suit coat draped over the back of his chair.

"And this is Buck Dolan," Phoebe finished.

Dolan, obviously several years younger than the others, wore a knit golf shirt, open at the throat. His complexion bore evidence of years-long exposure to the Gulf Coast sun, the age spots on his forehead and cheeks marring what must once have been a classically handsome face. His hair was thick and dark enough to make Callie wonder if it were his own.

"This is Callie Evers, everyone. She's going to be staying with me for a couple of weeks."

It seemed Phoebe didn't intend to share the distressing news about *why* Callie was staying with her. Of course, since Callie had spent the last three days becoming familiar with the town and its landmarks, especially those involved in the murder, and given the efficiency of small town grapevines, she imagined these three already knew exactly why she was here.

"Nice to meet you," Virginia Wilton said. "Phoebe says you're from Charlotte. I went to school with an Evers girl from the Carolinas. Belinda Evers. You any kin?"

"I don't think so."

"Her daddy was a doctor. Or a lawyer, maybe. Professional man in any case. *Very* good family. If I remember correctly, and I think I do, his given name was Robert."

"I don't believe I know them," Callie said, fighting another smile at the blatant attempt to trace her antecedents. It was such an accepted form of interrogation here that Virginia's questions couldn't possibly be construed by any Southerner as rude. This was simply the way one greeted new acquaintances—by trying to fit them into the convenient framework of one's old.

"Vacationing?" Tommy Burge asked.

Burge's expression seemed interested. He didn't look as if he were preparing to pretend to be horrified by her answer.

"No such luck," Callie said. "Actually, I'm working."

She was aware peripherally that Phoebe's thin body had straightened in her chair, almost as if she were trying to send her a signal. If these people were Phoebe's friends, however, they might have as long and as intimate an acquaintance with this area and its inhabitants as her hostess. Their insights about the people involved in the Delacroix case would be invaluable.

"Don't let us keep you, dear," Phoebe said.

"Working on what?"

There were all shades and gradations of accents in the South, but the cadence of Buck Dolan's speech was subtly different from the others at the table.

"The Katherine Delacroix case," she said.

At the words, there was a visible change in their postures. Almost a physical shrinking away, as if she had uttered a profanity in church.

"Callie's doing research for a book on Kay-Kay," Phoebe said too brightly.

Despite the danger of revealing the contents of her hand, she was fanning herself with her cards. Her other fist was pressed against her breastbone, the skin on the back stretched so tightly over the misshapen knuckles that it had whitened.

"Really?" Burge said. "I thought people had finally lost interest in that."

"I don't think they'll lose interest until the case is solved," Callie said.

"So you anticipate we shall be forced to endure unpleasant media attention in perpetuity."

Callie's eyes considered Dolan, whose tone had been far

less polite than the others. "Does that mean you don't believe it *will* be solved, Mr. Dolan?"

"Not in our lifetimes. They made too big a mess of the thing from the start."

"They?"

"Don't mind Buck," Virginia said. "He never liked Ben Stanton. He thinks Ben should have been able to prove his case, and instead…" She shrugged.

"You think the police mishandled the investigation," Callie said.

"I think the police never should have *attempted* to investigate. What kind of credentials did Stanton have that made him think he was qualified to investigate a homicide? A stint in the CID doesn't prepare one to deal with a murder. It was all right for him to play cop when all he had to do was write the occasional speeding ticket, but solving a homicide was beyond his skills. Way beyond."

"He called in the F-B-I." The initials were separate, precisely pronounced, Phoebe's accent making at least one of them multisyllabic. "You know that, Buck."

"After it was too late," Dolan retorted.

"I always liked Ben," Virginia offered. "Nicest young man you'd ever want to meet. Leastways up until the murder."

The murder. This was one of the few places in modern civilization where you could refer to a ten-year-old homicide as "the murder" and be certain everyone understood what you meant.

None of what they had said was new to Callie. Nor did it offer any substantive information about the crime. At least they were talking, and their initial hostility to what she was doing seemed to be fading.

She had known that the region's inherent interest in all things past would work to her advantage. As would its focus on people, that unfailing Southern emphasis on family and neighbors. The Delacroix had been "neighbors" to everybody in this town and probably related to half of them.

Besides, when you got right down to it, their daughter's

death had been the most exciting thing that had ever happened in Point Hope, Alabama. These people could disavow interest in that murder all they wanted. It was still there, clearly revealed in their faces and their arguments.

And that, too, was to her advantage. *Everybody knows everybody,* Phoebe had said. Secrets and human failings were common knowledge. Who was sleeping with whom. Whose child wasn't really his child. And whose behavior on Sunday morning was in direct contrast to his or her behavior on Saturday night.

"Stupid," Buck said dismissively. "Stanton should never have put himself in that position. He should have had sense enough to realize he was in over his head from the start."

"Didn't nobody *know* what was going on at the start," Tommy Burge said reasonably. "You wouldn't have either, Buck. You can't expect the police to be mind readers."

"Not mind readers," Virginia said. "You mean those people that can see into the future. Prognosticators. That's what you mean, Tommy. He couldn't be a prognosticator."

"He could have been a cop," Buck said. "A good cop looks at a scene like that and smells the wrongness of it. He didn't."

Ben Stanton had been called out that morning to find a child who had supposedly wandered out of her home while her father slept. According to most accounts, he had had no reason at the beginning to doubt what he'd been told. The back door was unlocked—from the inside—and there was no sign in the house itself of foul play.

"Were you in law enforcement, Mr. Dolan?" Callie asked. "You sound as if you might have some expertise."

Phoebe's laugh, the full, unexpected one, rang out. Dolan's eyes reacted by narrowing as they moved to her face. He doesn't like her, Callie thought, but the intensity of the look lasted only a second or two. When he shifted the focus of his still-narrowed gaze to her, she wasn't sure which of them he disliked.

"I was never a cop, Ms. Evers, but I'm also not a fool.

I read a lot of true crime. I know what the police are supposed to do. And in this case, they did everything *but*."

"You go talk to Ben," Virginia advised her. "None of us were in Ben Stanton's shoes that morning, so we don't know what we would have done. You don't either, Buck, so hush."

"Hindsight's always twenty-twenty," Tommy Burge agreed.

"Bullshit," Dolan said. "Any good cop—"

"You watch your mouth, Buck Dolan," Phoebe scolded. "You know I don't allow that kind of language in my house. Especially not with a young lady present."

Callie again controlled the urge to smile, thinking about the vocabulary used in the newsroom and by most of her friends.

"She's heard worse," Buck said, echoing her own thoughts.

"Not in my front parlor she hasn't. And she won't," Phoebe said firmly. "Now you hush about Ben. You'll have her thinking we're a bunch of ignorant rednecks. That isn't the way you want Point Hope portrayed in that book she's writing, is it?"

That had obviously been a warning, and Callie could only hope it wouldn't cut off the flow of information.

"It wouldn't be the first time," Burge said. "Didn't any of us come out smelling like roses from that thing."

"I'm sure that Callie—it was Callie, wasn't it?—doesn't have that agenda," Virginia said, without waiting for an answer.

"Just exactly what is your *agenda?*" Buck asked sarcastically, those faded blue eyes again locked on her face.

"To expose a murderer," Callie said. "I would think that would be what everybody here wants."

There was no response. The silence stretched, becoming uncomfortable enough that finally she broke it by adding, "Maybe we can all talk more later on. I'd really like to interview as many people as I can who were living here at the time."

"We play Rook every Tuesday and Friday," Virginia said, seeming relieved that the conversation had moved away from the word *murderer.* "We play at Phoebe's 'cause she doesn't drive anymore. Most days Doc stops by. Just for the company. Doc doesn't play cards. Never did, that I can remember."

"Doc?" Callie questioned.

"Doctor Everett Cooley. I expect you'll want to talk to him, too. He was the coroner back then. He'd have been here today except he had to go into Mobile."

"Driving Ida Sullivan to her ophthalmologist appointment." Phoebe supplied the information with a tinge of censure in her voice. "I told Everett when he called last night that he was letting that woman take advantage of him."

Callie wondered, given her tone, if Phoebe might be jealous.

"Doc lets *everybody* take advantage of him," Virginia said. "Lord knows he's done enough for you and me, Phoebe, that we shouldn't complain about him helping poor Ida out."

"I'm not complaining about *that,*" Phoebe said indignantly. "I just hate to see folks run him ragged," Phoebe said, turning back to Callie to explain. "Everett's supposed to be retired."

"I can't tell he's cut back on his hours much," Burge added. "Only doctor you'll find who still makes house calls."

"Thank goodness," Virginia said emphatically, moving one of the cards in her hand into another position.

There was another small, almost awkward silence.

"Well, don't let us keep you any longer, dear," Phoebe urged finally. "I'm sure that whatever you write, you'll be fair. After all, the people here didn't have anything to do with…what happened. We all got tarred with it just the same. You go talk to Ben. He can tell you more than any of us can. More than anyone else in town, for that matter."

"I intended to see Chief Stanton," Callie said. "This

morning, as a matter of fact. Could someone give me directions?''

Dolan's vulgarity was muttered under his breath this time. Still, it was enough to draw another chiding look from his hostess. And it was Tommy Burge who answered Callie's question.

"Get back on the main road and follow the signs that lead toward Mullet Inlet. Stanton's got a place down on the water. Anybody can direct you once you get there. Or stop at Galloway's Grocery and ask directions. Less chance of getting lost.''

"Thanks,'' she said, allowing her gaze to move around the small table and touch on each of them individually.

The collective attention, however, had clearly shifted back to the game. She had been handled, neatly and efficiently, and sent off to interview the man who had borne the burden of that unsolved murder for the past ten years. And judging by the reaction of these Point Hope inhabitants to her questions, she could imagine how excited Ben Stanton was going to be to have her show up on his doorstep.

CHAPTER TWO

WHEN SHE REACHED the end of the dirt road, overhung with more of the drooping Spanish moss that attached itself to almost every tree in the area, Callie realized Stanton's "place on the water" was nothing like she'd been imagining. And nothing like the old-moneyed, shabby-genteel atmosphere the rest of this community exuded.

The first thing that drew her eye was the pickup parked next to the house. Its color was so faded from years of exposure to sun and salt air that it was almost indistinguishable, especially under the layer of grime that overlay the finish. The house itself, built of cedar which had weathered to a muted silver, was little more than a cabin.

Behind it, the requisite pier projected far out into the water. At its end was a wooden boat shed, open on three sides and equally weathered. The boat inside had, at least in her uninformed estimation, probably cost more than the rest put together. And in contrast to everything else, it appeared to be both new and well maintained.

Callie took a breath, gathering control—or courage—before she opened the door of her car. As soon as she did, the heat, temporarily forgotten in the cocoon of the vehicle's efficient air-conditioning, assaulted her with a nearly physical force.

She stepped out, easing the door closed rather than slamming it. She didn't intend to give Stanton more warning than was necessary. She stood beside the car a moment, listening. There was a low background hum of insects from the surrounding vegetation. And nothing else. No sound of a television or radio drifting out from inside the cabin. No sign of its inhabitant.

If not for the presence of the boat and the truck, she might have gotten back into her car, willing to talk herself into believing Stanton wasn't home. Unless he had walked somewhere in this heat, however, it was obvious he must be inside.

She slung the strap of her purse over her shoulder, feeling the reassuring weight of her tape recorder inside. She resisted the impulse to turn it on. Honor among thieves, perhaps, but she wanted to play fair. If he refused to talk to her...

Suddenly, the hair on the back of her neck began to lift. She couldn't remember having experienced that sensation before, but she had read enough about it to know what was happening. The feeling that she was being watched was so intense that she looked up, her gaze fastening on the dark rectangle of the cabin's screen door. She could see nothing beyond it, certainly not enough to tell if someone were standing there.

Given the thickness of the palmetto and other scrub growing around the clearing in which the house was centered, the eyes she felt might be hidden anywhere. They might not even be human.

At that thought, there was a discernible check in her forward progress. She had to force herself to walk on toward the cabin, despite the strength of those physiological responses.

Never let them see you sweat. She gave in to the smile the phrase provoked, relieved to have something else to think about. Besides, whatever Stanton's response to her visit might be—

"That's far enough."

Again her eyes focused on the screen door. There was no question the voice had come from behind it. Because of his position, the advantage was all his. He could see her clearly, yet he was as effectively hidden as if he really had been standing somewhere in those thick woods.

"Mr. Stanton?"

"Who are you and what do you want?"

"My name is Callie Evers. I'd like to talk to you."

There was a silence, long enough that she was again aware of the buzz of the insects. "About what?" he asked finally.

There was something in the tone, a habitual wariness perhaps, that said he knew why she was here. She wouldn't be the first stranger to have approached Ben Stanton in the last decade. His radar was probably well tuned to curiosity seekers by now.

"About Katherine Delacroix."

As she answered, she crossed the remaining few feet until she was standing at the bottom of the low steps that led up to the porch. Unlike most of its counterparts in the region, this one didn't display a stick of furniture or anything green and flowering. Obviously, it wasn't intended to be welcoming.

"Then you're wasting your time," Stanton said.

"I have plenty to waste."

"I don't."

Deliberately, she allowed her gaze to move around the clearing, over the pickup that looked like it hadn't been washed in months and the encroaching vegetation. When her eyes returned to the screen door, she was smiling openly.

"I can see how *busy* the upkeep on your place keeps you, Mr. Stanton," she said, infusing that same feigned amusement into her tone, "so I promise I won't take up much of your valuable time."

"You won't take up any of it," he said, his voice colder than before. "Whatever you're looking for about the Delacroix case, you won't find any answers here."

"I thought you were the expert."

"You thought wrong."

"You handled the investigation."

"Don't you mean 'botched' the investigation?" There was a hint of mockery in the question.

"Did you?" she asked, wishing now that she had ignored her scruples and turned on the recorder.

"Get off my property."

Anger had replaced the mockery she had heard before.

"If it *wasn't* botched, then why won't you talk to me about it? Wouldn't you like to set the record straight?"

"I won't talk to you because you're a ghoul, Ms. Evers. And I don't like ghouls."

"You don't know anything about me. *Or* about my reasons for being here."

"If you want to talk about Katherine Delacroix, then you're a ghoul. She's been dead and buried for ten years. I'm not about to help you dig her up."

"Would you help me find her murderer?" The silence stretched, broken only by the low hum from the woods around them.

"Get off my property," Stanton said again, his voice flat, all emotion, certainly all humor, gone.

"Because I've read everything about this case I could get my hands on," Callie went on, ignoring the repeated demand.

"That only reinforces my original opinion of you."

"And I've come to the conclusion that Tom Delacroix couldn't have had anything to do with his daughter's death," Callie continued doggedly. If she couldn't charm Stanton into it, maybe she could shock him into talking to her. "What I think is that in your single-minded determination to convict somebody—*anybody*—for that murder, you ruined the life of an innocent man. And because you were so sure Delacroix was guilty, you let the real murderer get away with that…atrocity."

The screen door exploded outward so suddenly her throat closed in surprise, causing her to swallow the last syllable of the word she had settled on to describe the murder of Katherine Delacroix. And just as Stanton's "place on the water" had been nothing like her expectations, the man himself was totally different from the mental image she had brought to this meeting.

There had been plenty of photographs of Ben Stanton in the material she'd studied. She had studied them with an attention to detail which, she had finally admitted to herself, couldn't be credited solely to her interest in the case.

In most of them, he'd been wearing that neatly creased uniform, black utility belt fastened around narrow hips. Blue eyes had squinted into the strong coastal sun or were hidden behind mirrored sunglasses. Hair ruffled by the perpetual breeze off the bay, Stanton had appeared to be the picture of efficiency and dedication to duty. And none of those impressions fit with the reality of the man who had just stormed out of that door.

He wore nothing now but a pair of jeans, faded until they were almost gray. The waistband rode low on his hips, which were as lean as she remembered them. His chest, so brown it looked as if it had been carved from mahogany, was broader and more muscled that it had appeared under those crisply laundered uniform shirts. His feet were bare and they were as darkly tanned as the rest of his body. Even his hair was different. Longer than he had worn then, its ebony was streaked at the temples with silver.

And his eyes were no longer hidden. When hers lifted to meet them after that unthinking inventory, they were filled with fury, piercingly blue and incredibly cold.

"What the hell gives you the right—" he began, his voice taut with the force of his contempt.

"He signed his work," she said.

The angry rush of Stanton's words halted. His eyes, which had been narrowed in anger, widened. Even the pupils dilated, nearly destroying the rim of blue that surrounded them. Her heart leaped in response.

"Maybe you didn't know what that mark was or what it meant," she went on, forcing her voice to remain steady, her sentences measured and sure. "But you saw it. You *had* to have seen it. *Somebody* had to have seen it."

She hadn't intended to play her trump card so soon, but then she hadn't expected to be afraid of him, either. The force of Stanton's hostility had been palpable. And maybe

this was better than drawing it out. Better than slowly revealing what she knew, bit by bit, as she'd planned. After
all, the strength of his reaction had already confirmed that
she was right.

And now she had his full and complete attention. Ben
Stanton was literally hanging on her every word, the fury
in that ice-blue glare stunned into something very different.

"He drew a rose," she said, laying out for him what had
brought her here. "It was on the back of her neck, hidden
under her hairline."

Stanton said nothing, but his eyes had narrowed again.
And they were locked on her face.

"It was there, wasn't it?" she demanded.

Just as she had known from the initial shock in his eyes,
she also knew from his silence that she was right. And the
power of that affirmation roared through her body.

"It was drawn with a marker." Her excitement made the
words flow faster now, tumbling over one another. "Or
maybe just in ink. Red ink. But it *was* there, wasn't it, Chief
Stanton."

"Get off my property," Stanton said. He hadn't moved.
He stood on the edge of the porch, his eyes still too revealing.

"I know it was. It had to be. Because whoever killed
Kay-Kay did the same thing at least once before," Callie
said, and watched in satisfaction as his face changed again,
the tight, hard line of his jaw softening in shock. "Sixteen
years before he put that mark on Katherine Delacroix, he
did exactly the same thing to another little girl. Or don't
you want to hear about her?" she taunted. "Are you afraid
that if you do, you'll finally have to admit you were
wrong?"

THANK GOD he had recovered enough to convince Callie
Evers he wasn't going to talk to her, Ben thought, wielding
a mop over decking that had been spotless before he'd begun.

Physical activity always cleared his head, allowing him

to think more clearly, maybe by rushing blood to his brain. God knows he had needed that rush when Evers mentioned the rose. He had literally been light-headed with shock. And then he had been furious he'd let her catch him off guard. He still was.

That she knew about the drawing on the back of Katherine Delacroix's neck had stunned him, leaving him groping for some response other than "Get off my property."

Eventually he had said that often enough that it had had the desired effect. She'd gone, giving him a chance to fight in private the ghosts she'd revived. Ghosts he had, up until this morning, believed he'd exorcised.

"Damn you," he breathed. Struggling for calmness, he walked over to the bucket he was using to wring out his mop.

There was no way around it. She had done a number on him. At the remembrance of how well she'd succeeded, his hands twisted the cotton strands viciously, using them as a substitute target for his fury, most of it self-directed.

While he worked, he'd finally been able to fit what she'd said into some plausible scenario. Callie Evers, whoever the hell she was, had to have been given that highly privileged information. And she had tried to use it to get him to spill his guts, breaking his decade-long silence about Katherine Delacroix's death. It was the only explanation that made sense.

And he was going to have the hide of the person who had been responsible for that leak, Ben decided, shoving the head of the mop back into the bucket.

THE CURRENT CHIEF of Point Hope's two-man police department was leaning back, booted feet up on his desk, when Ben slammed through the door of his office. That relaxed atmosphere quickly dissipated as Ben launched into his tirade.

"What the hell were you thinking telling the Evers woman about that drawing?"

Doak Withers' feet had come off the desk as Ben came

through the door. As he listened to the accusation, his body straightened in his chair. Finally he stood and, leaning across the desk, pushed his nose within millimeters of Ben's, close enough that there had been a momentary danger they might collide.

"Screw you, Ben," he said.

"That *doesn't* answer my question," Ben said, ignoring the display of anger.

His own fury had continued to build on the way into town. He couldn't see any other way that woman could have found out about the rose, except from his former deputy.

"You *know* I wouldn't give out information like that," Doak said. "I ain't told nobody about the mark on that kid's neck, and I'm not likely to at this late date. If I did, it sure as hell wouldn't be some frigging female reporter.

"She'd already been out to your place when she came by here. She told me she'd talked to you. Told me she was writing a book about Kay-Kay. Not that that was a surprise. I've had half the town on the phone the last couple of days complaining about it."

"So what *did* you tell her?"

"Not a damn thing. I figured whatever you wanted her to know, *you'd* have told her. I didn't tell her anything, and that's the God's truth. I sure as hell didn't say nothing about the rose."

"Then who did?" Ben demanded.

He straightened, lifting the heels of his hands from the scarred top of the desk that had once been his, while allowing the tips of his fingers to maintain contact with its surface.

"How would I know?" Doak asked, his beefy face still flushed in spite of the fact that he, too, had straightened, mimicking Ben's action and putting them in a less adversarial position. "What makes you think *anybody* told her?"

"Because—" Ben stopped, his mind supplying an answer he didn't want to think about. If no one in this office had leaked the secret they had kept for more than ten years, then...

Then he would have to face the possibility that the other thing Callie Evers had said might be true. And that was something he wasn't ready to consider.

"Because there's no way she could have known about it otherwise," he finished, his logic pointing out the way, even as he mouthed those empty words.

He heard the huff of breath Doak released, his lips and cheeks fluttering slightly as he expelled it. "All I'm telling you is it didn't come from me," Withers said, his voice calmer.

"Simmons?"

"You think I'd tell Billy something confidential?" Doak asked scornfully. "You know better than that, too."

"There isn't anybody else."

"You put it into VICAP," Doak reminded him.

The national database maintained by the FBI held information about violent, unsolved crimes. Despite what Ben had believed about the identity of the murderer from the beginning of his investigation, he had checked the rose, as well as the other bizarre elements of Katherine Delacroix's murder, against what was already on file there. It had been done simply as a matter of course. A matter of doing his job.

According to the Bureau, there had been no match. There was no other murder on file with the same components as the Delacroix case. So whatever Callie Evers was claiming, Ben knew there hadn't been another unsolved child murder like this one.

That didn't explain how she had learned about that rose. And in order to put all this behind him again, if he ever could, that was something he needed to know.

"It's a closed system," he said, working his way through the possibilities, even as he explained why VICAP wasn't one. "No one gets in to see what's already there. We just provided the info on Kay-Kay's murder. It was checked against other unsolved cases. And in order for Evers to have someone do that..." He hesitated, trying to think if there were another way.

Doak filled in the pause. "To have someone do that, she'd have to already know about the drawing."

The silence grew, as Ben again rejected the other possibility—the one Callie Evers had suggested—as unthinkable.

"You want me to check the case file?" Doak asked, introducing a spark of hope into Ben's growing despair. "Make sure everything's still there. Verify it's not been tampered with?"

"You got some reason to think it might have been?"

The Delacroix file had always been kept locked in the office safe. In the beginning there had been too much media frenzy to chance anyone from outside the department getting their hands on what it contained—especially after the autopsy photographs had been stolen. That was something else that had been blamed on Ben Stanton's inexperience with a high-profile case.

And rightly so, he acknowledged bitterly. He had had no idea then the depths to which the tabloid scum-suckers would stoop. The theft of those pictures had been a wake-up call. One that had come too late.

"Nothing but what you're saying," Doak said, moving toward the old-fashioned safe, its gold script faded with age.

Ben watched as Withers worked the combination, which, he noted, hadn't changed in the years since he'd been gone. Nor had the brown accordion file in which the investigative reports were kept. Just the sight of it, even after all this time, made him sick at his stomach.

All the feelings from those endless days of frustration and resentment came flooding back. Frustration that he couldn't prove what he knew in his heart. Resentment that, despite the fact he had done everything he knew to do, despite the long, sleepless days and nights he had spent on this investigation, it was always going to be his failure. His shame.

A little girl had died, and her murderer walked free. And it had happened in his town. On his watch.

"Seal's intact," Doak said, bringing his attention back to the folder.

"Break it," Ben ordered.

Withers' eyes held on his, perhaps questioning the authority behind that order. They had worked together too long and too intimately, however, to let the fact that their positions were now reversed interfere with the natural chain of command.

Doak's thumbnail slid along the seal, splitting the gummed paper into two parts. He made no move to open the folder, simply holding it in his oversized hands. Surprised, Ben looked up in time to watch his former deputy swallow, the movement visible all along the thick, sunbrowned column of his throat.

"Opening this seems like… Hell, I don't know. Like some kind of desecration," Doak said, his eyes still on the file.

Exactly what he had accused Callie Evers of, Ben thought. Of digging up a child's murder to satisfy the unnatural hunger of the same people who had snapped up every copy of the tabloids that had carried those grisly photographs.

Was he any different? He had placed a seal on the contents of this folder eight years ago because he hadn't been able to do anything else with what it contained.

This was material he knew by heart. Every picture. Every comment. Every shred of evidence. None of it had gotten him anywhere. And he had always known that no matter what was in there, it could never bring Kay-Kay back to life.

"The desecration's going to be if anybody gets wind that we held that information back," he said. "We're going to be front and center again in every tabloid in this country."

Doak's eyes lifted, holding on his a long moment. Then his ex-deputy walked over to the desk. Tilting the accordion file so that the open edge of it slanted downward, he allowed the contents to spill out onto its surface.

"Help yourself," Point Hope's current police chief said. Then Withers laid the empty folder on top of his in-box and crossed the room to stand before the window that looked out on the main street of town.

Ben's gaze followed, briefly considering, as Doak seemed to be, the scene that lay beyond the tinted glass. There was no traffic. And no pedestrians. Everyone would be inside, either to avoid the heat or to eat their midday meal.

There was literally nothing out there to watch, so it was obvious what Withers was doing. If Ben wanted to paw through this stuff again, Doak felt he had the right. But he wasn't going to hand Ben a shovel and point him toward the grave.

Reluctantly he began to sift through the stack. When he came to the autopsy photographs, bound by a rubber band, bile crawled upward, burning his throat. He didn't look at them. If he ever wanted to view those images again, they would all be there, perfectly intact and terrifyingly vivid, in his subconscious. And in his nightmares.

He swallowed, forcing the nausea down, as he continued to methodically plow through the rest. He forced himself to compare what was here to the original list of the folder's contents, which he himself had composed.

This would all be on computer nowadays. They hadn't been that sophisticated back then, at least not in Point Hope, so he had kept hard copies of every report that had been generated by the Delacroix investigation. And he had kept his own notes, which were here as well. Just where they should be.

They included the drawing he'd made of that small red rose. He could still remember pushing aside the strands of hair that had been plastered against the fragile nape of Kay-Kay's neck that morning, exposing the tiny red bud.

There wasn't a shot of it among the autopsy photographs. Doc Cooley, who had been acting coroner at the time of the murder, had never seen it. The soft blond hair had dried by the time Doc made his examination, obscuring the flower.

And that had been another mistake. Ben had assumed Doc would see it. By the time he'd opened the folder containing the autopsy photographs and realized there wasn't one of the rose, the Delacroix had buried their daughter. At that point, they weren't about to allow the authorities, and especially not the Point Hope Police Department, to exhume her body.

So there was no way, Ben thought again, his fingers tracing slowly over the faded drawing. No way Callie Evers could have known about this. Not unless she was telling the truth. He moved his head in slow negation, swallowing to force down his building nausea.

"Something missing?" Doak asked.

He turned and found his former deputy watching him. The light from the window behind Withers provided a halo effect around his bulk.

"Not a thing," Ben admitted.

Nothing he had put into this envelope eight years ago was missing. Nothing except the absolute certainty he'd had when he sealed it that he knew who had killed Kay-Kay Delacroix. And that was the only thing he couldn't afford to have lost.

CHAPTER THREE

"I THINK I'LL SIT out here a few minutes longer," Callie said to her hostess. "If that's all right with you."

The peace of Phoebe's screened porch had been more than welcome. As had the glass of homemade scuppernong wine she'd been given. The lap of the water and the alcohol soothed nerves left raw by her encounters with Ben Stanton and Doak Withers.

She was already dreading the same song, second verse aspect of tomorrow's interviews. There were others she needed to talk to who had been as intimately involved in the murder as Stanton. And if they all reacted with the same hostility—

"You do just exactly as you please, dear," Phoebe said. "You don't have to get permission from me. You treat this like you would your mother's house. Or your grandmother's. I imagine I might be *almost* old enough to be that."

Apparently Phoebe had forgiven Callie's reasons for coming here. Or if she hadn't been forgiven, she had at least been accepted. Maybe that was nothing more than the usual Southern tolerance for an eccentric, granted routinely to writers.

"I thought I might walk down to the water. If you think it's safe."

"Safe?" Phoebe repeated, sounding amused. "Honey, you can walk anywhere you want to in this town. Any time of the day or night. We haven't had a crime since—"

Since someone murdered a little girl.

"In a long time," Phoebe finished, producing words

quickly to fill in that telltale hesitation. "Point Hope isn't like New Orleans or Birmingham or those other places you read about."

"I didn't want to bother your neighbors," Callie explained.

A row of more than a dozen houses, including Phoebe's, all built very close together, backed up to the bay. Between them and the narrow beach ran a dirt path, shaded with oaks and overgrown magnolias, which gave the neighbors easy access to one another's backdoors.

"I was afraid I might disturb someone's dogs or something. Cause an uproar," Callie added.

"We're all too old to have dogs. Outlived them. I wouldn't mind having a good watchdog, mind you. Let me know when somebody's coming. Give me a little warning so I can hide my clutter from my friends and the booze from the preacher," Phoebe said, her deep laugh ringing out in the nighttime stillness.

"You walk anywhere down there you want," she continued. "Along the path or down any of the piers. You can even walk on the beach. Just don't go too far out into the water. It's dangerous to swim alone, especially at night."

"Don't have to worry about that," Callie assured her. She wasn't that good a swimmer, and because of that, she had never been overly confident about the water.

"Well, good night, then," Phoebe said. "Sleep tight and don't let the bedbugs bite."

"You better not have any bedbugs, Phoebe. If you do, they'll take away your license," Callie teased.

"You know, I don't even know what bedbugs are," the old woman said. "That's just something I said when I put my boys to bed. I guess 'cause Daddy always said it to all of us."

"I didn't know you had children."

Callie couldn't remember seeing any family photographs around. Perhaps since Phoebe had opened her home to paying guests, those had been moved into her private rooms.

"Two boys. One of them was killed in Vietnam. Just

twenty-one. Had his whole life ahead of him." The voice in the darkness had lost all trace of its customary good humor.

"I'm so sorry, Phoebe. I didn't mean to stir up—"

"Oh, honey, that was a long time ago," the old woman said, dismissing her attempt to apologize.

"And your other son?"

The bang of the screen door drowned the last word of her question. Even in the short time she had spent as Phoebe's guest, Callie had discovered her hostess was a little hard of hearing. Or maybe, she thought, Phoebe's hearing was selective. Maybe she just avoided subjects that were apt to be painful, as her son's death obviously was.

Ghosts, she thought. So many ghosts.

Maybe that was simply the ambiance from the mysterious moss-draped oaks and old houses. Or the proximity to that dark water. The long history of the area, which stretched back to the Spanish exploration of the New World.

There was no doubt that Katherine Delacroix's small spirit was by far the most famous. And the image of Ben Stanton's face when she had told him about Mary's murder played over and over in her head as she finished her wine.

The last strands of color from the sunset had long ago faded from the sky, and with the overhanging rain roof, the porch had grown very dark. The night was clear and inviting, despite the fact that there was only a sliver of the new moon.

Phoebe's soft-soled lace-ups had made no sound on the wooden boards of the porch, but as Callie crossed them, the heels of her sandals echoed. The hinges of the screen door squealed when she pushed it open, evidence of the corrosiveness of the salt air.

The walk leading to the path was distinct, stretching between the overgrown foliage of what had obviously been, at one time, a well-kept back garden. Judging by the potted impatiens and geraniums on all her porches, Phoebe had a green thumb. The lawn and the shrubs were undoubtedly too much for her now. And the cost of having someone else tend to them probably a factor in her inability to keep their rampant growth controlled.

The breeze off the bay brushed Callie's face as she neared the water, carrying a tinge of brine and fish. Then suddenly, overriding those smells, was the stench of decay.

Something must have washed up on the narrow strip of sand between the bulkhead and the water. In this heat, it wouldn't take long for any organic flotsam to become unpleasant. Unpleasant enough to force her to turn back? she wondered.

As soon as the thought formed, the stench disappeared, replaced again by the not unpleasant smell of the water. She raised her face, nostrils distended, to breathe it in. The wind dislodged a strand of hair, which fluttered over her eyes.

She lifted her hand to push it away, but before she could complete the motion, her wrist was encircled by hard, masculine fingers. She jerked her forearm forward, pulling against their grip. She half turned, the movement stopped by the unnatural position in which Ben Stanton was holding her arm, behind and above her head.

"Aren't you afraid to be out here with a murderer running loose?"

"Let me go," she said evenly.

Obediently, those callused fingers unfurled, freeing her. She turned to face him, resisting the urge to rub at the place they'd gripped. It wasn't painful, but there was a lingering echo of their controlling force, which she didn't like. She felt like one of those gothic heroines who scrubbed at their lips after having been kissed by the villain.

Except this wasn't a villain, despite the fact that he had been accused of being that and almost everything else. And he hadn't kissed her. Judging by the coldness of his tone, that would be the last thing on Ben Stanton's mind right now.

At the realization of what must have brought him here, her heart began to race, beating so strongly it crowded her chest. She worked at mastering her breathing, determined not to let it be audible in the stillness.

"If I were afraid, I would never have come here." After all, if he followed the pattern, the man who had killed Kay-Kay was long gone from Point Hope. "Besides," she added, "I'm sure Chief Withers and his deputy are out on patrol. Making the world safe for democracy." The chief of police's refusal to talk to her still rankled.

"You like easy targets," Stanton said.

She shook her head, the movement small. She didn't understand what he meant, although his remark was obviously in response to hers. *Easy targets.* Withers? Southerners?

"The 'boys' in blue," he said. "The butt of all the jokes."

"Tan."

She was relieved to find her voice was steady, despite her excitement. Ben Stanton had come to talk to her, as unbelievable as that seemed after their confrontation this morning.

At her one-word response, his eyes narrowed. In this light she couldn't distinguish their color. Nor could she tell whether they were as cold as they had been earlier.

At least he was wearing clothes. She had discovered there are few things more intimidating than an angry, half-naked man.

"You wore tan, not blue," she said, wondering even as she did why she was explaining. What could it possibly matter?

"Am I supposed to be flattered you noticed?"

"I told you. I know everything there is to know about this case." *Including what you found on the back of Katherine Delacroix's neck.*

She didn't say that, but it was implied. And maybe the impact was stronger because she hadn't said it again.

"If you're going to make an accusation like the one you made this morning," Stanton said, "you damn well better have some evidence to back it up."

She was relieved they weren't going to play cat and

mouse. She suspected Stanton was better at that than she could ever be.

"I can show you," she offered.

She held her breath as she waited for his response. This was all she had hoped for. A chance to find out what Stanton knew. To combine it with what she knew. And maybe then—

"Show me what?"

"My material's inside. In my room. I think Phoebe's already gone to bed, so maybe we shouldn't—"

"Your virtue's safe with me, Ms. Evers." He sounded amused.

"I didn't mean that," she said stiffly.

His comment hadn't been sexually charged, but for some reason she felt her throat flush. Embarrassed that Stanton might think she was playing at that particular kind of coyness?

It doesn't matter what he thinks, she told herself, praying the darkness would hide that rush of color. *Nothing* mattered, not as long as he told her what she needed to know. And so she turned, leading the way back up the path.

"THAT COULD BE anything," Ben said, pleased with the tone. Dismissive, despite the nausea in the bottom of his stomach.

"Except you and I *know* what it is," Callie Evers said. "It's part of the stem of a rose. Just like the one he drew on his other victim."

At that quiet certainty, he looked up from the autopsy photograph she'd laid on the walnut secretary in her bedroom and straight into her eyes. They were gray-green, like the sea when you're far enough out to escape the shoals and bars. The color fit with her skin, which was almost Celtic in its fairness, heightened now by a subtle bloom of color along her cheekbones.

Nervousness or conviction? he wondered.

"I don't *know* anything, Ms. Evers, except what I hear you saying. So far you haven't shown me any proof. Not even that this other crime you keep talking about happened.''

"Hawkins Bluff, North Carolina," she said.

The words were low, but her voice had been filled with expectation, as if that was supposed to mean something to him. And it didn't. It didn't mean a damn thing.

"You're telling me a child was killed in North Carolina twenty-six years ago *exactly* like this?" he demanded, tapping his index finger on the photograph.

He didn't look at it again. He didn't need to. It was one he had examined a couple of hundred times—just as he had all the others—searching them for something he might have missed. Something that would allow him to put an end to the nightmares that had haunted his sleep for almost an entire year after he'd discovered Kay-Kay's body.

That was something he had never found. Something he wasn't going to find here tonight.

"Not...exactly like this," she admitted. "Maybe that's why no one ever made the connection before. That and the fact that you didn't reveal everything about the Delacroix murder.''

"Any cop who reveals everything he knows about an unsolved homicide is a fool. Whatever else you think about me, Ms. Evers, I'm *not* a fool. Tell Lorena this isn't going to work. Tell her it's time to quit wasting her money."

There was a small silence.

"You think...*Mrs. Delacroix* sent me here?"

The touch of incredulity was nicely played, Ben acknowledged. Of course, Lorena had the money to hire the best. That had always been part of the problem.

"Or maybe I'm supposed to believe you just enjoy examining autopsy pictures of dead children with a magnifying glass."

He could tell by her eyes that he was right. She'd never have been able to see that small curved line if she *hadn't* been studying the photo under magnification. Only the tail end of the stem was exposed, the line barely visible to the naked eye, even if you were looking for it. It couldn't have been identified as part of a drawing without the use of a glass.

Which was moot, he supposed, since he had never admitted there had been a drawing on Kay-Kay's neck. He wasn't going to. Not to her.

"I told you," she said. "I was looking for something like that. And I found it, just where the other one was."

"The other one?"

"The other rose. The other murder."

"In...North Carolina, was it?" The sarcasm was deliberate. If it had any impact, she hid it well.

"That's right."

"Give me year and day."

"In exchange for what?"

"In exchange for jack shit. You're the one who's trying to sell this cock-and-bull story."

"And *you're* the one who's trying to convince himself he couldn't possibly have been wrong," she countered, matching his mockery. "If you want that information, you're going to have to reciprocate with some of your own. Like a public admission that you found the drawing of a rose on Katherine Delacroix's neck."

He straightened, pushing his weight off the small secretary with enough force to rock it. She took an involuntary step back, her lips parting in surprise or in fear.

He had read that emotion in her eyes when he'd thrown open the screen door this morning and headed toward her across the porch. He had sensed it again tonight when he had grabbed her arm in the darkness. Of course, that had been deliberate, calculated to shock. He had wanted to throw her off balance to see how she'd react, and up until this moment she hadn't let him rattle her. He'd been impressed by how well she'd handled herself. Now, however, her anxiety was clear.

Way to go, Stanton. You're doing a great job scaring the bejesus out of a woman, he jeered silently, still watching her eyes. Reading in them the ongoing struggle to reassert control and to hide that telltale surge of anxiety.

"I'm not providing you with *anything*," he reiterated. "Whatever you think you've found in that picture, I wasn't wrong about Tom Delacroix. And you can tell Lorena that as long as there's breath in my body, I'll continue to say her husband was a murdering son of a bitch who strangled his own daughter to keep her from crying out while he raped her."

The impact of that brutal description was reflected briefly in Callie Evers' eyes. This time she didn't shrink away. Not from them or from his anger. Instead, she took the single step that would bring her back to the desk and touched the picture she had placed there.

"Then how do you explain the similarity between the two murders?" she asked. "How do you explain that other rose?"

"As far as I know, it doesn't exist. Unless, of course, you have some *proof*."

If she had, she would have put the two pictures on the table together. That's the way you did something like this. You laid everything out at the beginning if you wanted to force the person you were questioning to examine it and admit the implications. She hadn't. She had shown him only what he had already known.

"I can assure you the case is well-documented."

The flush of color had increased along her cheekbones. And he didn't think it was conviction this time.

"We're through here, Ms. Evers. I might have listened to you if you could have shown me—"

"July 9th, 1975. And in case you don't know where Tom Delacroix was on that date, I'll tell you. He was in the middle of a court-ordered alcohol abuse rehab. Under lock and key."

There had been one of those, Ben knew, although he wasn't sure of the dates. A six-month sentence, which should have been much longer considering the multiple D.U.I.'s, the last of which had involved leaving the scene of an accident. It would have been longer if it hadn't been for his father's money and position.

"Proof," Ben said, the word very soft and yet demanding.

"The courthouse burned. The records of the murder—"

He reached out and shoved the photograph that lay between them toward her. The picture sailed over the edge of the fold-down desktop. He didn't even watch it. He watched her instead.

Her eyes followed the photo as it floated to the floor. Only when it landed did they come back up to his.

"It *was* in the papers," she said calmly.

"Police reports, autopsy report, autopsy photographs," Ben enumerated. "You have *any* of those?"

"I told you. The courthouse where those records were stored burned in the early eighties."

"That's too bad," he said. "Or it's *really* convenient. I guess that depends on your point of view, doesn't it?"

"I have the clippings."

"Affidavits?"

She nodded. "From the reporter. He says the sheriff—"

"You have an affidavit from him? From the sheriff?"

The pause was too long, so that again he knew what her answer would be before she gave it.

"He's dead. I talked to his widow, who remembered him mentioning the rose. And the reporter—"

"Either one of those people claim to have seen this rose you're so excited about?"

"No," she said, her voice low.

"And that's your case?" he mocked. He hardened his voice. "You got *nothing,* Ms. Evers. Believe me, I wish you did."

She laughed, the sound harsh enough that its bitterness surprised him. "No, you don't. That's your worst nightmare. The thought that somebody might prove you were wrong. You hung your reputation on Tom Delacroix's guilt. You blamed the Delacroix's money and influence for your failure to solve a little girl's murder. You can't stand to even *consider* the possibility that you might have screwed up."

Maybe it wasn't his worst nightmare, but it was damned close. *Too damned close.*

He held her eyes, saying nothing. They weren't nose-to-nose as he had been with Doak, but they were close enough that he could see flecks of brown in the gray-green irises of her eyes.

And just as he had characterized the nature of the police chief's anger as mostly bluster, he acknowledged that hers was not. Whatever she had come here for, whether Lorena had anything to do with it or not, Callie Evers believed what she had just said.

"You don't know anything about my worst nightmare, Ms. Evers. For your sake, I'll pray you never have to find out."

Without another word, he turned and left the room, walking through Phoebe Robinson's darkened house as if he had lived here all his life. He didn't remember to take another breath until he was outside, in the familiar heat of a summer night.

He closed the front door behind him and allowed his body to sag against it. Then he closed his eyes, which were burning. He rubbed at them with the heels of both hands. When he realized what he was doing, he forced his hands away, pressing his palms flat on the door behind him. Finally, pushing against it he straightened, moving upright in stages like an old man.

As he started up the path to his truck, the smell of something foul drifted up to him from the water. His steps didn't slow, the odor slipping virtually unnoticed into the unwanted images that were bombarding his consciousness.

They would linger there all night, tormenting him. Just as they had ten years before.

CHAPTER FOUR

"CALLIE? WAKE UP, DEAR."

Her name, accompanied by Phoebe's genteel pounding on the door, pulled her out of the pit of exhausted, dreamless sleep she had finally fallen into. She opened her eyes, expecting to find daylight seeping in from behind the curtains she'd pulled over the windows of her room after Ben Stanton had left last night.

It was pitch dark instead. Her eyes sought the lighted numerals of the bedside clock, as her hostess knocked again.

"Wake up, dear," the disembodied voice from behind the door called. "You don't want to miss this."

Since she had just discovered it was 3:20 a.m., Callie decided that whatever Phoebe was talking about, she was perfectly willing to miss it. She closed her eyes, trying unsuccessfully to slip back into sleep. Lying in the darkness, she slowly became aware of a dull throbbing at her temples.

And she knew why it was there. Not only had she examined the photograph after Stanton left, even pulling out her maligned magnifying glass to do so, she had spent the following hours tossing and turning. Endlessly analyzing what she thought she had seen in that picture, as well as every word the ex-chief of police had said. Desperately trying to convince herself that, despite Stanton's denial, she hadn't been wrong.

"Callie, honey?"

She opened her eyes, focusing them on the ceiling above her head. She didn't answer, hoping that if she ignored Phoebe long enough, she'd give up and go away.

"You really need to get up, Callie. It's a jubilee."

Jubilee? The only meaning her sleep-deprived brain could assign to the term came from a hymn her grandmother had sung to her when she was a little girl. Something about Judgment Day.

The half-remembered reference to the end of the world and Phoebe's urgency were spur enough that she pushed up, propping on her elbow to consider the bedroom door. She felt disoriented, both from the lack of sleep and the too-abrupt awakening.

Her lips had parted, her mind trying to formulate an answer to a summons she didn't understand, when the door opened a crack. As she watched, the old woman's face, topped by its stock of disordered white hair, appeared within it.

"Oh, good," Phoebe said. "You're awake."

"What's wrong?" She considered possible disasters, ranging from fire to an approaching hurricane, that might require her hostess to wake her at this time of the morning.

"Nothing's wrong. It's a jubilee. Tommy called to tell me, and I didn't want you to miss it. I'll go get you my waders."

The face in the crack disappeared, although light from the hall continued to pour through it. Callie closed her mouth, feeling as if she must have come in on the middle of something.

She glanced again at the clock, just to make sure it really said what she'd thought. There was no mistake, and by now she was awake enough to know that she wasn't dreaming, as much as she might wish she were. Obviously, something was happening Phoebe felt she should see. Or that she would *want* to see. Something that involved water, if "waders" meant what she thought they did.

And suddenly, emerging from some dark recess in the back of her mind, an item she had run across while doing research on this area swam upward in her consciousness. Her writer's instincts had apparently filed it away for future reference. *Jubilee.*

"Here you go," Phoebe said, pushing the door open.

Despite the heat, the old lady was wearing a chenille wrapper over her nightgown, and she was carrying a pair of long rubber boots, one in each hand. Callie identified them immediately. *Waders.* At least she hadn't been wrong about that.

"What are those for?" she asked, although she was afraid she knew. She sat up, running her fingers through her hair.

"I'd just feel better if you wear them. Some don't, but Hobart always did. He made the boys wear them, too."

"Phoebe, I really don't think—"

"Anything out in that ocean can come ashore during a jubilee," Phoebe went on, ignoring her aborted protest. "The good *and* the bad. This way," she said, holding the boots up shoulder high, "you got some protection from rays and such."

Rays? As in stingrays? If so…

"Come on, now," Phoebe urged again. "You don't want to take a chance on missing this. No guarantee there'll be another one while you're here."

As soon as Callie had figured out exactly what rays Phoebe was talking about, her mind began formulating a couple of very *good* reasons for missing it. Before she could voice them, another, more practical thought intruded.

She earned a major portion of her income by writing local color stories for publications that specialized in exactly this kind of regional phenomena. She was sure there had been articles about jubilees through the years, but she couldn't remember any recent ones. Not in the magazine that was the primary market for her features *and* which represented her biggest paychecks.

She had always intended to produce a few freelance pieces while she was in the area. This one was being handed to her on a silver platter. And she literally couldn't afford to pass it up.

She threw the sheet off her bare legs and stepped onto the floor. The worn hardwood was cool under her feet.

Phoebe's eyes considered the length of thigh exposed by her little boy-leg pajamas before she pulled her gaze back up to Callie's face.

"And wear long pants," she advised, laying the waders across the footboard of the bed. "No telling what you'll run into. I'll be out on the back porch waiting for you."

No telling what you'll run into. Not the most enticing prospect she'd ever been offered. Money was money, however. She didn't have enough that she could pass up the opportunity.

As she pulled clothes out of the drawers of the old-fashioned highboy, she became aware of the sound of distant voices, their excitement clear. Despite Phoebe's unintentionally dire warnings, she could feel her own anticipation building.

As she dressed, she tried to dredge up what she could remember from the article she'd stumbled across. Not much, she realized, as she struggled into her jeans, sucking in her stomach to get the zipper up.

Jubilees were unique to the eastern shore of Mobile Bay. In spite of Phoebe's warning about "everything out there" rushing to the shore, they weren't fish kills. And that, she decided as she pulled a knit top over her head, was the extent of her knowledge.

There would be plenty of people willing to enlighten her about whatever was happening on the beach tonight. A lot more than would be willing to talk to her about the Delacroix case. Maybe she could use that to her advantage. Make some kind of inroads within the closemouthed local population.

She rummaged in the bottom of her closet, debating the best kind of footwear. She settled for a pair of worn sneakers. If they got ruined, it would be no great loss.

On her way to the door, she picked up the waders her hostess had draped over the footrail of the bed, holding them out to evaluate their size. They looked as if they would fit, which meant they hadn't been bought for Phoebe. They had probably been handed down, maybe from the father Phoebe was always talking about or from Hobart. Maybe even from one of her sons.

Callie slung the waders over her arm, their rubber feet bouncing against her thigh as she crossed the room to grab her camera off the table by the door.

Slipping its strap over her head, she took one last look around the bedroom. It felt as if she were forgetting something. Despite the nagging sensation, she couldn't think of anything else she could possibly need.

And since she wasn't planning on getting into the water, she realized she could leave the rubber boots here. Her arm had already begun the motion that would drop them on the table when she remembered she wasn't going out there to sightsee. It was possible she would need to become physically involved in the clamor she could hear in the distance.

Better safe than sorry, she decided. She'd take the waders and decide what to do with them when she got down to the bay.

IF THE POPULATION of Point Hope was almost a thousand, as she'd been told, at least a tenth of them were gathered on the strip of beach when she arrived. Someone had set portable lights up on the bulkhead and pointed them at the water. They illuminated the scene like a movie set.

She expected to find the bay churning with fish, fighting their way inland like whales trying to beach themselves. The shallows were filled with people instead, some in bathing suits and others in what appeared to be street clothes.

The containers they were using were as diverse as their attire, everything from nets to metal buckets to Styrofoam ice chests. Well beyond the area illuminated by the lights, a couple of skiffs patrolled, shadowy figures on board pulling up seine nets heavy enough that they were awkward to handle.

"First jubilee?"

Callie turned to find Tommy Burge, dressed in a dark polo-style shirt and khaki walking shorts, coming toward the beach from between the two houses behind her. He was carrying a long pole with a spike on the end in one hand and an open willow basket in the other.

She nodded, grateful to see a familiar face. "And I'm not sure what I'm supposed to do."

"Got a bucket of some kind?" he asked.

"I think I'd rather just take pictures of everyone else."

"Get out in the water beyond the lights and shoot back at them," Tommy advised, his eyes skating over the crowd.

She considered the people in the shallows, each of them intent on scooping up whatever was in the water. No one was paying attention to anyone else around them, which provided a great opportunity for some candid shots.

"Well, got to go," Tommy said taking a step toward the bay. "They never last long in August."

"Of course," she said. "You go on. I'll be fine. I may just watch from here."

Her eyes followed Burge as he jogged across the strip of coarse grass that separated the row of oaks from the water. She framed a couple of shots of the beach, realizing with the second that she couldn't manage the camera effectively and hold onto Phoebe's waders. She debated whether or not to put them on, but she was beginning to perspire. She could imagine how much hotter it would be with a layer of rubber covering her jeans.

She laid the boots on the ground, looking around at the surrounding landmarks to make sure she could find them again. Hands free except for the camera, she walked toward the bay.

Burge had been right, she realized when she reached the bulkhead. Since the beach was so narrow, she would have to be *in* the water to get the shots she needed. Not looking into those powerful lamps, as he had suggested, but taking advantage of them to light the scene. Maybe...to the side of the area that was the center of activity? she wondered, glancing in that direction.

Buck Dolan was sitting on the wall of pilings that formed the boundary between the land and the beach. He was smoking a cigarette, holding it affectedly between his thumb and finger. As she watched, he tilted his head, blowing a cloud of smoke upward. Illuminated by the lights, it drifted toward her.

"They're called floundering lights. Appropriate."

"Why appropriate?" she asked.

His profile, as classic as those on old Greek coins, was silhouetted against the lights he was describing. She thought again what a striking man he must have been, especially now that darkness hid the effects of age and climate she'd noticed before.

"Most of what's out there will be flounder. Plenty of crabs and shrimp. Some cats. Eels. The occasional mullet or spec, although the shrimpers have taken care of most of those."

The last part of that explanation meant nothing to her, but she assumed from its context that he was still talking about different species of fish. "Are they safe to eat?" she asked.

It was obvious they were, or these people wouldn't be out here. She needed to ask him something, however, to keep the conversation going. Dolan was a local resident, and he seemed willing to tell her whatever she wanted to know about this, even if he hadn't been willing to talk about the murder.

"They aren't sick. The oxygen in the water just gets too low. Nobody knows why. Maybe rain or the heat or an influx of fresh water from the rivers that empty into the bay. Whatever it is, it mostly affects the bottom dwellers. I've seen flounder going for pennies a pound after a good jubilee."

"Fishermen can't be too happy with that," she said.

He turned his head, looking directly at her for the first time. She wondered how clearly he could see her, considering the placement of the lights.

"They'll take whatever they catch to the markets in Mobile, Gulf Shores, and Pensacola, and they'll make a *very* good profit from just a couple of hours worth of work. You won't hear any fishermen complaining about a jubilee."

Turning back to face the water, he took another drag, blowing the smoke into the air.

"Are they shrimping out there?" she asked, nodding toward the distant boats. When she remembered that he probably couldn't see the gesture, she added. "The men in the boats, I mean."

"Shrimp and a little bit of everything else, I expect. Beggars can't be choosers."

There was a thread of amusement in the comment. As she watched, he threw the stub of his cigarette in a glowing arc toward the water. Her eyes followed it automatically, and she wondered for a second or two if it might hit one of the milling people. When no one reacted, it was apparent it hadn't, but the unthinking, or uncaring, gesture bothered her.

"You're not fishing?" she asked, bringing her eyes back to Dolan and trying to keep that reaction out of her voice.

"I'm an observer, Miss Evers. It is miss, isn't it?"

"It is," she agreed. "An observer?"

"Of my fellow man. It's a fascinating study."

"I can imagine," she said noncommittally.

She couldn't decide if Dolan were hinting that he could give her information about his fellow citizens. For some reason, despite her need for that, the suggestion made her uneasy, as encountering a tattletale in school might once have.

"Having any luck?" Dolan asked.

Despite what she'd been thinking, she wasn't sure if he were referring to her camera, the fish or her interest in the murder.

"With your book, I mean," he clarified.

"Some."

"I'm surprised. I thought people around here had just as soon forget that murder ever occurred."

"Why do you suppose that is?" she asked, injecting interest into her voice. Tattletale or not, this was why she was here. She might not like Buck Dolan, and she wasn't sure why she didn't, but he was a potential source of information.

"Fear," he said.

Fear? "Of what?" The interest this time was genuine.

"That all their dirty little secrets might get exposed."

"Are there dirty little secrets?"

"Dozens."

His voice was again amused, slightly cynical. Of course, what he said could only be the truth. Even in a town this small, there were bound to be things people didn't want exposed to the relentless glare of more publicity.

"Would any of those secrets make good stories?" she asked, wondering where he was going with this. Was there something he wanted to tell her? Was this his rather cryptic way of revealing information he thought she should know? Or was it something more personal. Something vindictive.

"A few. Isn't that what you're here for? To figure out which ones will and which ones won't?"

"I'm here because a little girl was murdered and the murderer was never punished," she said fighting to hide her distaste for what he was doing.

"Then I take it you don't buy into Stanton's theory?"

"Even if Delacroix did it, he was never punished," she said.

"Do you think he did?"

"That's what I'm here to find out," she evaded.

"Ever think about the consequences if he didn't?"

"I'm not sure I understand."

"The consequences of you stirring this all up again. Stanton let it drop years ago because he was convinced he knew who the murderer was and couldn't get him. However, if you succeed in proving that Delacroix didn't do it…"

He left the sentence hanging, but by now, she had figured out what he was doing. "Are you trying to warn me this could be dangerous?"

"I'm sure you were aware of that when you came. After all, there's no statute of limitations on murder."

"Then you believe the murderer is still alive?"

"I guess I'll have to read your book to find out, won't I?"

The amusement was back, along with a strong dose of sarcasm. Dolan stood, brushing sand off the back of his trousers.

"Well, this has been very pleasant," he said. "You have fun down there, you hear? Don't let the crabs get your toes."

Or the bedbugs bite. Everybody wanted to warn her against something.

"I won't," she said. "Maybe we can talk more later?"

"Of course. We'll all be at Phoebe's again next Tuesday."

The last was thrown over his shoulder as he headed up the slight rise toward the path that connected the old houses. Whatever message Buck Dolan had wanted to convey when he had spoken to her had been delivered.

She watched until she could no longer distinguish his shape in the shadows under the moss-draped oaks. And when she turned back toward the water, she realized that the people, still scooping fish into their containers, had drifted a few hundred feet further along the beach. A couple of men were moving the lights to that location.

Put up or shut up time, Callie thought, walking reluctantly down to the water. It looked as black as the night sky, and she could see nothing alive in it. The jubilee had moved past this stretch of beach, and if she were going to get any usable pictures, she would have to follow it.

A wave lapped over her shoes, soaking them and a couple of inches of the bottom of her jeans. The water wasn't cold, but it was cooler than the air around her. Surprisingly pleasant.

She glanced to her right, watching the crowd while Tommy Burge's words echoed in her mind. *They never last long in August.* She tried to pick him out, but she couldn't. Maybe he had already filled his basket and left.

His advice had been sound. The best shots would *be* from

the water. And she was now off to the side of the activity, just where she'd decided she needed to be for her pictures.

Another wave washed over her feet, and steeling herself, she stepped into the bay, walking into the water as it retreated. She had anticipated that it might get deep fairly quickly, since everyone was staying close to shore. Instead, even though she waded farther out than any of the townspeople, it was only slightly above her knees. And still pleasant.

Maybe if there had been any of the things Phoebe had warned her about visible in the water, she might not have been so brave. Once she was away from that line of cream that formed when the waves touched the narrow beach, the water seemed as calm as a lake. As warm as bathwater.

She lifted her camera, sighting through it. She touched the button to activate the zoom. It was so quiet she could hear the small mechanical purr as the motor sent the lens out. She framed a shot and squeezed. And then another, this one of a mother helping her little boy scoop fish into a plastic sand bucket, its fluorescent yellow vivid in the glare of the lights.

Smiling, she moved back a couple of steps, trying for a wider angle. Someone shouted, and several of the people she had been focusing on straightened, pointing down the beach.

Curious, she lifted her head, looking up at them over the top of the camera. At that moment something hit the back of her knees hard enough that she staggered forward.

Ray? Or, my God, a shark. Could that have been a shark?

The thoughts flew through her brain as she floundered, arms windmilling to maintain her balance. She knew she had to stay out of the water where whatever had hit her was swimming.

By the time she had remembered there were people on the beach and that she could scream to attract their attention, a hand had closed over her mouth. It pulled her backward, trying to topple her into the dark water. She fought to escape, clawing at the fingers that were clamped over her mouth, even as she staggered back. She had time for one terrified breath before something swept her legs from under her and she was pulled down into the brackish darkness of the bay.

CHAPTER FIVE

FRANTIC, no longer a sentient creature, but something primitive and unthinking, she struggled against the hand which inexorably held her under. Fighting to get her face above the surface. Fighting to draw another breath.

She was propelled relentlessly backward, pulled into deeper water as her fingers tore at the forearm that was wrapped under her chin. Her assailant had obviously been prepared for her initial reaction because he had placed his other hand, palm down, on her forehead to make sure she couldn't get her head above the surface. No matter how much she fought, she couldn't escape that implacable hold.

Her world had shrunk to a formless void of black water. There was nothing but its airless environment and those controlling hands. Sheer animal terror and a will to survive she hadn't known she possessed made her keep struggling. She twisted and turned, clawing futilely at his arm as she was towed farther and farther away from shore.

Finally, deprived too long of oxygen, she felt her strength and resolve begin to fail. She couldn't hold her breath any longer. The instinct to fill her lungs with something, even if it were the deadly water that surrounded her, was too strong.

There was one last cogent second when she knew with absolute clarity she going to die. Even in the midst of the terrifying realization, she understood, on some level at least, that only a few hundred yards away people moved along the beach, heads down, eyes locked on the teeming waters of this same bay. Not one of them aware of the life-

and-death struggle occurring in the moonless darkness behind them.

As the powerful hand on her brow held her under, consciousness began to fade. The mist formed first at the edges of her ability to think, blurring it. And then, moving with appalling suddenness, it spiraled inward, as if someone were turning a lens, closing the shutter of a camera.

Her body went limp. Her arms and legs, no longer capable of fighting, floated weightless in the water. She was no longer aware of its womb-like warmth. No longer capable of sensation.

Just before the last particle of light blinked out at the center of that collapsing vortex, the hand on her forehead and the arm around her throat suddenly released. His palms slipped beneath her shoulders, pushing upward with such force that her face broke the surface violently.

Either the shock of the blow or the abrupt change in position jerked her out of that apathetic surrender. Her first response was to draw breath, to pull life-giving oxygen into her starving lungs, which could then feed her dying brain. The second instinct, following within less than a heartbeat, was to expel the water she had inhaled. And those two vitally necessary acts were mutually exclusive.

Blind and deaf, she alternately gasped and choked and coughed. Water poured from her nose and gushed from her mouth in between the whooping, gagging breaths she drew. She flailed at the surface to keep afloat until she could reestablish the seemingly forgotten pattern of drawing air into her lungs.

Through the eternity that took, she never thought about where her attacker might be. All she was capable of at that moment was trying to restore an automatic, physiological process with which she had never before in her life had to be concerned. One which now seemed impossible.

Gradually—so gradually that she was almost unaware it was happening—she spewed forth the vileness she had swallowed and replaced it with gulps of air. The sound of them was so loud they echoed in her ears as her senses began to return.

She was alive. *She was alive.*

Then, just as that realization formed, hands grasped her shoulders again. Despite the numbing exhaustion which had, only seconds before, seemed overwhelming, panic gave her renewed strength. And a boundless determination. He would not pull her under again. She couldn't let him, because this time, weakened as she was, she knew she would die.

Screaming with rage, she raised her fists, beating at a face she couldn't see, flailing at it as wildly as she had at the water that had almost taken her life. In response the hands tightened painfully, digging into her flesh, even through the water-logged fabric of her knit shirt. Her assailant held her at arm's length, and still she struck out at him. And then suddenly, unexpectedly, the hard fingers released her.

Attempting to clear the water out of streaming, salt-seared eyes, she bobbed on the surface like a cork. Squinting first to the right, toward the blur of lights she knew represented the shore. Then to the left, blinking blindly at the void of sea and night sky. And then behind her.

There was nothing there. Nothing disturbed the tranquil water around her. Her relief lasted only long enough for her heart to begin to beat again. Long enough to allow her to draw another wheezing breath.

Directly behind her, the water exploded with the sound of something big breaking the surface. Two arms, their muscles like cables, wrapped around her body, locking hers to her sides.

"Stop it, damn it," a voice grated in her ear.

Her head, the only part of her upper body she could freely move, thrashed from side to side, as she twisted her torso. Neither had an effect on the man holding her captive. Desperate, she kicked backward, trying to drive her heels into his shins. The water defeated her, making those frantic blows puny.

"Stop it," he demanded again, shaking her hard enough that her head snapped back against the wall of his chest. "You're going to drown us both."

You're going to drown us both... The words were so illogical, given he was trying to kill her, that despite her terror, they reverberated in her brain. You're going to drown us both...

Stunned by the thought that he could believe she might not want to drown him or that he might not want to drown her, she stopped struggling. It was not a conscious decision so much as an admission that her reserves of strength were at an end. And if he really didn't intend to kill her...

"It's Stanton. I've got you. Now stop it," he ordered again. Unnecessarily, this time.

As soon as she ceased writhing, his arms loosened minutely, allowing her room to draw a breath. And another. They began to come faster, the harsh, jerking sound of them audible. Telling.

Not attempts to draw air into her lungs. She was sobbing because she had just realized she wasn't dead. And because she had finally decided that the man who was holding her from behind wasn't the one who had been trying to kill her.

Not a villain. She had thought that before, when he had grabbed her arm last night. She had known it on some instinctive level that was as primitive as the one which had forced her to struggle against whoever held her head under water.

She turned her body within Ben Stanton's embrace and wrapped her arms around his neck, clinging to him as if doing that were the most natural thing in the world. Her reaction caught him unprepared. For a fraction of a second, the powerful motion of his feet, kicking in the darkness below them, faltered.

They began to sink, slipping far enough into the water that its saline warmth trickled into her nostrils. Terrified again, she clutched Stanton tighter, attempting to climb him. Her legs wrapped around his and using the strong muscles of her thighs, she surged upward until her chin was above his shoulder.

He began to kick again, propelling them both above the surface. His arms tightened around her once more. Not in anger this time, but in comfort. To offer reassurance.

"I've got you," he said, his deep voice infinitely soothing. "It's okay. Everything's going to be okay."

She nodded, her chin rubbing against the cotton shirt he wore. Her sobs had lessened, sounding now like the snubbing noises a baby makes when it has cried too long and too hard.

"You got her?" a voice called from behind them.

She refused to turn her head. She rested her cheek against Stanton's shoulder, feeling the rise and fall of his breathing. She could feel his heart, beating beneath her own. It was racing, not from fear as was hers, but because of his exertions.

"Get in closer," he called, "and I'll hand her up."

His hands fitted under her armpits, preparing to lift her up to the owner of the other voice. A man, she realized, in one of the boats she had noticed earlier. It was right beside them, swaying gently in the low swells.

Her face buried against Stanton's neck, she could hear the slap of the water against its side. She could also hear the questioning shouts from the people on the shore, probably in response to her screams. She ignored both, clinging like a limpet to the man holding her.

"You're going to have to help," Stanton said. There was a thread of impatience in his voice now, but it was still calm, still reassuring. "I'll lift you up as much as I can, but you're going to have to pull yourself over the side."

She wanted to refuse. She didn't want him to stop holding her. She didn't want to have to take her arms from around his neck. She didn't want to move, not even to get out of the water, which she now abhorred.

There was something about the authority in that demand, however, that reached the innermost part of her. The part that was still a child, terrified by the darkness.

You're going to have to go back to your own bed, her mother would say, taking her by the hand. No matter how much she cried and begged, each night it was the same. *You're going to have to go back to your own bed.*

This was that same reasonable tone. And despite her fear, it evoked the learned response. She turned her head to look over her shoulder. A man she had never seen before was leaning over the side of the skiff. She turned back, searching Stanton's face for reassurance.

In the darkness, his features were indistinct, but she could distinguish his eyes from the surrounding skin. She couldn't read the expression in them, but like her mother's voice, coming to her in the middle of a nightmare, she knew they would be determined. A determination too strong for her present weakness.

She nodded, and then she released her death-grip on his neck, turning toward the skiff that was as close to them as the moving water would allow.

There was nothing graceful or athletic about the process she employed to get out of the water and into the boat. Once she had made the decision to do what Stanton had told her she must, she moved with an eagerness that belied her physical exhaustion.

She scrambled upward, Stanton pushing her from behind, his hands impersonally under her buttocks. The man in the boat pulled her up, his hands underneath her arms.

In a matter of seconds, she was sitting on one of the boat's flat metal seats. Her feet rested on top of a mass of tangled nets, which still contained whatever they had borne out of the sea. Dragged from it, just as she had been.

The hull rocked violently as Stanton pulled himself onboard. She clutched the sides of the boat, knuckles whitened, frightened it would overturn and throw them back into the bay. The skiff gradually steadied, and by the time it had, Stanton was kneeling beside her, wrapping the dry warmth of the other man's shirt around her trembling shoulders. It was only then she realized that she had lost the camera during that desperate struggle.

"Get out too far?" he asked, trying to pull the edges of the garment together, despite the fact that her fingers were still locked around the sides of the boat.

Stanton's gaze was level with hers, examining her face in the light of the flashlight the fisherman held. She couldn't imagine what he saw, but his eyes were both compassionate and concerned.

Relishing her safety, she didn't understand at first what he had asked her. *Get out too far?* Which implied...

"He tried to kill me," she said.

The blue eyes narrowed. "Tried to *kill* you?" The inflection had jumped at the end. "*Who* tried to kill you?"

Her teeth had begun to chatter. "A man," she managed through lips gone numb.

She wasn't sure how she could be so certain it had been a man, since she hadn't seen his face. The impression of his hands, their fingers incredibly powerful, was indelibly imprinted on her senses. It *had* been a man. Another woman wouldn't have been strong enough to control her frenzy.

"Who?" Stanton asked, as if he really expected she would be able to tell him.

He glanced up at his companion, who was still holding the flashlight. Her eyes followed automatically, and then she blinked, ducking her head against the intensity of its beam. She could see nothing of the face behind its glare.

"I don't know," she said. By now she was shaking so badly that the words came out as a stutter. "I couldn't see him. He held my head under."

Stanton's eyes had returned to hers, and he nodded as if that made sense. As if, thank God, he accepted the explanation. His next question ruined that surge of gratitude.

"You sure you didn't get tangled up with something?" he asked. "A lot of flotsam gets washed in with the tide."

Flotsam. The word brought back the stench of decay that had drifted up from the water's edge earlier tonight. Then it had been Stanton's hand, coming unexpectedly out of a similar darkness, that held her.

With that memory came the first splinter of suspicion. Ben Stanton had been out in the water with her. And apparently neither he nor the other man in this boat was going to admit to seeing anyone else out there.

"He put his hand over my face," she said, the words coming in spurts. "He held my head under. It wasn't flotsam, damn it. Somebody tried to drown me."

She could hear the edge of hysteria in her tone. What had happened to her was bad enough, but not to be believed—

"I didn't see anybody else," Stanton said.

Maybe it wasn't meant to be the accusation it seemed, but she was beyond trying to read nuances.

"Murderers usually don't want to be *seen*," she said.

It didn't come off quite as she'd intended, but it was difficult to be sarcastic when you were shaking hard enough to make the words quaver. The gratitude she had felt when she'd realized Stanton wasn't her attacker, but her rescuer, had faded, replaced by anger and resentment.

"Okay," he said, his voice still calm and as authoritative as it had been in the water. "That makes sense. Charlie, let's go take a look," he suggested to the man holding the light.

Whoever Charlie was, he moved quickly to obey, heading toward the seat beside the outboard motor at the back of the boat. He took the flashlight with him.

No longer pinned by its light, Callie lowered her eyes, and forced her fingers to loosen their grip on the sides of the boat. She brought them together, entwining them in her lap instead. The blood rushed back into their flattened tips, stinging, but she welcomed the pain. Something to feel besides fear.

She was breathing in jerky, too-audible inhalations. She worked on deepening them, determined to control the sounds they made. Stanton hadn't moved, still crouching on the balls of his bare feet in front of her.

She jumped when Charlie started the engine, and he reached out, putting his hand over hers. It was big enough to cover both of them, and it was warm and hard, the palm and the fingers callused. *Unmistakably masculine.* Just as those that had touched her face had been.

"He had big hands," she said. "As big as yours."

"Okay," he said again.

He sounded interested. And still calm, despite what she was telling him. *Professional,* she realized. This was probably a tone he had perfected through countless interrogations. And then, perversely, she wondered how many suspects Stanton could possibly have interrogated in a place like this.

A place where someone just tried to kill me.

"I'm not making this up," she said defensively.

"I never said you were. That's why we're going back to take a look." His eyes considered the water as Charlie slowly guided the boat in circles, his flashlight moving in all directions.

In the stillness, Callie realized that the sound of the motor, loud enough to block the voices that had been coming from the beach, was familiar. She had been aware of its vibration before. While she was under water? Or while she had been absorbed by that paroxysm of coughing? Recently, in any case.

Which meant that Stanton couldn't possibly have been the one holding her under. She felt guilty, as well as stupid, for having allowed herself even to consider that it *could* have been him. Ben Stanton might despise the media, but he wasn't the kind of man who would try to kill to keep the story of Kay-Kay's death from coming under public scrutiny again. No one—

No one? The thought was unbelievable and then unbelievably logical. *No one but the real murderer could possibly care enough about that to commit murder. Another murder.*

"It was him," she said, the words only a breath.

Despite their softness, Stanton turned, his eyes questioning. She replayed in her head the chain of logic that had led her to that conclusion and found no fault in it. There was no one else who would feel anything more than annoyance and aggravation if she produced the book she claimed she was here to write. No one except the person who had the most to lose by having the investigation of the Delacroix murder reopened.

"Don't you see?" she asked Stanton. "This *proves* it."

Her teeth were no longer chattering as the heat of excitement raced through her veins. She wasn't dead, thanks to Stanton, and now she knew she was right. She had been right all along. She had just had it confirmed in a way that not even he could deny.

"Proves what?"

"That was Kay-Kay's murderer in the water," she said. "It had to be. And now you'll have to admit I was right. Because whoever that was out there tonight, it wasn't Tom Delacroix."

"WHY DON'T WE go through the sequence again."

"Land sakes, Doak," Phoebe said, her accent stronger for her exasperation. "Even *you* ought to have it letter-perfect by now."

Callie glanced up at that, but there was no reaction in the broad brown face of the police chief. Either he hadn't realized he'd just been insulted, or he was honoring another long-standing regional tradition. The elderly were allowed to speak their minds, no matter how rude or insulting their thoughts might be.

Callie was grateful for Phoebe's intervention. They were sitting in the front parlor of her house, and they had been over everything that had happened out in the bay at least a half dozen times.

After they had finished searching the water, Charlie had guided the skiff to the shore. Then, in front of all those gape-mouthed people, Ben Stanton had picked her up, without asking permission or announcing his intent, and waded through the shallows with her in his arms. As embarrassing as that had been, she had been infinitely grateful he hadn't suggested she step out of the boat and back into that black water.

As soon as they reached the house, Phoebe had taken charge, helping her strip off her wet clothing and bundling her, still shivering, back into her pajamas. Withers' arrival, announced by the doorbell, had interrupted them as Phoebe was rubbing Callie's hair dry between the ends of a thick towel.

The old woman had gone to answer it, leaving Callie to finish the task. When Phoebe returned, she had belted her own chenille bathrobe around Callie and then led her down to the room where the two men had been waiting.

Stanton hadn't changed clothes. The whole time Doak was asking his questions, he leaned against the wall of Phoebe's front parlor, the water that dripped from the bottom of his jeans forming small, gleaming puddles on the hardwood floor.

During the course of the interview, he hadn't said much, but Callie had been aware of his eyes intently focused on her face. Maybe because she hadn't made the accusation she had blurted out in the boat.

It wasn't that she doubted the conclusion she'd reached. She had finally realized, however, that broadcasting something like that might make whoever had tried to kill her tonight more determined to succeed the next time.

"...Ms. Evers, so I'm not sure what you want from me."

Jarred from her internal reverie by the sound of her name, Callie looked up. Three pairs of eyes were on her face. And the expression within each of them was subtly different.

"I'm sorry," she said. "I'm afraid...I didn't get all of that." She *was* sorry. Not paying attention to Withers was only going to prolong this. And she needed it to be over.

She needed time to think about what had happened. More important, she needed time to decide what to do about it.

"Nobody sees nothing," Doak said patiently, looking at the notebook where he had written down what she'd told him. "Ben says there was nobody else in the water when

him and Charlie got to you. At least they couldn't see anybody. So…''

"So… What?'' she asked. ''So you think it didn't happen? Is that what you're implying? That I'm making this
up?''

"Of course, he doesn't think that,'' Phoebe said loyally.
"Tell her you don't think that, Doak.''

There was a revealing delay in the affirmation she had
demanded from Withers. He said instead, ''I'm just wondering if you could maybe have been a little bit *mistaken*
about what happened out there. About what you thought
happened.'' He sounded almost apologetic, although it had
been fairly obvious for a while this was the direction he
was going to take.

"Flotsam,'' she said bitterly.

"Ma'am?''

"I suggested Ms. Evers might have gotten tangled up
with some flotsam and panicked.'' Stanton's voice didn't
seem apologetic, although it was impossible to tell from the
inflection what he was thinking.

"Is that possible, ma'am?''

"No,'' Callie said, her eyes on Stanton's.

The moisture made his hair blue-black in the lamplight.
The shirt she had laid her cheek against was a gray T-shirt
that, because of its dampness, clung to his chest like a second skin.

"No,'' she said again, forcing her eyes back to Withers'
earnest face. ''It wasn't flotsam or jetsam or seaweed. Or
anything else the two of you are going to suggest. It was
a man's hands. He put one of them over my mouth so I
couldn't scream, and he pulled me under. Then he shifted
that same arm under my chin, so he could tow me out into
deeper water. Classic lifeguard carry, except he also put his
other hand on my forehead to keep my face under the water. Not flotsam. A man's hands. Believe me, I *know* what
a man's hands feel like.''

Again there was a small, awkward silence. She hadn't
realized the sexual connotation of that unfortunate construc-

tion until it came out of her mouth. Ignoring it, she stood, still concentrating on the current chief of police. For some reason that was easier than having to face Ben Stanton.

"If we're through here…" she said.

That's what Stanton had said to her, she realized. And it sounded like dialogue from one of the lawyer shows on TV.

"Folks are pretty stirred up about this book you're writing. I'd guess somebody's emotions just got a little out of hand," Doak said. "I'd like to apologize to you on behalf of this community, Ms. Evers. This isn't typical of Point Hope. I can tell you that."

"Just somebody having a little fun at my expense? Is that what you're suggesting?"

"Somebody trying to discourage you from what you came here to do," Withers acknowledged.

Someone out to discourage her? Maybe it was comforting to him to believe that.

"If you think of anything else," he continued, sounding almost as professional as Stanton had on the boat, "anything that might help us get a handle on who could have done this—"

Withers had risen as well. She had told her story and answered his questions. And she had heard the theory he was probably going to use tomorrow to explain what had happened to those people who had watched her being pulled from the water and then carried ashore. She couldn't see any point in either of them beating this particular dead horse any longer.

"If I do, I'll call you," she finished for him.

She walked past him, heading for the hallway that led to the stairs. Behind her, she heard Phoebe's voice, her tone querulous, though the words were indistinguishable.

Maybe that was just as well. She really wasn't up to listening to anybody's theories about anything. Not even if Phoebe's were about the police chief's stupidity. It seemed there had been more than enough stupidity to go around tonight. Including hers.

She had come here to discover a murderer, someone who had, to her certain knowledge, killed at least twice. And she had announced her intentions to the world. Then she had walked out into that water, never thinking about the possibility of danger.

Something important had come from tonight's fiasco, she told herself as she climbed the stairs. Because now she knew he was willing to kill again to keep a secret that was more than twenty-six years old.

CHAPTER SIX

"WHEN I HEARD what happened, I just had to come over and make sure you were all right."

Coffee mug suspended in midair, Callie turned her head and found Virginia Wilton standing outside Phoebe's back porch. Her hand was cupped along her forehead, and she was peering in through the screen, her glasses almost touching it.

By now, the whole town had probably heard what happened last night. She was surprised Virginia had been their only visitor. Of course, it was still early, a little after seven. *Give them time,* she thought, remembering the throng that had lined the beach, watching Ben Stanton carry her to shore.

"I'm fine," she said, completing the motion to bring the mug to her mouth.

Neither she nor Phoebe had tried to go back to bed after Stanton and the chief of police had left. Callie had known she wouldn't sleep. Even if she had, she would have dreamed about that endless struggle to breathe and the sensation of dark water rushing over her face as she was dragged farther and farther out.

The screen door creaked, announcing that her answer, not surprisingly, hadn't satisfied Virginia. Callie again turned her gaze away from the sunlight dancing on the surface of the bay and toward the door. Phoebe's friend walked across the porch to lower herself into one of the wicker chairs.

Once seated, she dabbed at her forehead with a lace-edged handkerchief before she asked, "Phoebe inside?"

Callie nodded, feeling no compunction to help the conversation along. Judging by their first meeting, Virginia would be more than willing to do most of the talking.

"So what does Doak think?" her visitor asked, right on cue.

Virginia lifted her hair off the back of her neck to dab the cloth along her nape. Her eyes were still on Callie, who hesitated, unsure how much of what she'd told Withers would be common knowledge. However, knowing small towns...

"He suggested I must have been mistaken about what I thought happened."

"Were you?" Virginia asked, the damp handkerchief balled in her unmoving hand. Her eyes, magnified by the thick lenses, made her look perpetually surprised.

"No."

"You think somebody was really trying to drown you?"

"Somebody held her head under water," Phoebe said from the doorway. "Doak thinks they were trying to scare her. To keep her from writing her book. You want some coffee?"

"Only if you got decaf," Virginia said. "That other stuff gives me palpitations."

Phoebe disappeared back inside the house.

"Doak thinks somebody held your head under the water to scare you?" Virginia asked, picking up where she'd left off.

"The other version is that I must have gotten tangled up in some seaweed and just *thought* someone was holding me."

Virginia's hoot of laughter was welcome, Callie decided, taking another sip of coffee.

"Seaweed," the old woman repeated after the cawing sound of it had died away. "That's what this town gets for driving Ben Stanton out of office. I swear Doak don't have sense enough to get in out of the rain."

"The seaweed was Stanton's idea." No need not to share the blame, Callie decided. There was enough to go around.

And she was finding that recounting the highlights of last night's interrogation before an appreciative audience was balm for her anger.

"You're kidding? Or maybe he was," Virginia said. "Because Ben *isn't* a fool. He'd know you aren't one either. Wonder what made him say something that."

"Well, it *is* hard to believe somebody would grab Callie and try to drown her with half the town watching," Phoebe said.

She was carrying a cup and saucer, which tinkled alarmingly in her trembling hand, as well as the glass carafe from the coffeemaker. She set the cup down on the table by Virginia's chair and began to fill it. Although the stream of coffee was wavering, its landing was fairly accurate. From the pocket of her slacks, Phoebe produced a spoon and a packet of artificial sweetener, which she handed over to her guest.

"You ready for a refill?" she asked, turning to Callie as Virginia began to doctor her coffee.

"I'm fine. Sit down and drink yours before it gets cold."

"If I drink any more, I won't sleep for a week. Callie and I been drinking coffee since the police left," Phoebe said, the last directed to her friend. "Beats all I've ever heard."

"I heard Ben made him turn you loose," Virginia said, her magnified eyes studying Callie over the rim of her cup.

"He heard the boat, I think."

"Ben's boat?"

"Stanton and another man, somebody called Charlie, had a skiff out there. I think he must have heard the motor."

In the hours since the incident, she had thought a lot about what had happened, reliving the sequence over and over in her head. Since she remembered hearing the approaching engine, subconsciously at least, she had to assume that her assailant, whose head was above water at all times, had heard it as well.

"He knew it was time to get gone," Phoebe said in agreement. "Good thing for you Ben was out there."

That was something else Callie had been forced to acknowledge. It hadn't been an easy admission to make, but it was nothing less than the truth. Stanton had saved her life, even if he hadn't believed it was in danger.

"I wonder why he was," Callie said. "Out there, I mean. Considering how far away he lives." The comment didn't come out as she'd intended, sounding ungrateful if nothing else.

"That's the way jubilees run," Virginia said, as if that explained everything.

Seeing Callie's blank look, Phoebe explained, "They move south to north like the tide. Ben was probably following it along the shore from the inlet. He'd know where it was headed. Ben knows these waters like the back of his hand."

"Stanton's a fisherman?" As she asked, Callie remembered the boat out at his place. Not the one he was in last night, but the larger, more expensive craft sheltered in the boathouse.

"Charters mostly. That's about the only way to make a living down here anymore," Phoebe said. "There's shrimping, but mostly Ben takes people out in the Gulf. 'Course, he knows all the bays and rivers, too, if they want to do that."

"You think he was bitter being forced to leave office after the murder?" Callie asked.

She should feel guilty about picking their brains. Despite Stanton's reluctance to talk to her, however, he was still one of the people at the very heart of this case. And neither Phoebe nor Virginia seemed averse to discussing him this morning. Distracted by what had happened last night, or sympathetic about her experience, they seemed to have forgotten Callie was an outsider as well as a member of the despised media.

"Bitter?" Phoebe asked, her puzzlement clear. "About what?"

"Well, he does seem to be struggling."

"Struggling? To make a living? That kind of struggling?'' Virginia asked. "What in the world makes you think that?''

"His house,'' Callie said. "How he lives.''

"Oh, the Stantons are just land poor,'' Phoebe said, seeming relieved. "No need to worry about Ben and money.''

"Land poor?''

"You know how those houses out on Mullet Inlet are all built right up next to each other? At least until you get to Ben's?''

They had been, Callie realized. Then there had been a long stretch of pine forest before she had come to the dirt driveway she'd been directed to at the grocery.

"And you saw how isolated Ben's place is?'' Phoebe went on. "Sitting all by itself out in the middle of nowhere?''

"He's the one that owns all that nowhere,'' Virginia chimed in. "That land's been in his family for years.''

"It's not worth what waterfront lots are worth here,'' Phoebe explained. "Not yet anyway, but you just have to look at what's been happening down on Fort Morgan Road to know how that land's going to skyrocket. If he wanted to, Ben could sell off some of it now and never have to work another day in his life. 'Course, the Stantons were never much for selling their land. That's why that tract is all in one piece.''

"So...he didn't need the chief's job?''

"Didn't need it and didn't want it. Ben came home from the army, and we drafted him all over again,'' Phoebe said.

She sounded pleased with the analogy. It was obviously something she had said before. Maybe the whole town had said it when they'd tried to convince Stanton to become their chief law enforcement officer. Given the aging population of this community, they had probably felt they'd pulled off quite a coup when he accepted.

"He was young, and he was smart,'' Virginia added, verifying that speculation. "Besides, he'd had experience with criminal investigations with the army. Whatever they call that.''

"CID," Callie supplied, remembering Buck Dolan's condemnation of that as Stanton's only qualification—and a poor one—for handling a murder case, especially a high-profile one. "So how long did he hold office?"

"Maybe…two years before the murder," Phoebe said. "Maybe a little bit more than that. Then those couple of years after it, while he was trying to solve the case. Up until Tom died, I guess. Then it was like he just gave up.''

"Delacroix died, and Stanton was fired?''

"Resigned. He thought that as long as Tom was alive, he had a chance of getting an indictment.''

"Do *you* think he did it?" Callie asked, watching her eyes.

"I *never* did," Virginia said, speaking eagerly into Phoebe's hesitation. "Tom purely doted on that little girl, and that's a fact. He took her everywhere with him. I never did believe he could do…what they said had been done to her," she said, clarifying without becoming explicit.

Callie didn't remind them that fathers and mothers killed their children all the time, often in ways that seem too bizarre and too horrible for normal people to comprehend. These women had known Tom Delacroix, probably for a long time. And she had asked for their opinions, which she understood would be subjective. That's what she had wanted. What they *felt* about Delacroix's guilt or innocence.

"And if not…?''

Callie deliberately let this question trail, still watching Phoebe's face. She had yet to answer the original inquiry. Maybe out of loyalty to Stanton or because she didn't know what she believed.

It seemed there was something she wanted to say, but for some reason, she was reluctant. Because Virginia was here? Or because she wasn't sure that her opinion wouldn't be repeated? Perhaps in Callie's book.

"If not Tom, you mean?" Virginia asked.

Callie nodded, glancing back at her. "There was another child murder twenty-six years ago in North Carolina. There were several unusual elements about it that were...very much like Kay-Kay's. Tom Delacroix was in rehab at the time, which means that he couldn't have killed that other little girl."

"My stars," Virginia said softly. "Ben know about that?"

"I've told him, but...he doesn't believe they're connected. Maybe because he doesn't want to believe it."

"So whoever killed Kay-Kay was like a serial killer? Is that what you're saying?"

"I'm saying it was someone who had killed before, at least once. And because of the timing of that previous murder, Tom Delacroix has to be excluded as a suspect. So, if it wasn't Delacroix...?" she asked again.

"An intruder," Virginia said, as excited as if she were answering a question in a quiz. "Just like they always said."

That had been the family's explanation. The only one they could make, given the situation.

"Do you believe a stranger would be able to walk into that house," Callie asked, "find the child, and get her out without her father hearing anything?"

"No," Phoebe said.

Callie turned back to her. Phoebe's face had changed, the lines that bracketed her mouth seeming to deepen.

"Whoever killed Kay-Kay had to know the house," she said, conviction strong in her voice. "To know Lorena was gone. And to know that Tom would be dead drunk that time of the night."

"A stranger couldn't have known," Callie reiterated.

Phoebe shook her head. "If it wasn't Tom, it had to be one of us. As much as nobody wanted to admit that, I think we've always known it was true. If you didn't believe Tom had anything to do with Kay-Kay's death, then you had to look at everybody in Point Hope differently after that murder."

"Stanton wasn't willing to do that?"

"I expect because Ben had more reason than just the evidence to want to blame Tom Delacroix," Virginia said.

"You hush," Phoebe hissed, turning angrily on her friend. "That's nothing but gossip, and you know it."

"What is?" Callie asked, feeling a surge of excitement, despite the pall last night's terror had temporarily cast over her enthusiasm for uncovering the secrets this town hid.

Virginia glared back at Phoebe, but she didn't answer.

"What kind of reason?" Callie prodded.

Virginia shook her head, her mouth pursed as if she were physically preventing what she'd hinted at from leaking out.

"Nothing," Phoebe said firmly. "Nothing that's going to be repeated in my house."

"Phoebe, a child was murdered," Callie reasoned. "A little girl you knew and loved. Surely, you want—"

"That's not got a thing to do with what she's talking about. Not one single, solitary thing."

Callie opened her mouth, prepared to argue that anything concerning Stanton and Delacroix probably had had a bearing on the crime. At least on the police chief's investigation of it.

"You see what you started?" Phoebe scolded her friend. "And it's got nothing to do with Kay-Kay's death. You tell her that."

"Ben thought it did, so who are you to say it didn't? You think you're smarter than the chief of police?"

"Ben thought *what* did?" Callie asked again.

Neither of them looked at her, ignoring the question as, eyes locked, they continued what was obviously a battle of wills. A battle in which the two opponents knew one another very well.

"Never you mind," Phoebe said. "That's water over the dam. And it's got no connection to that murder."

The noise Virginia made was both expressive and crude.

"If you're going to act that way, you just go on home,"

Phoebe told her. "We don't need that kind of commonness here."

Oh, yes we do, Callie thought. *We need whatever commonness will let Virginia spill her guts.*

"What the two of you are talking about is obviously old news," she argued. "Delacroix's dead, so what can it possibly hurt to repeat it? Since last night, I'm not sure we can afford to be particular about any aspect of this," she reminded Phoebe.

Not a very subtle plea for sympathy, but maybe a necessary one. *If* she were going to find out what they were talking about.

"They were just trying to scare you," Virginia said.

"He," Phoebe corrected. "There wasn't any *they.*"

With Virginia's about-face, Callie felt as if she had lost an ally. It made her defensive enough to hint at what she had suggested more openly to Stanton last night.

"You think someone held my head under water long enough to make me pass out just to *scare* me? Who in this town could possibly be bothered enough by what I'm doing to do that?"

"There was nothing enjoyable about what we went through at the time of that murder. Nobody who was here then is eager to have that mess stirred up again." Phoebe's eyes released her friend's to focus on Callie. "Nobody."

"Any idea who might be so determined *not* to have it stirred up that they would do that last night?" Callie asked. "And more importantly, *why* they would be that determined?"

She tamped down her disappointment that Phoebe's championing, which had been so welcome last night, had turned into the same resentment she claimed the other townspeople felt.

"I don't know," Phoebe said. "It's not my job to find that out. Doak will talk to the people who were on the beach. Somebody may have seen something. You can't tell until you ask."

Unlikely, Callie thought, since neither Stanton nor Charlie had seen anything. And they'd been *much* closer than anyone else.

"Phoebe—"

"Going on with all this questioning and investigating is just not smart," Phoebe interrupted, her voice almost pleading. "*Or* safe. Surely you can see that. Folks around here aren't happy about what you're doing. Stirring that up again. You need to examine your heart and see if this is really worth it to you."

Folks around here aren't happy about what you're doing. Maybe that was true, but it seemed to her that there was only one person in this town who couldn't afford to risk that she might produce some new evidence about Kay-Kay Delacroix's murder.

"Now Virginia's going on over to her house," Phoebe announced, "and I'm going upstairs to take a nap. And if I were you, Callie, I'd think seriously about packing my bags and heading on back home."

"Do you hear what you're saying?" Callie asked softly.

The fact that Phoebe seemed to be turning against her, even though she was couching her objection in the form of "for your own good," was very disappointing. And disturbing.

"You're the one claiming somebody's trying to hurt you," Phoebe said. "Whether that's true or not—even if they were just trying to scare you—I think if I was you, *I'd* stop doing whatever it is that got somebody angry enough to hold my head under the water. *If* I was you," she repeated, standing up. "You go on home now, Virginia. And try not to say something that'll get somebody mad at *you*."

"Don't you be telling me what to do, Phoebe Mae Robinson," Virginia retorted. "You aren't my boss."

"Well, I *am* your hostess. And *I'm* going upstairs for a lie down. You go on home. Callie needs to take a rest, too. And she needs to do some thinking."

It was obvious, as it had been before, who had the stronger will. Virginia sat stubbornly in her chair for another second or two, but eventually, draining the rest of her coffee in one long swallow, she banged the cup down noisily on the saucer and stood.

"Well, I guess I know when I've worn out my welcome."

"Good," Phoebe said.

She turned back toward the door that led into the house as her guest stalked toward the one that led outside. Just before Virginia reached it, she turned and said in a whisper, "Come on over to my house later. I'll tell you."

A little shocked by that flagrant breech of a long-standing friendship, Callie glanced toward Phoebe's retreating figure. Despite Virginia's whisper, her pace hadn't slowed. Apparently she hadn't heard the offer or had chosen to ignore it.

Callie turned back to find Virginia, her finger across her lips, nodding encouragement and winking at her. Then the old woman opened the creaking screen door and stepped out into the sunlight, leaving Callie alone on the porch.

Her mind on the recent conversation, her eyes again considered the water before her. Glinting in the morning sun, the bay looked serene. Incredibly peaceful. Just as Point Hope itself had when she'd first arrived. Now she knew that for both of them, that tranquillity was deceiving.

"VIRGINIA?" Callie called, tapping on the wooden frame of the screen door.

When she'd gotten no answer at the front, Callie had gone around to the back of the Wilton house, which, like Phoebe's, had a screened-in porch overlooking the water. Although it was early afternoon, too hot to be outside and hours before another of the spectacular eastern shore sunsets, she thought she should at least check to see if Virginia was out here before she gave up.

She had decided to drive out to Stanton's place again. The fact that he'd let Doak do all the talking last night might mean he agreed with everything the chief of police had suggested. Or it might mean that he had been thinking about what she had blurted out on the boat.

If nothing else, she needed to thank him. He had come into the water after her, which she knew he probably would have done for anyone else in that situation. She certainly wasn't attributing Stanton's rescue to any kind of personal concern.

To give him credit, however, he had persisted in his rescue, even after she'd attacked him, believing him to be her assailant. And when he'd realized how truly terrorized she was, he had treated her with a compassion that seemed genuine. All of which deserved some expression of gratitude, which she couldn't remember making last night.

And since Virginia's house was on her way, she had decided to accept the old woman's invitation to come over and hear the gossip Phoebe wouldn't let her repeat this morning.

"Virginia? Are you in there?"

She knocked again, and then tried the screen door. It wouldn't open. She put her hand along her forehead, as Virginia had done this morning, to examine the inside frame. There was an old-fashioned hook-and-eye latch, which had been secured.

So much for going out to Stanton's armed with Virginia's information. Disappointed, she stepped back far enough that she could look up at the second-story windows. There was an air-conditioning unit chugging away in one of the front rooms.

Phoebe usually lay down in her bedroom for an hour or so in the heat of the day. Callie would be willing to bet her neighbor did, too. Given the climate and their age, an afternoon nap was probably a smart move. With the noise the AC-unit was making, Virginia wouldn't be able to hear Callie calling.

Resigned to failure, she turned and began to retrace her steps to the street where she had parked her car. After Phoebe's warning, she hadn't informed her hostess about where she was going. And she certainly hadn't mentioned her intention to stop by the Wilton place on her way.

While they had eaten lunch, that same hint of reproach had been in Phoebe's manner. Maybe she was genuinely concerned for Callie's safety. Or maybe, since Callie was living in her house, she was worried about her own. And if someone *had* tried to kill Callie last night, perhaps she *was* putting Phoebe at risk.

They were just trying to scare you. That seemed to be the consensus. And after all, her attacker *had* let her go. She had attributed that to the arrival of Stanton's boat, but it *was* possible the two actions had had nothing to do with one another.

She had no idea how much time had elapsed between the moment her attacker had pushed her upright, inadvertently restarting the process of breathing, and the moment Stanton's hands had fastened around her upper arms.

Or *had* that hard shove in the center of her back been inadvertent? Had her assailant intended all along to bring her to the brink of unconsciousness and then to let her go? Had he intentionally pushed her upward with such force that it would bring her out of that oxygen-deprived stupor?

She reached her car, parked under one of the massive trees that shaded Virginia's front lawn. As she inserted the key in the door, she glanced down the row of houses. Heat rose off the pavement in waves, distorting the air. There was no one outside on either side of the street. No one sitting on the shaded front porches. No traffic to disturb the stillness.

She climbed into her car, hurriedly slipping the key into the ignition and starting the engine. As cool air began to pour from the vents, she adjusted the one to the left of the steering column so that it was blowing directly on her face.

She tilted her head, letting the cold stream touch the moisture on her neck. Then she turned her face to the right, allowing the vent to blow over her jawline and the dampness that had gathered around her temple. Finally she turned

her head the other way, rolling her neck, which was stiff
from a combination of tension and too little sleep.

As she did, something drew her eye to one of the windows on the second floor of the Wilton house. The twitching aside of a curtain, perhaps? To allow someone to see
out?

There was nothing there now. The white sheers hung
limp and still, presenting a blank, unrevealing face to the
outside world.

She wondered if Virginia had changed her mind about
sharing her gossip. Maybe having had time to consider
Phoebe's objection, she had thought better of her invitation.
Maybe she had realized that if she told Callie what she
knew, and it ended up in a book, she might very well alienate an old friend for life. Instead of telling Callie directly
that she'd changed her mind, had she chosen this way to
avoid the temptation to talk?

"You can run, Virginia, but you can't hide," Callie said,
the words very soft.

She had a feeling she could talk Virginia into telling her
that gossip, which she had obviously considered to be of
the "too good to keep" variety. And that would definitely
be to Callie's advantage. She'd come by again on the way
back into town, she decided, taking one last look at the
window where she had seen movement before she pulled
her car away from the curb.

CHAPTER SEVEN

THE SOUND of the car broke Ben's concentration on the vibration he was adjusting in the cruiser's engine. He shut it down and straightened, standing upright inside the engine well. His eyes were only slightly above the level of the housing, but he could see enough to make an identification of the vehicle he'd heard. It wasn't the one he'd been expecting.

He'd spent the morning getting ready for tomorrow's charter, so he hadn't been inside to answer his phone. And he had known Doak would want to discuss what had happened last night.

Thinking out loud, his former deputy called it. In reality, Doak's visits were a tacit request for Ben's input on some problem. Apparently Withers wasn't the only one who wanted to talk about what had happened last night, however, because Callie Evers had just parked her car in his yard.

He had left the house open, so it was going to become obvious pretty quickly he wasn't there. When it did, based on what he had learned from their previous encounters, she would come looking for him. The logical place to start would be out here, and he didn't want it to appear as if he were hiding. Not from her. Not from what she had said last night.

Mouthing a profanity, he reached down and retrieved the rag he'd laid on the casing. He used it to wipe grease off his fingers, not hurrying because he needed time to think. A few minutes to get prepared for what he expected her to say.

When he finally started up the steps, he realized she hadn't gotten out of her car. She was still sitting inside, the driver's-side window rolled down as a concession to the heat.

She's no more eager for this than I am, he thought, surprised by that intuition.

It didn't make a lot of sense. After all, she had driven all the way out here again. And there were only a couple of reasons for why she would. Either she wanted to talk about what she'd suggested in the boat last night or she wanted to thank him for getting her out of the water. He wasn't looking forward to either discussion.

He jumped onto the pier as she opened the car door. Eyes shaded with her hand, she seemed to be looking right at him, but she didn't start walking toward the water. Some kind of power play? To make him come to her? he wondered. Of course, since this was his home turf, he had all the advantages.

Still thinking like a cop, he admitted with a trace of bitterness. And he wasn't one. Not any longer.

Whatever had happened to Callie Evers last night wasn't his responsibility. If that's what she had come out here to talk about, he'd refer her to Doak. Not that she'd get anywhere.

Ben had realized that much as he'd listened to his former deputy's interrogation last night. He hadn't interfered, telling himself just what he was telling himself now. Not his responsibility. Not anymore, thank God.

He discovered he still had the grease rag in his hand. As he stood here, dreading another meeting with Callie Evers, his fingers tightened over the fabric, gripping strongly enough to be painful. Annoyed, he jammed the cloth into the back pocket of his jeans.

The same ones he'd been wearing last night, he realized. He hadn't seen any point in changing clothes to run his catch in. And then, knowing he had a full day's work ahead of him to get ready for tomorrow's charter, he had decided to delay showering until after he finished.

He probably reeked of fish and engine oil. He was so accustomed to those smells he was no longer aware of them, but he'd be willing to bet that Ms. Callie Evers would be. *And I really don't give a damn.*

As he stood watching from the far end of the pier, she turned and ducked back inside the car. She put her knee on the driver's seat and stretched across it, reaching for something.

When she stood up again, she settled a pair of sunglasses on her nose. She closed the car door, the sound echoing across the water as it always did. That's how he had found her last night. He had heard her wheezing, trying to get some air into her lungs, long before Charlie's flashlight had picked her up.

"Mr. Stanton?" she called, pitching her voice to carry across the distance between them, although she had already started to close it. "Do you think we could talk? If you have time. I promise it won't take long."

She had just offered him the perfect out. And he wouldn't even have to lie. He really did have a lot more to do before he'd be ready to take the cruiser out at dawn. The problem was, and it surprised him to admit it, there was some part of him that wanted to hear what she had to say. Maybe a natural curiosity about what had really happened out in the bay last night. Maybe even about the other murder she'd told him about.

Or maybe, Ben acknowledged, feeling a tightening in his groin as he watched her approach, his desire to talk to Callie Evers was based on something else entirely. On another, very different kind of desire. Because she looked a hell of a lot better than she had last night. A whole *hell* of a lot better.

She was wearing narrow white trousers, topped by a dark red shirt. The afternoon sun emphasized the blond streaks in her shoulder-length brown hair. He wasn't expert enough to say whether those were natural, but they looked as if they could be. Especially considering that nearly porcelain skin.

She seemed to have gotten some sun since she'd been down here. There was a sweep of color across the bridge of her nose and along the high cheekbones. The beginnings of a tan? With her complexion, that would be a real shame.

"What about?" he asked, raising his own voice.

"About last night," she said.

Her steps slowed the closer she came. As if, just as he'd thought before, she, too, was reluctant to have this conversation. Only, he couldn't figure out why she would be. Anymore than he had been able to figure out what she was after the first time she'd come out here.

Doak said she was writing some kind of true crime book about the murder. He hadn't been around many writers, but her interest in Kay-Kay's death had felt personal rather than professional. And more passionate than a ten-year-old murder should warrant. Even if she expected to turn this tragedy into a bestseller.

Personal, he thought again, jolted by the characterization. Maybe that was just wishful thinking on his part. The idea Callie Evers might be motivated by something other than money.

She came to a halt with less than ten feet of pier between them. He couldn't see her eyes, hidden behind those dark glasses. He had never liked being at that disadvantage. At one time he had considered himself skilled at reading people—especially their eyes. He liked to track the thoughts moving within them as they talked, using those to judge their veracity.

"I wanted to thank you for what you did last night," she said. "I couldn't remember whether I had or not. I guess I was a little…distraught at the time. I truly am very grateful."

There were a dozen responses he could make, some of them ungracious, even if they might also be true. Anybody in this town would have gone into the water last night. He would have done the same thing no matter who had been struggling out there. *With*, he admitted, *a couple of fairly obvious exceptions.*

He nodded without making any verbal response. The first time she'd come here, his reactions had given away more than he wanted them to. It was a mistake he didn't intend to repeat.

"And despite what Chief Withers suggested," she added, "I wanted you to know that I wasn't mistaken about what happened."

"Somebody got carried away," he said, echoing Doak's theory. "They were trying to scare you, and it got out of hand."

"Is that really what you believe?" she asked. "Even after what I told you? Even knowing Tom Delacroix couldn't have been responsible for his daughter's death?"

"I don't know anything of the kind. I've seen no proof of what you said about that other murder. *If* there was one."

"I have the affidavits I told you about in my car. If you'd only look at them—"

"Even if there *was* another murder with similarities to Kay-Kay's, it doesn't prove the same person committed both. Maybe Delacroix read about the other case. Maybe what he did was an attempt to make people believe just what you believe."

He was pleased that the old skills seemed to be coming back. Of course, he was more prepared this time. At his denial, her mouth flattened. After a few seconds, she shook her head.

"I don't understand why you aren't willing to at least consider the possibility. Supposedly, you were a good cop. Whatever you believed, you at least went through the motions. All I'm asking is that you do that again. Just go through the motions on the off chance that I might be right."

He was tempted, but he knew that had more to do with her than with her arguments. With the way she looked. Maybe even with the way she smelled, a subtle fragrance of flowers, which was probably her shampoo. The wind was whipping strands of sun-touched hair across her face, which she caught with her fingers, holding them away from her eyes.

His growing sexual attraction, and the resulting urge to please her, would be the only reasons to look at the material she wanted to show him. He had known from the beginning who had killed Kay-Kay. He had even known why. And nothing Callie Evers could ever show him would make him forget that.

"Sorry," he said, and on some level, maybe only hormonal, he really was. "It's not my job." He had already started back to the ladder when her voice stopped him.

"Someone tried to kill me last night. If you hadn't been there, they would have succeeded. It seems to me the only person who has that kind of stake in making sure I don't write about Katherine Delacroix's murder is the person who killed her."

He turned to face her. "That person's dead, Ms. Evers. You're eight years too late to make that accusation stick."

"But if I weren't too late, you'd buy into that idea, wouldn't you? Virginia Wilton hinted there had been bad blood between the two of you, long before Katherine's murder."

The question threw him. He wasn't sure what she was trying to get him to say. Or what she'd been told.

"Are you asking me if I believe Delacroix was capable of killing someone else? If, just for the sake of argument, we pretend he isn't dead?" He had intended the sharp sarcasm. If he had expected any reaction to it, he was disappointed.

"Just for the sake of argument," she agreed, her voice calm.

"I think Tom Delacroix was capable of almost anything."

"Even of what was done to his own daughter?"

Ben didn't understand why he hesitated before he could answer that. Maybe because of the way the question had been phrased. Even of what was done to his own daughter. Kay-Kay's death hadn't been the result of some drunken rage. Nor had it been an accident—a family argument that had gotten out of hand, claiming the life of an innocent victim. That had been the FBI's opinion, but Ben had known the murder hadn't been staged to cover up something like that.

It had been exactly what it had appeared to be. Cold and cruel and deliberate. There had never been any doubt in his mind about that aspect of it. There still wasn't.

"Even that," he said.

"You hated Delacroix," she said softly. "Maybe with good reason. I don't know. But all these years you've been terrified that your hatred made you screw up that investigation. You're afraid you let *it* convince you of his guilt, rather than the evidence, so that you did exactly what they all accused you of doing. You didn't look any place else for the murderer."

"You don't have any idea what I did," he denied, but she was getting to him, just as she had the first day she'd come here.

"Then why are you afraid to listen to me? Or to take a look at the information I've collected?"

"Is that supposed to be some kind of challenge, Ms. Evers? Something my ego just won't be able to resist? I'm supposed to jump into your little literary *investigation* because I can't stand being told I was wrong? Sorry, but I outgrew that kind of knee-jerk reaction a long time ago."

"It was supposed to make you think."

He laughed, the sound short and harsh. "Believe me, Ms. Evers, I think about Katherine Delacroix's murderer every day of my life. I think how sorry I am I didn't strangle that son of a bitch with my bare hands as soon I saw what he'd done."

"But he didn't," she said, her voice intense. "He *didn't* do it. That's what I've been trying to tell you. Tom Delacroix couldn't have killed his daughter."

The passion he had recognized was there again. And the surety. That's what had bothered him the first time. How damn sure she was about what she was saying.

"Because he didn't kill Mary Cameron twenty-six years ago," she went on. "He couldn't have. And if he didn't kill *her*, then he didn't kill Kay-Kay. Which means whoever did is still here."

"Or maybe he's moved back to North Carolina," he said, ridiculing her theory. Ridiculing her. It had no effect. Neither her face nor her voice changed in response to his mockery.

"He's here. I didn't believe that before. I didn't think it fit the pattern. But, after last night..." She took a breath, deep enough that it lifted her shoulders. "Whether you help me or not, I'm going to find out who he is, but...I'd really like your help," she finished softly.

He was even thinking about it, he realized, caught again in the spell of her conviction. Except his was just as deep.

"If you really believe someone tried to kill you last night, then if I were you, I'd get back in that car, and I wouldn't stop until I was too exhausted to drive. I wouldn't spend another minute in Point Hope. *If* I really believed that," he challenged. "Now if you'll excuse me, I have several hours work left. Good luck, and I hope goodbye. Because if you're smart, Ms. Evers, this will be the last time you and I see one another."

He turned and walked back to the cruiser. He thought he could feel her eyes following him, but he didn't look back. And a long time after he had the engine running as smooth as silk again, he heard her car start. He straightened, watching, as she drove back down the winding driveway toward the main road.

"MRS. DELACROIX?"

The slender blonde, stopped in the act of closing the door of the silver Mercedes sedan, turned at the sound of her name. The slight smile seemed automatic, probably her normal response to being addressed. As soon as she realized that the person who had called to her was a stranger, delicately shaped brows arched above the frames of the sunglasses she wore, questioning either Callie's right to be on her property or her identity.

Lorena Delacroix was more attractive than her pictures had suggested. Although her face was soft and pale, in keeping with the wheat-colored hair, it was not as full as the cameras had portrayed it. She was also more slender, and more fragile somehow, than Callie had imagined. Despite the fact that the woman had yet to open her mouth, Callie's preconceptions about Katherine Delacroix's mother shifted minutely.

"Yes?" Lorena asked, her tone sharply questioning.

Finally face-to-face with Kay-Kay's mother, Callie was inexplicably at a loss for words, uncertain how she should begin this crucial interview. And yet the whole time she had been waiting, standing in the shade of the oaks that lined the Delacroix's drive, she had been practicing what she would say.

Only occasionally had she let her eyes consider the second-story windows, two of which belonged to the room that had been Kay-Kay's. Whenever she did, "ghoul" had echoed unpleasantly.

"Who the hell are you?" Lorena demanded.

She took a step away from the car, putting her hand above her eyes to shade them from the sun. Even from this distance Callie could hear the soft jingle of the bracelets she wore. The sound seemed to break the spell that had held her.

"My name is Callie Evers, Mrs. Delacroix," she said, trying to find words that wouldn't get her thrown off the property. "I wonder if I could talk to you. It won't take long, I promise."

Almost the exact thing she had said to Ben Stanton. And if this interview had the same outcome as that...

"Talk about what?" Lorena's voice had lost all pretense to pleasantness. "You *do* know you're trespassing, don't you?"

"I know your husband wasn't responsible for your daughter's death. I know that he couldn't have been."

The hand that had been raised to shade Lorena Delacroix's eyes whipped the sunglasses off them instead. Although they narrowed reflexively against the sudden glare, they didn't waver from Callie's face. And they were not nearly as hard as they had appeared in those long-ago photographs.

"May I come inside and show you *how* I know?" Callie asked.

The silence lasted so long that she began to be afraid that using this approach had been another mistake. The cupid's bow mouth, carefully outlined in carmine, had a pinched look. Finally, it opened, revealing very even and very white teeth.

"If this is some kind of trick—"

"No trick, Mrs. Delacroix."

"If you're a reporter, I'm not telling you *anything*."

"I'm not asking you to. But…there are things I think *you* should know. Some things *I'd* like to tell you."

"Like what?"

"Could we go inside? I'm not used to this heat," Callie said, softening the blatant request with a smile. *And if you tell me it's not the heat, but the humidity…*

Another few beats of silence. Then Lorena set her sunglasses back on her nose, its perfection a dead giveaway that some skilled plastic surgeon had created it. The movement of the bracelets this time caught the sun, sending droplets of light glittering between them.

"You alone?" she asked.

"Of course," Callie said, feeling the same anticipation as when she had heard Stanton's voice in the darkness last night.

He was the ally she had wanted, but the barriers he had erected against any suggestion that Tom Delacroix might not be guilty were too firmly in place, and that had left her with only one other option.

"Come on in," Lorena Delacroix ordered.

Without waiting to see if Callie followed, she walked

around the front of the car and headed toward the dozen or
so steps that led up to the wide front door of her home.

"I CAN'T BELIEVE THIS," Lorena said. "How come nobody
ever told me about this drawing?"

"The police usually keep some piece of evidence from
the public so they can distinguish between the real murderer
and people who confess to crimes they had nothing to do
with."

"Wait a minute. Are you saying they thought somebody
who *didn't* have anything to do with the murder might confess?"

There had been no hesitation before the words "the murder." They had come out of Lorena Delacroix's mouth as
if they had no connection to her own flesh and blood.

"That happens all the time," Callie said. "If the police
hold something back, something only the real murderer
could know, it makes it easier to disprove those false con-
fessions."

The blue eyes had held intently on Callie's face as she
talked. "I'll be damned," Lorena said. "That's...crazy.
Somebody confessing, I mean."

"There are a lot of crazy people out there, Mrs. Delacroix. People who would do anything for the attention that
being a suspect in a high profile crime like this would give
them."

"Then you can bet your ass they've never *been* a suspect."

Callie was beginning to relax. Mrs. Delacroix had never
questioned that what she was telling her was the truth. Ad-
mittedly, it was very much to her advantage if it were.

"That son of a bitch," Lorena said, her eyes dropping
to the photograph on the coffee table.

Although it was only a shot of the back of a small blond
head, Callie had been reluctant to bring it out of her leather
portfolio. She had finally decided there was no way to discuss the drawing without providing some evidence of its
existence. And this photograph was all she had to offer.

That and the two affidavits she had collected in North Carolina were the only proof of her absolute conviction that the same person had committed both these murders. And unlike Ben Stanton, Lorena had been very willing to look at them.

"Stanton?" Callie asked, having little trouble figuring out who Kay-Kay's mother would consider a son of a bitch.

"This proves what a lying jackass he is."

"It's pretty standard police procedure."

Callie was trying to walk the fine line between being truthful and forming this necessary alliance. She had hoped to convince Stanton to work with her, but after this morning—

"You're telling me it's standard procedure to keep information like this from the parents of a murdered child?"

If those parents are suspects. "I'm afraid so."

"Let me make sure I understand what you're saying. The police have known about this…flower thing all along, but they never told anybody, because if they had, somebody might have discovered another child had been killed just like Kay-Kay."

"I wouldn't assign that motivation to—"

"I would." Lorena's words cut her sharply off in midsentence. "That lying son of a bitch."

Although Callie knew Stanton could care less if she defended him, withholding this kind of information *was* standard. It certainly didn't mean he hadn't investigated the drawing of the rose himself. She had never intended to imply that.

"I'm sure Chief Stanton ran the drawing through the national crime databases. When nothing turned up—"

"Why wouldn't it?" Lorena interrupted again.

"Police departments haven't always been good about sharing information," Callie said. "And when the national databases were established, no one could guarantee that all the cold cases were included. That was the intent, of course, but just the physical task of tracking down the information and submitting it would mean hundreds of hours taken away from their regular duties. Small police departments would have been hard-pressed—''

"So you're saying this other rose wouldn't have been in the database?'' Lorena demanded, again cutting off her explanation.

"Probably not. Especially since all the original records on that case burned in a courthouse fire. That, itself, was almost twenty years ago. I don't know that anyone has even looked at that particular murder since.''

The blue eyes seemed almost as hard now as they had in the television footage. "So how come *you* did?''

It was the question Callie had waited for Stanton to pose. And he hadn't. For some reason she hadn't expected it from Mrs. Delacroix. Again, her opinion of Kay-Kay's mother altered.

"I'm a reporter, Mrs. Delacroix," she said. "It's my job to dig up facts.''

The skepticism in that steady blue regard didn't change, despite the smile that moved the too-small mouth. "I wasn't born yesterday, Ms. Evers," Lorena said. "And I'm not a fool. You better start telling me the truth before I call Doak Withers and tell him I've got another trespasser for him to pick up.''

I'm not a fool. It was the third time in the past few days someone had made that claim. And, Callie acknowledged, they'd all been right. These people had been tempered by the fire of the media scrutiny they had passed through. There was nothing left in them that was naive or trusting.

"I knew the family involved," she said.

"In that other murder?''

Callie nodded, her throat tight.

"Twenty-six years ago," Lorena said, speculatively. "You must have been just a kid.''

With the speed and approximate duration of a flashbulb's explosion, the image of that basement was in Callie's head. She could smell the mold and feel the dampness.

"I'm surprised you remember it after all that time.''

Callie heard and even understood the words Lorena had

just said. She just couldn't concentrate on them. Not even when the memory faded. For a few seconds the after-image of that swinging lightbulb burned in her consciousness, as the retina will retain the glare of a flash after it's gone. It had been a very long time since that had happened. Long enough that she had almost forgotten how intense it was. And how devastating.

She allowed her lips to part slightly, trying unobtrusively to breathe through her mouth. Trying to pull in the oxygen she needed to defeat her lightheadedness. And the whole time she was doing that, she was also aware that she was expected to make some answer. Aware of the slow seconds ticking by as Lorena waited. Suspicion had begun to seep into the blue eyes before Callie could manage to align words into a coherent sentence.

"It's hard to forget something like that. Especially hard when you're a child," she added, wondering as she said it whether her answer made sense. And if it were too revealing.

Lorena nodded as if what she said had been perfectly rational. Then her eyes fell back to the photograph of the back of her daughter's head.

"The fact that there was this other case *proves* Tom didn't have anything to do with Kay-Kay's death."

For some reason, the triumph, the sense of vindication Callie would have expected, was missing from Lorena Delacroix's declaration. Her voice was flat instead, almost without emotion.

"It should. But I'm afraid there are…some problems."

"Problems?" The blue eyes lifted.

"The fire I told you about destroyed the official documentation. All we have is some secondary corroboration of the existence of that first drawing."

"What does that mean? Secondary corroboration?"

"Statements from people who talked to those who actually saw the drawing of the rose. People who, for one reason or another, were told it was an integral part of the investigation."

"Like that guy's wife? The sheriff's wife, whose statement you showed me?"

"That's right."

"So?"

"So...they probably won't be enough to convince the police to reopen the case. Especially since Stanton never acknowledged there was a similar drawing on...your daughter's body."

"Damn straight they aren't going to reopen the investigation," Lorena said, her voice bitter. "Not as long as Ben Stanton is alive. They wouldn't if you brought them the real murderer, begging to confess."

"If we can convince Withers—"

"Doak don't take a piss unless Ben tells him he needs to."

The crudity didn't fit with the persona Lorena had tried to convey, again shifting Callie's perceptions of the woman seated across from her.

"And you aren't ever going to convince Stanton," Lorena went on, seeming oblivious to the effect of her vulgarity. "This is personal with him. So...we go over his head."

"I'm not sure—"

"We don't mess around with the law," Lorena said, seeming to relish the words. "We go straight to the media instead."

"Without more concrete proof, they aren't going to be any more inclined to believe this than Stanton is."

"He hasn't got any authority to stop us."

"Maybe not," Callie admitted, "but the real question is whether or not the media would be convinced by what we say. Especially since no one involved in *this* investigation is going to admit that rose was there."

"They won't have to be convinced. Those people don't care about proof. The only thing they care about is whether or not this'll sell papers. You just give me those affidavits—"

"Mrs. Delacroix, I really believe—"

"Look," Lorena interrupted again, her voice harsh,

"I've lived with this hanging over my head for ten years. It killed my husband. Drove him to an early grave, God rest his soul. And all along there was proof that somebody outside this family killed Kay-Kay. And that son of a bitch Ben Stanton made sure we didn't know about it."

"*He* didn't know," Callie said, again wondering why she was defending Ben. "That's what I'm telling you. And even if he now admits it was there, the rose on your daughter's body can't exonerate your husband. Not alone. It can only do that in conjunction with proof of the existence of the other one."

"So that's what we show them," Lorena said, sliding the papers around until the two affidavits covered the photograph of the back of her daughter's head.

"If we release this information prematurely, and then they find out how flimsy our evidence is, we destroy our credibility. I think we have to wait until we find some solid link between the person who committed that first murder and this."

"What kind of link?"

"Something that ties him to the other family. Or at least to the area. I think that's the safest way. *And* the most likely to get the results we want."

The blue eyes considered her face a long time. "I've never much believed in playing it safe," Lorena Delacroix said finally.

"But surely if there's anyone who can understand the kind of harm that can be inflicted by having people speculate on someone's guilt or innocence..." Callie said, letting the suggestion speak for itself.

"You think I give a damn about somebody else being a suspect for a change? Hell, I wasn't even here that night, and they *all* think I had something to do with it."

Callie couldn't deny the truth of that. There were plenty of people who believed Lorena Delacroix knew more than she had told the authorities about her daughter's death.

"I think our best chance of putting this to rest, once and for all," Callie reiterated, "lies in working together to make that connection and waiting to go public until we have enough to convince any reasonable person.''

Lorena laughed again. ''Honey, if there is one thing I've learned, it's that reasonable people don't exist. Not when it comes to something like this.''

''I know it must feel like that—''

''You don't know anything,'' Lorena broke in. ''*Nobody* knows unless they've been there. Unless it's your picture on the covers of those sleazy little magazines stacked along every check-out counter in this country. You don't have any idea what we went through.''

''Mrs. Delacroix—''

''I'll wait,'' Lorena said, holding up her hand, its palm toward Callie. Jangling, the bracelets slid off her wrist and lodged on the fleshy part of her forearm. ''Hell, I've waited this long. A little longer isn't gonna kill me. But I'll tell you this, Ms. Evers. When it's time…''

''Yes?'' Callie asked, obeying the unspoken prompt as Lorena let the pause lengthen dramatically.

''I want to be the one who blows the whistle on that bastard. You understand me? I want to be the one who tells the press that for ten years Ben Stanton sat on evidence that could have cleared my husband of any suspicion in my daughter's murder. And I want to see the look on that bastard's face when I do.''

CHAPTER EIGHT

SHE SHOULD HAVE enough time for one more stop before Phoebe expected her for dinner, Callie decided, stealing a glance at her watch. She double-checked the numbers on the mailbox she was approaching, verifying the neatly lettered address.

The box itself was huge, carved and painted like a mallard decoy, with the opening for mail cut into the duck's broad breast. As she pulled her car into the gravel drive beside it, the wings attached to the wooden body spun madly in the hot wind.

Unlike most of the houses in the area, the cottage wasn't shaded by the ubiquitous live oaks. Instead, fruit trees stood like sentinels, guarding one side of the lot. On the other, neat wooden stakes defined the rows of a garden, green and flourishing despite the heat. Someone had devoted a lot of time and effort to seeing it stayed that way.

She turned off the engine and sat in the car a moment, studying the house. It was late Victorian, or at least it was garnished with the trappings of the period, including intricately cut gingerbread trim. Everything appeared to have been freshly painted; the shrubs and the lawn recently trimmed.

Glancing again at her watch, Callie gathered up her purse and the portfolio containing the photograph and affidavits. Then she stepped outside the car to be assaulted again by the heat, which had grown more oppressive as the long afternoon wore on.

"I got lemonade, but no air-conditioning."

The voice drew her eyes to the right-hand side of the

porch where an old-fashioned swing hung from the ceiling on chains. Seated in it was the man she had come to see.

"But air or not," he went on, "it's bound to be cooler up here than it is out in that sun."

"Dr. Cooley?"

"Now I know you're from out of town. Nobody's called me *Doctor* Cooley in forty years."

"What do they call you?" Callie asked with a smile, responding to the vein of humorous self-deprecation.

"To my face, you mean?"

She laughed, and after a second or two, the sound of his laughter, as deep and rich as his accent, joined hers.

"Come on up here where I can see you," he urged. "I don't get many good-looking women paying me afternoon calls anymore. They all act like I got old or something."

Relaxing at the warmth of his welcome, after the strain of the taut-string hour she had just spent with Lorena Delacroix, Callie climbed the low front steps. It took a moment for her eyes to adjust to the relative dimness of the porch.

The figure that materialized as they did was stereotypical. White-haired and portly, Dr. Everett Cooley looked exactly like what he was. A retired country doctor.

He wore an open-necked cotton print shirt. Khaki pants, held up by suspenders, stretched over a rounded belly. His feet were encased in beige tennis shoes. As their toes touched against the planks of the porch, propelling the swing gently back and forth, his trousers rode up a little, exposing white athletic socks banded at the top in red.

"Am I supposed to know you?" he asked, the movement of the swing smooth and measured, its chains creaking softly with each rhythmic push. "Neither my eyes nor my mind is as good as they used to be. And don't you be insulted if I delivered you or something. I've seen a heap of baby bottoms in my day. Can't be expected to try to sort all of them out at my age."

Callie laughed again. "You can relax. We've never met."

"You selling something?" he asked.

A different version of an old story, she thought. A story Everett Cooley was very familiar with.

"Makes me no never mind if you are, you understand," the old man hurried to assure her. "I like visitors, even salesmen. And I might just buy whatever it is you got for sale. Except magazines. I already take more of those than I can get read."

"Not a salesman, but a writer," Callie said.

The white head tilted slightly, as the shrewd brown eyes examined her face. "What you write?"

"A column for a weekly up in Charlotte. And a lot of freelance articles. Maybe even for some of those magazines you subscribe to."

"Well, why don't you sit down and talk to me about what you're writing," Cooley said.

Callie chose the rocker aligned at an angle from the swing. She set her purse and the portfolio on the floor beside it, and then leaned back, setting her own chair into motion. Neither of them said anything, listening to the creak of the chains and the low thump of the rocker against the wooden planks.

"You famous?" the old man asked after a moment or two.

"I'm terribly afraid I'm not, Dr. Cooley," Callie said.

"But you're hoping to be. Every writer's hoping to be or you wouldn't stick with it. Too damn hard, otherwise."

She laughed. "Then maybe I am hoping, at that."

"So what do you write?"

"Articles about dogwood festivals and art shows. Nature things. Caves, forests, rivers. Articles telling people where to go for their next vacation. You name it, I've done it."

"I probably read something of yours. What's your name?"

"Callie Evers."

"Evers. Don't ring a bell. You making any money?"

"Not as much as I'd like to," Callie said, laughing again

in response to the overt teasing. His good humor was infectious.

"And I expect that just might be why you're here," Doc Cooley said, the amusement suddenly stripped from his voice.

At the abrupt change in tone, there was an increase in Callie's heart rate and the beginnings of a blush spread upward into her throat. She had been lulled into relaxation by the old man's friendliness—just as he'd intended.

Obviously, Cooley was as shrewd as the stereotype suggested. She wished she'd remembered that part. Her smile had become strained, but somehow she managed to hold onto it.

"You came here looking for fame *and* fortune, I'd imagine," the old man said softly. "Or would I be wrong about that?"

"I came here to write a book."

"About Kay-Kay Delacroix. Well, you ain't the first. Unfortunately, I doubt you'll be the last. 'Course, it's been a while, 'cause there's nothing new to write. But then I forgot we got the tenth anniversary coming up. Guess folks'll be wanting to speculate some more about what *really* happened."

"And you believe you already know," Callie suggested.

"Me? Hell, no. I never claimed to know any more than *how* that baby died. Medically, I mean. That was my job, and I did it, sick as it made me. You want theories about anything else, you go see Ben Stanton."

"Do you think his is the *right* theory?"

"Ben shore believes it is."

"You didn't answer my question, Dr. Cooley. Do *you* think Tom Delacroix killed his daughter?"

"Tom was a friend of mine. We grew up together. Hunted and fished together a thousand weekends. Slept in the same tent. Ate the same food out of the same pan. So I'm not exactly what you'd call an impartial observer." His mouth moved, lips pursing, and then he leaned back in the swing, looking up at the ceiling above their heads. "You want the God's truth about what I think?'' he asked, his eyes still raised.

"Yes."

"I've seen a lot of purely awful things in my time. Some I don't like to think about. But what they did to that baby—"

"They?" Callie broke in, her voice sharpened with surprise.

His chin came down at the tone, eyes meeting hers. "Him. Her. Whoever did it."

"Are you saying…it could have been a *woman?*"

Despite the speculation about Lorena's complicity in her daughter's death, Callie had never seen any suggestion in print that Kay-Kay Delacroix's murderer might have been female.

"Why not. It might have been easier for a woman to lure her out of the house. And the rest wouldn't have taken any more strength than a normal-sized woman would have. 'Course it never was the strength that was the sticking point for me. It was the other.''

There were so many possible "others" that Callie was afraid to guess which he might mean, so she didn't interrupt again.

"Tom Delacroix doted on that little girl. Never seen anything like it. She went everywhere with him, almost from the day she was born. And despite all I know about the sorriness of the human condition, I can't believe a man who loved a child like Tom did Kay-Kay could do that and *then* have the presence of mind to take the precautions he took afterward.''

"You mean the water," Callie said softly.

"Washed her as clean as she was when I handed her to her mama to take home from the hospital. Cleaner maybe.''

The killer had lured or carried Kay-Kay Delacroix from that pink-and-white bedroom on the second floor of the house Callie had just left. The site where the murder had taken place had never been determined, not to anyone's satisfaction. It was another of the anomalies that had made the case so fascinating to the media.

But after the murderer had finished, he had taken the little girl's body down to the dark waters of the bay and washed it. He had wrapped her in a sheet, one that had been taken from the Delacroix linen closet. Then he'd hidden the body in the marshy grasses near the edge of the water behind the Delacroix house. Where Ben Stanton had found it the next morning.

"Whoever killed her even scrubbed under her nails," the old man said. "Scrubbed 'em clean, too. There wasn't nothing on that little girl's body that gave us one single clue we could use to find her killer. Not a hair or a thread or a scraping of skin. And in my opinion, professional *and* personal, it would take somebody a lot colder and a lot less drunk than Tom Delacroix would have been by that time of the night to do that."

The silence after Cooley finished lasted so long that the low buzz from the yard seemed to fill Callie's head.

"He left *something*," she said, her voice no louder than the creak of the chains. "Something I think you found when you examined the body."

Cooley had to know about the rose Stanton wouldn't admit existed. He *had* to. And that was why she was here, of course. If she could get an affidavit from him—

"Something *I* found? You tell me what you think I found. I'd be real interested in hearing that."

"He cleaned the body, to remove any evidence that might link the murder to him, but then he marked it."

"What kind of a mark?" he asked, sounding genuinely curious.

Obviously he was testing her. Trying to find out how much she knew. He had been fairly forthcoming so far. Maybe when he realized that she really did know what she was talking about, he would be even more so.

"Whoever killed Kay-Kay drew a small red rose on the back of her neck, hidden under her hairline."

The doctor's eyes widened, but not in the same way Ben

Stanton's had. Not at all in the same way, Callie acknowledged. Cooley looked bemused rather than shocked. And he shook his head, smiling a little.

"I don't know who you been talking to, young lady—"

"The end of the stem is visible in one of the autopsy photographs."

"And I'll bet you got that photograph real handy in that satchel there."

"Would you like to see it? To refresh your memory."

"My memory's fine," the old man said. "I don't need it refreshed. Not about what was done to that little girl."

As the silence stretched, it became obvious he wasn't going to respond to what she had told him about the rose. There were other questions that only Cooley could answer, however.

"She was your patient, wasn't she?" Callie asked. "Before the murder."

Even after all these months, Katherine Delacroix was only a series of photographs to her. Everett Cooley had known her. And as he had talked about the murder, the sense of Kay-Kay as a real child, a person, an individual, came through more clearly from the old man than it had from Lorena Delacroix herself.

"I brought her into this world, and I saw her laid out for the next. And there weren't nearly enough years between."

At the sudden quaver in his voice, it seemed a sacrilege to continue. Except two little girls were dead. And there was no one to speak for them. No one was looking for their murderer. No one but her. So Callie steeled herself against Cooley's emotion.

"About the rose, Dr. Cooley…"

"I didn't find any roses on that baby's body, Ms. Evers. I took those pictures myself, and I expect whatever you think you see in that photograph was just that—something you *think* you see. Now I'm telling you flat out it's time to let this thing go. Let it rest. Let *us* rest. Whatever you write ain't gonna bring Kay-Kay back. It's just gonna stir up a lot of pain and unhappiness. And you sure ain't gonna solve that crime, if that's what you're thinking. Not after all this time. Ben Stanton couldn't, not as bad as he wanted to. And he *did* want to. Believe me.''

''But he was wrong,'' Callie argued. ''His premise was wrong from the beginning, and it tainted everything he did.''

''I know there's folks who'll tell you that—that the police didn't look at anybody but Tom—but I know for a fact that ain't so. Ben's a good cop, and he conducted a good, thorough investigation. Once he knew what he had, he went at it from every angle you could imagine. There wasn't nothing there. Nothing that could *prove* who did it.

''Ben thought he'd figured it out, all right. He'll probably think that until the day he dies, but I can tell you for a fact that he didn't leave any other possibility unexamined. If that baby's murder *could* have been solved, Ben would have done it.''

The brown eyes were earnest. And she found that she believed what Cooley was telling her. There had been no shock in his eyes when she revealed that she knew about the drawing. Not as there had been in Stanton's. And there hadn't been any pictures of it included with those that had been stolen and released to the media, which must mean...

What? she wondered. That Stanton had never told *anyone* about that mark? Had that been for the very legitimate reason she had just suggested to Lorena Delacroix? Or because it didn't fit with his theory about the identity of the murderer?

''Now you pick up your purse and your picture with whatever you thought you saw in it, and you carry them on back home with you,'' Dr. Cooley said. ''Let these good folks here alone. And let Ben Stanton alone, too. He did all a man *could* do. He don't need you and everybody else second-guessing him. Stirring everything up again. Don't you think he feels bad enough?''

''Does he?'' Callie asked. ''You know him. I don't. I don't have any way of judging how he feels.''

''Ben would have given his life to protect that little girl.

He wouldn't have thought twice about it. He couldn't do that, so he did the only thing he could do for her. He devoted two years of it trying to catch her murderer. And when he couldn't do that either, I thought it would break him, strong as he is. I'll tell you the truth, Ms. Evers. I prayed God it wouldn't. And my prayers were answered. That baby's murder changed Ben Stanton, but thank God, it didn't destroy him. Now you get on home. Take your roses and your photographs and your book writing with you. And you leave that man *and* this town alone."

IF IT HAD BEEN Doc Cooley's intention to change her opinion of Ben Stanton, it had worked, Callie admitted, as she drove the now familiar route back to the bed-and-breakfast.

Ben Stanton would have given his life to protect that little girl. He wouldn't have thought twice about it...

Just as he had come into the water last night to rescue her. Without any hesitation. Without any idea of what he might find out there. Without any consideration of his own safety.

He devoted two years of it to trying to catch her murderer. And when he couldn't do that either, I thought it would break him, strong as he is.

The phrases ran through her head like a litany, more powerful because she knew they were true. Instinctively, from the beginning, she had known this was the kind of man Ben Stanton was, despite his refusal to help her.

And why should he? To him, she was exactly what he had called her. A ghoul. And that's all she was.

What she had never realized was the depth of his emotional involvement in this case. She had believed Stanton was belligerent to her because he couldn't stand to give up his cherished theory about the identity of the murderer.

But maybe his reluctance to consider her evidence had more to do with what would be an unbearable sense of failure than with any personal animosity he had felt for Kay-Kay's father. Even as she acknowledged that possibility, she realized she still didn't know the source of that supposed animosity.

She had just turned down the street beside the bay—the quiet, shaded avenue on which both Phoebe and Virginia lived. She looked at her watch again as she approached the Wilton house.

She was already late for supper because she had spent so long with Cooley. If she didn't take one more shot at getting Virginia to talk to her, she might never understand the relationship between Ben and Delacroix. And on the chance that it had some bearing on the identity of the real murderer...

She pulled the car up to the curb in front of the Wilton house, looking up at the second-story windows as she turned off the ignition. The sheers covering the one where she had seen movement earlier this afternoon were still.

She opened the car door, slipping her keys in the pocket of her slacks and leaving everything else where it was on the passenger seat. She stepped out onto the sidewalk, hit the auto-lock on the handle and closed the door.

When she turned to face the house, she felt a strange reluctance. In the emotional aftermath of Cooley's tribute to Stanton, this felt very much like a betrayal. As if she were going behind Ben's back in an attempt to acquire damaging information about him.

Did it really matter what personal hatreds had once existed between him and Tom Delacroix? Cooley had assured her that Ben had conducted a thorough investigation, no matter what he had felt about Kay-Kay's father.

Her hand dipped back into her pocket, closing around her keys. Then, remembering what was at stake, she forced her fingers to release them and walked up to the door. She pushed the bell, listening to its old-fashioned chimes in the distance.

As she waited, she turned to look along the street. A few of the neighbors on the other side were sitting on their front verandas. With this row of houses between them and the bay, she wondered if they could see from that vantage point the nightly display the setting sun provided.

She turned, pressing the bell again, and waited once more as the long seconds of silence slipped away. Finally she turned, intending to head back to her car.

Out of the corner of her eye, she caught sight of the brick walkway that led to the back of the house. It wouldn't take half a minute, she thought, to see if Virginia were sitting on her screened porch, preparing to watch the nightly spectacle.

It didn't, but because of the rain roof and the approach of dusk, the porch was too dark to see into. As she had this morning, Callie put her hand along her forehead and leaned close to the screen door. The wicker chairs, almost identical to Phoebe's except for the colors of the flowers in their cushions, were all empty.

She noticed the latch that had been hooked earlier this afternoon no longer was. It would take only another half minute to cross the porch and knock on the back door. Virginia was probably in the kitchen fixing supper. It was entirely possible, considering the volume of her whisper this morning, that her hearing, like Phoebe's, wasn't what it used to be.

Callie eased the door open, the movement almost furtive. She walked across the porch, sandals echoing on the planks. The curtains over the glass portion of the back door had been drawn to each side, but there was no light on in the kitchen.

There seemed to be a faint glow from the front of the house. She hadn't noticed it when she'd pulled up to the curb, so obviously it wasn't coming from any of the rooms facing the street. Again she put her hand against her forehead and pressed it against the pane of dark glass, trying to determine where the light was originating.

As she leaned against it, the door opened, swinging inward without a sound. She straightened, startled and slightly off balance. The door continued to move, exposing an expanse of black-and-white floor tile and old-fashioned metal cabinets that had been painted white.

There was a wicker table, with colorful place mats and two settings of china on it. Matching napkins were folded on each plate. There was no smell of food. And no evidence in the sink or on the counters that anyone had cooked tonight.

Maybe Virginia had decided to walk down to the shore before supper. Callie turned, looking out through the screen of the porch at the colors the sinking sun painted over sky and water. She scanned the area under the trees, starkly silhouetted against that backdrop.

There was no one there. Nothing but the row of long piers, reaching out into the water. And an equally empty darkness inside, she acknowledged, turning to look across the kitchen.

"Virginia?"

She waited, listening to the tree frogs and the low, soft lap of the water. *Close the door,* she told herself, *get back into the car, and drive three houses down the street to Phoebe's.*

Her growing sense of unease prevented her from doing that. For some reason—a reason that had nothing to do with the gossip she had come here to hear—she wanted to see Virginia Wilton. She wanted verification that the old woman was all right. That she was as sharply contentious as she had been this morning.

Without allowing herself time to think about the propriety of what she was doing, Callie stepped over the threshold and walked across the kitchen. The sound of her footsteps seemed magnified by the tile, the metal, the emptiness.

"Virginia?" she called, when she reached the opposite door.

There was no answer. As she strained to hear one, she became aware of the music, filtering faintly downward from somewhere upstairs. Her lips relaxed into a smile.

She couldn't have named the song if her life depended on it, but she knew the era to which it belonged. The 1940s

Big Band sound fit with the peaceful, dusky atmosphere of the house, and it would also explain why Virginia hadn't answered the bell or heard her calling.

Reassured by the simple explanation, Callie stepped into the hallway, walking forward boldly now, guided by the music. From the foot of the stairs, she could see an open door on the second floor. Muted light flooded from it into the dark hallway.

"Virginia?" she called again, more as a matter of courtesy than because she expected the old woman to be able to hear her over the strains of Glenn Miller or Tommy Dorsey or whatever orchestra was playing.

She was surprised that, if Virginia had retreated upstairs for the night, she'd left the back door unlocked. Of course, in Point Hope that probably wasn't all that unusual.

We haven't had a crime… The remembrance of Phoebe's claim triggered in her consciousness the same response it had then. *Not since someone killed a little girl.*

The sense of apprehension she had felt before she heard the music washed over her in a great, roiling wave of anxiety. She hurriedly climbed the carpeted stairs, her footsteps this time making no noise at all. She intended to call out again, but the volume of the music increased as she neared the open bedroom door and her throat tightened.

She had at last recognized the song. A half-remembered snatch of lyrics echoed through her memory as she climbed. *I'll be seeing you in all the old familiar places…*

She topped the stairs, the thickness in her throat a hard ache now. *Something was wrong. Something…*

She would wonder later if she had smelled the blood before she had seen it. Or if the scent she had unconsciously attributed to an old house occupied by an old woman hadn't also been a memory.

One as elusive as the words of that song, which had played over and over again on Virginia's record player as her blood had inexorably seeped out of the wound in her head, slowly congealing in a glistening, ever-expanding puddle.

There was no need to check for a pulse. No need to call 9-1-1. Callie had never known anything in her life with such absolute certainty as she knew that.

Virginia Wilton was dead. She had been dead for a long time. And the secret she had promised to tell Callie this morning would never be revealed. Not by lips that were so ghastly white.

CHAPTER NINE

CALLIE TURNED, stumbling in her haste to get away. The
banister wavered into sight, and her hand reached out for
it. She leaned weakly against the balustrade—eyes closed,
mouth open, breathing deeply.

After a few seconds, she pushed away from its support
and ran down the stairs. She never even considered trying
to find the phone and calling the authorities. She wanted
out of the house. The smell of it, combined with what she
had seen in that upstairs room, was more than she could
bear.

She turned at the foot of the stairs, skidding on the hardwood floor. She hadn't headed toward the front door, which
was nearer, but unthinkingly retraced the path she had taken
here. Only as she neared the end of the hall into the kitchen
did she slow. While she'd been upstairs, the sun had sunk
into the bay, leaving the back of the house in total darkness.

She hesitated on the threshold, unable to see anything
but the white tiles of the floor, paler than the alternating
black ones. That same sense of foreboding she had felt as
she approached the house closed over her again.

She did not want to cross that dark expanse. Not even
to escape what she had found upstairs. Not even to summon
help from the neighbors, sitting tranquilly on their porches
across the street. Not even to avoid the stench of blood and
mildew.

Trembling, she collapsed against the wall. She put the
back of her head against it, listening to the harshness of her
own breathing. Her mother's voice, calm and reasoned,

echoed in her memory. *You're going to have to go back to your own bed.*

This was the same nameless terror she had fought so long ago. And into it came the shrilling of the phone, the sound so unexpected she jumped. Hanging on the wall beside the doorway where she was standing, it seemed preternaturally loud. Panicked, she ran across the kitchen and slammed into something big and solid, something that grunted with the impact.

"What the hell?"

Her recognition of that voice was instantaneous. And just as she had in the water last night, Callie put her arms around Ben Stanton, clinging to him mindlessly. Exactly as she had once clung to her mother, fighting the formless horror of nightmares she could never articulate.

After a few seconds, as the phone continued to ring, Ben's arms closed around her. She laid her cheek against his chest, listening to his heartbeat. Reassured by its steadiness.

And then she remembered what she had to tell him. She raised her head, looking up at his face. She could barely make out his features in the darkness, and she wondered how she could possibly have known with such certainty whom she had run into. There had been no doubt in her mind. No question. And no fear.

"She's dead," she said. "Virginia's dead."

"Dead?" he repeated, as if the word or the concept it conveyed were unfamiliar.

"Upstairs. In the room with the music." In the silence between the measured ringing of the phone, she could still hear the tinny strains of that old melody drifting down the stairs.

"What happened?" he asked.

She shook her head, the motion so slight it was barely movement.

"Callie?"

"I don't know. She was just...lying there."

"Are you sure...?"

"Oh, yes. Oh, God, yes."

She was. Even now, even at this distance, she was sure.

"Stay here," he ordered, stepping back to break her hold.

It didn't work. She wasn't about to let him leave her here alone. Not in this darkness. "No," she denied.

She clung to him, even when he put his hands on her upper arms, attempting to set her away.

"I have to go see about Virginia. You know that."

"No," she said again. Despite the knowledge that she was acting like a child, she thought she couldn't stand it if he left her alone. Not in this house. Not with that miasma of rot and mold and blood still in her nostrils. In her head.

"Then come with me."

The lesser of the two evils, but she wanted to be out of here. Away from what she had seen upstairs. Out in the fresh, heat-laden night air.

"*Damn* it."

For an instant she thought that had been directed at her, but he stepped to the side, breaking her hold by pushing her arms downward. He succeeded because he finally used his strength against her. He strode across the kitchen and picked up the receiver, mercifully cutting the phone off in midring.

"Hello?" And then he listened.

As he did, Callie crossed the room. She positioned herself behind him, her back to his, facing the blackness where she knew the outside door to be. She stood as near to Ben as she could get without physically touching him. Shoulders hunched, she crossed her arms over her chest as if she were cold. She was. She was shivering, from fear or reaction.

"It's Ben Stanton, Phoebe," he said into the receiver.

Eyes gradually adjusting to the darkness, Callie could make out the shadowed shapes of table and chairs. And then the door to the screen porch, standing open, just as she had left it.

"I'll have to call you back," Stanton said.

His voice reflected a calmness that was as comforting to

her as the rhythm of his heart, beating steadily under her cheek, had been. He reached out, wrapping his arm around her shoulders and drawing her against his side.

Tears burned her eyes at the gesture. Gratefully, she pressed her face against the cotton of his shirt, and took a deep breath, seeking control of the terror that had seized her upstairs. The fabric under her cheek smelled of washing powder. Underlying that was the unmistakably masculine scent of his body. A hint of soap. The clean, salt-tinged fragrance of the sea.

"As soon as I can," Ben promised. Then he listened, briefly this time, before he spoke again. "Callie's here. She's fine. Give me a few minutes, and I'll call you back. I promise I will, Phoebe. Don't you come over here until you hear from me."

He put the receiver on the hook, still holding Callie against his side with one arm.

"You sure you want to go back up there?"

If the option is to be left down here in the darkness...

She nodded, her skin brushing against the cloth-covered wall of his chest. His fingers squeezed her shoulder reassuringly, and then he turned, guiding her through the doorway and leading the way toward the stairs. Back toward the light and the faint, hauntingly familiar music.

THE STREET that had been so peaceful when she had parked her car in front of Virginia's house was alive with activity. Emergency vehicles, their light-bars garish in the darkness, were parked along either side, blocking traffic. People stood on the sidewalks, the alternating colors of the strobes reflecting off their shocked faces.

Even though she had gone upstairs with Ben, his arm around her, she hadn't gone into Virginia's bedroom. Not even to the door. She had stood at the top of the stairs, leaning against the banister. Ben had left her there only a matter of seconds.

It had taken him no longer than it had taken her to arrive at the same conclusion. He had reacted to it far more effi-

ciently, however, calling the dispatcher as soon as they got
back downstairs. Callie had retreated to the veranda when
the first of the emergency units arrived.

That had been maybe thirty minutes ago. Now Ben and
Doak Withers were standing out in Virginia's front yard,
talking to one of the paramedics who had been upstairs.

They were too far away for her to hear any of the conversation, but the medic kept shaking his head. Once Doak
raised both hands, palms up, the gesture questioning.

Remonstrating with the opinion he'd just been given? she
wondered. An opinion about the cause of death? Whatever
that was, no one had bothered to share the information with
her.

Finally, Doak put out his hand, talking the whole time.
After the fireman had gripped it and then Ben's, he stepped
away, heading toward one of the units parked along the
curb. The two men watched his retreat, their backs to Callie.

Withers said something to Ben. Then both of them turned
to look up at the porch where she was standing. Ben shook
his head, the movement slight. His mouth never moved,
although Doak made another comment. Without answering
it, Ben started across the yard, his ex-deputy following.
They climbed the steps together.

"Ms. Evers?" Withers said. "Like to ask you a few
questions, ma'am. If you don't mind."

Despite the way that had been phrased, she knew it
wouldn't make any difference if she did.

"What happened to Virginia?" she asked, instead of
bothering to agree to something they both knew was a fore-
gone conclusion.

"The paramedics think she must have fallen and hit her
head hard enough to knock herself unconscious. Hard
enough to open up a gash on her temple. And then…she
just never woke up."

Callie allowed the scene she had just spent the last half
hour trying to forget to reform in her head. The explanation

for what she'd seen upstairs seemed to be that Virginia Wilton had bled to death as a result of a minor accident.

"Fell over what?" she asked disbelievingly. "She was in her own bedroom, for God's sake."

Virginia had lived in this house for years. She would have known the position of every piece of furniture, especially that in her own bedroom.

"I don't guess we'll ever know what happened for sure," Doak said. "Maybe she got up too fast and felt a little faint. Paramedic said that kind of thing happens all the time."

She had heard about cases like that. Usually there was something else involved. Drugs or alcohol. Maybe in this instance the contributing factor had simply been age.

"There was so much blood," she said, her voice low.

"They think with her history she may have been on medication that contributed to that," Ben said.

"What kind of history?"

"A couple of strokes, the last one only a few months ago. They were relatively minor, but still..."

Callie nodded. Apparently there had been nothing sinister about Virginia's death. A simple accident. One of thousands that befall the elderly every year. This one with more tragic results than most.

"We were curious as to why you were here," Doak said.

Their eyes were fastened on her face, the same detached, professional interest in both. Her gaze met Ben's, wondering if he suspected what had brought her here. And then, suddenly, wondering if her careless revelation this afternoon had been what had brought *him* here.

She hadn't thought to question why Stanton was standing in the middle of Virginia's kitchen in the darkness. She had been far too relieved to find that he was.

"Ms. Evers?" Withers prompted.

"I wanted to ask her some questions," she said, pulling her eyes away from the steady regard of Stanton's.

"Questions about...?"

"The Delacroix case. I told you when I came by your

office. I'm writing a book about Katherine Delacroix's murder."

She didn't look at Ben again, but those unanswered questions still troubled her. Had he come to Virginia's to try to find out what the old woman had told her? Had he been that concerned about whatever Virginia knew?

"You thought *Mrs. Wilton* would have some information about the murder?" Doak asked skeptically.

"I'm trying to talk to as many people as I can who were residents at the time of the murder. To get a feel for atmosphere. For the town's reactions, if nothing else."

Withers nodded as if that made sense. What Virginia had intimated she knew was none of his business, Callie decided. Phoebe had been adamant that the old gossip had nothing to with Kay-Kay's death, and Virginia hadn't denied her contention. Although that begged the question of why Callie had been so determined to hear it.

"You come in the back?" Doak asked.

"The door to the screened porch was unlatched. I thought Virginia might be cooking supper. I came in, intending to knock on the back door, but…" She hesitated, trying to remember.

"Yes, ma'am?"

"It was unlocked. Actually, it wasn't completely closed. It opened when I tried to look in. I wondered why Virginia would go upstairs at night and leave the door unlocked."

"Most people around here don't bother to lock their doors," Withers said, his tone a little patronizing. "We aren't like other places where you have to be afraid all the time."

We haven't had a crime…

"Virginia locked *hers*," she said.

There was a small silence.

"How would you know that?" Ben's tone was more assertive than Doak's. And again professional.

"It was locked when I came by earlier this afternoon."

"The back door?"

"The door to the screened porch. The hook was latched."

"Did you knock?"

She nodded. "I rang the bell, and when there was no answer, I went around to see if she might be out on the back porch."

"About what time would that have been," Doak asked.

Right before I drove out to his place, Callie thought, her eyes locking with Stanton's. "Maybe…one. One-fifteen," she guessed. "After lunch."

There was a subtle change in the blue eyes, and she knew Stanton had just put those times together, but he didn't mention her visit to his place either.

"And that's when you found the screen locked?" Doak asked.

"I called up to her, but the window unit was so loud I knew she wouldn't be able to hear me."

"Maybe she was out shopping or something," Doak suggested.

She shook her head. "I saw movement. At the window upstairs. Someone pushed aside the curtain." She turned and looked up, as if she could see through the roof of the veranda. "It was the window right above our heads."

Both men looked up, and then quickly back down, as if embarrassed by that lapse of logic. And neither of them voiced the obvious. The room directly above their heads was the corner bedroom where she had found Virginia's body.

"You're sure of the time?" Ben asked.

She turned, again meeting his eyes, wondering why he had asked. "I stopped by here on the way out to your place."

Withers' brows lifted in surprise, but he didn't question the reason for that visit.

"Is she right?" Doak asked. "Between one and one-fifteen?"

"About then," Ben acknowledged.

There was a prolonged silence. A radio in an emergency

vehicle out on the street squawked, its message unintelligible.

"That doesn't make sense," Withers said finally.

"What doesn't?" Callie asked, sensing that the atmosphere had altered somehow, without understanding what she'd said to bring that change about. "Ben?"

This was the first time she had called him by his given name, and despite their physical proximity in the kitchen, saying it felt strange. Out of place. Less comfortable than his arm around her shoulders had felt.

"The paramedics placed the time of death earlier," Stanton said. His features were set, his mouth almost stern.

"Earlier? How much earlier?"

"Around eleven o'clock this morning. That's just an estimate," Doak said. "And very preliminary. Based on their observations of the condition of the body. Amount of rigor. The way the blood had settled. But hell, in *this* heat…"

Withers continued to talk. After the phrase "in this heat," however, Callie heard nothing else, her mind racing along its own track instead. She had just realized that, despite the late afternoon heat, the window unit in the bedroom hadn't been running. As loud as it had been this morning, she would have noticed it. There had been no sound in that room but the record, playing over and over again on the old-fashioned turntable.

She looked up to find Ben watching her again, a question in his eyes. As if he knew she had just thought of something that didn't fit.

"…so don't go feeling this was your fault," Doak was saying. "They're probably right about the time of death. They're usually right on the money."

The statement was just bizarre enough that it broke through her abstraction. "That *what* was my fault?" Surely he couldn't mean Virginia's death.

"I don't want you to worry that she got up too quick when she heard you calling her and fell."

Was that possible? The idea that this might be her fault

hadn't crossed Callie's mind until he'd planted it. And now that he had...

"If that were the case, then who unlocked the screen door?" Ben asked.

The possible answers to that were undoubtedly running through their minds just as they were through hers. The simplest was that it had been Virginia at the window this afternoon, just as Callie had thought at the time. And Virginia who had shut off the window unit in the bedroom and then come back downstairs sometime later in the day to unlock the screen door.

If the paramedics were right about the time of her death, however, then it would have had to be someone else at the window. Someone who had entered the house and locked both doors behind him. Someone who had watched through that upstairs window as Callie drove away. Someone who had turned off the air conditioner—to make it more difficult to pinpoint the time of Virginia's death? she wondered—and had then left the house through the kitchen, leaving both doors at the back unlocked.

"Are you saying...?" Doak paused, seeming to want someone else to put it into words.

Callie wasn't sure she was capable of doing that, although she understood what Ben was thinking.

"I'm saying that Virginia might not have been alone when she died. Not if Ms. Evers is certain about the time she was here this afternoon."

"It was after lunch," she said, trying to remember if she'd looked at the clock before she'd left. "Phoebe and I ate late because we'd been up most of the night. She took a morning nap."

She didn't mention Virginia's early morning visit. And she wasn't sure why she didn't. Maybe to avoid questions about why she hadn't conducted the interview she'd mentioned then?

"What you saw could have been the air conditioner blowing on the curtain. Making it flutter or something," Doak suggested.

"Then who shut the air conditioner off?" she asked. "It *was* off, wasn't it?"

The last was addressed to Ben, and he nodded.

"Now let's not go off half-cocked here," Doak protested. "There are probably a dozen explanations. We need to wait until the coroner gives us a definite time of death. Until then—"

"Secure the scene," Ben said.

The chief of police didn't respond immediately. Finally, as he realized the implications of that quiet command, Withers' brows lifted.

"Hell, Ben," he said, his voice subdued, "it's too late for that. There must have been ten paramedics tramping around up there. Volunteer fire department," he explained to Callie. "We get an emergency, and everybody wants in on the action."

"Do it anyway," Ben urged. "At least keep anybody else out of there."

"You were the first one here," Doak said, turning his attention back to his ex-boss. "You see anything strange?"

"I wasn't looking for anything strange."

Just like before, Callie thought, the realization chilling.

The same scenario Stanton had faced with Kay-Kay's death. And it must be a cop's worst nightmare: to believe you are dealing with one situation, which calls for one kind of reaction, and then to find out after it's too late that you were dealing with something very different.

"Secure it now, Doak," Ben said, the note of authority clear. "And tell the coroner we need something definitive on time of death as soon as possible."

"Look," Doak said, "I understand what you're suggesting, but...if Mrs. Wilton died at eleven, why would someone still be up in that room at one?"

"Most of the houses along this stretch are occupied by the elderly. Lying down after lunch is the norm rather than the exception. And those who are awake aren't going to be out in the heat of the day. Waiting a couple of hours to leave would mean less chance that whoever was here would be seen.''

Doak nodded. "Anything else?"

"Dust it. And do it yourself. Check for prints on the air conditioner. The arm of the turntable. Both back doors. You didn't touch the knob on the door into the kitchen?"

It took a second for Callie to realize he was talking to her. She shook her head. "It opened when I leaned against the glass. I never touched the knob."

"That door first," Ben ordered, turning back to Withers. "My prints will be on the inside knob of the front door where I let the paramedics in. Both our prints will be on the handle of the screen at the back, but I don't think anyone else came in that way."

I don't think anyone else came in that way. She wanted to ask why he had come in through the back, walking into Virginia's kitchen in the dark. She didn't, though. Not in front of Doak. And she couldn't explain why she was so reluctant to do that.

Of course, she herself had been less than forthcoming about several things. Like why she had come here twice today to talk to an old woman who had nothing relevant to tell her about Kay-Kay Delacroix's death. And why she hadn't mentioned Virginia's visit and the argument she'd had with Phoebe this morning.

"Is that it?" Withers asked.

"It'll do for a start," Ben said. "Just keep everybody else out. That's the most important thing we can do now."

Doak nodded, and then he hurried down the steps toward the patrol car he'd parked on the street. Behind him there was a small, strained silence. Both she and Ben had left things unsaid. Things Withers might need to know if this turned out to be what Ben was suggesting it was.

"Did you call Phoebe back?" Callie asked.

She didn't want her to come over here and discover what had happened without some prior preparation.

"I phoned Doc Cooley and asked him to go over there. I asked him to tell her what had happened to Virginia and, whatever he had to do, to keep her from coming over here.''

''I'd like to go see her. If I'm free to leave.''

The inflection of the last was questioning. Not that she expected him to tell her she couldn't. Even after the possibility had been raised that there might have been someone in Virginia Wilton's house this afternoon, no one seemed to be questioning any of Callie's actions.

''I'll go with you,'' Ben said.

''Don't worry. I'm not planning to leave town,'' she said, stung by his mistrust.

''I'd feel better if you were.''

''If I were leaving?''

That hurt, too, and she couldn't imagine why it should. Just because he had put his arm around her when she'd been terrified didn't mean he owed her any special consideration.

''It might be safer,'' he said.

She shook her head, holding his eyes as the implication washed over her. ''You think...'' She didn't finish, because she didn't want to articulate what she believed he was thinking.

''I don't like what's going on. I didn't like what happened last night. I don't like the idea that someone else might have been inside Virginia's bedroom this afternoon. I don't like the way any of this looks.''

A good cop looks at a scene like that and smells the wrongness of it. From everything she'd been told since she'd been in Point Hope, Ben Stanton had been a good cop.

''You think someone murdered her,'' she said flatly, finally putting into words what they all had been avoiding.

''I never said that.''

He didn't have to. His instructions to Doak had implied the possibility. The unavoidable conclusion to be drawn from those precautions was that this was now a crime scene.

''Whoever it was...whoever was at that window,'' she

amended, "saw me. And he had to have known I was here to talk to Virginia. I haven't made any secret of what I'm doing."

"If they're right about the time, Virginia was dead long before you arrived."

"That's what bothers me," Callie said softly. "The possibility that Virginia really did know something about Kay-Kay's murder. And the possibility that someone killed her to keep her from telling me what it was."

CHAPTER TEN

PHOEBE'S KITCHEN was crowded with neighbors and friends when they arrived. Some, like Doc Cooley and Tommy Burge, Callie knew. A couple of women she didn't recognize were attempting to make coffee, searching through the cabinets and setting mugs and spoons and neatly folded linen napkins out on the counter.

She was surprised Buck Dolan wasn't here. She thought she'd seen him while she'd been standing out on the veranda at Virginia's. As the neighbors gathered in quiet groups along the sidewalks, a man leaned against one of the oaks across the street. She had followed the glowing tip of his cigarette in the darkness as he periodically brought it to his lips.

Maybe Buck was still out there, watching as Doak and his deputy carried out Ben's suggestions. More concerned about observing the investigation of one friend's death rather than seeing to the welfare of another.

"Phoebe," Callie said gently.

The old woman was sitting at the kitchen table, forehead in her hands. At the sound of Callie's voice, she straightened, turning toward her almost eagerly. Her eyes rimmed with red, nose and cheeks blotchy, it was obvious she'd been crying.

"I didn't mean it. You know I didn't mean it," Phoebe said, reaching out to take her hand.

Callie nodded, as she knelt beside Phoebe's chair. Freeing her hand, she put her arms around the thin shoulders and hugged her close. The old woman sobbed audibly, melting into her embrace. After a few seconds, she pushed away, wiping her eyes with the paper towel she held crushed in her hand. She sniffed, and then took a deep, ratcheting breath before she spoke.

"Everett says she must have fallen."

It was almost a question. As if she expected Callie to tell her the details of Virginia's death. Resisting the urge to look at Ben or Cooley for guidance, Callie nodded again. With that encouragement, words spilled from Phoebe's lips in a torrent.

"The paramedics told him it looked like she hit her head on something. I think it was that bedside table. I *told* Virginia it wasn't a real bedside table, but she said it held a lot of things. That table was way too tall to use for a bedside table. If I told her once, I must have told her a dozen times."

Callie nodded again, as if that could make a difference now. Her eyes held on Phoebe's face, trying to evaluate her emotional stability.

"She knew I didn't mean it, didn't she?" Phoebe asked, her voice lowered to a whisper so that the question was only between the two of them. "I was upset about... You know." Her eyes lifted, quickly touching on either Ben's face or Dr. Cooley's before they came back to Callie. "Virginia never did know when to keep her mouth shut, but...I loved her. She was my best friend for more than fifty years. Ever since she married Beau Wilton and moved into that house."

"She knew you loved her, Phoebe. Don't worry about what happened this morning. Virginia knew how much you loved her."

With the questions that had been raised about Virginia's death, Callie had almost forgotten the spat. Now she felt guilty that her curiosity caused the breech in the two women's long-standing friendship.

"Everett says it was her medicine that killed her," Phoebe continued, pushing the crumpled paper towel against her nose and sniffing again. "It was supposed to thin her blood." She shook her head, eyes focused on a spot beyond Callie's shoulder. "If I'd just gotten my nose back in joint and gone on over there to make up with her, maybe..." She shook her head again, her shoulders trembling with the force of her breathing.

"There's nothing you could have done."

"Now what'd you get your nose out of joint about in the first place?" Doc Cooley asked.

Callie turned, realizing that he was standing right beside her. His tone seemed a little condescending, almost as one might talk to a child. Or, Callie acknowledged, as a long-time friend and physician might talk to his elderly, hard-of-hearing patient.

"Me and Virginia had words this morning," Phoebe admitted.

"So what else is new?" Doc asked, smiling down at her. "Virginia would *really* have thought you didn't love her if the two of you didn't go at it now and again. What was this one about? Whether the Winn Dixie or the Piggly Wiggly has the best price on broilers?"

Despite her true and heartfelt grief, Phoebe's lips moved into a reluctant smile at his teasing. "That was last week."

Doc laughed, reaching down to pat her hand. "Now I ain't seen Virginia, so what I'm telling you isn't a medical opinion, you understand. But if the drug she was taking is what I'm thinking it was, there wasn't anything you could have done to save her, even if you'd been over there with her. So I want you to quit worrying about that. Virginia would want you to. You know that, Phoebe. You just buck up, now, you hear me. And put that kind of foolishness out of your head."

"You really think that's true, Everett? That I couldn't have done anything even if I'd been there."

"I doubt you could. I doubt *I* could. So don't you go worrying anymore about that fuss y'all had."

Phoebe nodded, obviously comforted. Callie didn't see how Cooley could make that assessment without knowing Virginia's prescription. Of course, maybe what he'd said had simply been a kindness. And if it was a white lie, Callie couldn't blame him for having told it. She put her hand on the back of Phoebe's chair and got to her feet.

"Callie was gone most of the afternoon," Phoebe said. "Working on her book. The whole time, I kept thinking I ought to go over to Virginia's, but I just kept putting it off. My daddy used to say not to let the sun set on your anger, so the later it got, the more I knew I needed to put things right. To tell you the truth, I was halfway expecting her to come over here."

Having watched that battle of wills this morning, Callie imagined that would have been the usual sequence. Virginia would be the one who would give in. She would have been the one to make the first move to set things right between them.

"Then, as the day wore on, and she didn't come, I got real uneasy. I just had this feeling that something wasn't right. I called her a couple a times, but she didn't answer. Then the last time I called... That's when you picked up," Phoebe said, looking up at Stanton as she wiped her nose again. "And she'd been lying there dead all that time I'd been thinking about her."

"Doc's right, Phoebe," Ben said. "There was nothing you could have done."

"Did she go peaceful, you think?"

That was addressed to Ben, although it might have made more sense to ask that question of Cooley. It seemed especially ironic that Phoebe would ask Ben. After all, he was the one who had suggested there might have been foul play involved in Virginia Wilton's death. And if he were right, then her last few minutes wouldn't have been peaceful. Not if she had realized what was about to happen.

Callie shivered, just as she had in Virginia's dark kitchen. Again, she crossed her arms over her chest, unconsciously rubbing her hands up and down them. The silence between Phoebe's question and Stanton's answer seemed revealing, but his tone was completely normal when he gave it.

"If the paramedics are right, she just bumped her head

and never woke up. There's lots worse ways to go, Phoebe.''

For a second the scent of blood and mildew was strong in the room. Or maybe that was only in her head. She had never before noticed the musty, old-age smell that had seemed to permeate Virginia's house this afternoon in this one.

"Come on, Phoebe. Why don't you let me take you upstairs," Callie said, closing her mind to that. She had noticed that the old woman's hands were trembling more then they usually did. If they weren't careful, Phoebe would have a stroke. "Maybe Doc can give you something to help you sleep," she added.

She glanced at the doctor and found his eyes on her face. She tilted her head, questioning.

Cooley looked down at Phoebe, reaching out to take her hand. He lifted her arm and placed his fingers around her wrist, obviously checking her pulse. No one said anything, waiting until he released the bony forearm. Finally he took Phoebe's hand between both of his and smiled at her again.

"Steady as a rock. You're gonna outlive all of us, Phoebe Mae," he pronounced before he turned to look at Ben. He continued to hold Phoebe's hand in his left palm, his right hand stroking the top of it. "I asked Tommy to call Phoebe's son. Going to stay with him for a couple of days will be better for her than staying here alone and working herself into a state."

"Sam said he'd be here in about an hour," Burge said.

"I told Everett I don't *need* to go to Sam's," Phoebe said, looking up at Callie. "That's my son that lives in Mobile. As soon as he heard, though, he told Tommy he was coming over to get me. Promised to bring me back as soon as we know about the arrangements. You called Peggy Ann, didn't you, Tommy?"

"I called her," Doc said. "That's not the kind of call anybody wants to make, I can tell you. She's gonna come up as soon as she can get a flight out of Tampa."

"That's Virginia's daughter," Phoebe explained for Callie's benefit, since everyone else seemed to be aware of these relationships. "I don't know if they'll want to bury her here. Surely they will, though. Beau's buried here. All her friends."

"That's not anything for you to fret about, Phoebe," Cooley said. "Her family'll handle that. You just let it be."

An echo of what he'd told Callie this afternoon, she realized. And in the same tone. *Let it be. Let that man and this town be.* She hadn't, and now...

"Land sakes, Callie, I didn't even *think* about you," Phoebe said, shocked at her lack of consideration for a guest, even a paying one. "You're welcome to stay here. You'll have to do your own cooking, but I can give you back part of the rent—"

"Phoebe," Callie protested, stopping the spate of words. "It doesn't matter. I'll be fine, I promise."

"Well, I don't feel right leaving you, but once Sam and Debbie have made that trip... It'll just be for a couple of days. Just until Peggy Ann gets here and makes the arrangements," Phoebe promised.

Callie nodded. She knew, however, that no matter how long it was, she wouldn't stay in this house alone. She raised her eyes, looking directly into Ben's. He'd been watching her, just as Doc had. And she wasn't sure what her face revealed.

She had come to Point Hope assuming that Katherine Delacroix's murderer had killed and then moved on, as he had so long ago. She had been a fool not to consider the possibility that he might still be here. And that what she was trying to do might put her—or others—in danger.

That she should be afraid of Kay-Kay's murderer, however, had never crossed her mind. Not until last night. And even then, everyone else's explanation had been more palatable.

Someone was trying to frighten her, they had suggested. If they were, she acknowledged bitterly, they had succeeded. It seemed that every ounce of courage she possessed was gone. In the course of the last two days she had been reduced again to that frightened little girl, crying in the darkness.

Holding her eyes, Ben moved his head from side to side. Obviously a negation. Of Phoebe's suggestion? If so, she was in complete agreement. She would get a motel room. Or she would pack her bags and get out of Point Hope.

This was a case that had been unsolved for ten years. The other murder for more than a quarter of a century. What idiocy had made her believe she could figure out what had happened to those two little girls?

"I'll help you pack," she said again, the offer out before she had time to acknowledge her reason for making it. One last chance. *One last chance to learn the truth.*

PHOEBE FINISHED folding the worn nightgowns and cotton underwear she had laid out in a stack on the bed. Callie watched her, trying to think of some way to ask her questions without revealing that there had been something suspicious about Virginia's death.

As Phoebe started to fold the first of the three pairs of slacks and the matching knit tops she had taken out of the closet, Callie admitted there might not be a way. And since she had been thinking only five minutes ago that it was time to leave Point Hope, she wasn't sure why it seemed so important she learn the secret Virginia had hinted at.

She didn't suspect Ben of any wrongdoing, despite the fact that he'd been in Virginia's kitchen tonight. She couldn't explain her surety that he had had nothing to do with either Virginia's death or what had happened during the jubilee.

Not logically, anyway. And in a situation as fraught with danger as this, logic, not emotion, should be the guiding force in everything she did. Instead, she was basing her judgment of Ben Stanton on factors which involved nothing *but* emotion.

The feel of his arm around her shoulders, comforting, drawing her close. The way he had looked at her as he'd knelt beside her in the boat, his eyes concerned and compassionate.

Only last night, she thought, watching Phoebe's palsied hands move over the garments, smoothing them one by one as she laid them in her suitcase. Last night. Time had telescoped since her arrival here.

Everything was moving too quickly. A new and far more terrible event had occurred before she had had time to understand the significance of the threat against her that had preceded it. There were too many things she was missing. And if she didn't figure some of them out before Phoebe left—

"I need to know what Virginia meant," she said aloud.

Phoebe's eyes, looking old and tired, lifted. "Meant about what, dear?"

"About why Ben Stanton hated Tom Delacroix. About the bad blood that had nothing to do with the evidence. Why Ben was so sure Delacroix killed his daughter."

"That's nothing but gossip. Virginia should never have brought it up."

But she did. And now she's dead. And I have to know if that gossip had anything to do with her death.

She couldn't say any of that to Phoebe. Or to anyone else. Officially, Virginia's death was an accident. Right now at least. And it might very well *have* been. Just as what had happened to her last night *might* have been someone trying to scare her. She doubted both those suppositions.

"Virginia thought it was important," she said.

"Well, it wasn't. Virginia was wrong. Kay-Kay's dead, and so is Tom. Digging up that old dirt isn't going to bring either of them back to life. I'm not about to let you or anybody else speak ill of the dead."

Something that reflected badly on Delacroix then, and not on Stanton. With that realization there was an easing of the unacknowledged dread she hadn't realized she harbored.

"Was it true?" she asked.

A crease formed between Phoebe's eyes. "True?"

"The gossip Virginia was talking about? Just tell me if it was true, Phoebe."

"I told you it isn't important—"

"But it *is*. I promise you that. I won't put it in any book, if that's what you're worried about. It'll stay between you and me, I swear. Just tell me that much. Was it true?"

The old lady's eyes held on her face, and Callie waited, unconsciously holding her breath.

"Only three people know the answer to that," Phoebe said finally. "And one of them's dead. If you want the truth…"

She hesitated, looking down on her trembling hands. Suddenly, she pressed them together so tightly the swollen knuckles whitened. She brought them to the center of her chest, holding them against her breastbone.

"I hate being old," she said, tears welling. "I hate never knowing anymore what's right and what's wrong. You'd think I would by now. You'd think I'd always be sure what was the right thing to do." She shook her head, the palsy making the gesture infinitely sad. "I don't gossip," she said softly. "I don't hold with those who do. You can ask Ben if it's really all that important."

"Phoebe—"

"That's all I'm saying, so don't you ask me anymore. I don't think I can bear it tonight," she said, with a break in her voice. "You ask Ben. And whatever he tells you—if he tells you—then you'll know it's the truth."

"SHE'LL BE ALL RIGHT," Cooley said, as the four of them stood in Phoebe's front yard, watching the taillights of her son's van disappear down the again-peaceful street. "Phoebe's a tough old bird. All that generation is."

Callie realized that she had mentally assigned Cooley and Phoebe to the same generation. Forced to think about it, she acknowledged that there could indeed be a generation's span between their ages. Phoebe was in her eighties, while

Doc, only semiretired, might very well be in his early sixties.

"They survived a depression and a world war," Burge said.

"And lost their sons in Korea and Vietnam," Cooley added.

Phoebe had, Callie remembered. And then she had lost her beloved Hobart, too. Facing the deaths of those she loved was not unfamiliar to someone who had lived as long as Phoebe.

"I'm heading home," Tommy said. "Let me know if there's anything else I can do, Ben." Again, there was that unconscious assigning of authority to Ben Stanton.

"Guess I'll get on back, too." Doc said. "Give you a lift, Tommy? You're on my way. Unless you need me for something else." The last was addressed to Stanton.

"Thanks," Ben said, shaking hands with Burge. Then he turned to the doctor, enclosing Cooley's hand in both of his. "You always get stuck with the dirty work, Doc. Thanks."

"Goes with the territory. I knew that going in."

"Does it get any easier?" Callie asked, thinking about having to tell someone a friend was dead. Or having to tell a daughter that her mother was gone. Cooley had done both tonight.

"At least I know what to expect. That's the main difference between now and when I started practicing."

"I appreciate you coming over to check on Phoebe," Ben said. "I was afraid she was going to show up at Virginia's."

"Phoebe's not only my patient, she and Hobart were friends."

Tommy had started off across the lawn, heading toward Cooley's car. The doctor, however, didn't seem in a hurry to put his decision into action.

"How about you, Ms. Evers? You gonna stay here like Phoebe suggested?" he asked.

"Long enough to straighten up in the kitchen at least,"

she said. Her eyes touched on Ben's face before they moved back to Cooley's. "I'll decide what I'm going to do after that."

"You need a little something to help you sleep?"

The offer was tempting. Wherever she ended up for the night, she suspected the events from this day would play over and over in her head.

"I don't think so," she said. She had never used drugs as an escape, not even a temporary one. She was too old to start now. "Thanks for the offer, though."

"Suit yourself," Doc said.

He turned, following Burge across the lawn. His back to them, he lifted one hand, waving goodbye with a single, side-to-side motion of his wrist.

"How about it, Tommy? You game for a nightcap?" he called.

Burge's reply was unintelligible, but whatever it was, it made Cooley laugh. She and Ben listened as their voices faded away under the shadows of the oaks. After a few seconds, car doors slammed, followed by the sound of an engine starting. Then, just as they had with Sam Robinson's car, she and Ben watched the taillights disappear down the street.

"You aren't staying here," he said.

"I know."

"Were you serious about straightening up?"

"I can do it in the morning," she said. "I need to make sure everything's turned off. Check the coffeemaker. And then I guess I should find a motel. Any suggestions?"

She looked up, but his eyes were still directed toward the end of the street where Doc's car had disappeared. Toward Virginia's house, she realized.

"Come home with me," Ben said.

She examined the words, unsure that he'd said what she thought she'd heard. They had been straightforward enough, however, not to lend themselves to any other interpretation.

"Why?"

"Because I think you'll be safer. Safer than being by yourself in a motel."

She let the silence build as she thought about the offer. *Come home with me.* Protection wasn't usually the motive for a man to issue that kind of invitation. And in this case...

Logic versus emotion. Despite her instincts, it certainly wasn't logical for her to trust Ben Stanton. Not in this situation. Not enough to be alone with him. Especially since no one would know where she was or who she was with.

No one would know where she was...

"Callie?"

"I need a few things from inside," she said.

"I'll go with you."

Protection, she thought again. Maybe Stanton didn't have any motive other than that for his invitation. But, of course, she did in accepting it.

Ask Ben, Phoebe had suggested. *And if he tells you anything, you'll know it's the truth.*

There were a lot of truths that had not been revealed about what happened the night Kay-Kay Delacroix died. Just as there were other truths about what had happened today. *Ask Ben.*

She turned, walking up the sidewalk to climb the front steps of Phoebe Robinson's old house. Very much aware of the man who followed her.

CHAPTER ELEVEN

"YOU HUNGRY?"

She was, Callie realized with a sense of shock. It didn't seem as if she should be, not after what had happened today. But it had been a very long time since she and Phoebe had shared lunch and some very strained silences during the conversation that had accompanied it.

It was too dark to see her watch. The last time she remembered noticing the time was when she had been helping Phoebe pack. It had been after eight then, and that had been at least a couple of hours ago.

"Actually...I am."

She was aware that Ben turned toward her, pulling his eyes from the road for a few seconds. "What sounds good?"

The exchange was surreal, given their previous relationship and the events of the past few hours. It reminded her a little of those two women, laying out linen napkins and Phoebe's silver spoons alongside the too-weak coffee they'd made, as if those acts might in some way ease the pain of Virginia's death. There was something very human about going on with the ordinary things of life, no matter the chaos that surrounded you.

"Nothing really," she said. "I just know I need to eat."

She was both nauseated and lightheaded. Almost disoriented. Maybe part of that was because she was riding in a truck with Ben Stanton *and* planning to spend the night with him.

Despite however practical her reasons for that might be, the situation was decidedly unreal. It was suddenly made more so by the abrupt turn Ben made, heading the pickup down an unpaved road, without any lessening of its speed. And it was not the drive that led to his house.

Through the open driver's-side window, she heard the music before they topped the rise, revealing the restaurant below. The ramshackle structure seemed to totter on top of its stilts, hanging haphazardly over the edge of the water.

Someone had wrapped strands of miniature Christmas tree bulbs along the top railing of its attached pier. Their lights were reflected in the bay like stars. That touch of elegance warred with the reverberating bass from the country ballad that was blaring through an outside speaker.

"I know it doesn't look like much," Ben said, guiding the pickup over a series of bone-jarring potholes in the dirt parking lot. "But the food's good."

It would have to be, she thought, as he pulled in between a mud-splattered SUV and another truck, bass boat attached. He shut off the engine and rolled up his window, mercifully lowering the volume of the music.

"We have to eat somewhere," he said in explanation, maybe even in apology. "We'll have to go inside," he added, when she made no move to get out of the truck. "They don't do takeout."

Meaning they would have to sit at a table like an ordinary couple out for the evening. *And if there had ever been a less ordinary evening… Or two people who were less likely to be a couple.*

"Unless you'd rather not be seen with me."

Surprised, she looked up to find he was watching her again. The flickering red neon sign atop the restaurant gave a ruddy glow to his sun-darkened skin.

"What does that mean?"

"I tend to forget what the world out there thinks of me."

Son of a bitch. Botched investigation. It was all right for him to play cop when all he had to do was write the occasional speeding ticket…

All the derogatory remarks that had been made about Ben Stanton since she'd been in Point Hope echoed in her mind. And considering them in light of what he'd just said, she laughed.

His head tilted, questioning her reaction.

"I should probably tell you that there are a few people *here* who aren't exactly admirers of yours."

His lips flattened, and then, as she watched, the corners lifted. Almost a smile.

"I ignore them, too. I'd forgotten how many people you've talked to."

"Not nearly as many as I'd intended to. Things…" She shook her head, thinking about the past couple of days. "Things keep happening."

He turned, staring out at the bay through the windshield. He laid his forearms on top of the steering wheel, crossing them at the wrists. She was relieved to escape, even briefly, the intensity of those eyes.

"I think you may be right," he said. He hadn't turned his head, his gaze still focused on the water.

She almost asked, "Right about what?" Then, as the possible connotations of that statement filtered through her exhaustion, she found she was incapable of saying anything for a long time.

"Right about Delacroix?" she asked finally, her voice husky from the constriction of her throat.

"I don't think this is about scaring you away."

"Then you think… You think whoever is doing this might really *be* the same person who killed Kay-Kay?"

His head moved slowly from side to side, the motion not strong enough to indicate denial.

"I would have staked my life," he said softly.

On Tom Delacroix's guilt. In a way, he had. Ben Stanton had spent two long, frustrating years trying to indict Kay-Kay's father for her murder. And he had just confessed he was no longer certain Delacroix had committed the crime.

"Why did you go to Virginia's?" she asked.

He turned to face her. A crease had formed between the dark brows, and she supposed her question did seem a non sequitur.

"Tonight?"

She nodded.

"You said Virginia told you there was bad blood between me and Delacroix. I wanted to know what she meant."

"Was there? Bad blood, I mean? Before the murder?"

"Lorena didn't tell you?"

She wasn't sure if that was another accusation that she was aligned with Mrs. Delacroix, or if, given the efficiency of small-town gossip, he was aware she had met with Kay-Kay's mother this afternoon. She decided to give him the benefit of the doubt and go with the latter interpretation.

"She told me you were a son of a bitch," Callie said. "I don't know if that's got anything to do with her husband, but I took it to mean there was bad blood between you and her."

He laughed, the sound unexpected, and without amusement. "You could say that."

"Because you accused Delacroix of murder?"

The tempo of the music changed, becoming more upbeat. The bass wasn't strong enough anymore to rattle the windows, but it filled the silence, which lasted long enough to become edgy.

"Virginia didn't tell you anything, did she?" Ben asked. "I couldn't figure out why you'd go back to see her, when I knew damn well she didn't have any information about Kay-Kay's murder. But that wasn't why you wanted to talk to her. She hinted there was animosity between me and Tom. *That's* what you wanted to ask her about."

Cooley had told her Stanton was a good cop. A good investigator. From their previous encounters, she had known he was bright, so she supposed she shouldn't be surprised that he'd arrived at that conclusion.

"Her exact words were that you had more reasons than just the evidence to think Delacroix had killed his daughter. Phoebe wouldn't let her say anymore, but when her back was turned, Virginia promised she'd tell me what she meant. *If* I'd come to her house later on."

"When did she tell you to do that?"

"She came over to Phoebe's this morning to make sure I was all right. That's what she said, anyway. I think she was just curious."

"Did you tell her you thought somebody tried to kill you?"

She hadn't. Not in so many words. Certainly not words as blunt as those she had used to Ben.

"I suggested someone had a reason to try to keep me from asking questions. Something more than just to prevent interest in Kay-Kay's death from being stirred up again."

"Make any suggestion as to who you thought that might be?"

"I don't *know* who that might be," Callie said truthfully, bewildered by the question.

"Obviously someone who had a connection to that other murder in North Carolina."

She had said that to Lorena Delacroix, and for a moment, she wondered if Lorena had relayed that information to Ben. But the necessity of such a link would be obvious. It was what had brought her to Point Hope.

She nodded. "To the location. Or the family."

"But you haven't found that connection?"

"Not yet."

"And Virginia didn't offer any possibilities?"

No one had. She hadn't really told all that many people about the other murder, she realized. Ben. Lorena Delacroix. The two old women this morning. She wasn't sure she had mentioned it in her conversation to Cooley, but she knew she hadn't said anything about it to Withers or Dolan or Tommy Burge.

"She... Actually, I'm not sure how much of what I said made an impression on her. That there had been another murder did, but... She asked me if you knew about it. I told her that you did now. That I'd told you."

Again the music from the speaker was the only sound in the cab of the truck. The nasal twang of the vocals, something about lost love, seemed out of place with what they were discussing. She had time to listen to a couple of verses of the lament before Ben spoke again.

"Did you tell Virginia and Phoebe about the flower?"

She had told Lorena. And Cooley. She knew she should confess those disclosures, and she would at some point. But that wasn't what Ben had asked. And after all, neither of those people had turned up dead.

"I told them the murders shared some unusual aspects."

"But you didn't mention the drawing specifically?"

She shook her head, again feeling a trace of guilt that she had mentioned the information to the others. Ben had kept that secret for ten years, and it now felt like a betrayal that she had revealed it.

"We need the phone records," he said.

"*Phone* records?"

"Virginia wouldn't have been able to keep that kind of information to herself. She would have wanted to tell somebody about the other murder. About the similarities to Kay-Kay's. Since Phoebe was there when you mentioned it, that wouldn't have been who she called. Not after their argument about gossiping."

"You think she *called* someone to tell them what I'd said."

"Knowing Virginia, I'd be willing to bet on it. At least we have to hope she did."

Because if they could find out the name of the person she'd called, then...they'd know who had killed her? And who had killed Kay-Kay? It seemed too easy. Too simple a solution for this convoluted, decade-old mystery.

"Unless she called everybody in town," Ben added, putting that speculation into perspective.

"Or nobody."

"Knowing Virginia, I don't believe she could have managed that."

"I don't know. Phoebe was pretty hard on her. I thought that's why she wouldn't let me in this afternoon."

"Hard on her how?"

"When she mentioned whatever had been between you

and Delacroix, Phoebe told her that it was nothing but ugly gossip and then she sent Virginia home. She told her...'' As she remembered them, Phoebe's words seemed eerily prophetic, but she made herself repeat them. "Phoebe told her not to say something that would get somebody mad at *her*. When I went to see Virginia and the door was locked, I thought she'd had second thoughts about sharing her gossip, since Phoebe felt so strongly about it.

"But...even if she did call someone, we can't know what she talked to them about. Maybe she talked about the old gossip or her fuss with Phoebe and *not* about the other murder." She hadn't asked him directly, but it must be obvious that she wanted to know about the bad blood Virginia had mentioned. After all, she had gone to her house twice today to find out. "Unless everyone in town already knew whatever she was alluding to."

Phoebe and Virginia had. Maybe this wasn't nearly the dark secret she had supposed it to be this morning.

"In Point Hope everybody knows everything," he said. "At least they think they do."

"Do they know this?"

"Most of it. Lorena and I have...some history."

The pause had been infinitesimal, but with his linking of their names, Callie had already arrived at that conclusion before he confirmed it. For some reason, the nausea she had been blaming on an empty stomach stirred again.

"A sexual history?" she asked.

And felt like a fool as he let the words lie, unanswered, between them. That pale, round face with its perfect nose and shrewd blue eyes was unforgivably clear in her mind's eye.

She was disappointed, she realized. Disillusioned with the image of Ben Stanton that she had created in her own mind. A creation begun long before she'd arrived in Point Hope.

She couldn't imagine why she was. After all, he was very attractive, obviously virile and an unattached male. He undoubtedly had a long and varied "sexual history," involv-

ing a lot of women. She had to have known that, somewhere in the back of her mind. None of it had mattered.
Not as long as it *stayed* in the back of her mind.

Hearing him confess to a liaison with Lorena Delacroix,
however, created pictures she didn't want in her head. It
wasn't as if she herself had made impeccable decisions in
her personal relationships. And it was patently ridiculous
for her to presume to be disapproving of anything in Ben
Stanton's past, even considering her unfavorable impression of the woman involved.

She hadn't liked Lorena Delacroix. Everything about her
had rung false. From her pious invocation for God to rest
her husband's soul to her lack of emotion over her daughter's death to her blatant hatred of Ben Stanton.

Just as her instinct had been, almost from the beginning,
to trust Ben, her emotional responses to Lorena Delacroix
had all been unfavorable. She had fought them because she
needed the information Kay-Kay's mother could provide,
but from the first, she hadn't liked her.

"We come from the same place," Ben said, his voice
low. "Share the same background. I've known Lorena all
my life. And I understand why she is…what she is."

His gaze was again directed toward the dark water.
Hands crossed at the wrist, the long, tanned fingers hung
relaxed on the back side of the steering wheel.

"Maybe it's hard for someone who's not from here to
know what it's like to grow up on the wrong side of the
tracks in a place like Point Hope. You're always on the
outside looking in. It's more than money. More than family.
Mine and Lorena's have been here as long as anybody
else's, but…

"Maybe it's because they made their living from the bay.
Suffered through the good times and the bad associated
with it. For Lorena's family, those times were mostly bad.
Her daddy was a drunk. A mean drunk. I never thought
she'd end up with another one."

"Tom Delacroix," Callie said.

"Except for his drinking, he represented everything Lorena had ever wanted."

"And that's why she married him?" *Him instead of you?* "Because he came from the 'right side' of Point Hope?"

"I guess it's easy to judge that kind of ambition, too."

"I'm not *judging* it. I'm trying to understand it." But as she made the denial, she knew that what he'd accused her of was true. She had already made her judgment of Lorena Delacroix during this afternoon's interview. "So...if it was her choice, why does she hate you?"

"I don't think she does," he said.

"She gives a pretty good impression of it."

A muscle tightened in the line of his jaw, knotting and then releasing. Callie watched the movement, illuminated by the glow from the neon sign.

"Lorena needs a lot of attention," he said finally. "Tom didn't always provide it."

"So you did." The tone was flatter and harsher than she'd intended. It sounded like an accusation.

He turned his head, looking at her in the semidarkness. "*Not* after she was married. If that's what you're thinking."

It had been, of course. She had thought that's what they were talking about. Small-town adultery. The kind of ordinary, everyday gossip someone like Virginia would probably relish.

Phoebe had been right, she realized. This didn't have anything to do with the murder.

"And that's what Virginia wanted to tell me? The fact that you and Lorena had once...been involved, and she married Tom Delacroix instead?"

"I don't *know* what Virginia wanted to tell you."

She waited, the music again filling the silence between them. "What does that mean?" she asked finally.

She was too tired to deal with this, she thought. She felt empty, both physically and emotionally. And this whole story seemed to have been drawn out past the point of relevancy.

What the hell could it matter if Ben and Lorena Delacroix had once slept together? Especially if, as he claimed, that relationship had ended before she'd married Delacroix.

Ben took a breath, expelling it so that it was almost a sigh. And then he turned to face her again.

"I was stationed at Fort Polk. In Louisiana," he explained, probably aware from her expression that she wasn't following. "I hadn't been home in a couple of years. My mother was dead and my daddy wasn't the kind to write, so I didn't have any idea what was going on back here. Then, all of a sudden, Lorena shows up."

"At Fort Polk?"

"I didn't think anything about it at the time. It was exactly the kind of silly, thoughtless thing she'd do. The kind of thing she'd done all her life. A little wild. Not very smart. She'd ridden the damn Greyhound bus, all that way to Louisiana. Just to see me, she said. And I have to confess, I wasn't opposed to her being there. A little flattered, I guess. Homesick, maybe. I hadn't known that until I saw her."

"So you...renewed your acquaintance," she said, her voice still too flat, so that his mouth tightened in response.

"We had sex," he corrected, his tone matching the lack of expression in hers. "We spent most of that weekend in bed in a motel room. I put her on the bus back here on Sunday afternoon. And I didn't see her again for three years."

"Were you in love with her?"

It was a woman's question, the kind of thing that had seemed important to ask until she had. Then it seemed only ridiculous.

"No. And before you start judging *that,* I can tell you she wasn't in love with me either."

"She just needed some *attention.*"

"I thought so. I found out later that there was a little more to it than that."

"Meaning?"

"Meaning she'd been sleeping with Tom Delacroix for several months before she made that visit."

"And you were supposed to be her last fling before the wedding?"

It made sense. According to him, he and Lorena had a history. Maybe she had been reluctant to give that relationship up. To give *him* up. And that was something which, as another woman strongly attracted to Ben Stanton, Callie could certainly understand.

And there had been a more than twenty-year gap between Tom Delacroix's age and that of his wife. The tabloids had speculated at the time of their daughter's murder that Lorena had married Tom for his money.

So none of what Ben was telling her should come as a surprise. Before she married Delacroix, Lorena had arranged one last meeting with a man she had probably found sexually attractive most of her life.

"Everything she'd ever wanted was right at her fingertips," Ben said, "and she couldn't get him to commit. She couldn't get him to marry her. Why should he? He was getting what he wanted. Lorena wasn't the kind of woman anyone could imagine Delacroix choosing for his wife. When he did, as hard as she tried, she never fit in. Never was accepted by his friends. Certainly not by his family."

"Then why did he marry her?" Callie asked, throwing the question out, not because she cared, but because it seemed called for. Expected.

"He married her because she turned up pregnant," Ben said. "Carrying the child Tom Delacroix had always wanted and his first wife hadn't been able to give him. A little girl," he added softly, as the slow chill of realization began to make its way up Callie's spine. "A little girl they named Katherine."

CHAPTER TWELVE

"SHE WAS YOURS." Callie whispered the words as the implication of what he had just said hit her. "Kay-Kay was *your* daughter."

It made sense of the years he'd spent trying to solve her murder. Not the devotion of a good cop, but a father's desire to bring to justice the murderer of his own child.

"I don't know," Ben said flatly.

"But given the timing…" She knew this was something he must have gone over again and again, trying to prove, if only to himself, whether Kay-Kay could have been his.

"By the time I got out of the army and came back here, Lorena was married. At some point I learned she had a child. I don't remember how or when because it didn't make any great impression on me.

"I even saw Kay-Kay occasionally. No bells went off. There was no instant recognition of kinship. No blood called to blood." His voice was still low, the tone almost mocking. "I didn't know how old she was. I hadn't been around enough kids to even make an educated guess about her age. And frankly, trying to do that never crossed my mind."

"You *never* suspected?"

"She looked like Lorena. Like she had when she was little. There was nothing about her that would make you think she might be anything other than what she was supposed to be. Tom Delacroix's heir. And the absolute light of his life."

Tom doted on that little girl, Virginia had said. And Doc Cooley's assessment had been much the same.

"Then how in the world could you believe he killed her?"

"Because Lorena told him."

It took a few seconds for her to comprehend what he meant because it seemed so bizarre. "She *told* him Kay-Kay wasn't his? Why would she do that?"

"I told you. She needs *lots* of attention."

Emotion, which had been carefully contained when he had talked about the possibility that Kay-Kay could be his child, was now in his voice. It was the same anger she had heard the day she confronted him with the similarities between the murder in North Carolina and the one in Point Hope.

"She told him Kay-Kay wasn't his daughter to get *attention?*"

"Maybe being married to Tom was getting dull. Or maybe Lorena had finally realized that the things she'd thought she wanted all her life hadn't made her happy and they weren't going to. I don't have any idea why she decided to tell either of us anything. And after all this time, I don't know that what she told us was the truth. All I know is that in my case—"

He stopped the words, cutting them off abruptly, and again she waited.

"For some reason, she had decided she wanted me back in her life. Maybe she thought that knowing Kay-Kay was mine would somehow…" He made that small negative motion with his head again, his eyes once more on the water. "Who knows what she thought. I've given up trying to figure Lorena out. All I can tell you is that she came out to my house one night and told me Kay-Kay was mine and that she'd finally told Tom the truth. Less than forty-eight hours later that little girl was dead."

"And you believed Tom had killed her…in *revenge?* Oh, Ben, that doesn't even make sense."

"None of it ever did," he said. And then, after a moment, "I don't suppose you still want something to eat?"

Without waiting for an answer, he turned the key in the

ignition, the movement of those long fingers somehow conveying the same fury his voice had held. The engine of the pickup roared to life, and he gave it enough gas that the wheels sprayed dirt and gravel as he backed out and headed across the parking lot toward the road. He made no attempt to ease their passage over the potholes this time.

"Ben," she said, putting her hand on his arm.

It wasn't protest. It was, perhaps, more in the way of comfort. Or apology. Because she had finally recognized that she had brought about exactly what Doc Cooley feared for him.

Ben Stanton had put this pain behind him once. As much as it would be humanly possible for him to do. He had gotten on with his life. Living in the same town. Living among people who knew every detail of what they, and he, viewed as his failure. He had been able to do that because he didn't give a damn what they thought about him. Only for what he thought about himself.

And he had cared about bringing Kay-Kay's murderer to justice. He had cared desperately about the death of a little girl, who might have been his own daughter. Now, after the agony had faded to something bearable, Callie had convinced him that his failure had been even more damaging than he had once believed. And his guilt greater.

He understood now that he had been wrong in his original hypothesis about the cause of Kay-Kay's murder. Because of that error in judgment, he had gone after the wrong man. And in doing so, he had let the real murderer escape.

Cooley had warned her, but she hadn't listened. *I thought it would break him, strong as he is. That baby's murder changed him, but thank God, it didn't destroy him.*

Another failure might. If it did, that was a guilt *she* would have to live with. Just as she would have to live with the knowledge that her questions might have led to Virginia Wilton's death. And in spite of it, Kay-Kay Delacroix and Mary Cameron were still dead. Their killer still unpunished.

"I have to make that call to Doak," Ben said, turning his forearm so that her fingers slipped off.

His voice was again controlled. He wanted a record of the phone calls Virginia had made this morning. And he would have to rely on Doak to get it. It would take an official request to obtain that information. Despite the air of authority Ben Stanton carried, an authority Withers still willingly obeyed, he no longer had the power to demand its release.

"Did Virginia know?" Callie asked, trying to come to terms with the repercussions of what she had set in motion. "About Kay-Kay, I mean? About the possibility…?"

"Despite Lorena's peculiarities, I can't imagine that would be something she'd want to broadcast. Surely she wouldn't want to bastardize her own daughter."

"But if Delacroix had divorced her for that reason, the question of her daughter's paternity would have come out."

"You didn't know Tom Delacroix," Ben said. "The Delacroix always had more pride than money. And they had a hell of a lot of both. Tom would never have admitted someone else had fathered *his* daughter, not even to keep her from inheriting.

"Besides," he continued, "it wouldn't be that easy to disavow her, even if he took Lorena to court or demanded proof of paternity. His name was on her birth certificate. Kay-Kay was in his will and had been since her birth. He had *always* acknowledged her. I'm not sure he could have gotten out of paying child support, at the very least, even if tests proved she wasn't his. Knowing Lorena, I'd be willing to bet she had checked all that out before she dropped her bombshell."

"So…why tell him? What *did* she possibly hope to gain?"

"Freedom. With a guarantee that she'd always be provided for—as Kay-Kay's mother. Or maybe she believed it would give her power. Something to hold over Tom's head. Something to use against him if he didn't let her do whatever she wanted."

"I don't understand."

"Maybe she threatened to reveal his impotence. Or to reveal that she'd tricked him into marrying her. To reveal to the world that the child who would get at least some of the Delacroix money, no matter what he did, wasn't even a Delacroix."

"Would he have given in to that kind of blackmail?"

"Opt for an ongoing private humiliation rather than a public one? If you knew Delacroix, that would make sense. I'm not claiming to know what Lorena was thinking. I never have."

"But at the time of the murder you believed that instead of living with those threats, Delacroix just decided to kill *Kay-Kay*? Why not kill Lorena? That I *could* understand."

That would have been a far more normal reaction. Believing Delacroix would kill a little girl he adored made no sense. She couldn't believe it had to Ben. Not even back then, dealing with all he'd been dealing with. Of course, she didn't know these people, and he did. All his life.

"There would still be the problem of Kay-Kay," Ben said. "If Tom managed to get away with killing Lorena, he couldn't afford to announce to the world that her daughter hadn't been his child. That would have appeared to be a pretty powerful motive for him to be his wife's murderer."

"That seems convoluted," she said doubtfully.

"Look, I never claimed to be objective about this. At the time, I thought the idea that he'd put his whole heart into loving a little girl who wasn't his had gotten to Tom. He thought about it through those two days, and then, when he was drunk enough, he snapped. Killing Lorena wouldn't have been nearly so easy as getting rid of the bastard she had foisted on him was." The bitterness underlying that accusation was clear.

"And then they just stayed together? He didn't divorce her. She didn't leave him. That should have been some indication—"

"United front. The world thought one or both of them

had killed their daughter. Those accusations necessitated
that they stay married. Or maybe she really didn't know
that he'd done it. At least…that's how I read it then. A few
months later Tom had his first heart attack. Lorena played
at being devoted wife, along with her continuing role as
grieving mother. Eventually, when the second heart attack
killed him, she got what she had wanted all along. Her
freedom *and* the Delacroix money.''

"Except Delacroix didn't kill Kay-Kay,'' Callie reminded him. "He couldn't have because he didn't kill
Mary. And the two murders have too many elements in
common, even if you discount the rose, for all of them to
be coincidence.''

"The Bureau's profiler told me something I've never forgotten. At the time…'' His voice faded.

"Ben?'' she questioned as the silence went on and on.

"He said drawing that rose was a sign of love. Like
murderers who arrange their victim's body so that they look
comfortable and at peace. Posing them, so the pain they
just put them through won't be so apparent.''

"A sign of *love?*''

Of all the motives she had imagined behind the drawing,
that one had never crossed her mind. And she wasn't sure,
at least in Mary's case, that she could ever accept it.

"A sign of his affection,'' Ben verified. "He drew something beautiful. Delicate, small and tender. And he hid it
underneath her hair, protecting it from anyone else's eyes.
It was just for her. When they told me that, it all seemed
to fit. I thought the rose meant that, in spite of everything,
Tom loved her. He needed to tell her that he did, even as
he killed her.''

As he talked, the words realigned themselves in her consciousness, shifting to form another kind of pattern. Not the
one Ben had thought they formed ten years ago.

"Hidden,'' she said. "Hidden under her hair because
what he felt about her was a secret. A secret affection.''

He turned his head, looking toward her in the darkness.
The speed of the pickup diminished, slowing as he thought

about what she said. And then, without comment, he turned his eyes back toward the road, his foot again pressing down on the accelerator.

BEN STOPPED the truck in the exact spot where it had been parked the first time she'd come here. He cut off the engine and killed the lights, but neither of them made any move to get out.

After a few minutes, the noise of the tree frogs resumed in the thick woods around the clearing. There were no lights on inside the cabin, but a halogen lamp set high on a pole beside the pier provided some illumination, filtering outward to fight the darkness in the front. Enough that she could see his eyes when he turned toward her.

"Stay here," he ordered.

"Why?"

She didn't want to stay here. Not alone. It was finally hitting home to her what she had done. A murderer had lain unexposed for more than twenty-five years, and she was responsible for bringing him out of hiding to kill again.

"I want to take a look around," he said.

"No."

"Callie—"

"Nobody knows I'm with you. They couldn't. We just need to go inside and make that call. The sooner we have the information about who Virginia talked to…"

The sooner they would know the name of the murderer? Could it really be that simple? Maybe it would be. They wouldn't know unless they tried.

She put her fingers around the handle of the door. At the thought of stepping out into that unknown darkness, however, she hesitated. She heard the door on Ben's side open and then close, the sound loud in the nighttime stillness.

She watched him walk around the front of the pickup. He opened her door and offered his hand, waiting for her to put her fingers into his. That's all she had to do. Trust him to protect her. She had no reason not to. No reason except…

Secret affection. The troubling phrase echoed again in her head. An affection such as a man who had just discovered Kay-Kay was his daughter might have felt?

"What's wrong?" Ben asked.

She shook her head, forcing herself to place her hand in his as she slid off the high seat. His fingers closed strongly around hers. As they did, in the diffuse glow cast by the lamp over the pier, she saw his mouth move. He was smiling at her.

He used his hold on her hand to urge her away from the truck, and then he slammed the passenger-side door. She jumped at the sound, just as she had tonight when the phone rang in Virginia's kitchen. And as he had then, Ben put his arm around her shoulders, guiding her toward the front door of the cabin. His home. His territory.

Was this where he had brought Kay-Kay that night? Was this the crime scene that Ben Stanton, despite the thoroughness of his investigation, had never been able to discover. No neighbors to watch his comings and goings. No one living near enough to hear anything. The perfect place for a murder.

She shivered involuntarily, thinking, too late, how completely isolated they were. *Hidden. Hidden affection.*

"Cold?" he asked.

As death. The words formed in her head, and as they did, she pulled away from his hold. She turned toward the truck, trying to visualize, even as she began to run toward it, if he had left the keys in the ignition.

"Callie?"

The sound of her name was accompanied by a soft *phut,* which seemed to come from the woods to the right of the cabin. And then, just as it had out in the bay, something hit her from behind. Her knees buckled as she was thrown to the ground.

Stanton's arms were around her. He rolled, carrying her with him. And then she was again facedown on the ground, his body spread-eagled over hers. He held her down, the side of her face pressed into the dirt.

She was too shocked to offer any resistance. She opened her eyes and realized she was facing one of the tires of the truck. She was so close she could smell the rubber, still hot from its recent contact with the highway.

There was another of the strange, pneumatic noises, and dirt sprayed over them. She closed her eyes, putting up her hand in an ineffectual attempt to protect her face. Another *phut,* and the tire she was facing deflated, sinking into the sandy soil with a hiss.

"Under the truck," Ben demanded. "Get under the truck."

At some time between the dirt hitting her hair and his command, she had finally realized someone was shooting at them. Using her elbows and knees, she scrambled under the protection of the pickup, canted now at a slight angle because of the flat. She turned her head in time to watch Ben join her.

"What the hell is—" she began.

"Shh," he whispered.

They listened together. Her wildly beating heart sent blood roaring through her ears, so that she was afraid she wouldn't be able to hear anything but its pulse. In the still-ness that had fallen after those three quick shots, however, she clearly heard movement in the bushes.

And she heard Ben's instructions. He turned his head, his mouth near enough that his breath brushed the sweat-dampened hair at her temple.

"Crawl out on the other side," he whispered. "Just far enough to give me room to follow. Then lie there and wait. When I tell you to run, head for the boat. Keep low and keep moving."

The boat. The one at the end of the pier? Under the light?

"Now," Ben said.

Despite her confusion, she obeyed, dragging herself by her elbows toward the other side of the pickup and then, reluctantly, out into the open on the other side. Ben was right behind her.

"Stay down," he ordered.

As soon as his body cleared the truck, he strained upward, fingers closing over the handle of the driver's-side door. He eased it open, but apparently the noise was enough that whoever was in the woods figured out what was going on.

Three more bullets, fired through the same silencer as the first had been, struck the pickup and whined away into the night. Ben had flinched from the sound, ducking automatically to protect his exposed head. Before the scream of the ricochets had faded, however, he was clambering up into the cab again. As he did, a bullet shattered the glass of the passenger-side window.

"Son of a *bitch*."

She had time to wonder what had prompted that before he dropped to the ground beside her.

"Okay?"

She had nodded before she realized he wasn't looking at her. Nor was he waiting for an answer. Instead, he was pulling himself along the ground toward the front of the truck, using his elbows, knees and feet, just as she had, to propel the movement.

She lifted her head, trying to understand what he was doing. She could see the stock and then the barrel of a rifle moving back and forth as he shifted his weight from one side to the other as he crawled. He had gone back inside the cab to get the gun from the rack above the back window.

The fact that he was armed *should* make her feel better. Despite the adrenaline flooding her system, however, the initial shock was wearing off. She was becoming aware of the signals her body was sending to her brain. Her elbows were raw, and her breasts and knees ached from where Ben had thrown her to the ground. Her palms, abraded when she'd used them to try to break her fall, stung.

Another shot rang out, this one not muted by the silencer

and much closer than the previous ones had been. Ben's gun. His shot. And just as she arrived at that realization, he barked out the command he'd told her to expect.

"Go."

CHAPTER THIRTEEN

TO THE PIER. To the boat. Just as everyone else always did, Callie reacted automatically to the authority in Ben Stanton's voice. She scrambled to her feet. Crouching behind the protection of the truck, she raised her head in an attempt to spot the pole that marked the beginning of the pier.

It was gone. At least the light on top of it was. For a few seconds, she didn't know where to go, disoriented by the darkness and by the time she'd spent crawling along the ground without any visual references.

As she hesitated, Ben's fingers closed around her upper arm. He began to run, for the first few steps literally dragging her along behind him. Eventually, her feet began to move of their own accord. She was totally dependent on his guidance because she was running blind. Not only did she not know the terrain, but in the darkness she couldn't see a thing.

Suddenly the toe of her sandal caught on something—a root or a vine. It held her foot momentarily, pitching her forward. Ben's fingers dug into her flesh. The strength of his hand managed to keep her upright, despite her stumbling, off-balance stagger. After a few steps she regained her equilibrium.

She concentrated on maintaining it as he tried to pick up the momentum they had lost. He pulled her along as shots from that muted rifle followed them, destroying the sense of security she'd felt when Ben asked her to come home with him.

As they ran, her eyes began to adjust to the darkness, and their surroundings swam into focus. She could see the pole. The long dock that extended out into the water. Even the boat at the end of it, gleaming white and beautiful in the faint moonlight.

As they approached the pier, a bullet hit one of the planks, sending up a shower of splinters. They sprinted through them, the sound of their feet hammering across the boards. She could hear her own breathing, seeming as loud as their footsteps.

Behind them, their assailant continued to fire. A few shots hit wood, their impact coming a split second before she heard the rifle's throaty *phut*. Several struck the surface of the water, the noise almost lost under the pounding of their feet. As soon as they reached the boat, Ben shoved her against its side.

"Climb," he ordered, turning to provide covering fire.

Her hands fumbled for the rungs of the ladder, and she pulled herself up and over the side as his rifle barked again. Once onboard, she stopped to catch her breath.

Almost immediately, she heard Ben storm up the ladder. Then he was beside her, pausing long enough to push her down into the bottom of the boat. He headed toward the bow and after a few seconds, she heard the powerful engine come to life.

She wondered briefly about the mooring ropes, but apparently that's what he had been doing after he'd directed her to climb the ladder. Huddled on deck, she listened as the boat roared out of the boathouse and into the bay, leaving the steady cough of gunfire that followed it farther and farther behind.

"WE SHOULD BE safe here," Ben said.

He had returned from securing the line around a cypress knee to find Callie sitting on the deck, her head back, eyes closed. At the sound of his voice, she opened them, looking up. She would be able to see nothing more than his silhouette, a blacker shape against the dark, moss-draped branches arching over the slough where he'd hidden the boat.

When he'd left the boathouse, he hadn't had any destination in mind. His sole purpose in taking the cruiser had been to get them away from the shooter. With the truck disabled, the bay had offered their best chance to do that.

Once out on the water, he'd remembered this place. Secluded and remote, it would serve their purposes, at least for tonight. Although there were people in the area who knew these backwaters as well as he did, he hoped the murderer wouldn't be one of them.

"You okay?" he asked, concerned by her lack of response. He stooped beside her, balancing on the balls of his feet.

"I think so," she said. Her voice sounded remarkably steady, considering all she'd been through. She took a deep breath, audible in the stillness, before she added, "A little bruised and battered, but...nothing serious."

"You weren't hit, were you?"

She had probably never had to dodge bullets in her life, but he couldn't fault the way she'd handled herself. As he had from the beginning, he found himself admiring her ability to remain cool under fire. Literally under fire this time.

"No," she said. "You?"

It was a rhetorical question. A returned courtesy. Except he hadn't been as lucky.

"I caught a ricochet," he said. "A fragment of one, anyway."

In the sudden silence, he evaluated the sound of the water lapping against the boat. Their passage had caused those ripples. Eventually they would die away, and he'd be able to hear if anything else came up the slough. Not that he was expecting company, he reassured himself.

"You were hit by a ricochet?"

"Nothing serious," he said. "There's a first aid kit in the cabin. I thought maybe you might..." He hesitated, feeling awkward about the request.

"You want me to take a look at it," she said.

She didn't sound particularly eager. Of course, neither was he. He didn't think the damage was enough to put him out of commission, but his shoulder hurt like hell. And the wound had continued to bleed sluggishly, which wasn't a good sign.

He was feeling pretty rough around the edges. Hunger, lack of sleep, maybe even a touch of shock from the loss of blood had all taken their toll. As soon as they got below, he could do something about a couple of those.

"Would you mind?"

As he asked, he wrapped his fingers around the top of the railing, using it to pull himself to his feet. She didn't move, so he extended his hand to her.

He had done that before, he remembered. Offered to help her down from the truck. She had put her hand in his, and then, after they'd walked a few feet toward the house, she had broken away from him and headed back to the pickup.

She must have heard something he hadn't. And her quick reaction to it had probably saved her life, taking her out of the path of that first bullet.

"I don't mind looking at it," she said, "but you should understand that isn't my area of expertise."

She put her fingers in his, and he pulled her to her feet. This time he resisted the urge to put his arm around her shoulders, realizing only belatedly that might have been what she had been reacting to back at the cabin. An unwanted familiarity. If so, it was a mistake he wouldn't make again.

"SO HOW DOES IT LOOK?" he asked.

"I told you I'm no expert," she said, cool fingers pressing carefully along the torn flesh, "but I think it's just a gouge. There doesn't seem to be anything under the skin. It looks as if the fragment just tore some of the flesh away."

That should be good news, he thought. His nausea had returned with a vengeance as soon as they'd exchanged the fresh air above deck for the humid staleness below. And the image she had just painted of a piece of metal scoring a furrow across his back didn't help.

"Peroxide?" she asked.

"What are my other options?"

He listened as she rummaged through the contents of the first aid box. "Mercurochrome." The noise continued briefly. "I don't see any alcohol. Wouldn't that be better?"

"Beats me," he said. It would hurt more, but that hadn't been her question. "I've got bourbon. Too good for pouring over a scratch, but I wouldn't be averse to drinking it."

"Me, either," she said.

Before he could offer to fix those drinks, she poured the peroxide over his shoulder. He could hear it, sizzling against the raw flesh, before it rolled, cold and wet, down his back. His body jerked in reaction, more from the unpleasantness of the sensation than from any pain.

"That can be our reward when this is over," she said, putting her hand, almost comfortingly, on his spine. "A good stiff drink."

And I'll be out like a light. That idea was more appealing than it should be, considering someone had been lying in wait at his cabin with a rifle and a silencer. Someone who was still out there in the darkness, maybe searching for them right now.

And whoever that person was, he'd been a step ahead the whole way, Ben acknowledged bitterly. From the morning he had found Kay-Kay's body, that bastard had played him like a fish. Making him dance to his tune.

Except fish didn't dance. And he had. For ten long years, he had done exactly what he'd been expected to do. Even to bringing Callie home with him tonight. He had done exactly what that son of a bitch had known he would.

"Ben?" she questioned, squeezing the top of his shoulder.

Compared to the antiseptic, her fingers were warm. Warm and soft. Just as the rest of her would be. Which was a hell of a thought, he admitted, given what was happening around them.

"What's wrong?" he asked aloud.

"Nothing. Just checking. You swayed a little."

"I'm okay. Slap a bandage on top of that, and I'll fix us both a shot."

"I'm not crazy about your word choice," she said. The attempt to inject humor into the situation wasn't completely successful, but he'd give her credit for trying. "A drink does sound good, however."

"Does anything ever rattle you?" he asked.

"What the hell does *that* mean?"

"It was supposed to be a compliment. I was thinking about all that's happened since you've been here. You haven't let any of it shake you."

"*All* of it shakes me," she denied, pressing a gauze pad over the wound on his back. He flinched from the pressure, which eased immediately. "Sorry," she said.

She taped down the sides of the bandage without touching the injury again. He listened as she put the things she'd used back in the box and closed the lid.

"Especially Virginia's death," she said, obviously a response to his earlier comment. "I feel responsible for that."

"Responsible?" he repeated, sliding off the edge of the table and turning to face her. "Why the hell would you feel responsible?"

"Because I stirred this up again. If I hadn't come here and started asking questions—"

"He would have gotten away with murdering a child. Two children," he amended. "He *had* gotten away with it."

"Maybe. But at least Virginia would be alive."

"And maybe another little girl would be dead. Did you ever consider that? You had *nothing* to do with Virginia's death," he lied. "She said something to the wrong person."

"She wouldn't have if I hadn't come to Point Hope."

"You can't know that."

She didn't argue, but he could tell by her face that she didn't believe him. Her eyes revealed the same bone-weary fatigue he was dealing with. The same near-shock.

He picked up his shirt and shrugged into it. The sticky,

blood-soaked dampness was unpleasant against his heated skin, but he couldn't risk running the air conditioner. Not the way sound carried across the water.

"How about that drink," he offered. At least there was plenty of ice.

She nodded, leaning tiredly against the wall. He walked over to the provisions cabinet and worked the combination lock. He took out the bourbon and two plastic cups from the overhead cupboard. He poured two fingers in each and, leaving the whiskey out, carried the drinks over to where she was standing.

He handed one of the cups to her and tossed back the contents of his as if it were a dose of medicine. When he lowered his head, she was watching him, her own drink untouched.

"Bottoms up," he ordered.

"Do you have any idea who it is?" she asked instead.

"Who was shooting at us?"

"Who killed Virginia and Kay-Kay. Who killed Mary."

He shook his head. "Disappointed?" She said nothing, so he answered his own question. "I don't know why you would be. I haven't had a clue about any of this from the start."

"What Virginia knew…"

He cocked his head at the pause, questioning it, but before she completed the thought, she raised her cup, taking a sip of the bourbon. She grimaced at the taste, rolling it around on her tongue before she swallowed.

"I think what she knew had something to do with the other murder," she said.

"Why?" He wanted to know what she was thinking. And since he needed to stay awake anyway…

"Because that's the only new element. What I told her this morning. If it was something she had known all along, then she might have let it slip before now. The fact that there was another murder was new information. Apparently it triggered some memory. Later on, she must have acted on that and..." She paused again, drawing breath before she took another sip.

"What exactly did you tell her and Phoebe?"

She shook her head. "I don't remember word for word. I mentioned North Carolina, but not the town. I told them when. Not the exact date, but...I think said twenty-six years ago."

"And you didn't mention the rose."

There was a small hesitation, but eventually she shook her head. She took another swallow of the whiskey, her reaction to the taste less apparent this time.

"You're sure?" he prodded, following up on the hesitation.

Her eyes came up too quickly. Widened. "I'm sure," she said. And then she added, "I did mention it to Doc Cooley. I had assumed he already knew, but he claimed he hadn't seen it. I didn't see how he could have done the autopsy and not have found it, but...it didn't feel like he was lying."

"He *didn't* see it. That's why there were no pictures of it in the photographs that were stolen. When I finally made myself look at them a couple of days after the funeral, there weren't any of the rose. I should have mentioned it to him, but I assumed he'd find it. And by the time I realized he hadn't, it was too late. At that point, Lorena and Tom weren't going to give permission for an exhumation."

"It must have been hard for Doc," Callie said. "To do the autopsy, I mean. Maybe that's why... He told me he delivered Kay-Kay. She'd been his patient all her life. I could hear in his voice how much he cared."

"I know now I should have sent the body to Mobile or Birmingham. Gotten a forensic pathologist to do the autopsy. But...I wanted Doc to do it. I knew he'd treat her right. With dignity."

She nodded, and then her eyes dropped to the remains of her bourbon. She rolled the cup, watching the liquid tilt from side to side.

"How did you get interested in the first case?" he asked. "The Cameron girl's murder?"

Again, there was a slight hesitation before she answered. And she didn't look at him this time. "I knew the family."

"What made you put the two together? You couldn't have spotted the stem in that photograph. Not unless you were looking for it. And not unless you *knew* what you were looking for."

The silence expanded. As he waited through it, he could feel the effects of the alcohol. It had hit his empty stomach and was already racing through his bloodstream. Strangely, he felt more alert, but also slightly disoriented. He eased his hip onto the edge of the table and reached across it, fumbling for the box of saltines he kept there, handy for any customer with a bout of seasickness.

"She was my sister."

His fingers had already closed around the top of the box of crackers before the sense of what she had just said hit him. He turned to face her, moving slowly. Wondering if the bourbon had had more of an effect than he'd suspected.

"Mary Cameron was your *sister?* But...*Cameron?*"

"When my father died, we moved back to Charlotte. To live with my mother's family. She began to use her maiden name. She said it was easier for me to use it, too, because of school. I didn't understand then that was because of Mary's murder. Because of the notoriety. No one in that house ever talked about Mary. Maybe, because I was so young at the time, they thought I didn't remember her death."

"Did you?"

"Not consciously, although there were always the dreams... Maybe what I *think* I remember now is only what I've read. I can't be totally sure anymore."

"How old were you?"

"I was three. Mary was six," she said softly. "We slept in the same room."

The words were almost stark in their simplicity. *We slept*

in the same room. If Mary Cameron's murder had followed the pattern of Katherine Delacroix's...

"You were there," he said, realization closing around his heart like a cold hand. "My God, Callie, you were in that room the night he came for her."

SHE REALIZED only as she talked that she had never before told anyone all of it. Not like this. And as she had told him, she had never been sure she would be able to distinguish what she remembered and what her mind had reconstructed from what she had read. She knew that if there was anyone for whom she needed to make this attempt, it was Ben.

"There were no signs of forced entry," she said, her voice still as low as when she'd begun.

"Yet somehow he got in," Ben said. "And he took her out of her bed without waking anyone." It had not been a question.

She looked up from the bourbon she was still toying with. "Or he lured her out. Doc said that to me yesterday. He was talking about Kay-Kay, of course. I'd never thought of that possibility before, but...he might have done that with Mary."

"How?"

She shook her head. "I don't know. I can't imagine. We slept in twin beds, one on each side of the room."

Nothing had changed about that bedroom, not even after Mary's death. There had been too many other things for her mother and father to worry about, perhaps, including their own grief. And every night they had sent her to sleep in that same dark room, lying across from the empty bed from which her sister had disappeared.

"And he didn't kill her there," Ben said.

She knew by the way the comment had been framed that he was comparing everything she told him to Kay-Kay's murder. The one about which he already knew every detail.

"There was a basement..."

As soon as she pronounced the word, she could smell it. The odor dark and cold, like some ancient evil.

A bare bulb had hung down between the floor joists on an old-fashioned, fabric-wrapped cord, the kind you never saw anymore. When the chain was pulled, it would set the bulb into motion. It swung in slowly diminishing circles, dimly illuminating different parts of the basement as it moved.

"He took her there?"

She couldn't remember ever going into the basement of that house. After Mary's death, the door was always kept locked. Yet despite how young she had been when Mary had been killed, Callie knew she must have gone there at least once. Because she had never forgotten that circling light or the smell.

"Can you tell me...?"

The pause in Ben's question forced her to raise her eyes to his. They were compassionate, just as they had been when he had knelt beside her in the boat. And because they were, she found the strength to tell him the rest.

"She was raped. And strangled. Then, maybe for good measure, because she was almost certainly dead when he did it, he cut her throat."

There was no sound in the cabin after those whispered words. They both knew that was a major difference between the manner of Mary's death and Katherine Delacroix's.

Callie had no idea of the significance of that difference, but she had almost reached the end of Mary's story. Now there were only two things she had to tell him. He knew about the rose. She wouldn't have to tell him that, but the others...

For some reason, they had always been the worst to her, even though she had long ago recognized that her horror was illogical. Far worse things than these had been done to her sister.

"Mary's hair... She had long blond hair, so light it was almost white. Like an angel's. Everybody commented on it."

There were pictures of her and Mary, identical towheads

bent over their dolls or playing with one of the kittens. As Callie matured, her own hair had darkened. Mary's, however...

"After she was dead, he cut it all off," she said, the words harsh, abrupt, breathless. "He cut off her hair, and then he stuffed it into her mouth."

"To keep her quiet," Ben said softly.

Anyone with an understanding of abnormal psychology would have recognized the symbolism. Mary's killer had closed her mouth, filling it so that she could never reveal his secret.

"That was one reason everyone believed it must have been my father. That and the fact there was no forced entry. Even after they found her in the basement, even after he must have realized they thought *he'd* killed her, he swore the doors had all been locked when he went to bed. He swore he'd checked each one of them himself. My father couldn't *not* tell them the truth. Not even after he understood they might use it to convict him for his daughter's murder."

"They tried your father for Mary's murder?"

"They wanted to, I think, but...they never brought formal charges. My father was a minister, one of only two in town. His congregation believed he was incapable of doing what had been done, of course. Maybe the world was more innocent then, but the police never charged him. It didn't matter. People always wondered. You could see it in their eyes when they looked at him. And he knew what they were thinking."

There was only one more thing she had to tell Ben. And then she would never have to think about the smell or that slowly circling light again.

"There was a sink there. In the basement," she clarified, thinking that perhaps he had lost the thread of the narrative because it had taken her so long to get to this point. "It had been used for laundry, I think, long before there were washers and dryers. I don't know if my mother ever used it herself..."

Her voice faded. She turned her head, as if she were looking out to where the bay stretched toward the horizon. Out to the dark water in which Kay-Kay Delacroix's body had been ritualistically washed.

"He bathed her," she said. "He washed Mary's body in that sink, just like he did with Kay-Kay. But…" She took a breath before she told him, knowing how important this was. "That couldn't have been done for the same reasons everybody believed it was done in the Delacroix case. There *was* no DNA evidence twenty-six years ago. Even if he hadn't washed her body, there would still have been no way to connect him to Mary's murder."

CHAPTER FOURTEEN

BEN OPENED HIS EYES to a darkness that was almost total.
Moisture-laden air pressed against his skin like a weight.
And he had no idea what had awakened him.

He listened to the stillness, concentrating on finding
within it any sound that might represent danger. Footsteps
on the deck above his head. Water lapping too strongly
against the hull. An unfamiliar creak or rattle.

There was nothing. Only the peaceful, late-summer insect noises from the surrounding woods. And gradually, as
he listened to them, his wariness dissipated. Nothing but a
bad dream, he told himself, willing the tension from his
muscles. Of course, he had heard enough tonight to precip-
itate a nightmare or two.

He searched his consciousness, trying to remember what
he'd been dreaming, but there were no images left in his
brain. Only those from the nightmare he'd lived with the
last ten years. And those that had formed as he had listened
to Callie.

Callie, he thought, jolted again by the sense that something was wrong. He had intended to stand guard all night,
despite his conviction that no one could find them out here.

Of course, only a fool would be looking, considering the
vastness of the area in which they had to hide. With that
comforting thought, he closed his eyes. He needed to sleep.
He needed to be clearheaded tomorrow to decide what had
to be done.

And then his eyes opened again, that nagging uneasiness
too strong to deny. He pushed up on his elbow, wincing as
the wound on the back of his shoulder protested, and looked

toward the bunk where Callie was sleeping. Totally exhausted, she had been out almost before he'd laid the rifle across his lap and leaned back against the wall facing the companionway. He had listened as her breathing settled into a slow, steady—

Realizing finally what had nagged at him, he listened again, ears straining in the stillness. Then, gripping the rifle, he surged up off the floor. The flood of adrenaline was overwhelming, making his hands tremble and his mouth go dry.

Not again, he prayed. *Dear God, please not again.*

Soundlessly, he crossed the cabin. He had taken off his shoes because he'd gotten them wet securing the lines. His toes gripped the polished floor as he shifted the rifle in his hands, his finger wrapping around the trigger.

He couldn't see a damn thing, but he didn't need to. He knew every inch of the cruiser by heart. Every plank that would squeak under his weight. The location of every piece of equipment he might stumble over.

As he climbed the stairs, the darkness gradually lightened. And when he reached the top of them, he could see Callie at the stern, outlined against the faint moonlight. His eyes scanned the perimeter of the boat. Then he turned, examining the bridge, charcoal against the shadow of the overhanging trees. There was no one there, and his gaze came back to the figure at the stern.

"Callie?" he questioned, keeping his voice low. She turned toward him, but there wasn't enough light to read her expression. "What are you doing up here?"

"I couldn't sleep," she said, turning back to the water.

There were always the dreams... Had she had one tonight? Another nightmare about her sister?

Still watching her, he bent his knees and, reaching behind him, propped the rifle against the bulkhead. Then he crossed the deck, stopping beside her. Her eyes were focused on the entrance to the slough. Beyond it, dark and vast, stretched the waters of the river and the bay. And everything that had driven them here.

"What's wrong?" he asked.

She shook her head, still without looking at him.

"It might help if you talk about it," he suggested.

She laughed, the sound devoid of amusement. "No one *ever* talked about it. When my mother moved back with her family, it was as if it had never happened. We all conspired to pretend it hadn't. It wasn't until she died that I felt free to read about Mary's death. When I did, I realized that the person who had killed her had never been caught. Never been punished. And no one cared. It was over, it was done, and no one cared about what had happened to Mary *or* to my father."

"I know it was hard for him—"

"Four years to the day after Mary died," she broke in, "he took out the gun he kept in his desk drawer and he shot himself with it. It was his birthday. That's why he had gotten up so early the morning he found Mary was missing. We were going on a picnic. A special birthday celebration. And every year after that—"

Her voice broke, but after a moment she strengthened it and went on. "He left a note. I was never allowed to see it. I found it with my mother's things after she died. There was only one sentence. No message for her—or for me—although we were as much victims of what had happened as he was. He had to know that. He *had* to know. I think he just…lost his way. After so long, living with something like that, maybe you do."

Ben didn't want to hear this, and yet there was a terrible fascination in knowing about this man. Mary's father, who had so much in common with Delacroix. An innocent man *he* had pursued.

"What did it say?" he asked. "That one sentence."

"I didn't kill my daughter."

After years of ignoring those doubting eyes, which must have haunted him every minute of his life since his daughter's death, that was the only thing her father had had to say to his family. And to the world. *I didn't kill my daughter.*

"I didn't kill mine either," Ben said, "but...there were times after her death when I thought about doing what your father did. And that's something I've never told a living soul."

There was no response to that confession. And after a moment he turned away, sorry he'd told her.

He started toward the bridge. By the time they got back to civilization it would be daylight. And finally he would be able to take some action against this bastard. To make up for his failure ten years ago. This was still his town. His case. His watch. Maybe he no longer wore the badge that made all that official, but it always would be. At least until he had put the person who'd killed Kay-Kay behind bars.

Callie's hand closed over his forearm, stopping him. He looked down at it, her pale fingers such a contrast to the darkness of his skin. After a moment she removed them, but he didn't move, other than to raise his eyes to meet hers.

"I came here to find *you*," she said. "To enlist your help. I knew that if there was anyone who cared as much as I did about finding justice for the two of them..." Her lips trembled on the last, but the movement was quickly suppressed.

He knew she wasn't asking for his sympathy. Although she *had* been a victim of her sister's murder, Callie hadn't chosen that path. She had come here instead to clear her father's name and to find her sister's killer. A murderer that everyone else, including him, had stopped looking for years ago.

Unexpectedly, she leaned toward him and, holding his eyes, stretched upward until her lips were a fraction of an inch from his. He didn't move. Couldn't move.

She was again close enough that he could smell the fragrance of her hair. This time it mingled with the warm, woman-scent of her body, caught and held in the moisture the humid air left on her skin. Intensified by the heat.

She closed her eyes and leaned forward to press her lips against the corner of his mouth. The kiss was insubstantial, obviously *not* an invitation or provocation. His body didn't respond in quite the way his intellect interpreted it, however.

She stepped back, opening her eyes to look up at him. As he watched, his eyes locked on her lips, they slanted upward. When he didn't answer it, the smile became tentative. Uncertain. As if he had rejected some tender of friendship.

Except, as he had admitted to himself at least, friendship wasn't what he wanted from Callie Evers. Maybe it was time to clarify what she wanted from him.

Almost of their own accord, his fingers reached out to touch her upper arm. His thumb trailed down to the soft fragile skin inside her elbow. Then, still holding her eyes, he ran the pad of it back up, following the muscle that underlay the pale, smooth skin. Definitely a caress.

Her eyes widened, but they held on his as if mesmerized. And she made no effort to pull away, not even when his fingers closed around her elbow to pull her toward him.

He put his other hand on her opposite arm, and then, holding her by the shoulders, he drew her close, lifting her a little so that her mouth was again millimeters from his. Her body rested against his, her toes barely maintaining contact with the deck.

He tilted his head, aligning his lips to fit over hers. He expected her to recoil or resist. Maybe he wanted her to, finally giving him a chance to control *something*.

Her body stiffened, but she didn't struggle. Not even when his mouth fastened over hers. Not even when his tongue probed, demanding entrance.

He hadn't thought about what he would do if she refused. This had been sheer impulse, fueled by his admiration of a woman who knew when to be afraid, but not when to quit. And by his growing sexual attraction, an unconscious seduction on her part, which had begun the day she stood at the foot of his front steps, challenging everything he believed.

By the time he had been forced to consider the possibility

that she might refuse to respond, her mouth had opened. And then there was no pretense of reluctance. Their tongues met and melded as her lips clung to his. As hungry for this as he had been.

When her arms went around his neck, he released her shoulders. His palms cupped under her hips instead. He bent his knees, lifting her into his erection, which was hard and hot and uncomfortable, straining against the confines of his jeans.

Her body molded itself to his, two halves fitting together as they were intended to. Except there were too many barriers for them *really* to be together. And he wasn't thinking right now about psychological ones. He was thinking only of physical barriers. His jeans. Her slacks.

He wanted them off. He wanted to take her right here, the decking cool beneath her bare back as he drove again and again into her yielding softness. As their tongues continued to explore, he removed his right hand from her hips, bending his knees even more to maintain that elemental contact between them. He slipped his fingers, flattened, between their bodies, working by feel over the buttons of his fly.

His knuckles were moving against the most intimate part of her anatomy, so she had to know what he was doing. *And* what he intended. She made no protest. Not even when he succeeded, freeing his arousal from the constriction of both his jeans and his briefs.

He slipped his hand inside her waistband, the tips of his fingers tracing along the top, searching for the opening. When she realized what he was doing, her arms released their hold around his neck. Her hand fastened over his fingers, trying to pull them away. He ignored it, concentrating on her waistband.

Side opening, he discovered. Using only his thumb and forefinger, he slipped the button through the buttonhole and found the tab of the zipper.

Again protesting fingers got in his way. He pushed them aside, determination driven by need. By desire. By a hunger as hot and wet as the grass-clogged backwaters around them.

As soon as he'd lowered the zipper, he brought his other hand around, hooking his thumbs in the waistband of her slacks, one on either side of them. He pushed downward, forcing the waistband over the curve of her hips. Once past that slight resistance, they fell, pooling around her feet.

The panties she wore left most of her buttocks exposed. Her skin was cool, incredibly smooth under his palms as his hands again cupped under her hips. Despite her slenderness, there was a satisfying, womanly roundness to them.

He lifted her again, bending his knees and coming up strong and hard under her. He could feel the cleft between her legs, covered now by only that thin band of silk, damp and hot against his bare erection. The sensation was electrifying. He gasped, breath sucked inward as if he'd been plunged into ice water.

The sound was a louder than her answering moan, which seemed to originate from somewhere deep in her throat. Low, guttural and wordless, it didn't sound shocked, as his rasping inhalation had been. It had sounded... *Pleased?*

He wasn't sure of his assessment until she moved, intentionally deepening the contact between them. He pushed upward again, responding to that encouragement.

His hands still under her bottom, he lifted her, near enough that he could see the film of moisture above her parted lips. Near enough that he could feel her breath moving against his cheek. Near enough that the almost dazed look in her half-closed eyes made him remember all she'd been through the last two days.

And that was the last thing he wanted to do. He didn't *want* to think about how vulnerable she was. He didn't want to be noble or controlled. He didn't want to be any of the things he knew he should be. He just wanted to be inside her.

Inside her heat and wetness. The dampness of his skin sliding over hers. Hipbones impacting together as he drove into her again and again, burying everything bad that had ever happened to either one of them in the hot, mind-numbing sweetness of hard sex. Destroying evil with something that was as old and primitive. And just as powerful. Life-giving instead of life-taking. They both needed that affirmation right now.

"Ben?" she said.

Her voice was hoarse. Pleading. And the sound of his name, whispered in that particular tone, changed the dynamics of what was happening between them.

Maybe not enough to make him back off, but enough to let him know that with this woman it couldn't be *only* physical. Not just sex, as much as he needed the sheer mindlessness of that, the escape from thinking it would provide.

"If you're fixing to say no," he warned, the words clipped and demanding, fighting that emotion he hadn't want to feel for her, "then you damn well better do it quick."

"I'm not like this," she said, her voice almost plaintive.

"Like what?" he mocked, pulling her body into closer contact with his.

"Like someone who would…do something like this."

"It's called making love."

"I *know* what it's called," she said. For the first time, there was an edge to her denial. "What I don't know is why *we're* doing it."

Despite the ache in his groin, the trembling muscles, the too-rapid heart rate, he didn't laugh or get mad because, God help him, he understood exactly what she meant. They'd gone from being adversaries to physical intimacy in a matter of days. And despite the fact that he'd made love to a lot of women through the years, one-night stands had never been his style.

"Maybe we're 'doing it' because someone tried to kill us tonight," he said, "and we've just now figured out we aren't dead. And we know we could have been."

For some reason, her eyes, holding on his, filled with tears. She blinked, trying to control them, and he realized he'd never seen her cry. No matter what was happening. No matter what horrors, past or present, she was forced to confront.

"Don't you start crying," he said, his voice harsher than he'd intended. He hated it when women cried. He always had.

"I'm not *crying*," she said forcefully.

She put her hands on his chest, pushing him away. He took a deep breath, trying to think, but he refused to move.

Her objection had been only that. An objection. He knew from her first response that if he pressed her, if he just went on with what he was doing, she would eventually let him make love to her. She was as aroused as he was. And there was some part of her that needed this release as much as he did.

She said no, but I knew she really wanted it. And how many times, he wondered, had some guy with a hard-on used *that* justification? How many goddamn times?

Slowly he straightened, releasing her. She slid down his body, inadvertently moving against his arousal, sending a powerful aftershock shuddering through him. She held onto his shoulders until she'd regained her balance, and then she took a step back, trying to put some necessary distance between them.

As she did, her feet tangled in her slacks, which were still lying in a small, white puddle on the deck. She glanced down at them, reaching out with one hand to steady herself. The tips of her fingers encountered the ribbon of dark hair that arrowed down across his stomach.

She jerked her hand away as if it had been burned, but her eyes had risen to lock on the place where she'd touched him. Stubbornly, almost angrily, he made no attempt to cover himself.

She hadn't objected when he'd undone his fly. And she had played a major role in getting him this aroused. It didn't seem she had any right to be offended by the results.

Even as he thought that, her eyes came up. And what was in them didn't indicate she was offended. Instead...

"Callie?"

She said nothing, her eyes on his. Then her fingers, the ones which had just brushed his body by accident, reached out again. Their touch was almost as tentative as her smile had been, but this time it was clearly no accident.

It was permission. Or invitation. And he needed no other.

He took the single step that closed the distance between them. Bending, he lifted her into his arms and started toward the stairs that led to the cabin below.

"Not there," she whispered.

Unsure what she'd said, he inclined his head, bringing their faces so close his nose touched her cheek. His steps slowed.

"Please," she begged. "Not down there in the dark."

With that request, a pain acknowledged but unspoken, moisture unexpectedly burned behind his eyes. He raised his chin so that she couldn't see his face, lips flattened against any expression of the emotion that welled up inside him.

And as he looked up, he realized the sky had lightened. The first hint of dawn. Without comment, he carried her back to the stern, kneeling to lay her on the cool, smooth decking.

Despite what he had thought before, despite their mutual hunger, this was no longer about release, however much that might be desired.

She had never asked for his pity. He knew that would be the last thing she would want from him, so he wouldn't sully the courage that had brought her to Point Hope by offering it. There was now, however, undeniably, an element of protectiveness in what he felt for her.

And a recognition of the fragility she hid so well. *Not down there in the dark.* Not in that place of endless nightmares. And as he lowered his body over hers, he vowed this was a shadow he would defeat and then erase from her life.

Her eyes opened, looking up at him in the subtle half-light. His palms shaped her face, thumbs caressing away the dampness at the corners of her eyes. And then, lowering his head, holding her eyes until the last possible second, he allowed his mouth to fasten over hers.

THE FIRST TIME Ben had taken her had been about need, both his and hers. Their lovemaking had been almost frenzied. And despite his obvious intent and her body's responsiveness, ultimately it had been mostly for him.

The second time, however, there was no sense of urgency at all. She had been aware of the difference from the moment his hands and his tongue had begun to move again over her body.

She couldn't remember when he had removed the rest of her clothing. She was aware of her nudity only because she could feel the roughness of his unshaven cheek and callused fingers against her breast, as well as the warmth of his tongue, laving with an unconscious authority over its hardened nipple.

Her body shifted, her back arching to create a closer contact with his lips. In reaction, his mouth closed around her breast, its hard suction creating a matching pull deep within her lower body. She shivered, feeling her responses build so that every touch, every flick of his tongue, every movement of his lips, brought her nearer the edge.

We've figured out that we aren't dead. And we could have been... Reason enough, had they needed one, for taking comfort in each other's arms. Taking comfort in still being alive, if nothing else. And after all, the need to procreate after danger was an ancient and potent biological urge.

For her, she had finally been forced to acknowledge, this was far more than that. More than a confirmation that they had survived the night. It had been, almost from the first time she'd studied those grainy newspaper images of this man.

Now he was flesh and blood. A physical reality. And to her, he was truly larger than life. Perhaps because he had saved hers on more than one occasion.

Or because, despite the effect it had, he'd been brave enough to do what she'd asked of him. To move beyond his circumstances and convictions to arrive at the truth about Kay-Kay's killer.

He had been strong enough to survive even that. And to come through it to the other side, still capable of the gentleness with which his hands were moving over her body.

Without warning, his mouth abandoned her breast. His thumb replaced the warmth and dampness of his lips, moving back and forth across the sensitized nub as his tongue began to examine her ribs on its journey down her body.

Slowly and without any haste, he traced each individual arch of bone, leaving a trail of heat and moisture on her skin. Lower and lower, until finally his tongue began an equally unhurried exploration of her naval. And then lower still, until it moved with unquestioned skill against the very heart of her sensuality.

Her breath caught, the inhalation sharp enough to make him hesitate. In protest of that hesitation, her hand fastened in his hair, silken between her spread fingers. And when his tongue moved again, increasing the tempo of its strokes, her hand closed too tightly around the strands she'd captured.

With movements sure and powerful, his mouth continued to caress. Waves of sensation built within her body, radiating upward from its heated core. Traveling along nerve pathways that had been created for this one purpose, serving no other.

Her lips parted, her breath releasing in a low sigh as the spiraling vortex began to collapse around her. With an exactitude that demonstrated untold experience, his body moved on top of hers. With one hand, he guided his erection. The other slipped beneath her hips, lifting them. He drove against the most hidden and vulnerable part of her, so hard and deep that despite his painstaking preparation, she flinched.

"Shh," he whispered, breath warm against her temple, lips moving against the sweat-dampened hair. "Shh."

His hips rocked forward, the moisture of their first encounter easing his passage. When he moved again, it was little more than a shift of weight, and the soreness became something else. Something anticipated. Known. Desired.

The muscles that had tensed relaxed, her bones melting and then reforming around him. It was his inhalation this time, a softly indrawn breath that presaged the next, deeper thrust. And then deeper still, until finally he filled her completely. Beyond fullness. An intensity that was again almost frightening.

She was incapable of movement. Incapable of response. Incapable of anything but breathing in the salt-fragrance of his skin. She turned her face, feeling the rasp of his beard against her cheek. So dear. And dearly familiar.

Unconsciously, her muscles clenched around his erection, reacting to that surge of emotion. An emotion which had almost nothing to do with their physical intimacy. Far more to do with her growing feelings for the man who held her.

As he began to move above her again, she opened her eyes, looking over the dark, broad shoulder that strained against her breast. And only then did she realize it was morning.

Another night had passed. Another endless darkness to be lived through. And they had.

Slowly, the sensations that had spiraled away when he'd shifted over her returned. Like summer lightning, they flickered and roiled throughout her body. Building. Until they became a wave, overwhelming everything in its path as it rushed to crest, slowly and powerfully, against the beach.

Her hands found purchase in his. She held them, their fingers interlocked, as they rode that crest together. Sensation peaked and then retreated, leaving them spent and exhausted, muscles trembling in the aftermath.

He lifted his head, his breathing ragged and uneven, to look down into her eyes. "When this is over—"

"Over?" she interrupted, the pall of sadness almost inevitable at the reminder. "Will it *ever* be over?"

His mouth tightened, and then he brought their joined hands to his lips, brushing a kiss, as insubstantial as the one that had begun this, against her knuckles.

"Ben?"

He raised his head again, his eyes as clear as the sea. "I'll find him, Callie. I was wrong before, but…it's been long enough. No more victims. No more, I promise you."

And slowly, still holding his eyes, she nodded.

CHAPTER FIFTEEN

"GET A COPY of the calls Virginia made during the last forty-eight hours. If you have to, ask Judge Morehouse to subpoena the records," Ben said, his instructions rapid-fire.

He was speaking into the phone at Phoebe's. They had come straight here from the slough where they'd spent the night, tying the cruiser up at her pier. It made more sense than going back to Ben's, and Callie had a key. Besides, her car was still here.

Ben listened for maybe twenty seconds before he said, "I don't give a damn if it is Sunday. This is police business—" The sentence was cut off abruptly, obviously in response to what Withers was saying. "Son of a *bitch*," Ben exploded. "You *make* them get to it, Doak. This morning. And don't take any of their crap about what they can and can't do. Tell them you've got a murder on your hands. What about the fingerprints?"

The pause was longer this time, and his eyes found Callie's as he listened.

"Somebody was lying in wait out at my place last night," he said after a moment. "Somebody with a rifle and no qualms about using it. I can damn sure prove *that*."

She could tell by his expression, even before he spoke again, that he hadn't liked Withers' response.

"If the two *aren't* related, then why the hell would somebody be out there shooting at us?" As he listened this time, he shook his head, lips compressed. "Because she's right, damn it. Tom Delacroix *didn't* kill Kay-Kay. Somebody else did. Somebody in this town. Somebody with a connection with that other murder in North Carolina. And we have to figure out what it is."

Another pause.

"We need those phone records," Ben said, his voice calmer. "We have to know who Virginia talked to between..." He hesitated, brows raised in inquiry as he looked at Callie.

"Around seven," she supplied.

"Between seven and two yesterday. And we need the autopsy results as soon as possible." He listened once more, his mouth again tightening in frustration. "Okay," he said finally. "Do what you can. I'll call you back in a couple of hours."

He set the receiver on its cradle with more force than was necessary. When he turned back to Callie, his eyes were bleak.

"Nothing usable on the prints. Doak says it looked like the surfaces in the bedroom had been wiped. Even if he's right, it doesn't prove anything. Other than Virginia dusted."

"I can't believe there weren't prints on the screen door."

"Nothing clear enough to be read. And now Doak's trying to say that it could have happened like the paramedics thought."

"It didn't. You know that."

"But I'm not sure we'll be able to prove it, even with an autopsy. Judging from where that wound on her head was, it's going to be tough for the coroner to say with absolute certainty whether she fell and hit her head or whether somebody hit her."

He pulled out a chair at Phoebe's kitchen table and sat down. He leaned back, and then straightened, grimacing.

"You ought to have somebody take a look at that."

He nodded, but she knew the injury was the last thing on his mind right now. "I could fix us some breakfast," she offered.

"I had a charter scheduled for this morning," he said. "I never even thought about it until now."

"Can you call someone else to take them out for you?"

He nodded again, but didn't make any move toward the phone.

"How about some coffee at least?" she asked.

"Coffee sounds good."

"Buck Dolan's not a native, is he?"

The crease she had noticed before formed between the dark brows. And she supposed that *had* been a leap. Her mind had been making those all morning. Trying to find a way to get from where they were to what they needed to know.

"His accent's different," she explained.

"People retire here or they move down for the climate. Half the people in this town weren't born here."

"And were any of them born in North Carolina?" she asked. It had felt as if he were dismissing her idea out of hand.

"Maybe, but I'm not sure how we could go about finding out which ones," he said, his tone considering. "Maybe cross-reference the tax records. I think some of those require you to give your place of birth. Maybe voter registration. I can tell Doak to put Billy on it when the courthouse opens on Monday."

"But you think it's a long shot," she said, mollified by the seriousness with which he'd discussed the idea.

"No more than any of the other things we're looking at. After all, Virginia may not have made *any* phone calls yesterday."

"And if she didn't?"

"Then I'll go out to my place and take a look around. I need to do that anyway."

"Look for what?"

"Footprints. Tire tracks. Casings. Whatever he left. And he *will* have left something. Whether it leads us anywhere…"

He started to shrug and winced. He rolled the damaged shoulder in an attempt to loosen the muscles. When he realized she was watching him, he pushed up from the table, walking over to the counter to begin making the coffee.

Callie didn't offer to help. She didn't even want to move. She felt worse than she had last night. Too little sleep and too little food, combined with too much stress and adrenaline.

After watching Ben fill the carafe, she made herself get up and open the refrigerator door. She wasn't sure she could face scrambling eggs, if they both starved to death. Thankfully, there were several plastic containers, neatly covered with colored tops, on the shelf next to the eggs.

She would have been hesitant to open anything enclosed in plastic in her own refrigerator. Phoebe, of course, would never let food go bad, not even leftovers.

Callie took out the largest container, holding one edge of it against her stomach as she eased the lid up on the opposite side. The sensation of the cold plastic against her midriff was welcome. Almost refreshing.

And the contents, the remains of a peach cobbler left from dinner two nights ago, seemed surprisingly inviting. She walked back to the table and set it down in the center before she looked up. Ben was watching her.

"Peach cobbler," she said. "Not exactly breakfast food, but…it looks good to me."

He turned and opened the drawer beside the sink. He took out two spoons, holding one out to her with a small salute.

"Want it warmed?" she asked.

He shook his head and walked back to the table. He handed one spoon to her and then sat down, dipping the other into the cold pie. He had taken a couple of bites before she joined him.

She didn't bother to pull out a chair. She propped her hip on the side of the table, their spoons alternately dipping into the plastic bowl until the contents were gone. Ben picked up the dish and tilted it to scrape the juice out of the corner.

"I like the way you think," he said, putting his spoon

and the container down before leaning back in his chair. As soon as his shoulder made contact with the cross bar at its top, he straightened. "Son of a bitch," he said under his breath.

"That's probably inflamed."

"Just sore."

"How long's it been since you had a tetanus booster?"

"How the hell do I know? Do *you* know how long it's been since you had one?"

"Of course," she said truthfully.

He shook his head, avoiding her eyes by looking across the room toward the sink. "Coffee's ready," he observed.

"*I* fixed breakfast."

His eyes came back to her face, widened a little. After a moment, amusement replaced the surprise.

"You union or something?" he asked.

"Or something."

He pushed up again, sighing theatrically. He poured two cups, leaving it black, and brought them to the table. He set hers down rather than handing it to her. Then he took a long swallow of his before he put his cup down on the table.

"In lieu of toothpaste," he said.

He cupped his hand behind her neck, drawing her toward him. He didn't hurry the movement, giving her time to pull away if she wanted to. She didn't. She wanted him to kiss her.

When he did, it was in marked contrast to last night's heat and passion. His lips met hers, caressing, and then, after a moment, his tongue invaded. Her mouth opened willingly. She could taste the coffee, the flavor darkly rich and pleasant.

He broke the kiss, his mouth hovering just above hers. "How do you think Phoebe would feel about our taking a shower?"

"Individually or together?" she asked, a little breathless.

He laughed, releasing his hold on her neck. His thumb

brushed along her cheekbone and was then pressed briefly against her lips before he stepped back.

"I *know* how she'd feel about our showering together. And I don't think that's a game we can afford to play right now."

His eyes were serious. She had forgotten how very blue they were, surrounded by that sun-darkened skin.

"You go first," she offered. "You want me to throw your clothes in the washing machine?"

She could tell from his expression that the idea was appealing. She knew how much she was looking forward to getting out of the clothes she'd been wearing for the last twenty-four hours and into something clean.

"I guess not," he said finally. "Take too long for them to dry. You don't suppose Phoebe's got something I could wear."

"I can look."

She wasn't hopeful. According to Phoebe, her husband had been dead for more than twenty years. Callie doubted there would be a single masculine garment in this house, especially something large enough to fit Ben.

"Double-check the back," he ordered. "I'll do the front."

He picked up the rifle he'd brought in from the boat and headed toward the front of the house. Obediently, she checked the lock on the backdoor and the night latch. Both were secure.

On her way to the hall, she picked the two cups of coffee up off the table. Ben was waiting at the foot of the stairs, and they climbed them together.

"Towels are in the cupboard with the bird decals," she said.

"What are my chances for a razor with a decent blade?"

"I'll bring you one of mine."

He nodded. They stood awkwardly in the hallway at the top of the stairs for a moment.

"Don't go back downstairs alone," he said finally.

"Nobody knows we're here."

"It won't be hard to figure out. Not with my cruiser and your car sitting out there in plain sight."

"You don't think he would try something in broad daylight."

"I don't want to take any chances. Just stay close. As a matter of fact," he said, holding the rifle out to her.

She looked down at it and then up at him. "I don't have a clue how to use that. I think I'll be a whole lot safer if you just keep it with you. I'm going to look in Phoebe's room for something for you to wear, and then I'm going to grab a change of clothes from mine. I'll stay within screaming distance."

"Scream loud. I'll have the shower going."

"Believe me, if I start screaming, you'll hear me."

THE FIRST COUPLE of drawers were the hardest. By the time she finished searching those, she had realized Phoebe had nothing to hide, except a propensity for hanging on to garments long past their expiration dates. As someone had said last night, Phoebe's generation lived through the Great Depression. The "waste not, want not" lessons they'd learned then were hard to give up.

Callie closed the top drawer of the dresser and turned. Closet, she decided, walking over to it. There was a vertical row of pictures hanging on the narrow wall beside its door. She stopped to look at them, her hand already reaching for the knob.

A bride and groom, the occasion obvious only because of the cake on the table and the bouquet in the young woman's hand. She was dressed in street clothes, a style that Callie guessed would be pre-war, late 1930s or early 1940s.

She leaned closer, trying to determine if this was Phoebe. The era was right, but it was hard to recognize the familiar wrinkled features in the glowing face of the bride. Her eyes moved to consider the groom, who looked even younger. He was grinning at the camera, obviously pleased with his day's work.

Above the black-and-white wedding photograph was a hand-tinted picture of a young man in uniform. Hobart? she wondered momentarily. The uniform he wore, especially the beret, and the style of photography itself indicated this was from a different era. Her gaze moved back and forth between the groom and the young soldier. Phoebe's son, she decided, the one who had been killed in Vietnam.

The third picture was a family grouping, taken when the children were much younger. Two sturdy little boys, dressed in matching cowboy outfits, smiled at the camera. The smaller held a broomstick onto which a cloth horse head had been attached.

She tried to remember the name of the son who lived in Mobile, the one who had picked Phoebe up last night. Older or younger? She didn't know and of course, it didn't really matter.

She opened the closet door and was struck immediately by the slightly musty smell of its contents, reminiscent of the odor she'd been aware of at Virginia's house yesterday. She fought the urge to slam the door. Instead, she willed her hand to reach up and push aside the dresses and knit pants suits hanging from the bar. After a few seconds it became obvious there was nothing here that had belonged to any of the men in Phoebe's life.

She had already stepped back, preparing to shut the door, when she noticed that someone had installed shelving down the right-hand side of the closet. She reached inside again, pushing the clothing all the way to the left, thinking these would be a more likely place to store unused clothing.

Her quick survey revealed there was none of that among their contents. Certainly no masculine garments. The top two held quilts, neatly folded, their bright patchwork patterns intricate enough that her fingers reached out to touch them, tracing over the thumbnail size pieces with their myriad tiny stitches. Then her hand moved downward, still caressing. The next shelf contained a mixture of items, including a crocheted afghan and a set of hand-embroidered sheets. And on the final shelf...

Her fingers hesitated. The most prominent item was the blue field and white stars of a folded American flag. She had certainly seen enough movies to know what it meant when the flag was folded in this tight, triangular shape. And beneath it was a scrapbook. Her grandmother had had one exactly like this—black pages, a thick cardboard front and back, fastened together with laces that ran through the holes and tied in front. Inside would be more photographs. Phoebe and Hobart. The boys.

Her fingers stroked the cloth of the flag, moving almost reverently over the shape of one of the stars. She raised her head, listening to the distant sound of the shower. Then she pulled the scrapbook from under the triangle of cloth.

Still standing in the doorway, she opened the cover of the album. Its size made it awkward to hold and turn pages at the same time. She'd been right about the photographs, but it was too dark in the closet to see any details in them.

She closed the book, cradling it against her chest, to walk over to the windows. Once there, she opened the album, propping the top of it on the sill. As she turned the pages, her eyes moving from one photograph to the next, she felt a pang of guilt. Looking for something to replace Ben's bloodstained shirt had given her a quasi-legitimate excuse to search Phoebe's bedroom. This, however, was sheer voyeurism.

Not that there was anything here that she thought Phoebe would object to her seeing. There were more pictures of the children—Christmas mornings and birthdays. The kind of innocuous family events of which everyone took photographs.

"Callie?"

Ben's call startled her. She half-turned, thinking he might be in the doorway, watching her unwarranted invasion of her hostess's privacy. As she did, the scrapbook slid off the sill, the top dipping downward before she could right it. A yellowed newspaper clipping fell out of the back, drifting to the floor as Ben called again.

"I thought you were going to bring me a razor."

She closed the book and, holding it against her chest, bent to retrieve the clipping. She tried to slip it inside without opening the album, wondering as she did if Phoebe would notice it wasn't in the right place. If it had had a "right" place.

She hurried to the closet, trying to get the pages of the scrapbook, still clutched against her chest, open enough to allow her to slide the clipping inside. Finally it slipped down between two of them. One arm around the album, she reached out with the other to open the closet door, and the clipping fell out the bottom, again floating to the floor.

"I'm coming," she called, stooping.

This time the article had fluttered open on its way down. As she leaned down over it, the headline caught her eyes. Remains Of U.S. Servicemen Returned To States.

Phoebe's son? The date at the top was July 12, 1975. And she would realize only later how strange it was that there was no sense of recognition. No chill of premonition. Not until her eyes dropped to the byline. *Fort Bragg, North Carolina.*

She sank to her knees, laying the scrapbook on the floor beside her. She scanned the article, searching for names. And there was one she recognized. James Hobart Robinson, age twenty-one, of Point Hope, Alabama. *Phoebe's son.* Whose remains had been returned to the United States in July of 1975.

"What are you doing?"

She raised her eyes to find Ben standing in the doorway. Wearing only jeans, he held a towel, with which he was drying his hair. Seeing her face, the hand holding it stilled.

"Callie?" And when she didn't answer, "What's wrong?"

Wordlessly, she held out the article. He hesitated a second or two before he stepped into the room. Draping the towel around his neck, he reached out to take the clipping, his eyes examining her face instead of looking at it.

"What's this?"

"Read it," she said, trying to think what this meant. It

had to mean something. It was too great a coincidence *not* to. Too close to the time and the place of Mary's murder.

"Phoebe's son," Ben said. "He was killed in Vietnam."

"Look at the date."

He looked back down at the clipping. "He was on some kind of covert mission. Special Forces. I don't remember the details, but there was a delay in bringing the bodies back to the States. They had to negotiate for the remains after the war."

"*July, 1975.*" Maybe it was only a coincidence. Maybe she had become obsessed with this, so that everything, every event, seemed to have a bearing on those two murders.

"Your sister," Ben said. And then he did exactly what she had done. He looked at the byline, and his eyes lifted to hers. "North Carolina. They brought the bodies back to Bragg."

"Did Phoebe and Hobart go up there?"

"Damned if I know," Ben said.

"Who *would* know?"

"You aren't suggesting that Phoebe or Hobart…"

But she could tell he was thinking about it, even as he denied she could be suggesting it. And of course, Hobart Robinson had been dead by the time of the second murder. After a moment Ben shook his head.

"There's no way Phoebe could have been involved in either of those murders. You can get that out of your head."

"A five-year-old and a six-year-old? You don't think a woman would be strong enough to strangle a child that small?"

"And rape her?"

"No semen was found on either body."

"Maybe not, but there was physical evidence—"

"Of *penetration,*" she argued. "It didn't have to be rape. If you're a woman, what better way to divert suspicion."

"That's insane."

"So is murder. Especially the murder of a child."

"And the murder of your best friend?"

"Virginia knew something. Something she promised to tell me. Phoebe's the only one we know for sure who knew that."

"That's ridiculous, Callie. This whole…idea is absurd. We don't even know that they went there. The army may have shipped those bodies home. Jimmy's buried here. All we know is that the remains came back to North Carolina."

"In the same month and year that Mary was murdered."

"You can't think—" he began before she interrupted.

"Don't do what you did before. Don't make up your mind before you have evidence to prove or *disprove* a hypothesis."

His face changed, its features seeming to harden before her eyes. She wasn't sure whether that was in response to what she had just said or because he couldn't believe Phoebe might be involved. She didn't want to believe it either, but too many things fit together to completely ignore the possibility.

"I'm trying to gather that evidence," he said tightly.

"What if Virginia didn't make any phone calls? Will you consider this then?"

"I *am* considering it. I'm just finding it damn hard to believe. I've known Phoebe Robinson all my life. Hobart, too."

"But you *don't* know if they went to North Carolina to pick up their son's body?"

"I was…what? Fifteen? I wasn't keeping up with who went where. They buried him here. That's all I know."

"And Hobart was still alive?"

"In '75?" He thought about it, and then he nodded. "I'm pretty sure. We can check that easily enough."

"He *wasn't* alive when Kay-Kay was killed," she said.

Phoebe was. And Phoebe's son had to be the connection they had been looking for to North Carolina. Same month. Same year.

"What about last night?" Ben asked.

It took her a second to realize he was referring to whoever had shot at them. Phoebe hadn't even been here. They had watched her drive away with her son.

Her other son? Callie wondered. Was it possible—

"And do you really think it was Phoebe holding you under the water that night?"

"No," she admitted, remembering the feel of that hand pressed against her forehead. The hard, masculine strength of the arm around her throat. "Maybe Doak was right. Maybe that had nothing to do with what's happened since. Or with the murders. Just...someone trying to scare me away."

Phoebe had been the one who had been so insistent that she go out to the bay that night. And Phoebe had been the first one she'd told about the book she was supposedly writing.

Maybe Phoebe had put someone up to making that first attempt to scare her off. Burge or Buck Dolan? Both were there that night. And either one of them could probably have been convinced to pull that prank. *If* Phoebe told them to. Phoebe of the strong, dominant will.

"I'm not buying this," Ben said.

"She taught her in Sunday School." *Secret affection?*

"Did she know Mary?"

Her eyes lifted, focusing on his face.

"Phoebe's only connection to the area was that her son's body came through there," Ben reminded her. "*If* she even went to Bragg to collect it. You think she just stopped off at some house in the middle of the night to murder a kid? With Hobart's help? Or did he wait for her out in the car?" The last was coldly sarcastic. And it was a perfectly reasonable question.

"I don't know. That doesn't seem to make any sense..."

She shook her head, knowing there were too many unexplained elements to make the leap she had made. There *were* coincidences. Even of this magnitude.

But she didn't understand why Phoebe hadn't mentioned this link to North Carolina when Callie told her and Virginia about Mary's murder. Maybe she hadn't given them enough information. Or maybe it had been nothing but a coincidental convergence with a horrible, grief-stricken time in Phoebe's life. Maybe she had never made the connection between the dates and the location.

"When you're looking for suspects, you have to consider what people are capable of," Ben went on, hammering home his point. "Phoebe wouldn't be capable under *any* circumstances of doing what was done to those two little girls. Besides, you're leaving out something very important. *Why* would she kill them? There has to be a reason for those two deaths."

"Is there *ever* a reason to murder a child?"

"Fear," Ben suggested.

"Fear?"

"Usually fear of discovery."

"If...they were being sexually abused?"

"That's always been a possibility. And that's not a woman's crime, Callie. Neither is this kind of repeat pattern."

"There have been women serial killers," she argued, but logic, reason or maybe just sheer humanity was already making her doubt the conclusion she had jumped to only minutes before.

"Not like this. Not that we know of."

"So where does that leave us?"

"Right where we were before you found this," he said, lifting the clipping. Then he folded it and slipped it into the pocket of his jeans before he held his hand out to help her up.

CHAPTER SIXTEEN

SHE SHOULD HAVE KNOWN Ben wouldn't be able to leave it alone. Within an hour after their showers, he had been trying to touch base with Withers again. And having no success.

There were a dozen explanations for Doak not being home, including the possibility that he had gone to the airport to meet Virginia's daughter. It was also possible that he didn't want to talk to his former boss again, since they were having such a fundamental disagreement over the cause of Virginia's death.

"Maybe he's out at your place, doing all that stuff you said you were going to do," she had made the mistake of suggesting.

Ben's eyes had come up from the receiver he'd just slammed down in frustration. "Want to ride out there?"

They had, but that had turned out to be another wild-goose chase. The soil was too sandy for the smudged tracks they found to tell them anything. Based on a few broken twigs, Ben thought he'd located the spot where the sniper had hidden, but there was a disturbing lack of physical evidence. No casings. No footprints. Nothing that would lead them anywhere.

And to add insult to injury, the windshield of Ben's truck had been smashed in. It looked as if someone had taken a baseball bat to it, although they didn't find whatever had been used in the attack. Nor was there any logical explanation of why it had been carried out. Callie was beginning feel that while they were out chasing their tails, whoever had committed the two murders was sitting back, laughing at them.

"Now what?" she asked on the way back into town.

"Let's go by the police station. Doak might be there."

"On a Sunday morning? Besides, I thought you were convinced he wasn't taking this seriously. At least not the possibility that Virginia was murdered."

"But he can't deny what happened to us last night. And that says panic to me."

Doak's panic? Or the killer's? "I don't understand."

"That looks like an overreaction. All of this does. Everything that's happened since you arrived. You haven't come close to identifying the murderer. So why try to kill you?"

"Because he thinks I might," she suggested.

"But no one has. Not in a quarter of a century. Whoever this is has been safe for a long time. He has to have been thinking he'd gotten away with it. So why react so strongly to someone taking another look at Kay-Kay's murder? There have been other people down here during the past ten years, trying to do the same thing you said you were doing."

"Because no one's ever put the two murders together before."

"Exactly," Ben complimented. "Which means he thinks he *can* be tied in some way to the other murder. There's some thread that leads from there to here. And he knows it."

"But...we *don't*. We haven't found any connection, other than Phoebe's son's body being returned to Bragg that same month."

"He can't afford to give us time to find it. That's why things are happening so fast. So we won't make that connection."

"Then it must be something obvious."

"At least to him," Ben said. "What are you doing?"

She had slowed because they were approaching Dr. Cooley's house. "Cooley still sees patients. If he's here, he could look at your back."

"He'll be at church."

"Not unless he goes to Sunday school," she said.

As she turned into the drive, it was obvious she'd been right. Cooley's car was parked beside the veranda.

"We don't have time for this," Ben protested.

"Ten minutes. And if you don't get that checked out, you're going to end up with an infection that could put you in the hospital. Frankly, I don't think *I* can afford *that*."

She pulled to a stop behind Doc's car, shutting off the engine and turning to face him. "No one else is concerned about what's been going on. Doak is perfectly willing to believe Virginia's death was an accident. So are the paramedics. Everyone thinks what happened to me the night of the jubilee was a prank. They'll say the same thing about your windshield.

"You're the only person here who believes Kay-Kay's murderer is active again. And the only person who knows he's trying to kill me. Besides, it's not just me he's after now. That damage to your truck looked like an act of sheer rage. He...or she," she amended, "thinks *you're* a danger to him now. He didn't think that before, at least not for the last eight years. Now he thinks I've told you enough about Mary's murder that you could discover his connection to it, even if he gets rid of me. And apparently he knows you well enough to know that once you get your teeth into something..."

"I wasn't much of a threat to the bastard before."

"Well, you are now. Unless you go down with lockjaw," she said, opening her car door.

"Mighty early on a Sunday to come visiting," Cooley called.

Callie looked up to find the old man standing at the side of the porch, hands on the banister, looking down at them.

"Not that you ain't welcome," he said. "I told you before. I'm always hoping for a visit from a pretty girl."

He was dressed for church. His trousers were linen, the

untreated, old-fashioned kind that wrinkled. With them, he was wearing a blue shirt with a wide white collar and a navy tie with small white polka dots.

He had probably been waiting until the last minute to put on his jacket. After all, he'd told her he had no air-conditioning. Callie could see the sheen of sweat at his temples, the thick hair damp with humidity or his recent shower.

"Business and not pleasure, Doc," Ben said, moving a little stiffly as he climbed out of the other side of her car.

"Business?" Cooley questioned. "What kind of business?"

"Your kind," Ben said, smiling up at the old man. "Got a scrape I want you to look at."

"You been fighting again? How many times I got to tell you that it's a gol-darn fool pair of legs that'll stand around and let their head get beat up."

Ben laughed, walking around the back of the car. Callie had started up the front walk as Cooley's laughter joined his.

"This wasn't a fight, Doc. Not unless you'd call something so one-sided that I didn't get in a single lick a fight."

"I'd like to see the man who could keep you from getting in your licks, boy."

Doc walked across the porch as he talked, meeting them at the top of the steps. He looked closely at Ben's face, clearly evaluating. Then he put the back of his hand against Ben's forehead. When he took his fingers away, he shook them as if they were hot, his lips pursing in a long, low whistle.

"What you got against modern medicine, boy? Or are you just trying to suffer in silence in front of this sweet young thing. What do they call that now? Being macho?"

Neither of them pointed out that no one had called anything by that term in more than twenty years.

"No lectures, Doc. She's given me enough of those. Just shoot me full of some expensive miracle drug, and we'll be on our way," Ben suggested. "Then you can get on to church."

Cooley turned, opening the screen door and ushering Callie into the front hall with a sweep of his hand. The inside walls were covered with a patterned paper, and the rooms she could see from the foyer were dominated by huge pieces of furniture.

The house was definitely Victorian, just as she'd originally surmised. And she'd bet the furniture was original to it, bought or made for the house when it had first been built, and lovingly maintained through all these years.

"I expect I've got a few sample miracles lying around," Doc said. "If you ain't picky about expiration dates."

Once inside, Callie had turned back toward the front door, not sure in which direction she should head. Cooley was waiting for Ben to precede him into the house.

"He doesn't know when he had a tetanus booster," she said as soon as they were both inside.

"I expect I've got a record of that, too," Doc said, directing her toward one of the doors on the right of the central hall.

The room had obviously been his office. There was a small anteroom, which had been created by the addition of a partition. A door in the middle of that was open, and Cooley led the way through it into his examination room. A paper-covered table, complete with metal stirrups, stood in its center. Around the walls were several tall cabinets, painted a glossy white, which held instruments and an array of dark bottles.

Callie could vaguely recall this same kind of home medical office in her own small hometown. Even the smell of it, slightly antiseptic and anxiety-producing, was familiar. Nostalgic. Apparently this kind of setup had been fairly widespread in the rural South, at least up until the '70s.

"Now where's this scrape you want me to look at?" Doc asked, motioning Ben onto the table.

Callie looked around, but there was no seating in the room except a metal stool. Its position at the head of the examination table left no doubt it wasn't intended for visitors. She had already leaned against the wall before she realized that, although she had seen a lot more of Ben than was about to be revealed, this examination should, by tradition, be private.

"Should I maybe...?" She hesitated, gesturing vaguely toward the door through which they'd entered.

"You ain't bothering me," Doc said, watching Ben shrug out of his shirt as he pulled on a pair of latex gloves he had taken from a box at the top of the table. "She bothering you?"

Ben shook his head. "She's already seen this. Poured peroxide over it. I don't know how the hell it got infected."

"Let's take a look at what's going on," Doc said, lifting his chin to view the wound through the bottom of his bifocals.

Apparently the gauze square Callie had taped over it last night had loosened during Ben's shower. There was nothing covering the gouge now, and looking at it, she understood why he had been unwilling to lean back against anything. The wound was ugly, the flesh around it swollen and discolored.

"How in the world did you do this?" Doc asked, gloved fingers feeling gently along the gash.

"Ricochet," Ben said. "Somebody was lying in wait for us out at the house last night. Somebody with a rifle."

The big fingers hovered just above the injury, as Doc lowered his head, looking at Ben through the top of the glasses.

"Are you telling me somebody shot at y'all?"

"More than once. Shot out a couple of tires, too. We made it to the boat, but when we went back out there this morning, we found whoever it was had bashed in the windshield of my pickup."

"Good Lord," Cooley said, his hands suspended in midair. "Over what she's fixing to write about?" He tilted his head toward Callie, but he didn't turn to look at her.

"Over Kay-Kay's murder," Ben said.

"'Cause they don't want all that mess stirred up."

"'Cause they don't want it *solved*."

"There ain't but one person who don't want that baby's killing solved, boy. And that's whoever killed her."

"Then I guess that's who we're talking about," Ben said.

There were several beats of silence before Doc said, "So you finally come around to her way of thinking." His hands began to press around the wound again.

"I didn't have any choice. Two different murders. Two little girls. Two towns, hundreds of miles apart. And Tom Delacroix couldn't possibly have committed the first."

"You sound mighty sure."

"He was under lock and key at the time. One drunk driving incident too many for even his daddy to stomach."

"You know as well as I do how slipshod those rehab places are. Who's to say he didn't sneak out?"

"He was there that night. I checked the patient logs."

Callie hadn't realized he'd done that, but then, knowing his thoroughness, she shouldn't be surprised. He must have made that call the morning after she'd shown him the information she'd accumulated on Mary's murder.

"And what day would that be?" Cooley asked.

He walked over to one of the cabinets and returned with something long and slender, encased in cellophane. He stopped in front of Ben to tear it open, extracting a pair of surgical tweezers. He used the foot pedal to open the metal garbage can under the table, dropping the wrapping he'd removed inside it.

"July 9, 1975," Callie said.

Doc's eyes focused on her briefly before they came back to Ben. "And you're sure he was locked up on that day."

"I checked it when Callie told me about the first murder."

Doc nodded, his lips pursed. "So what does that mean?"

"That someone besides Tom Delacroix killed both of them. That other little girl in North Carolina *and* Kay-Kay."

"And you're thinking it was somebody from around here? From Point Hope?" Doc asked, stepping around to the side on the table.

"Based on what's been happening," Ben agreed.

"And he was out there shooting at you last night."

"*And* in Virginia's bedroom the morning she was killed."

"*Killed?* That sounds like... Hell, you ain't thinking somebody murdered Virginia? I told you what happened. Paramedics told you the same thing. She fell and hit her head and bled out because of the medication she was on."

"Except I don't believe that's what happened. I think she knew something, Doc. Something the killer couldn't take a chance on her telling Callie."

"Something...like what?"

"You remember when Jimmy's remains were returned?"

"You talking about Jimmy Robinson?" Doc asked. He focused his bifocals on Ben's back. "You want a shot 'fore I do this?"

"Do what?"

"I think there's some trash in here. Fleck of metal maybe. I'm gonna be digging around a little bit, but it probably won't be any worse than a needle. Up to you, though."

"Just do it," Ben ordered.

Although Callie couldn't see Cooley's hands, she could tell from Ben's face when the doctor began probing for the debris. Ben didn't make a sound, but his lips compressed. After a moment, the crease formed between his brows and the muscle in his jaw knotted. His eyes met hers briefly before they fell to concentrate on his hands, which were resting flat on his thighs.

Suddenly she decided this was a procedure she preferred not to watch. She turned her back to the examination table, taking a breath and focusing on the row of certificates on the wall behind her, determinedly ignoring what was going on across the room.

The nearest frame held Everett Cooley's diploma, which had been issued by a university she wasn't familiar with.

Probably regional, she decided, her gaze moving on to the one beside it.

"So what about Jimmy Robinson?" Doc asked.

Callie took a step to her left, physically moving down the line. The next three frames held documents concerning Cooley's medical degrees and certifications. While she studied them, she listened with half an ear to the conversation behind her.

"You know how his body got home from Fort Bragg?"

"I didn't even know it came from Bragg," Doc said.

"Apparently all the remains from Jimmy's unit were originally transported there. Maybe because they were Special Forces. Or maybe that was standard procedure after the war."

"Beats me," Doc said. And then, in an entirely different tone, "Gotcha." There was a ping as if he had dropped something metallic into an equally metallic container.

Callie didn't turn around, but her neck and shoulders ached with sympathetic tension over what he was doing to Ben.

"If Phoebe went up there, either for some kind of memorial service or to bring Jimmy's body home, would Hobart have gone with her?" Ben went on. "Would he have been able to, I mean?"

"Tell me when this was again."

"July '75."

Then there was a prolonged silence, broken finally by a gasp. Callie half-turned at the sound. Ben's head was down, however, the hands that had been flat on his thighs clenched into fists as Cooley continued to dig around in the wound.

After a few seconds Callie made herself return to the wall display. There was nothing she could do to make this any easier for Ben, and she knew what Doc was doing was necessary.

She had run out of diplomas and degrees, though. She turned her attention to a grouping of photographs. Most were black-and-white, scenes and people she recognized from the time she'd spent in Point Hope. More interesting than the documents.

"I doubt Hobart would have been able to travel any distance by car that summer," Doc said, "Neither him nor Phoebe would fly. Can't think how they would have got up there. *If* they went."

"Then I guess the army flew Jimmy's remains home," Ben said, his voice sounding strained. "The other was a long shot."

"You aren't trying to put Hobart Robinson at the scene of that other murder, are you? That one in the Carolinas."

"Callie found a clipping about Jimmy's body being returned to Bragg. Same month and year. It seemed worth following up."

"I doubt Hobart ever killed a rat, much less a child."

"Like I said," Ben agreed. "It was a long shot. The dates are probably just coincidence."

"This is gonna sting," Doc warned.

Callie took another step to the left to study a photograph of a group of men, all in uniform, standing in front of a Quonset hut. A few wore sunglasses, but most were squinting into what appeared to be strong sunlight. She leaned forward to read the tiny, precisely printed line of white lettering in the bottom right-hand corner. *Free Clinic July 1973.*

She looked back at the row of faces, maybe eight or nine of them. The word clinic had a medical ring. Despite the unexplained uniforms, she tried to find Everett Cooley's features in one of the faces. Just as it had been with that smiling bride, whom she had known must be Phoebe Robinson, it was impossible. The passage of nearly thirty years, the sunglasses, dark hair—all served to disguise Cooley, if he were there.

She looked at the picture above the first, which contained a similar grouping. Fewer soldiers this time, and there were several children lined up in front, looking shyly at the camera. Most of them were barefoot, and there was a telltale thinness to both their bodies and their garments that bespoke real poverty. At least it did to someone who had grown up in Appalachia.

The neat lettering on this photograph was no more enlightening than the other. *Our patients July 1974.* Again she searched the faces of the men. Most of them seemed to be in the prime of life. Late thirties or early forties. There was a scattering of younger faces—leaner and harder.

"Were you in the military, Dr. Cooley?" she asked, looking over her shoulder. "Is that where these pictures were made?"

"Reserves," Cooley said, his eyes still on Ben's back.

"Who are the children?"

There was a small silence, and it was Ben who answered her.

"Doc doesn't like to toot his own horn, but instead of going to summer camp, he and some of the other reservists who had medical training used to run free clinics during those two weeks. Doctors, dentists, whoever had medical expertise they were willing to share. Y'all did that for years, didn't you, Doc?"

"A while," the old man agreed. "We enjoyed it, and it got us out of drilling. Okay, looks like that's everything that was in there. A shot of antibiotics and a bandage, and this ought to heal up nicely. I'll check about that tetanus booster."

As Callie listened to his footsteps cross the room, her eyes returned to the wall, studying the next photograph. In this one the photographer had arranged the people so that behind them in the distance was a series of mountain peaks. There was something tantalizingly familiar about them, evoking a sense of near-recognition. The same kind of mountains where she had grown up, old and heavily wooded, weathered by time and the elements.

"I know the Army kept your shots up to date," Doc said, "but I can't find any record of you having a booster since you came home. You been treated by anyone since I retired?"

"Haven't had any call to be," Ben said.

"Everybody needs an annual. Even you." Cooley noisily slammed the file drawer which had contained the records he'd consulted, and his footsteps recrossed the room.

Callie's eyes dropped to the precise white letters at the bottom of the third picture. *My last clinic, summer of 1975.* And then her eyes found the mountains again.

Aware of Doc moving behind her, opening cabinet doors and shifting their contents around, she looked back at the dates on the first two pictures. July 1973. July 1974. And then on the last. Summer of 1975.

That summer. The summer Mary had been murdered. Moving almost frantically now, her eyes skimmed the faces of the men again, trying to find something familiar in any of them. Something that would tell her—

And when she found it, her heart stopped, her breath literally freezing in her lungs. There was no mistaking the long, silver-gilt hair she remembered only from the photographs her mother had kept of the two of them. Identical fair heads bent together over a book.

She turned in time to see Everett Cooley push down the plunger of the needle whose point he had injected into Ben's upper arm. And then Doc's eyes rose, meeting hers. In his was a malevolence of such incredible force, she couldn't imagine how he had kept it hidden so well. And for so long.

"It's Mary," she said, pulling her gaze from Cooley's to focus on Ben, who had been watching the fluid from the needle go into his arm. "She's in one of these. I think he knew her."

She was afraid none of that made sense. Despite her near-incoherence, however, Ben immediately surged up from the table, trying to push the old man away from him. Cooley didn't release the needle, holding onto it and Ben's arm with a strength that seemed unnatural for a man of his age. Of course, he was a big man, his body bulkier than Ben's muscled leanness. And she had always thought of him as being older than he really was.

Ben shoved him again, reaching out at the same time for

the needle, trying to pull it out. This time, Doc released his arm, stepping back and taking the needle with him. He backed away as far as he could, still watching Ben, his eyes almost feral.

"Tell me you didn't kill her, Doc," Ben demanded, his hands curling into fists. "Tell me you didn't butcher my daughter."

"She wasn't *your* daughter, no matter what Lorena told you."

"How the hell do *you* know what Lorena told me?" Ben asked, taking a step toward the old man.

Cooley pressed against the wall, but his voice showed no sign of fear. "Tom always told me everything. Including what that slut said about the two of you. She played us all for fools, boy. You ought to have figured that out by now."

Ben shook his head, the movement strangely uncoordinated, as if he were trying to clear his vision. Involuntarily Callie started toward him, drawing the old man's eyes. Again, she was struck by the raw hatred within them. Then, as Ben took a staggering step toward Cooley, they shifted back to him.

"What'd you give me, you bastard?" Ben demanded, the words thick, as if he had been drinking.

Cooley didn't answer, his eyes still watchful. Ben shook his head once more, and then he lunged forward, aiming a roundhouse punch at the old man, who dodged instinctively.

The blow didn't even come close. All it did was unbalance Ben so that he was carried forward by its momentum, his body crashing into a wheeled instrument cart. He slid down the side of it, trying to stay upright by grabbing hold of its edge.

The cart shifted under his weight, turning over to land with a crash beside the examination table. Ben rolled onto his back, closing his eyes tightly and then opening them, trying to get them to focus.

"Get out," he commanded, the words slurred, distorted by the effects of whatever Cooley had given him.

Instead, Callie ran to him. She wasn't sure whether her intent was to get him to his feet or to defend him from Cooley. She stooped down, pulling on Ben's arm. "Get up," she begged.

His eyes were open, but he didn't move. The movement came at her peripherally instead. From Cooley, who was running toward them. She looked around, searching for something she could use against him.

The only thing within reach was the metal garbage can. It was heavier than she'd expected, but somehow she managed to lift it. And despite the awkwardness of her semi-kneeling position, she heaved it toward the doctor.

Cooley warded it off, and the can landed on the floor with a distracting clamor. Left off balance by the throw, Callie tried to right herself by putting her palm on Ben's chest, aware that she hadn't even slowed Cooley down.

And then suddenly he was there, right beside them. She realized belatedly that she would have to get to her feet if either of them was going to have any chance against him. Because there was no doubt in her mind that he intended to kill them. Just as he had killed Mary and Kay-Kay.

Cooley's sudden lunge had a purpose that she hadn't been aware of, however. As she tried to stand, he bent, gripping the leg of the metal stool that stood at the head of the table. With one fluid, powerful motion, he swung it at her.

She had time to get her left arm up. She heard a bone snap as the metal seat hit her wrist. And then, virtually unchecked, the stool continued its upward arc, slamming viciously into the side of her head.

CHAPTER SEVENTEEN

EVEN BEFORE she opened her eyes, Callie knew where she was. The smell that lingered in her nightmares was all around her. A wave of terror washed over her, so strong it left her weak. She fought back the sob that ached in her throat.

If she cried out, he would hear her. He would find her, despite the darkness. And then he would do to her what he had done to Mary.

She wanted to clamp her hands over her mouth. She had done that before, stifling any sound that might betray her. Huddled in the darkest corner under the stairs, palms crossed over her lips, she had watched him. And she hadn't cried. If she could only do that now...

Despite her instinct not to move and draw his attention, the impulse to put her hands over her mouth was irresistible. When she tried, however, a shard of agony lanced through her left arm.

There was something wrong with it. Something wrong with both her arms, she realized, because she couldn't move them.

Panic bubbled upward in her chest, demanding a verbal release. Instead, she pressed her lips together as tightly as she could, rolling them inward and clamping her teeth over them to keep from crying out.

As she did, she opened her eyes and slowly turned her head to the side, trying to locate him in the dimness. Pain roared through her skull, its intensity making her sick.

She swallowed the building bile and closed her eyes against the onslaught. Willing the agony to fade. Willing herself to silence. After a moment the pain in her head dulled to something bearable, a level that allowed her to think. She couldn't remember how she had hurt her head. She didn't remember…

And then, like an image from a dream, there was a flash of something silver impacting against her temple. She had put up her arm to ward off the blow—

That must be what was wrong with it. Whatever he had hit her with had made contact with her forearm before it had hit the side of her head.

But that hadn't happened here. That had been somewhere in the light. Somewhere with a different smell. Somewhere…

Another image floated up through the fog that obscured her brain. She had been bending over someone.

Ben. The name was in her consciousness before she really remembered him. But Ben hadn't been there the night the man had taken Mary, so she was confused again. She hadn't known Ben when she was a little girl. Which meant…

She raised her head, trying to see her surroundings. The agony in her skull, which had eased, came back with a vengeance, pounding through the bones until she thought they would break apart.

And suddenly, in the midst of it, she remembered something else. The flash of silver had been a stool. That's what he had hit her with. Because she had been trying to get Ben up, so they could get away. So they could get out of there.

There. Which was…Doc Cooley's office.

The thoughts formed in her brain, as if an unseen hand were pushing pieces of some scattered jigsaw puzzle back into place. Making sense of what had been, seconds before, only chaos.

The dark figure from her nightmares had a face, but it was not the one she had seen that night, bending over Mary as that bare bulb had circled, illuminating and then hiding what he was doing. This face was different, but still she knew it. Everett Cooley. Beloved doctor. Brutal murderer.

And he would kill her and then he would kill Ben if she didn't get them out of here.

The resulting rush of adrenaline energized her. She struggled to sit up. And failed. All she could do was lift her aching head a few inches. Far enough that she could now see the thick leather straps which tied her to the table. One stretched across her hips, pinning her hands to her sides. The other was just below her breasts.

The sob she had fought escaped then, echoing off the walls. It was followed by another, slipping out before she could gather control. *Too loud. Too loud.*

Despite the sickening jolt of pain, she turned her head, her eyes searching for him on the other side of the room and then as far behind her as she could. They scanned over glass-fronted cabinets that seemed replicas of the ones in his office upstairs. These, too, were full of instruments and bottles.

There was no one else here. Not unless he was hiding in the shadows. Watching her. Enjoying her panic.

She worked to calm her breathing, which, like the sobs, seemed to echo too loudly in the stillness. As she did, she heard a noise, something that had been there for a while, hovering on the rim of her awareness.

It was coming from above her head. Her eyes focused on the ceiling over the table. It was too dark to distinguish anything beyond the straight, even lines of exposed beams and the patches of shadow between them.

Beyond them, from the house above, she could hear what she had now identified as footsteps. They would move, the rhythm plodding and regular, and then they would stop. Then, after a moment or two, they would start again, repeating the pattern. Back and forth across the room over her head.

She listened for endless seconds, her breathing suspended as she strained to make sense of what was going on. That was not Ben, of course. The image of his lifeless body, stretched out on the floor of Cooley's office, eyes staring upward unseeingly, negated that possibility. He might even be dead, she admitted, fighting another building sob. She had no idea what had been in the needle Cooley had shoved into his arm.

All she knew for sure was that she was in the basement alone. And whatever Cooley was doing upstairs, he wouldn't leave her alone long. At least, he wouldn't leave her here alive.

Frantically, she began to struggle against the unyielding restraints, setting off every screaming torment in her battered body. After a moment she was forced to stop in order to control the growing nausea.

Obviously she was suffering from the effects of a concussion. The blow to her head had caused a period of unconsciousness deep and prolonged enough that Cooley had been able to drag or carry her down the stairs without her being aware of it. And she knew enough to know that her loss of consciousness was not a good sign. Nor were the nausea and disorientation she had experienced when she'd awakened.

She desperately needed to think. She had to do *something,* or she and Ben were both dead. And then Cooley would slide their bodies into the dark waters of the bay, and no one would ever know what a monster he was.

Slowly, closing her eyes and forming a wordless prayer, she began to try to work her right wrist, the one that wasn't broken, out from under the strap. The leather was tight enough that it bit cruelly into the flesh of her forearm. She pressed her hand into her thigh, trying to create enough space between it and the strap that she could pull it free.

There wasn't much room to maneuver. The top strap held her upper arms against her body so that she could barely bend her elbows. She twisted and turned that arm, trying to slide her hand from under the stiff leather.

As she worked, she realized that the pattern of footsteps over her head had changed. They had headed off in a different direction now, seeming to move away from her. Efforts to escape suspended, she tracked them until they faded away.

Was he coming here? Would the next sound she heard be those plodding footsteps on the stairs that led down to the basement where she lay, strapped to a metal table like a lab animal in some medical experiment? *Like a lab animal...*

Slowly, she turned her head again and surveyed the instruments behind the glass-fronted cabinet doors with a new and terrifying understanding. She had just remembered that Doc Cooley had not only been Point Hope's beloved doctor through the years. He had also at one time been this rural county's coroner.

And finally, she knew where she was. She even understood the purpose of the table where she lay. She was in what once had been Doc Cooley's morgue. In his home, just as his office was.

IT WAS THE VIBRATION that woke him. And the effort it took to force his eyelids up far enough to create even a slit of light in the swirling darkness was enormous.

At first, he didn't understand what he was seeing. It was only after it had moved away that he realized the object that had literally been in front of his nose was a shoe. *Doc's shoe.* He made the identification without much interest in it, his eyes slowly closing again. *Doc's summer, church-going white bucks.*

As he listened to the sound of those retreating footsteps, he gradually became aware of sensations other than the slight vibration they communicated through the old wooden floor. The coolness of its surface beneath his cheek and temple. The cotton-like dryness of his mouth. The dull ache in his head.

And underlying all of those was again that nagging sense that something was wrong. There was something he should be doing. Something important. Whatever it was, however, it seemed too difficult to think about.

His mind began to drift, retreating into the peaceful world it had occupied before Cooley came into the room and woke him up. He wondered, the thought floating almost idly through his consciousness, what Doc had wanted. And then, the question only slightly more troubling, he wondered why he was lying on the floor. That seemed...wrong. Yet Doc hadn't even asked him why he was here.

He heard a door open somewhere, unoiled hinges creaking. He put his tongue out to lick his lips, trying to gather enough moisture in his parched mouth to swallow. He needed water.

Water. The word reverberated in his head. Maybe he was out on the water. There was that same feeling of undulation, as if the waves were moving beneath the hull. Except he knew he was in Doc's office. On the floor. And a second ago Doc's Sunday shoes had been right beside his face.

He tried to lift his head, pushing onto his forearm. The room spiraled sickeningly around him. He put his hand out to steady it, touching an object on the floor beside him that he hadn't been aware of before.

It was the wheeled cart he'd overturned when he'd fallen. And he had fallen because...

He shook his head, trying to clear the mist that not only blurred his vision, but his ability to think. And to remember. Callie had been looking at some pictures while Doc had treated that gouge on his back. And then...

Tetanus, he remembered, pleased by that small success. Doc had been going to give him a booster. Or maybe it was already too late. Maybe that's what was wrong. Maybe that's why he felt like this—so thickheaded and lifeless.

He managed to get the other hand under him, putting it flat on the floor and using it to push his upper body up. He still had to get to his knees, he discovered. Once he had, he rested, swaying slightly. Head hanging, he tried to find some reserve of strength that would allow him to climb to his feet.

Maybe Doc could give him something. Something to stop the fever. There was too much to do for him to be out of commission. Callie had told him that. It's why they'd stopped by Doc's in the first place. And he couldn't imag-

ine why they had both left him alone, so sick and lying on
the floor.

Maybe Doc would do that, if he thought he was drunk.
Doc might just let him sleep it off. But not Callie. She'd
be in here trying to make him get up. She'd be trying to
make him—

She had been.

He could remember looking up at her. And then… And
then something had hit her, hard enough that he had heard
the blow. Hard enough to knock her backward and onto
the floor. He searched his memory, but there was nothing
else there. Nothing until Doc's footsteps had awakened
him.

He turned his head, looking at the place where Callie
had knelt beside him. There was nothing but a dark smear
on Doc's heart-pine floor. It looked like something had
been spilled. Had he done that when he'd knocked over the
cart?

He reached out with his left had to touch the smear. His
right elbow gave way, his body collapsing, almost gently,
onto the floor. His reaching hand fell short, inches from its
target.

His cheek was again flattened against the cool, smooth
wood, the feeling too pleasant to resist. His eyes closed,
and then, nagged by the thought of that something he
needed to remember, he forced them open. In spite of how
hard he tried, however, whatever it was that was so important wouldn't come to him.

It would, he told himself. Eventually. He just needed a
minute. If he could just close his eyes and rest, he knew it
would all come back to him.

DESPITE THE FACT that she had recognized the seriousness
of her predicament from the time she'd awakened, the cold
horror of this new discovery made her efforts to escape
even more frenzied. Frantically, she twisted and turned her
wrist, fighting to slip her hand beneath the leather band that
held it.

It wasn't until she slid her arm at an angle across her body that she succeeded. Sucking in her stomach as much as she could, she was able to work her hand from under the strap. Elation roared through her, creating a renewed determination.

She knew she would never be able to do what she had just done with the wrist Doc had broken. Incredibly sensitive to movement, it was probably swollen as well. She would have to unfasten the strap that held it, working blind and one-handed.

Her fingers skimmed over the leather, searching for a buckle or a fastening. She started on the right-hand side, working her way across the strap by feel. She was able to touch the far side with only the tips of her outstretched, straining fingers.

And there had been nothing along the entire length of the leather. No release. No buckle. Which meant...

She started back on the right side again, feeling carefully along the edge of the table. The strap came from underneath, but, even stretching her arm as far as she could below the edge, she could feel nothing that would release it.

The urge to scream out her frustration was so strong she had to stop the movement of her hand to concentrate on defeating it. She forced herself to remember what was at stake. Not only her life, but Ben's. And to remember what this bastard had gotten away with through the long years. Mary and her father. Kay-Kay. If she gave up now...

Breathing in small, sobbing inhalations, she made her fingers search again, reaching as far as she could toward the left side of the table. No matter how much she strained, she could go no farther than the edge. She closed her eyes, again denying the urge to panic, as she tried to think.

All she had to do was to turn her upper body a little under the band across her chest. The leather must have some give. After all, she had gotten her hand out by working against it.

She began to push her right shoulder against the strap's

unyielding strength. *Fraction of an inch. Fraction of an inch.*

Aching fingers, their tendons stretched beyond endurance, touched the metal of a buckle. Straining with every ounce of will she possessed, she got her fingernails under the side edges of the tongue. She began to pull it slowly upward, drawing it out of the buckle. Away from the tooth that held it.

As she worked, inching the tongue upward with her nails, millimeter by millimeter, the footsteps came back into the room above. Moving back and forth again directly above her head.

Despite the fact that she had thought she couldn't extend her reach any farther, now she did, tugging desperately at the leather. When the tongue finally came free, she repositioned her fingertips, drawing it toward the table so that the hole pulled away from the point of the prong. She threw the strap to her right and, without pausing to celebrate, immediately went back to work on the one across her chest.

The reach was easier this time. Confidence growing, she stretched her arm across her body, fingers searching under the table for the buckle. And, although she was able to reach farther underneath the edge this time, it wasn't there.

Either the fastening was literally under the table or the upper strap had been buckled on the other side. And since the pieces of leather were obviously not original to the table, given its purpose, it was entirely possible Cooley had done exactly that. Diabolically clever in thwarting any attempt to escape? Or simply a chance occurrence that had had that same effect?

After only a few seconds spent trying to make her good arm bend backward into a position only a contortionist could assume, she knew she was going to have to unfasten that buckle with her left hand. The one attached to that damaged wrist.

It isn't broken, she told herself fiercely, dragging the arm across her body. *Bruised. It's only bruised. Ignore the pain. It's only pain. All it means is that you're still alive....*

With the first stretch she knew the truth that litany couldn't hide. At least she could move her fingers, which meant there was hope. Forcing her eyes to focus on the instruments that waited behind the glass doors of the cabinets, she extended her fingers until her vision blurred with tears.

It felt as if she were literally tearing the bones in her wrist apart. She envisioned a crack in them, spreading and then splintering, but despite the pain, she couldn't quit.

Above her head the footsteps retraced their path, fading away once more. She was panting now, her terror that he would come down here before she'd succeeded almost destroying her ability to stay calm and think rationally.

Finally, her desperate fingertips touched the tongue, the nails of her thumb and forefinger gripping the edge of the leather and beginning to draw it upward. She tried to count the seconds between the disappearance of the footsteps and the time it took to free the hole from the prong. The numbers wouldn't stay in her head, and so she had no idea of the passage of time.

At last it released. She closed her eyes, allowing the strained muscles and tendons to relax, trying to will away the excruciating pain. After a few seconds, she pushed the strap off her body with her right hand.

Then, using that arm to lift herself, she sat up on the edge of the table. Her right leg reached for the floor. As she prepared to jump down from the table, she cradled her damaged forearm against her stomach.

It was farther than she had anticipated. Weak-kneed, she staggered when her feet hit the floor. The air thinned and then blackened around her head. She leaned against the table, panting again, waiting for the vertigo to subside.

When it had, she pushed away from the table, her eyes searching for an exit. There had to be some other way out. Other than the stairs which led to the house above, which were clearly illuminated by the light that came from the top. It seemed to lure her toward them. *Some other way,* she told herself, eyes examining the shadowed corners.

Apparently, the basement had been only partially finished. Most of it was only a darkly yawning crawl space. She considered hiding there, but eventually he would find her. Or, if there was no other exit, he might lock the door at the top of the stairs, leaving her here to die. Alone. And in the dark.

She drew a long, deep breath, fighting that lifelong fear, as she continued to examine her surroundings. Beyond the last of the cabinets, far from the bulb at the top of the stairs, a fainter light filtered into the dimness.

Still cradling her arm against her body, she ran toward it. There was a narrow passage between the last cabinet and the wall, which led into the other half of the basement.

High on the opposite wall was a window. It had been morning when they'd entered Cooley's house, and yet there was only a smudged grayness coming through the glass. She hurried toward it, wondering again how long she had been unconscious.

When she was close enough, however, she realized the sunlight was blocked by a decades-long accumulation of grime. Given the pristine conditions of the rest of the house, she knew that had to be deliberate. Someone might question why a basement window was boarded, but who would question why it wasn't clean.

She looked for something to climb up on. And when she found it, she struggled to drag a wooden crate, one-handed, across the concrete floor. It made too much noise, but she couldn't help that. She had to get out of the house and get help. It was their only hope.

She pushed the box against the wall and stepped up on it. With her right hand, she scrubbed at the dirt, exposing a small area of glass that looked out on the driveway.

Cooley's car was still there, the trunk standing open. She couldn't see hers. She enlarged the area she was looking out of, allowing her to see more of the drive, but her car was definitely gone. It had been moved from where she'd parked it. He had hidden her car, just as he would hide their bodies. And then no one would ever know.

She straightened, running her fingers around the edge of the window, looking for the latch. When she found it, she pushed it upward, relieved that it moved as smoothly as if it were kept well-oiled and frequently used. Then she shoved at the sash, trying to slide it up.

Unlike the lock, however, it resisted. Dreading the pain, she forced her other hand up, adding its feeble strength to the effort. Still the window wouldn't budge.

Too many coats of paint, she thought. All that meticulously painted trim. She ran her fingers along the edge of the frame, encountering not the multiple layers of paint as she'd expected, but a line of small, round depressions. Despairing, she traced their pattern, reinforcing what she had known instantly. The bastard had nailed the window shut, countersinking the nails, so there was no way they could be removed.

She sagged against the wall in defeat, leaning her forehead against the window. The glass was cool, temptingly soothing against her throbbing head, but she couldn't stay here. She had to do something. She had no choice but to keep trying until he came for her.

As if on cue, she heard the sound she had been dreading—and expecting—since she had awakened and realized where she was. The door at the top of the stairs opened with a small, revealing creak. And then the plodding, deliberate footsteps she had listened to crossing back and forth above her head started down the basement steps.

CHAPTER EIGHTEEN

SHE MADE A QUICK, despairing survey of her surroundings, looking for some kind of weapon. There was nothing in this part of the basement but the crate she had shoved under the window. And it was too heavy to pick up. Besides, other than throwing it at Cooley, she couldn't imagine how she could use it.

Hide, her mind screamed. She had done that before, and she had survived. *She* had survived, but he had gone on to kill another child, another little girl, exactly as he had killed Mary. And now there was no one else left to stop him. No one else who knew what a monster he was.

And so, instead of cowering in another nightmare corner, she ran back toward the section of the basement where Cooley had set up his morgue. There would be something in those glass-fronted cabinets she could use against him.

Just before she rounded the corner formed by those cabinets, the measured footsteps stopped. Either Cooley had reached the bottom of the stairs or he had come down them far enough to see she was no longer strapped to the table.

Or maybe he had heard *her* footsteps, running back toward the room where he'd left her. Maybe he was waiting in there for her.

She didn't care if he was. She had only one thought in her mind. One goal. She was going to do now what she had been incapable of doing twenty-six years ago.

As she came through the narrow opening, she glanced toward the stairs and then around the perimeter of the room. There was no sign of Cooley.

Which doesn't mean he isn't here, she thought, trembling fingers opening the first of the glass doors.

Her eyes traced over the array of implements, a confusing assortment of saws and scalpels and plier-like instruments she didn't recognize, all laid out in neat rows on metal trays. Her hand hovered over them, hesitating. And then it darted forward, her fingers closing over one of them. Clutching her choice, she had begun to turn when he hit her.

It was that aborted motion which saved her. The downward chop of his hand, aimed at her neck, landed on her shoulder instead. The shock was so great that for a second or two she was almost paralyzed. Then, completing the movement she'd begun, she drew her elbow as far back as she could, until it banged hard against the cabinet behind her.

She drove her hand forward again, plunging the scalpel she held into the soft, yielding belly of Everett Cooley. He sagged against her, and she fought the urge to pull the blade free in order to get away from him. Instead, she used every ounce of willpower and a lifelong rage to push it deeper.

He moaned, and she felt a rush of exhilaration. She had hurt him. She had hurt the bastard. Vindication, however small, for all the years of fear and survivor's guilt she'd suffered.

Then, like a wounded animal, Cooley roared an inarticulate expression of his own rage. He threw up his arms and staggered backward. She didn't have time to release her hold on the handle of the scalpel. When he moved back, it slid out of his stomach.

Almost reflexively, Callie looked down at the blade. There was no blood on its shining surface. It seemed as clean as when she had selected it from the metal tray.

Despair welled, replacing that momentary exhilaration. It was as if he truly were a creature from some nightmare. Invincible and indestructible.

With an infuriated scream, she rushed at him, the scalpel held low, her fingers wrapped around its handle, positioned exactly as they had been when she'd first picked it up. She drove the blade into his stomach again.

As she did, she finally realized that his bulk made that area less vulnerable than many others. She should have repositioned the weapon, driving it downward, into his neck or his chest instead.

It was too late now. She drew back her hand, determined to strike again. He raised his arm to ward her off, and then the intent of the gesture changed, becoming a blow. Awkwardly aimed, the back of his hand struck the side of her head, knocking her away as if he were swatting aside an annoying insect.

The force of it was powerful enough to send her stumbling into the cabinets behind her. She careened off them, and he hit her again, using his fist this time, the blow coming from the opposite direction.

It struck her temple, almost exactly where he had hit her with the stool. Her head snapped back, recoiling with enough force to crack the glass in the door behind her.

His fingers closed around the wrist of the hand in which she held the scalpel, banging it again and again against the thin pane of glass in the other door until it shattered. As her fist broke through, one of the shards that had remained in the frame sliced open the skin on the back of her hand, and the blade fell from her fingers.

Holding her wrist with one hand, Cooley reached behind her, driving his other through the panel her head had starred. Glass fell noisily over the metal trays and the instruments they held. And suddenly, with that sound, she understood what he was doing.

The image of that grisly array of blades behind her flashed through her mind. She surged forward, pushing the old man back, trying to drive him away from them. Trying to put those deadly instruments out of his reach.

The element of surprise succeeded, at least briefly. She managed to get her forearm up, positioning it under his chin. In spite of the near-electric shock from the impact on the broken bone in her wrist, she shoved his head back.

And then, as he had before, he roared, charging forward and driving her back into the tall cabinet, which teetered dangerously. Again his hand reached behind her, grabbing for something on its shelves.

She could see his face, lips drawn back from yellowed teeth, a sheen of sweat on his smoothly shaven cheeks. She could even smell him. Soap. Aftershave. Toothpaste. A murderer on his way to church.

Fury at the success of his long deception gave her renewed strength. Once more, she managed to push him back an inch or two, but he was better prepared this time.

He rushed forward, his bulk overpowering her. He slammed her body against the cabinet behind her. There was a loud report, as it tilted and then went over, carried backward by their combined weights.

It landed on the concrete floor with a crash. The glass doors at her back shattered completely. And as the cabinet collapsed, she fell into it, with Cooley on top of her.

Stunned, she lay unmoving for a second or two, held immobile by his weight. She opened her eyes—face-to-face with the horror from her nightmares. Her forearm was still beneath his chin, holding his head up, his face only inches from hers.

His eyes were glazed. Staring. Even in the dim light it was obvious that the pupils were dilated and fixed.

She waited for him to move, adrenaline-driven blood rushing and throbbing in her ears. There was no other sound. The only smell was the scent of mildew. And as they lay together in a bizarre lovers' tableau, the dust from the cabinet's landing swirled and drifted and finally began to settle around them.

"YOU'RE OKAY," Ben said again, while he held her, rocking her back and forth as if she were a child.

They were huddled together on the basement stairs. Shell-shocked. Unable to move. Unable to do anything other than struggle to comprehend that they were still alive.

And that the enemy who had haunted both their lives was finally dead.

She hadn't even heard Ben's shot. Or if she had, she hadn't recognized it for what it was. And only now was she beginning to understand the near impossibility of what he had done.

Just as the cabinet had begun to topple, Ben had fired the hunting rifle he'd taken from Doc's collection. And despite the effects of whatever drug Doc had injected into his arm, he had managed to hit a moving target in the dimly lit basement.

He had been afraid that he might hit her. That was the first thing he'd told her after he'd pulled the old man's body off, freeing her physically from its burden.

Cooley's death had freed her from the rest. She had been three years old when Mary was murdered. Although she had blocked the memory in order to survive, apparently she had never forgotten the events of that night. They had colored almost every aspect of her life since.

"We have to call Doak," Ben said.

"I know," she whispered.

She didn't want to move from his arms, and yet she wanted out of here. Out of the darkness. Away from the smell. Away from Cooley's stiffening body. Away from his private morgue where, she now believed, he had brought Kay-Kay that night.

"Come on," Ben said, using the stair railing to pull himself up. He reached down, taking her elbow, but she gasped as he touched her arm. He released it immediately. "What's wrong?"

"My wrist. I put it up when he swung that stool at my head. Reflex action. I think it cracked a bone."

"Probably saved your life," Ben said, stooping beside her to put his arm around her waist instead.

He was right. The stool had still hit hard enough to cause a concussion. And if she hadn't partially deflected it…

"Worth a broken bone," she said, glancing up at him.

He looked as bad as she felt. The pupils of his eyes were

wide and dark. The light shining down on them from the top of the stairs illuminated his face, gray under the tan.

"I can't believe it's finally over," she said.

She couldn't. Although the pace at which events had unfolded since she'd arrived in Point Hope had been frenetic, it seemed she had lived with this nightmare forever.

Ben used his thumb to wipe something off her cheek. She wasn't sure if it was blood or tears, or maybe a smear of dirt. And she didn't care. She did care very much, she had found, about what that gesture conveyed.

"What now?" she asked, fighting the ache in her throat.

"We get the authorities in here. And then—" He shook his head, his eyes moving to the room at the foot of the stairs. "This is going to devastate this town."

It would. Everett Cooley had been more than a respected member of his community. He had been venerated. Worshipped.

"At least it's closure," she said. "For you. For Kay-Kay. Even for Lorena. Her husband's been exonerated. And so has she, I suppose. There were always people who thought she had something to do with her daughter's death."

"Maybe she did," Ben said, his eyes still focused below. "Just not in the way they thought."

"What does that mean?"

"Doc said she played us *all* for fools."

"I don't understand."

Perhaps it was the trauma they had been through, but there was too much of this she still didn't understand. Maybe, with Cooley dead, they would never know all the details.

"I've been trying to figure out what he meant," Ben said. "And now, I guess there's only one person left who can tell us."

LORENA DELACROIX'S eyes widened when she opened the front door and saw him standing on her porch. Ben knew Doak had called her early this afternoon to give her the news about Doc, but it had taken him all day to get a chance to come over here.

By the time he had taken Callie to the hospital in Baldwin County and had waited for the results from the CT, the morning had been gone. Because of the severity of her concussion, the doctors had decided to keep her overnight for observation.

Knowing she was in good hands, Ben had spent the afternoon helping with the search of Doc's house and doing some of the paperwork on what had happened. He had lost track of time, but it must be pretty late because Lorena was already undressed.

The robe she was wearing was nothing like the ones his mother used to wear, Ben acknowledged bitterly. The material of this one was thin and silky. Obviously expensive. And it managed to cling in all the right places.

Despite the hour, Lorena's hair and makeup were still carefully in place. He shouldn't be surprised at that attention to her appearance, even given the news she'd received today. Since she'd married Tom Delacroix, Lorena had taken pains to live up to that image of old money. At least, to her version of it.

The shock in her eyes when she recognized him lasted only a few seconds before it changed into something that looked suspiciously like satisfaction.

"I guess somebody warned you," she said.

Ben had come to demand an explanation for Doc's comment. He couldn't make sense of what she'd just said or of that smirk, not in context with the events of today. "Warned me about what?"

His head still ached from whatever Doc had given him. He couldn't remember the last time he'd gotten more than a couple of hours of uninterrupted sleep or had anything to eat. And when he did—remembering also the way Callie's mouth had tasted, sweet and cold from the peach cobbler— that memory didn't make him any more willing to put up with Lorena's poisonous tongue.

"I've already told the media how you sat on information

you knew would exonerate us," she said. "And that it wasn't until Callie Evers came down here and called your hand that you did anything about it. That's gonna be included in every headline trumpeting the news that you finally caught Kay-Kay's murderer. So don't think you're going to come out of this with anything to your credit, Ben Stanton."

"I was wrong about Tom. I've admitted that publicly," he said, feeling his anger build. He didn't know yet how much of that was justified and how much was the result of the stresses of the last twenty-four hours. "But maybe if you'd told me the truth from the beginning, I might not have come to the wrong conclusion about your husband."

There was something in her eyes, a flicker of surprise or of fear. It was quickly controlled. And then they were again hard. And very cold.

"I don't know what the hell you're talking about," she said, "but I'm not interested in hearing your excuses. It's over, Ben. This is a done deal. There's nothing you can do to stop it."

She began to close the door, but at the gloating expression on her face, something snapped inside him. He put his hand flat against one of the imported leaded-glass panels and shoved it inward, hard enough that she was forced to step back, her eyes widening once more.

"You told me Kay-Kay was my daughter, but that was a lie, wasn't it?" he demanded. "You lied to me, just like you lied to Tom. I'm here to find out what lie you told Doc."

The blood drained from her face, leaving two spots of color on her cheeks. And the emotion this time wasn't hard to read.

"I don't know what you're talking about."

"Before he died, Doc said you played us *all* for fools. I got to thinking about what he might have meant. And that made me remember a couple of nights when I saw Doc's car in your driveway. Him and Tom being friends, I didn't think too much about it. But his car was here at least one night when I knew Tom was out of town. I remember think-ing at the time that was strange. Wondering what Doc was doing here so late.''

"Everett Cooley was my personal *physician.*''

"And he was also your lover," Ben said, the words dis-tinct. He couldn't prove that, but given what they had found at Doc's—

"How dare you?" Lorena said. Her breasts heaved under the thin robe.

"I've got the pictures." Seeing her face as that registered was almost satisfaction enough to make up for what she had done to them all, Ben thought. Almost enough. "They're evidence now," he went on, "but when it's all over, you may be able to get them back. Or maybe your lawyer can.''

She swallowed, the movement strong enough that he could trace it down the smooth line of her throat. "Evi-dence?''

"The thing is those aren't the only pictures Doc took," he said, showing her no mercy. He wasn't feeling merciful right now. Not with Callie in the hospital, and Lorena call-ing the media to do all she could to blacken his name. "Did you know about the others? Quite a hobby old Doc had.''

"I don't have any idea what you're talking about," she said, pushing the door toward him. His hand on the glass stopped it.

"I'm talking about the pictures he took of your daugh-ter.''

There was again that telltale flicker in her eyes before she said, "Kay-Kay was very photogenic. A *lot* of people took pictures of her. People loved her.''

"Except Doc loved her a little too much. And he had kind of a strange way of showing it. By the way, the pic-tures he took of Kay-Kay are a lot more revealing than the ones he took of you.''

She hadn't known. That, too, was obvious in her eyes. She looked like he'd felt when they found them. And of course, the ones of Kay-Kay weren't the only ones they'd found.

That's what Doc had been doing while Ben had been lying unconscious on his office floor. He'd emptied everything from those secret files into his battered black medical bag, the one he carried with him wherever he went. They had found it sitting on the front seat of his car.

They would never know what he intended to do after he'd packed up all that pornography. *And* after he had taken care of him and Callie. Was he going to leave town this time? "Retire" somewhere. Or was he just destroying the evidence of his hobby in case anyone got suspicious when they found the bodies.

"Every time I took her in to see him I stayed in the room," Lorena said. "He never asked me to leave. There's no way—"

"And when she went on those hunting trips with him and Tom? To the beach. Or how about the time they took her to Disney World? There are pictures of all those, too. Daddy's little darling, invited along everywhere the two of them went."

"If you're trying to suggest that Tom—"

"I'm *suggesting* that Tom was dead drunk almost every night. You *knew* that. And that's when that sick old man—"

"Stop it," she demanded, turning away. "Just...stop it."

"You told Doc she was his daughter, too, didn't you? And then when he found out from Tom that you'd told me the same thing, he figured out that you'd not only been two-timing Tom, but you'd been two-timing him as well."

She looked back at him then, a sickness to match his own in her eyes. "Tom told him?" She shook her head, her eyes distant, unfocused. "You'd think a man wouldn't want *anybody* to know something like that. I never dreamed Tom would—"

"What the hell kind of game were you playing, Lorena?"

Her chin almost quivered, but at the last second, she lifted it, her lips tightening before she opened them to spit the words at him. "I was tired of being married to a drunk."

"Then you get a divorce," he said coldly. "You don't play with people's lives." And finally it hit him—why she hadn't done that. The piece of the puzzle that had been missing. "Except you couldn't get a divorce. If you did, you'd have to give all this up. Tom's lawyers made you sign a pre-nup. You divorce him, you get nothing. You leave Tom, and you're screwed.

"*Unless,* of course," he went on, realizing some of it only as he talked, "you can find somebody who's able to support you in the style to which Tom's money had made you accustomed. And Doc and I were the logical candidates. You'd slept with both of us, near enough to the right time. You figured your daughter was a pretty good bargaining chip. And we both had money. In my case, the possibility of it, at least. Only something went wrong. It didn't quite work out the way you planned."

Ben hadn't bitten on the bait. He would have done right by his daughter, but he would never have married Lorena.

"I must have been the backup. Doc was obviously the one you were really after. Richer than me. And older. Not as long to live. Only he didn't bite either. So...what went wrong, Lorena? You can tell me or you can tell a grand jury. I think one will probably be convened to look into your role in your daughter's death."

"You wouldn't do that," she said.

He couldn't, but he could tell she wasn't completely sure of it. And having any of this come out would destroy the social position she wanted so desperately to maintain here in Point Hope. She was too stupid to know there wasn't one.

"You just try me, Lorena. Believe me, I'd love to drag you through the same cesspool Doc dragged this town through."

There was a long silence before she said, "He wanted a paternity test."

"And you couldn't afford that," he said, "because it

might prove the very thing you didn't want it to. That Kay-Kay *wasn't* Doc's. So instead, you told me, and then you told Tom, that *I* was Kay-Kay's father, hoping I'd offer to marry you when he asked for a divorce. Only that didn't work out quite the way you planned it either. And two days later, she was dead.''

"It wasn't my fault," she said. "Kay-Kay's death had nothing to do with—"

"You broke his heart, Lorena. Tom loved that little girl more than his own life, and you told him she wasn't his. So Tom got drunk and cried on his best friend's shoulder, and then Doc knew you'd been lying to him, too."

"It doesn't mean that that's why—"

"No, it doesn't," he agreed before she could finish. "Maybe Kay-Kay was getting old enough that he knew what he'd been doing was dangerous. Or maybe he'd reached a point were he couldn't stop. I suspect we'll find some others who'll come forward once this comes out. Or maybe," he added softly, "maybe Everett Cooley just knew you better than the rest of us."

Her eyes came up at that. Filled with moisture, they were starkly revealing.

"Maybe he knew the best way to get back at you for lying to him. You were playing us all for fools," Ben said, repeating the old man's words. "And if there was anything Doc didn't like, it was being played for a fool. He wouldn't like it at all that somebody like you had tried to put something over on him.

"So he figured out how to get back at you and to protect himself at the same time. He killed the only thing, besides yourself, that you've ever loved. He killed your little girl because of what you did to him. And that's something you're going to have to live with, Lorena, for the rest of your life."

EPILOGUE

SHE HAD ASKED the nurse to leave the light on, but when she opened her eyes, there was only darkness. She turned her head, locating the closed door by its thin rim of light.

By that time, she was awake enough to realize she wasn't alone in the bed. And to know who was lying beside her.

She laid her cheek against Ben's chest, breathing in the scent of his body. The clean, laundry-starched fragrance of his shirt was such a pleasant contrast to the medicinal smell of the hospital, which had been too reminiscent of Cooley's office.

Afraid she'd wake him, she resisted the urge to put her fingers over the muscle that rose and fell with reassuring regularity. Her lips lifted, wondering how he'd managed this. Wondering, too, about the reaction of the nurses who would be coming by for those hourly observations.

And then, deciding she didn't care about either, she settled more closely against his chest, curling her hand beneath her chin. She had already closed her eyes when she felt him stir.

"You okay?" he asked, his voice rumbling under her ear.

"What are you doing here?" she asked.

She allowed her fingers to touch his chin. It was obvious he'd recently shaved. Bathed. Changed clothes. And then he had driven all the way back to the hospital to lie down beside her.

"Couldn't sleep," he said.

She thought about the possibility that that was really why he was here, at least briefly, before she challenged it.

"Seriously," she demanded, and felt the depth of the breath he took before he answered her.

"I knew I'd feel better if I were with you."

She examined the words, deciding she liked the sound of them, whatever they meant. They lay without speaking for a few minutes, only the faint nighttime noises from the corridor beyond that closed door intruding on the relaxed silence.

"Did you talk to Lorena?"

"Yeah, and before you ask, you really *don't* want to know."

"I want to know why he killed them," she said reasonably. "I need to know that before… Maybe before I can let it all go. It shouldn't matter, I know, but…"

"He was a sick old man," Ben said, the words clipped and harsh. "Leave it at that, Callie."

"He *wasn't* an old man when he killed my sister."

More silence, less comfortable this time. She understood why Ben didn't want to talk about this, but it was there between them. It always would be. At least until she understood.

"He liked adulation," Ben said, his voice flat as if he were reciting a lesson. "Adoring patients, like Phoebe and Virginia. Kids like me who had grown up looking up to him. He liked doing the pro bono stuff, those free summer clinics he organized within the reserves. He especially liked it if it got him recognition. And it did. Community leader. Church deacon. The wise and benevolent physician, who also had a fondness for white-haired, angelic-looking little girls. The younger the better."

"There were others," Callie whispered, sickness moving into her throat at the thought.

"Dozens, but none that he murdered, as far as we know."

"Then…why? Why them? Why the two of them?"

"Kay-Kay to get back at Lorena, although…"

"Although what?"

He shook his head, the small familiar motion that didn't

denote denial. "We'll probably never know why he killed Mary. Maybe he couldn't resist touching her. Maybe she threatened to tell what he'd done. And he would know your father was someone who couldn't be bought off or intimidated into keeping quiet."

An uncannily accurate assessment. Based, she supposed, on what she had told him about her father's insistence that the doors to the house had all been locked that night.

And her father would have been thrilled to be involved in something like the clinics Cooley had organized. He would have seen them as a wonderful boon for his poorest parishioners. He might very well have taken Mary with him when he carried the other children from his church to see the visiting doctors.

He loved to show off his girls. With that memory, the first she had allowed herself in a very long time about that sweet, gentle man, her eyes filled with tears.

"I don't know how Doc got into your house that night. Maybe Mary let him in. Maybe he told her he was going to bring by a special gift for your father's birthday. I know Kay-Kay opened the door to him. He might have thrown a pebble against her window, and seeing Doc outside, she would have gone down and let him in. And then he could have taken her wherever he wanted. She loved him, and he was always good to her," he said, his voice bitter with the knowledge of the price Katherine Delacroix had ultimately paid for Cooley's favors. "With Mary..."

His voice faded, and Callie waited through the stillness, seeing that circling bulb again. Enclosed in his arms, and with Cooley dead, the power it had over her had lessened.

"Maybe he never intended to kill Mary," Ben went on. "I don't know what went wrong. Maybe she cried out, and he thought he had to make her stop..."

The halting words touched a chord of memory buried so deeply in her mind no clear image surfaced to accompany it, not like her father's face had done. That explanation *felt* right.

Mary *had* cried out. She had struggled and fought. Then

she had gone very still. And when the light circled again, that man had been bending over her.

"And then he never did it again? Not in all those years? Is that possible?"

"Doc was all about control. When they opened the new outpatient clinic, he moved his practice there. They wanted him. Enticed him. It didn't last more than a couple of months because he couldn't stand not being in charge. He couldn't run things the way he wanted them run. Eventually he retired, raised his garden and kept his parents' house exactly as it was when he was a boy."

"It doesn't make sense, not that he could kill two little girls, and then...nothing."

"He valued the community's good opinion of him. He couldn't bear to lose that. Besides, he probably viewed what he had done to Mary as an accident. Maybe it was. At least her death. Maybe he never intended to kill her."

"And Kay-Kay? Are you suggesting that was an accident, too? And what he tried to do to me?"

"You endangered everything he'd worked for his whole life."

"Because I could tie him to Mary."

Ben had told her that was the key. She had been a threat because she had a connection to the murder in North Carolina.

"How did he know?" she asked. "The first time, out in the bay, he hadn't even seen me yet. And I hadn't told Virginia and Phoebe about Mary. I hadn't told anyone but you. How could he possibly *know* I was that threat?"

"Callie," Ben said softly.

For a second or two, she thought he was giving her a warning that he didn't want to talk about this anymore. And then...

"He recognized my name."

"Phoebe would have told him all about her new guest and where she was from. She always told him everything. Your name was unusual enough that he put two and two together. He'd been waiting, all these years, for something like that to happen. Waiting for someone to show up who could connect him to Mary.''

''Then why follow the same pattern with Kay-Kay's murder? Why draw the rose on her neck? Why bathe her?'

''The same reasons he did those things in the first place. Because there are compulsions that are stronger than logic. Or the intellect. And remember, if I hadn't seen that rose...''

Cooley hadn't included it in the autopsy report or the pictures, of course. He didn't know Ben had seen it. And if Ben hadn't, no one would ever have known it was there.

''Virginia knew about the clinic,'' she guessed.

''A lot of people knew. She called Doc that morning, by the way. I don't know that she'd really put it all together, or if she just said something that made him afraid she might. It might not even have been the clinic. Phoebe and Hobart may have asked Doc to go to Bragg. He was there, in the same state. It would have been reasonable. Maybe that's what Virginia remembered.''

And what Phoebe had thought of? Callie wondered, remembering those trembling hands clasped beneath the old woman's breasts as she had talked about never being sure about the right thing to do. Was it possible Phoebe had been trying to decide whether she should implicate an old friend in something so terrible she must surely have believed he couldn't have had any role in it?

''Poor Phoebe,'' she whispered.

''A lot of people aren't going to be able to believe it was Doc, no matter what we turn up. Cooley was a hero to the people of this town. Somebody they looked up to. Somebody they loved.''

The word seemed to echo in the darkness. *It's called making love.* Ben had said that last night. Making love.

''So...what now?'' she asked.

He didn't answer for a long time. Long enough that she turned her head, looking up at him for the first time. His eyes were focused on the ceiling.

''There'll be a lot of media interest. That's already

started. Lorena's been helping it along, but...I suspect she'll back off now. Things will eventually die down again. An unsolved murder is always more interesting than a solved one.''

"They'll want to know about Mary," she said, beginning to realize the implications of the media's interest for her.

"And about your father's suicide. About you.''

"God," she said, the word low.

There was another silence.

"I've got a boat," he reminded her.

Despite the things they had talked about tonight, there was something in his tone that made her smile. He turned his head, leaning back a little in the narrow bed so he could see her face.

"Are you offering me an escape?" she asked.

"I'm offering...'' He hesitated, and she felt the breath he took before he said, "I'm offering whatever you're willing to accept.''

Whatever you're willing to accept. "That's a pretty open-ended invitation," she said, smiling at him.

"Yes, it is.''

He hadn't answered the smile. His eyes seemed very blue in the dimness. After a moment, she shook her head.

"I'm not exactly sure...'"

Suddenly, in the face of that steady regard, she ran out of words. If they were monitoring her heart rate, someone from the nurse's station would probably be in here fairly soon.

"You don't have to be," Ben said. "I'm not *sure* either, but...I want us to try. Maybe we'll find out that we don't even like each other—''

"No," she said. "No, we won't.''

"There's been nothing even slightly normal about our relationship. Almost nothing normal," he amended, the stern line of his mouth relaxing.

"Yes," she said.

"Yes?''

"Yes. Whatever.''

"Dammit," he said. "You're crying again."

"No, I'm not," she denied. "I'm just tired. Concussed. I have a cracked ulna. But I'm *not* crying."

"A cracked what?"

"Ulna. It's the smaller bone in—" She stopped, because even in this light she could read the laughter in his eyes.

"Just checking," he said. "I didn't want there to be any nasty surprises once I get you onboard."

"I think we've had our share of nasty surprises."

"Enough to last a lifetime," Ben agreed.

In a way, this had been far harder on him than on her. Ben had freely admitted his lifelong admiration of the old man.

She, on the other hand, had succeeded in what she had come here to do, although the effects had been more far-reaching than she could have imagined. The only thing that *had* happened like she'd imagined it...

"So where are we going on this boat of yours?" she asked.

"Some extremely secluded beach. Despite all the development, there are still plenty of them along the coast. Or maybe an inlet on the bay."

"Like the one where we were last night."

"Maybe," he said. He leaned forward and put his lips against her forehead. "Or maybe we need to stay closer to civilization for a day or two. Until we're sure you're okay."

"I'm okay. At least I will be..." She hesitated, the commitment too new, almost too tenuous for that confession.

"Me, too," he said. "Maybe that inlet's a pretty good idea. We lie low there until this dies down again...."

She waited a long time before she asked, "And then what?"

"I don't know how you feel about Point Hope, but...despite everything, it really isn't a bad place to live." Her throat closed against the promise of that, so that she couldn't answer him for a moment. "Unless there's something or someone waiting for you in North Carolina?" he added when she didn't respond.

Only memories. All of them ones she didn't want. She wanted new ones. And the best possibility of making those...

"Nobody's waiting for me. Not back there."

"Footloose and fancy-free," he said, lips nuzzling her hair.

She smiled a little at the nice, old-fashioned sound of that phrase. And then she told him the final secret she had kept. Because she thought he needed to know.

"There *was* a man once..." she began, but her throat closed again as she thought how near this reality had come to her expectations. Not many people in this world could say that.

"A man?" he repeated. He had gone very still, even his breathing suspended. "Somebody I should know about?"

"I knew him only from his pictures. From some newspaper clippings. Stories about how long he had tried to find the murderer of a little girl. How much he cared. And I think I knew even then, that if there was anybody in the world... I came here to find *you*," she said, "because I knew you were the one person who would help me find Mary's killer, but...I think I also knew, even then..."

"Callie," he said, and this time she knew what he meant.

She turned her head, looking up to smile at him again. Instead, his mouth closed over hers, his tongue invading with the sweet mastery she remembered. Far more powerful than any of her expectations.

Author Note

Thank you for reading SECRETS IN SILENCE. This book is very special to me, not only because it is set in Alabama, but also because it is dedicated to the wonderful school where my son teaches. If you enjoyed SECRETS, I hope you'll look for the stories I have coming up in the very near future. Next month NIGHT AND DAY, a two-in-one Intrigue, in which Anne Stuart and I have connected novellas, will be on the shelves. Anne's wonderful Blackheart hero is "night" to my ex-CIA Man of Mystery's "day," a clash of opposites sure to set your pulses racing. In December, my contribution to the exciting Trueblood, Texas continuity, THE COWBOY'S SECRET SON, hits the stands—just in time for some Christmas stocking stuffing. Please put that one on your Santa wish list. And then in the spring of 2002 watch for the third book in The Sinclair Brides trilogy from Harlequin Historicals. You don't want to miss out on how the youngest of the Sinclair brothers, Sebastian, wins his wife.

With gratitude,

Gayle Wilson

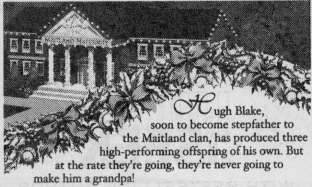

*H*ugh Blake,
soon to become stepfather to
the Maitland clan, has produced three
high-performing offspring of his own. But
at the rate they're going, they're never going to
make him a grandpa!

There's *Suzanne*, a work-obsessed CEO whose Christmas spirit
could use a little topping up....

And *Thomas*, a lawyer whose ability to hold on to the woman
he loves is evaporating by the minute....

And *Diane*, a teacher so dedicated to her teenage students she
hasn't noticed she's put her own life on hold.

But there's a Christmas wake-up call in store
for the Blake siblings. Love *and* Christmas miracles
are in store for all three!

Maitland Maternity Christmas

A collection from three of Harlequin's favorite authors

Muriel Jensen
Judy Christenberry
&Tina Leonard

Look for it in November 2001.